RESISTANCE

BOOK I

First Second

New York & London

Text Copyright © 2010 by Carla Jablonski
Illustrations Copyright © 2010 by Leland Purvis

Published by First Second
First Second is an imprint of Roaring Brook Press,
a division of Holtzbrinck Publishing Holdings Limited Partnership,
175 Fifth Avenue, New York, NY 10010

Distributed in Canada by H. B. Fenn and Company Ltd.
distributed in the United Kingdom by Macmillan Children's Books,
a division of Pan Macmillan.

Design by Colleen AF Venable

Colored by Hilary Sycamore and Sky Blue Ink

Cataloging-in-Publication Data is on file at the Library of Congress.

ISBN: 978-1-59643-291-8

First Second books are available for special promotions and premiums.
For details, contact: Director of Special Markets, Holtzbrinck Publishers.

First Edition May 2010
Printed in January 2011 in China by C&C Joint Printing Co.,
Shenzhen, Guangdong Province
3 5 7 9 10 8 6 4

RESISTANCE
BOOK 1

Written by
Carla Jablonski

Art by
Leland Purvis

Color by
Hilary Sycamore

First Second

WORLD WAR II BEGAN ON SEPTEMBER 1, 1939, WITH THE INVASION OF POLAND BY NAZI GERMANY AND RUSSIA. BUT IT WAS NOT UNTIL 1940 THAT THE GERMANS INVADED FRANCE. THE FRENCH WERE FORCED TO SURRENDER WITHIN WEEKS.

ON JUNE 22, 1940, THE FRENCH AND THE GERMANS SIGNED AN ARMISTICE AGREEMENT. THE FRENCH WOULD STOP FIGHTING AND AGREE TO GERMAN DEMANDS. NOT EVEN A YEAR HAD PASSED SINCE FRANCE AND BRITAIN DECLARED WAR ON THE NAZIS. BUT FRANCE COULDN'T WIN AGAINST THE GERMAN ARMY.

FRANCE WAS DIVIDED INTO TWO ZONES: OCCUPIED, WHERE THE GERMANS WERE IN CHARGE, AND THE FREE, RUN BY THE NEW FRENCH GOVERNMENT, NOW IN VICHY.

THERE WERE MANY REASONS TO AGREE TO THIS PLAN. FRANCE WAS STILL RECOVERING FROM THE DEADLY BATTLES OF WORLD WAR I. IT SEEMED AS IF THE GERMANS WOULD WIN THIS SECOND WAR AND TO GIVE IN NOW, SOME BELIEVED, WOULD PROTECT FRANCE FOR THE FUTURE. ALSO, MANY OF THE FRENCH AGREED WITH NAZI IDEAS, OR WANTED A CHANGE IN GOVERNMENT, AND THERE WERE PEOPLE WHO TOOK ADVANTAGE OF THE CIRCUMSTANCES TO MAKE MONEY.

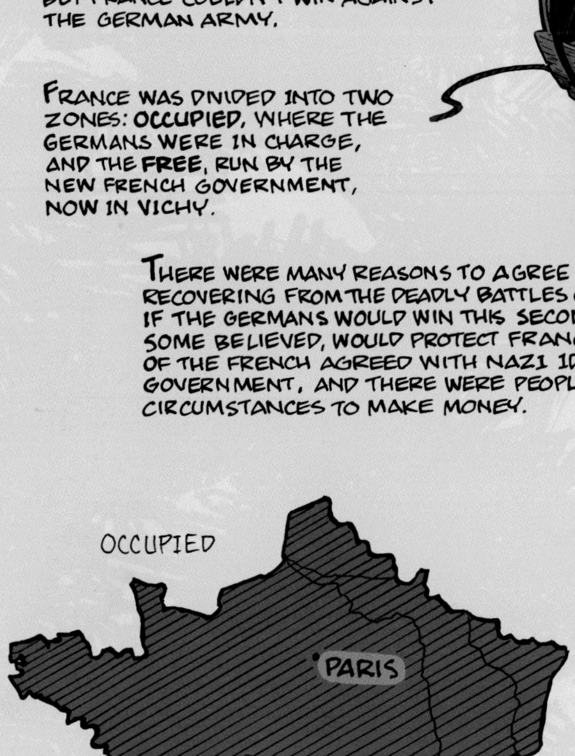

BUT THERE WERE THOUSANDS (SOME SAY TENS OF THOUSANDS) OF FRENCH MEN, WOMEN AND EVEN CHILDREN WHO RESISTED IN WAYS LARGE AND SMALL FROM THE BEGINNING. THEY JOINED WELL-ORGANIZED NETWORKS OR SIMPLY ACTED ON THEIR OWN.

IN THE OCCUPIED ZONE, LIFE WAS SEVERELY RESTRICTED. CURFEWS, RATIONS, ROUND-UPS, ARRESTS, SEARCHES, AND EVEN TORTURE BECAME A WAY OF LIFE. THERE WERE GERMAN SOLDIERS EVERYWHERE. IN THE SOUTHERN "FREE" ZONE THERE WERE STILL SHORTAGES, STILL GERMANS PRESENT, BUT PEOPLE WERE NOT LIVING WITH THE SAME LEVEL OF FEAR AS THOSE NORTH OF THE DEMARCATION LINE. THEY WERE LIVING IN DEFEAT, BUT NOT LIVING UNDER OCCUPATION.

OCCUPIED

PARIS

VICHY

"FREE"

UNTIL 1942.

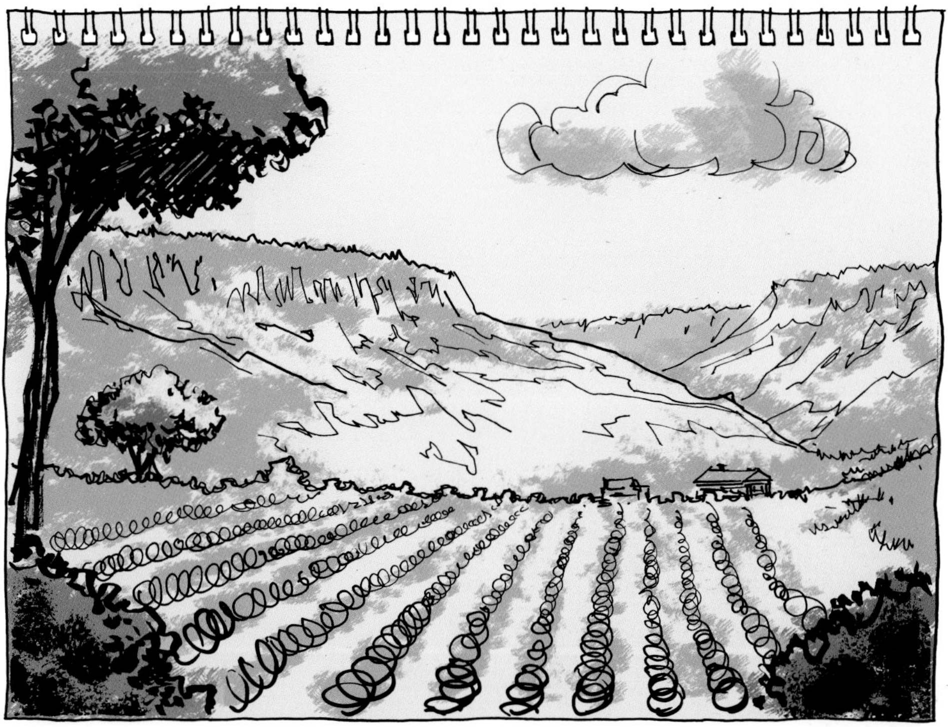

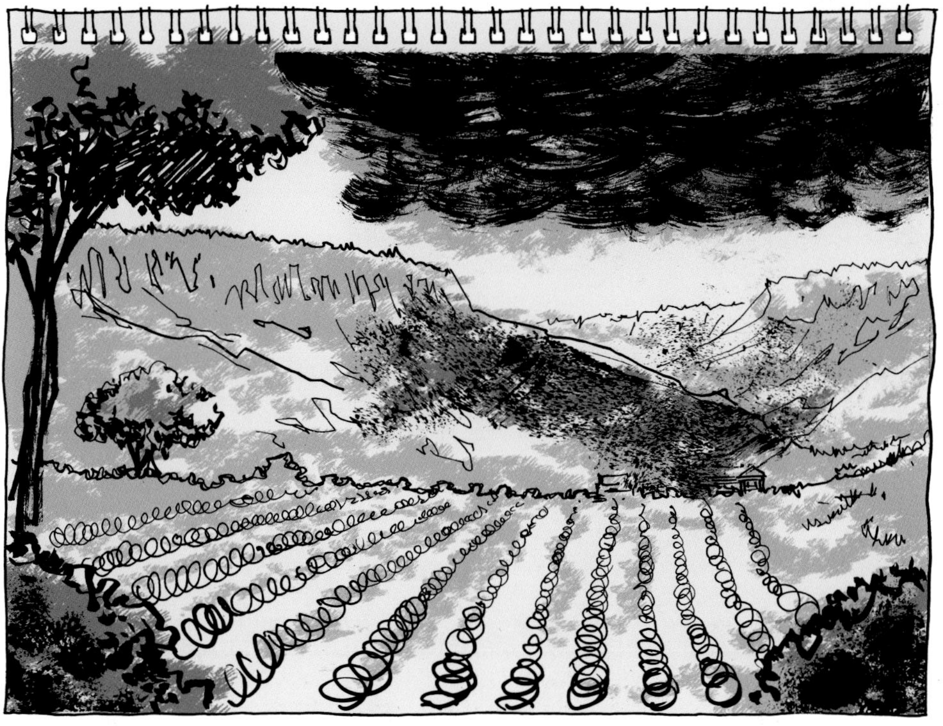

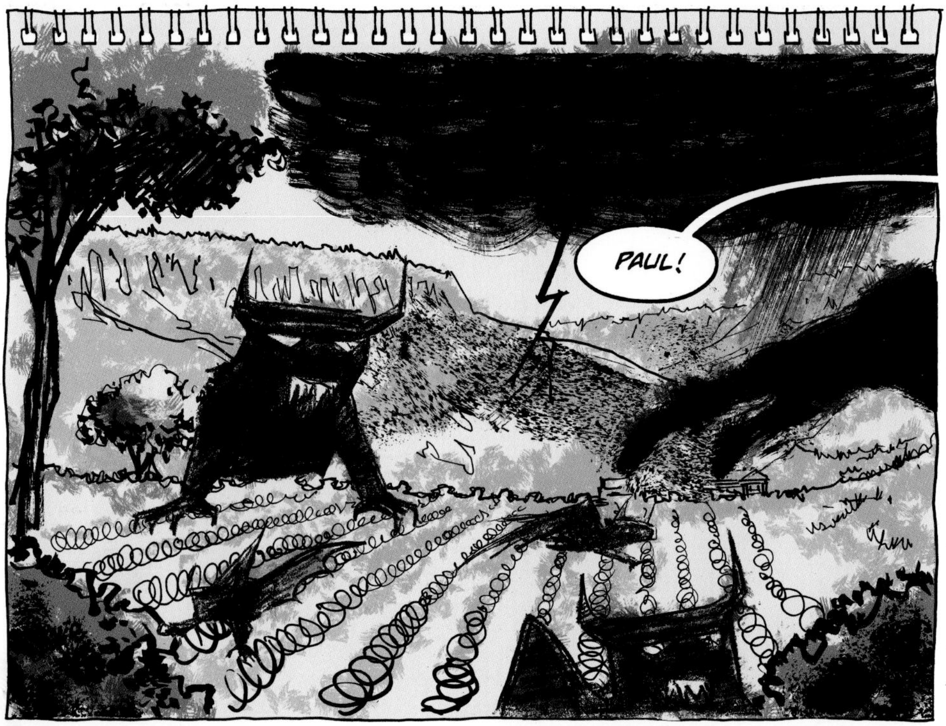
PAUL!

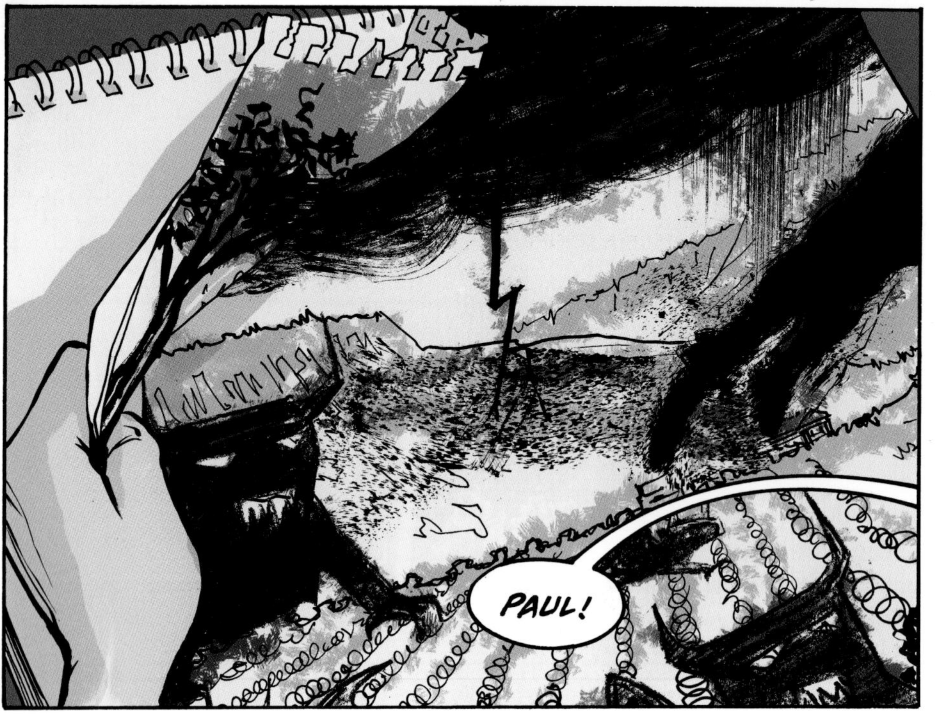
PAUL!

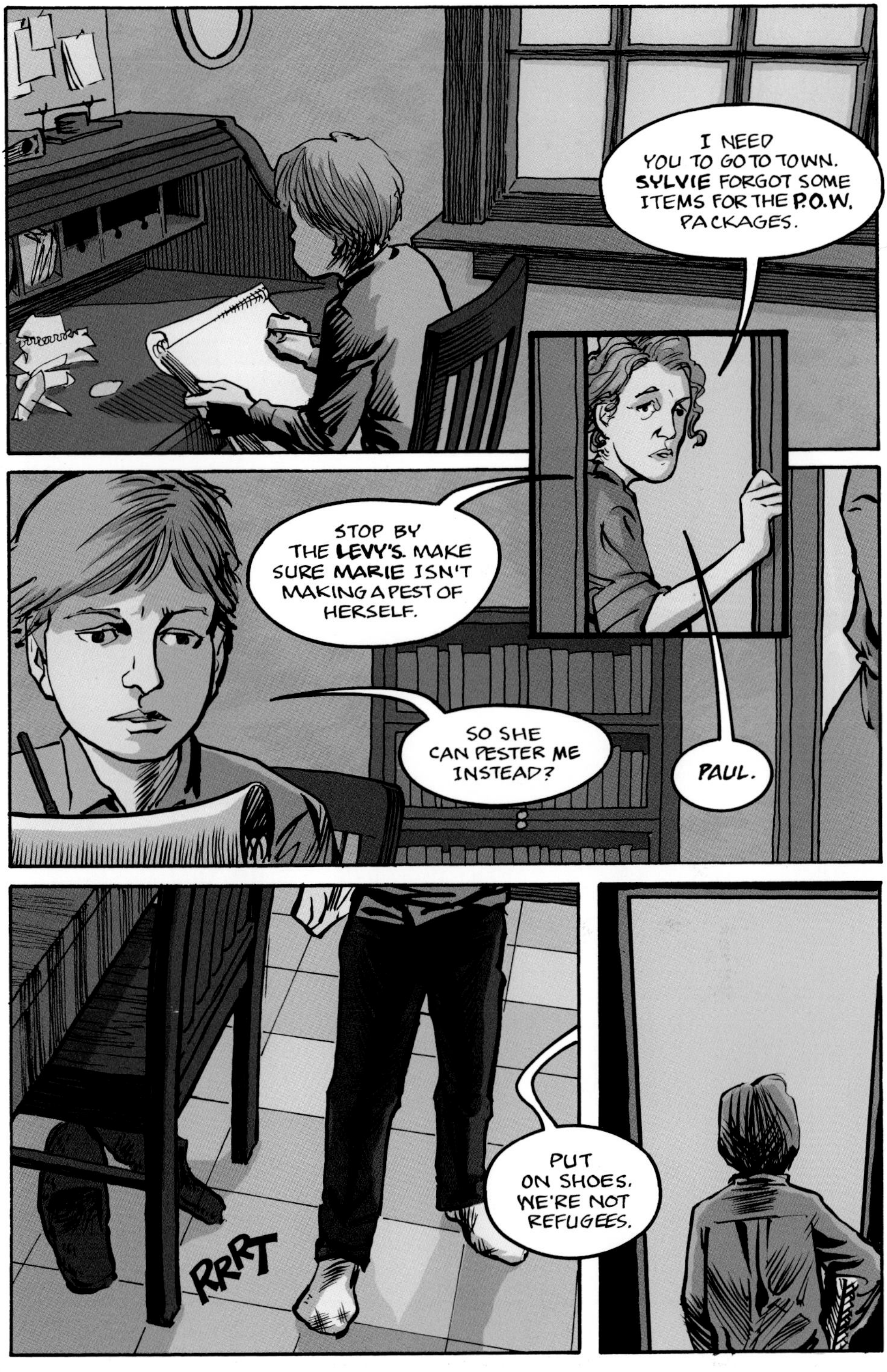
I NEED YOU TO GO TO TOWN. SYLVIE FORGOT SOME ITEMS FOR THE P.O.W. PACKAGES.
STOP BY THE LEVY'S. MAKE SURE MARIE ISN'T MAKING A PEST OF HERSELF.
SO SHE CAN PESTER ME INSTEAD?
PAUL.
RRRT
PUT ON SHOES. WE'RE NOT REFUGEES.

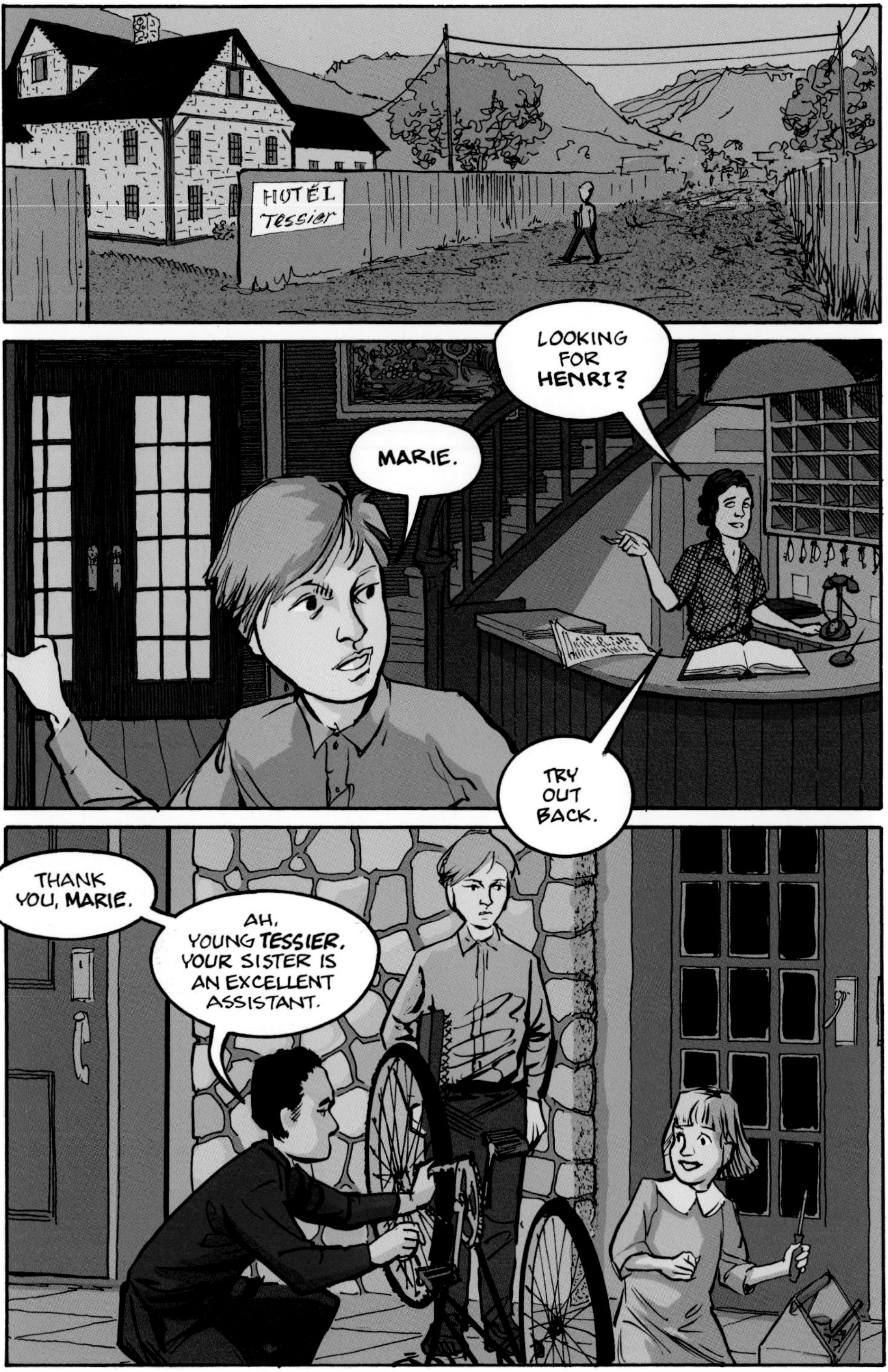
HOTÉL Tessier
LOOKING FOR HENRI?
MARIE.
TRY OUT BACK.
THANK YOU, MARIE.
AH, YOUNG TESSIER. YOUR SISTER IS AN EXCELLENT ASSISTANT.

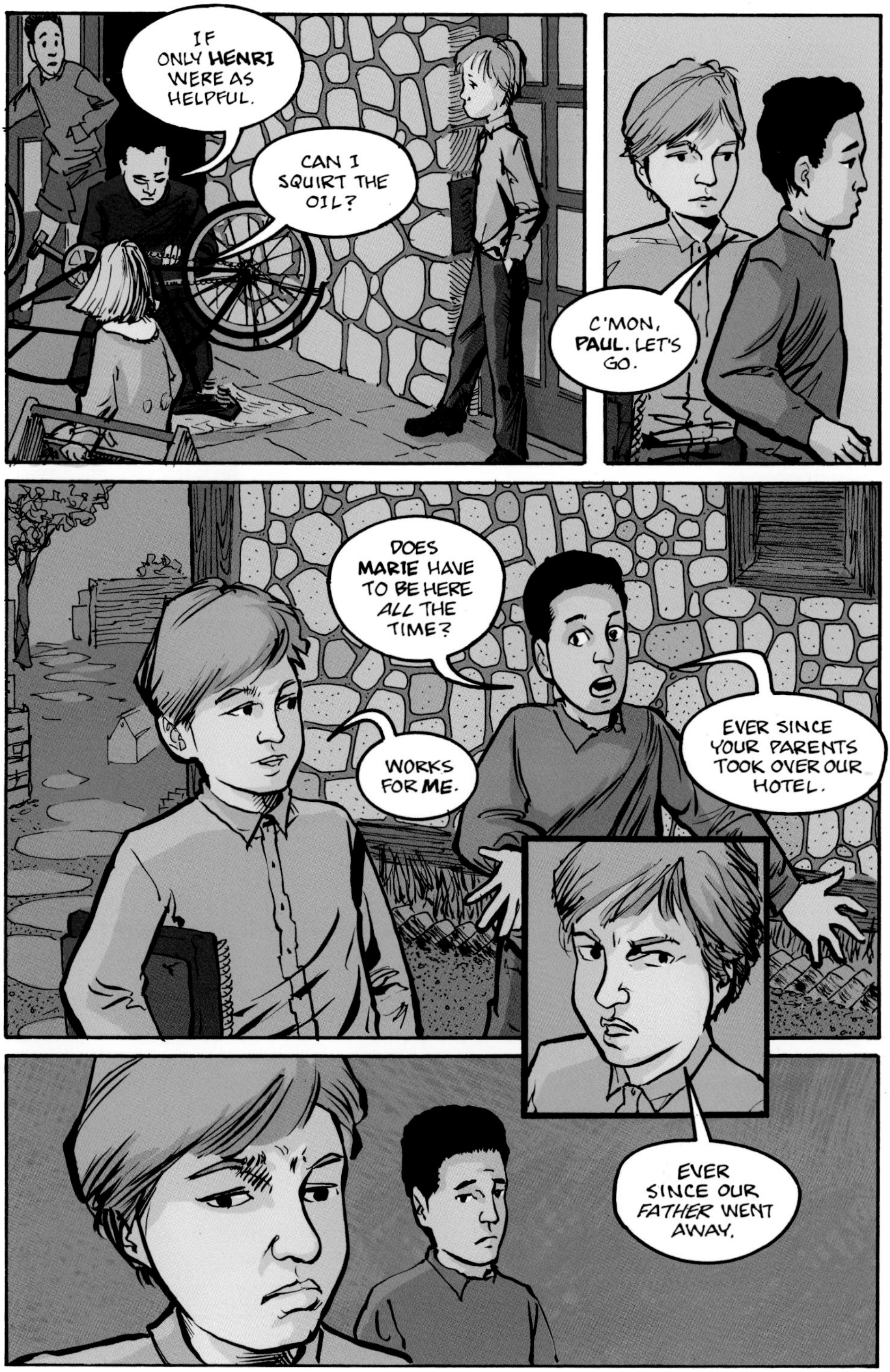
IF ONLY **HENRI** WERE AS HELPFUL.
CAN I SQUIRT THE OIL?
C'MON, **PAUL**. LET'S GO.
DOES **MARIE** HAVE TO BE HERE *ALL* THE TIME?
WORKS FOR **ME**.
EVER SINCE YOUR PARENTS TOOK OVER OUR HOTEL.
EVER SINCE OUR *FATHER* WENT AWAY.

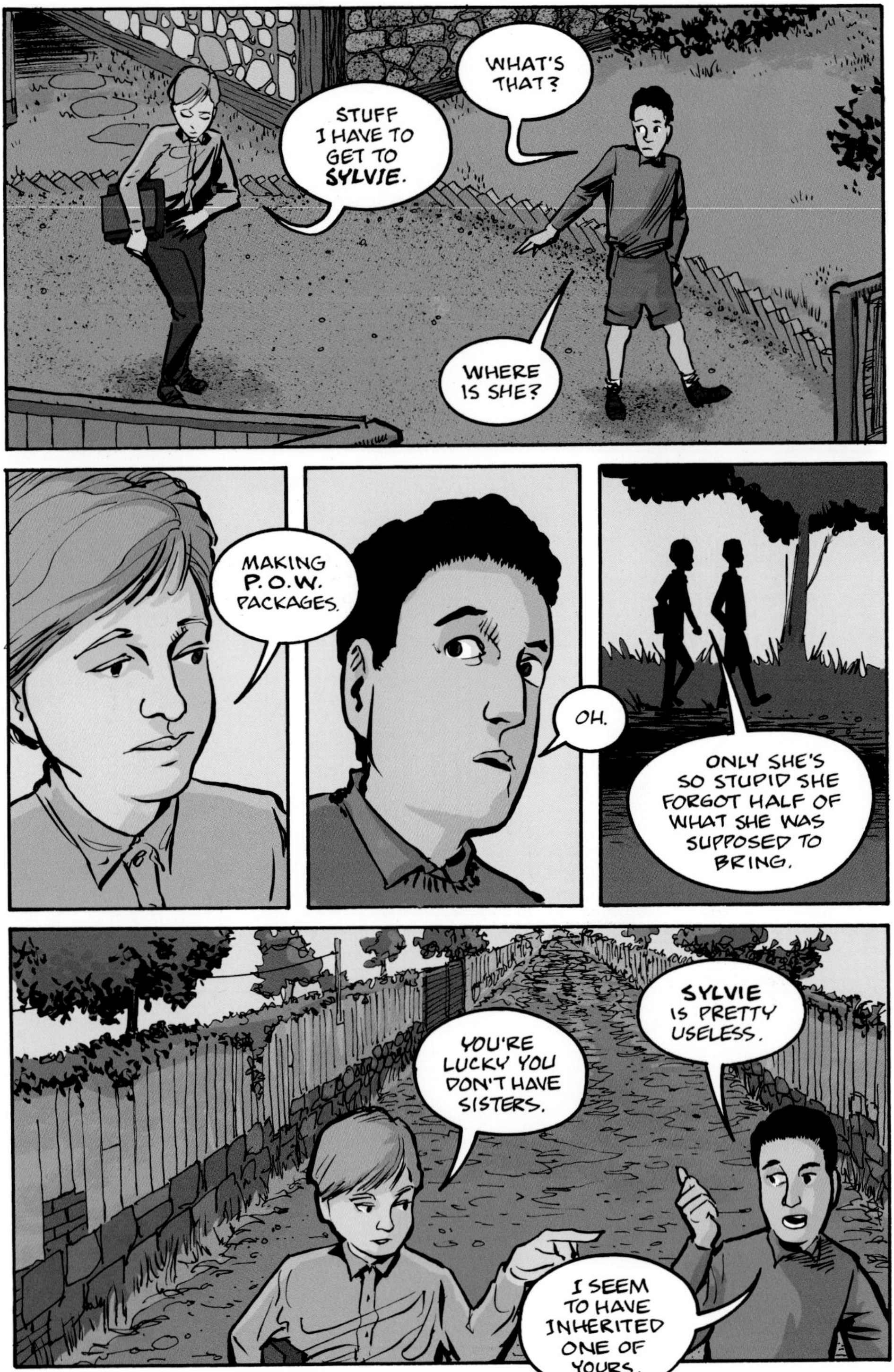
STUFF I HAVE TO GET TO SYLVIE.
WHAT'S THAT?
WHERE IS SHE?
MAKING P.O.W. PACKAGES.
OH.
ONLY SHE'S SO STUPID SHE FORGOT HALF OF WHAT SHE WAS SUPPOSED TO BRING.
SYLVIE IS PRETTY USELESS.
YOU'RE LUCKY YOU DON'T HAVE SISTERS.
I SEEM TO HAVE INHERITED ONE OF YOURS.

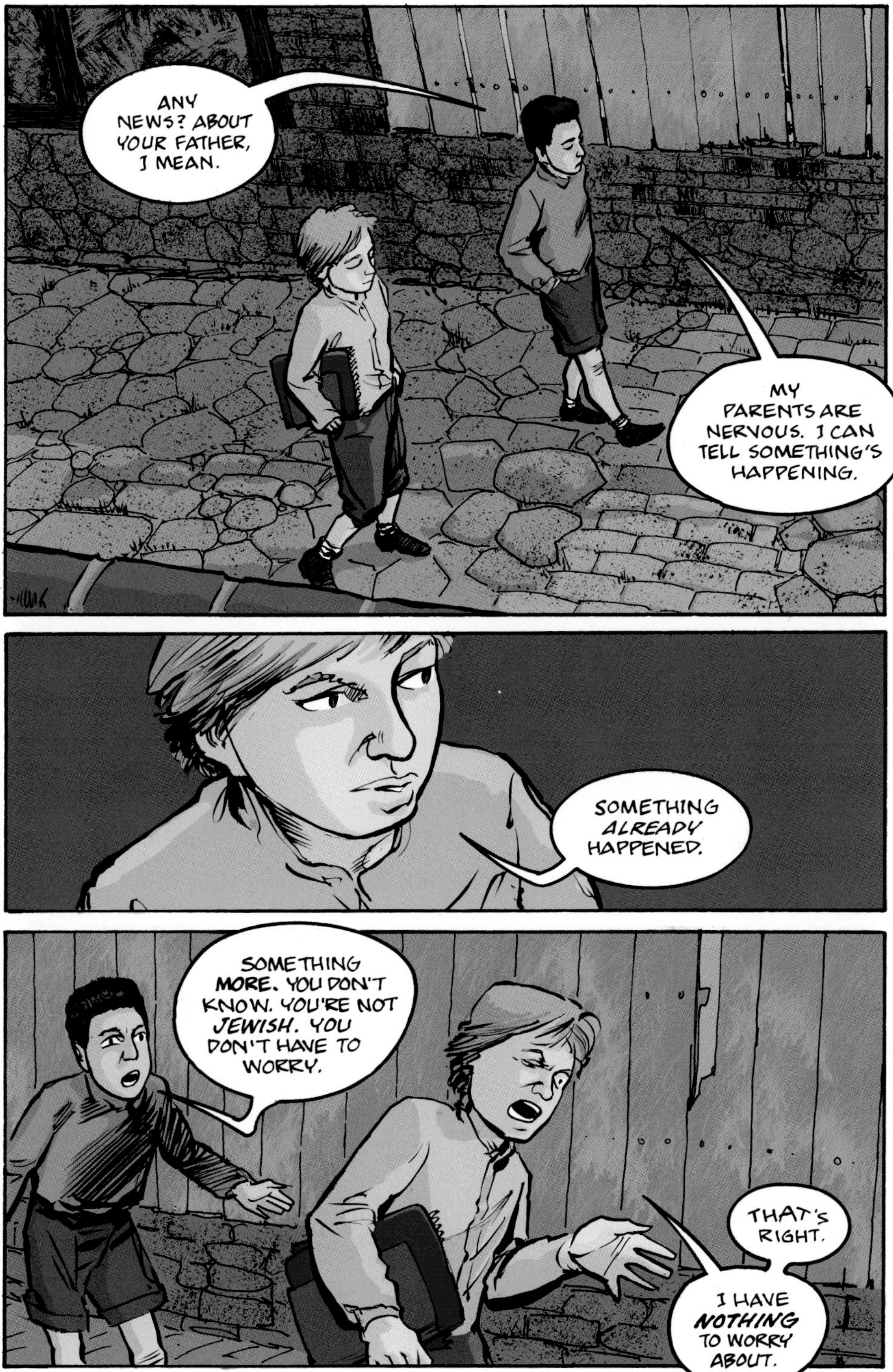
ANY NEWS? ABOUT YOUR FATHER, I MEAN.
MY PARENTS ARE NERVOUS. I CAN TELL SOMETHING'S HAPPENING.
SOMETHING *ALREADY* HAPPENED.
SOMETHING **MORE.** YOU DON'T KNOW. YOU'RE NOT ***JEWISH***. YOU DON'T HAVE TO WORRY.
THAT'S RIGHT.
I HAVE ***NOTHING*** TO WORRY ABOUT.

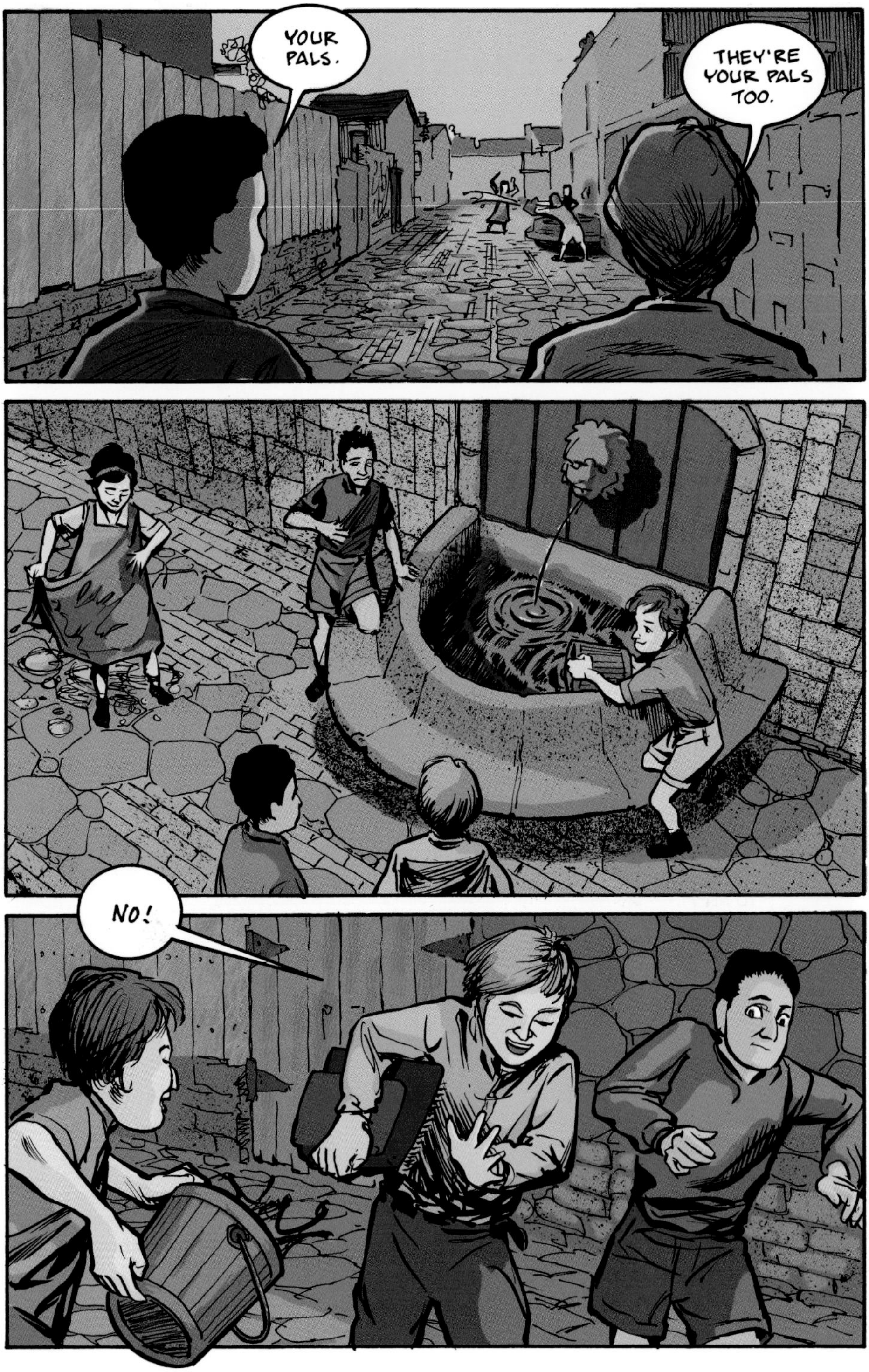
YOUR PALS.
THEY'RE YOUR PALS TOO.
NO!

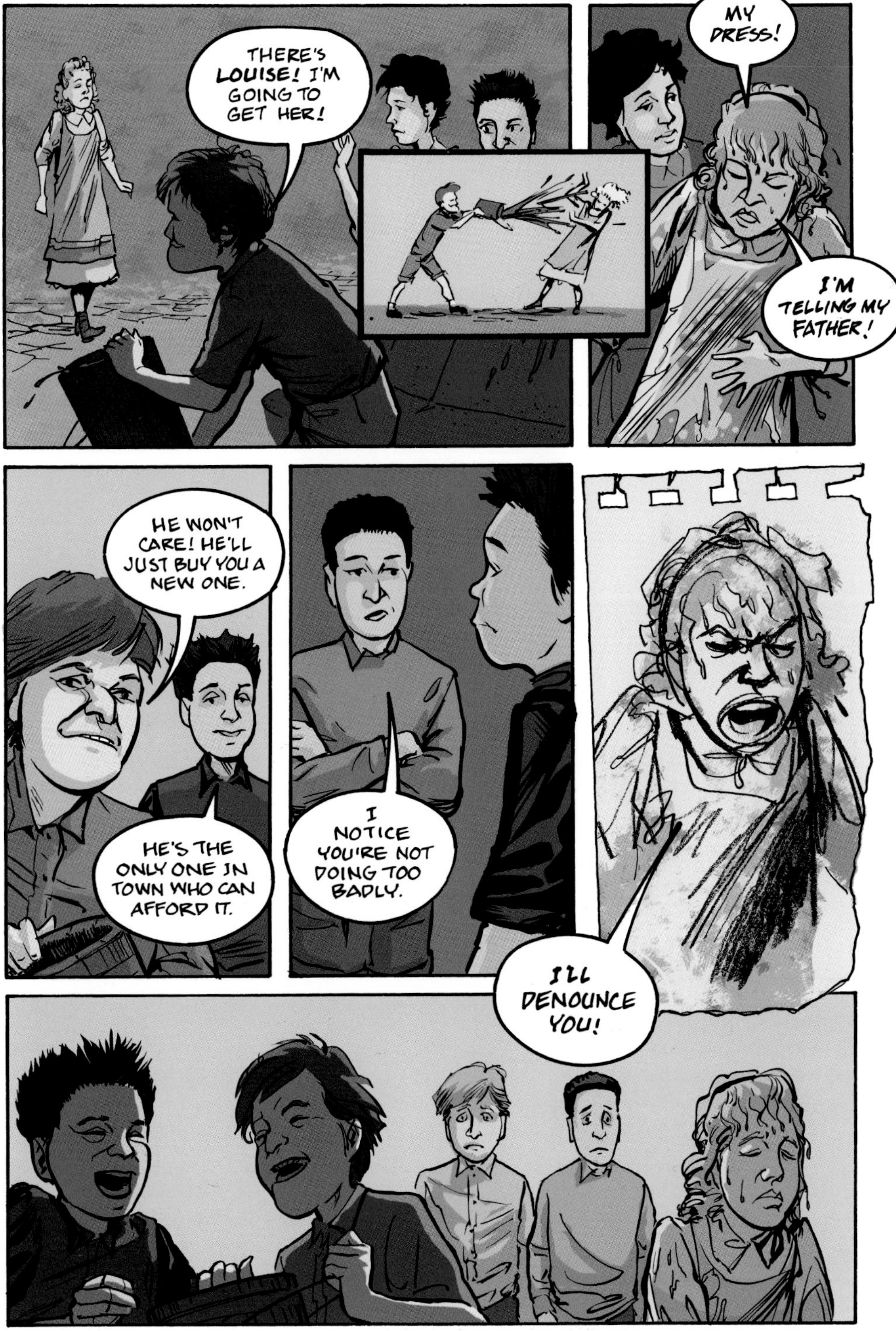
THERE'S LOUISE! I'M GOING TO GET HER!
MY DRESS!
I'M TELLING MY FATHER!
HE WON'T CARE! HE'LL JUST BUY YOU A NEW ONE.
HE'S THE ONLY ONE IN TOWN WHO CAN AFFORD IT.
I NOTICE YOU'RE NOT DOING TOO BADLY.
I'LL DENOUNCE YOU!

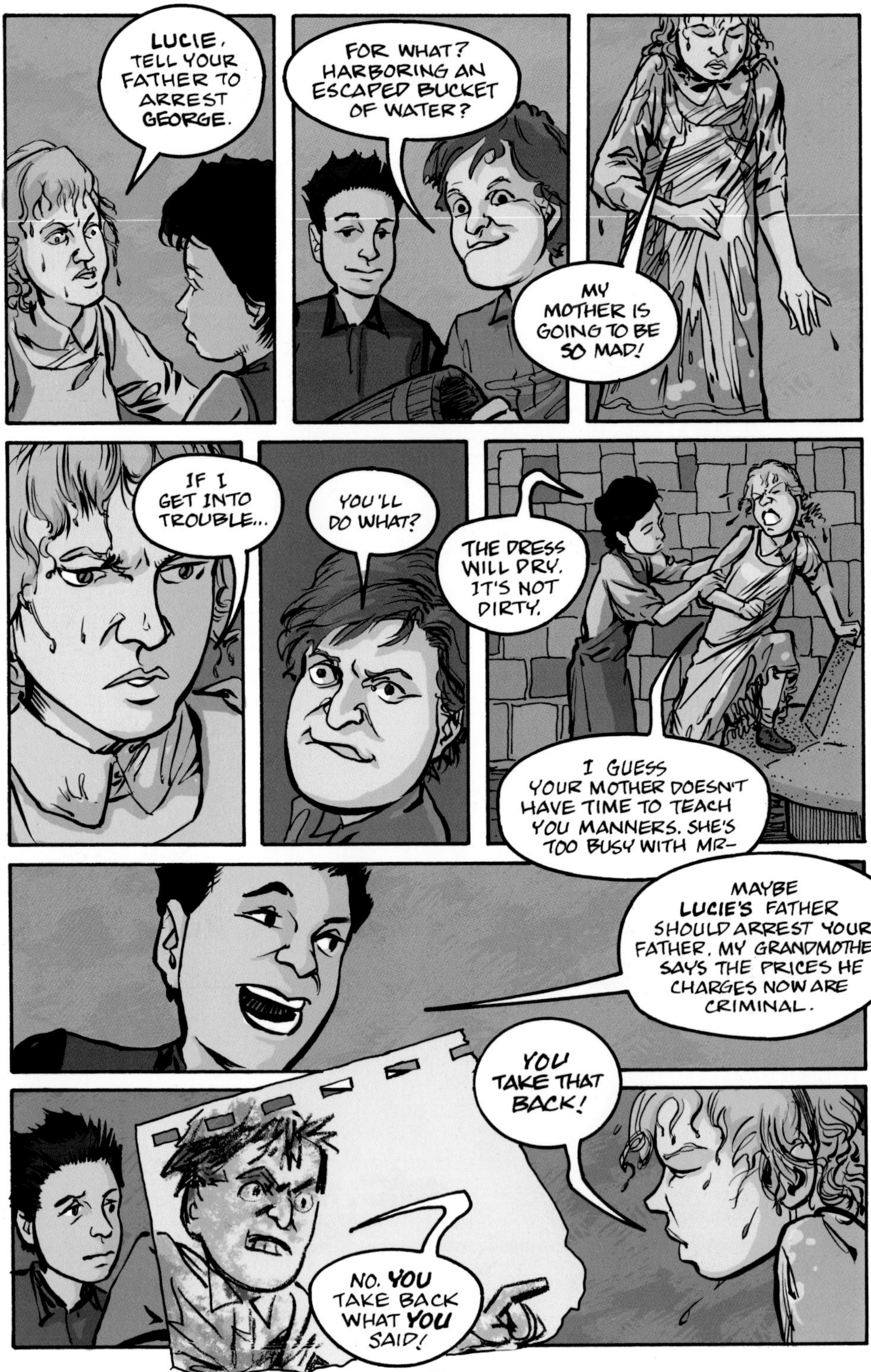
LUCIE, TELL YOUR FATHER TO ARREST GEORGE.
FOR WHAT? HARBORING AN ESCAPED BUCKET OF WATER?
MY MOTHER IS GOING TO BE SO MAD!
IF I GET INTO TROUBLE...
YOU'LL DO WHAT?
THE DRESS WILL DRY. IT'S NOT DIRTY.
I GUESS YOUR MOTHER DOESN'T HAVE TIME TO TEACH YOU MANNERS. SHE'S TOO BUSY WITH MR-
MAYBE LUCIE'S FATHER SHOULD ARREST YOUR FATHER. MY GRANDMOTHER SAYS THE PRICES HE CHARGES NOW ARE CRIMINAL.
YOU TAKE THAT BACK!
NO. YOU TAKE BACK WHAT YOU SAID!

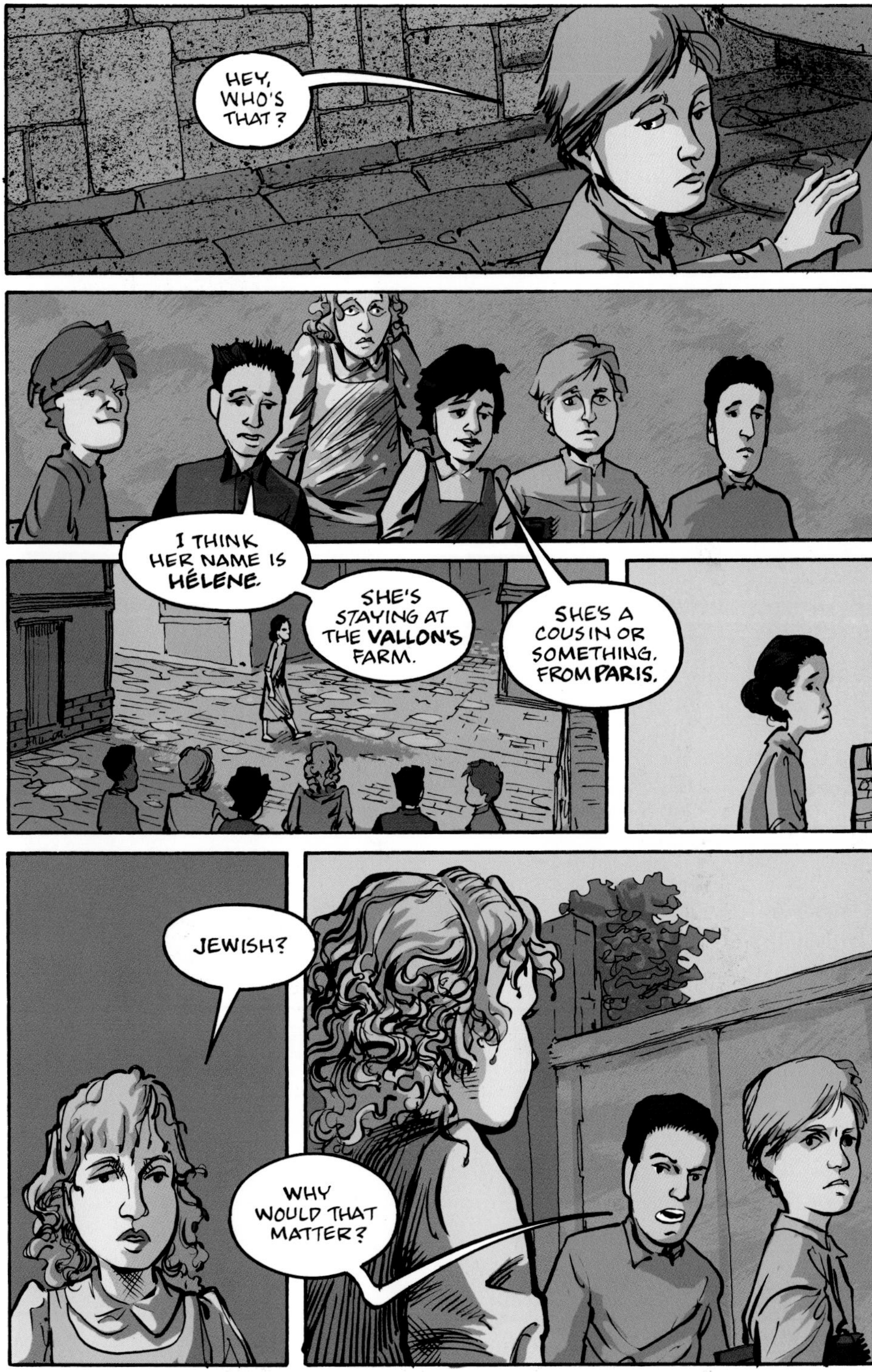
HEY, WHO'S THAT?
I THINK HER NAME IS **HÉLENE.**
SHE'S STAYING AT THE **VALLON'S** FARM.
SHE'S A COUSIN OR SOMETHING. FROM **PARIS.**
JEWISH?
WHY WOULD THAT MATTER?

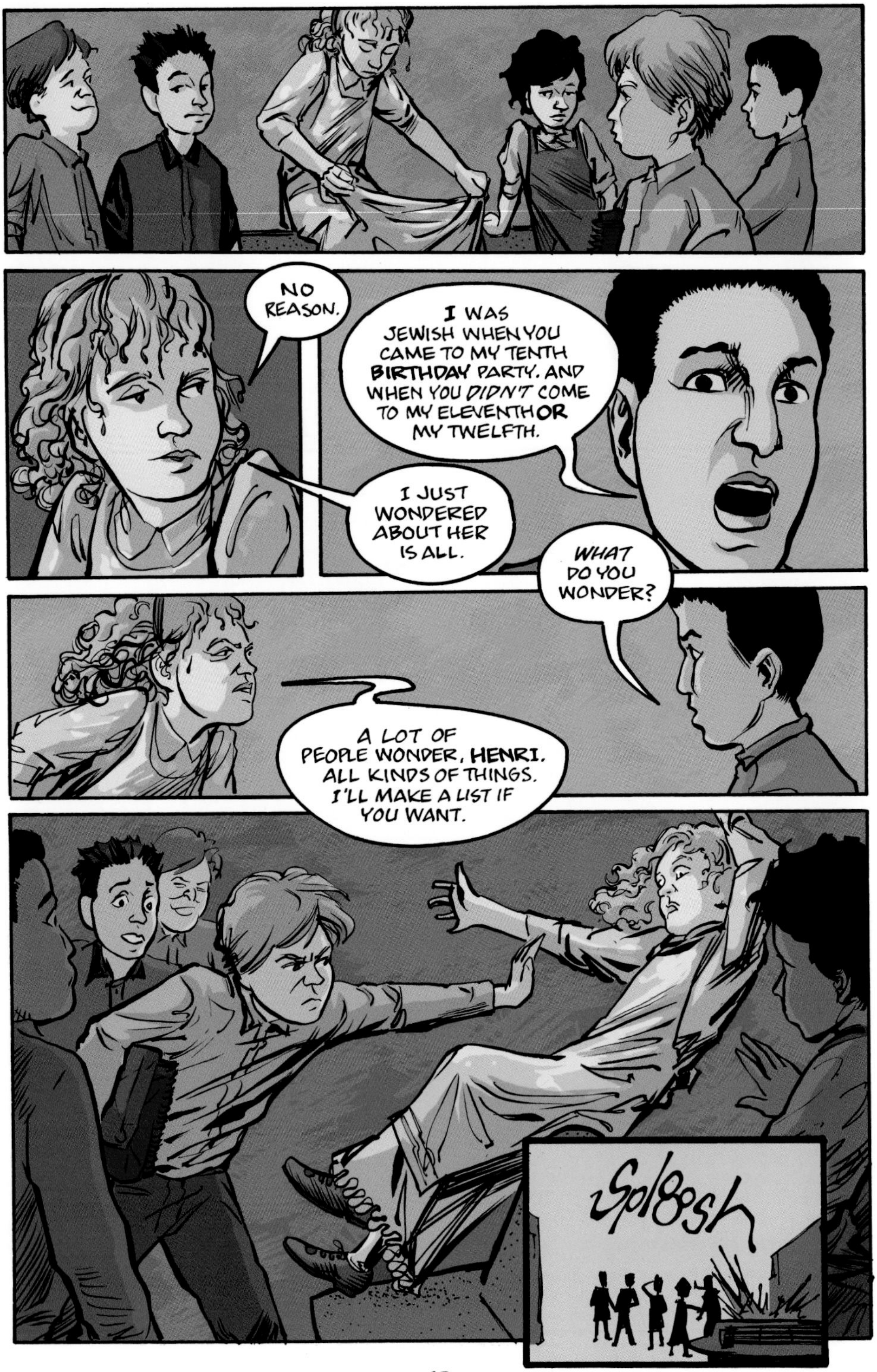
NO REASON.
I WAS JEWISH WHEN YOU CAME TO MY TENTH BIRTHDAY PARTY. AND WHEN YOU DIDN'T COME TO MY ELEVENTH OR MY TWELFTH.
I JUST WONDERED ABOUT HER IS ALL.
WHAT DO YOU WONDER?
A LOT OF PEOPLE WONDER, HENRI. ALL KINDS OF THINGS. I'LL MAKE A LIST IF YOU WANT.
Splosh

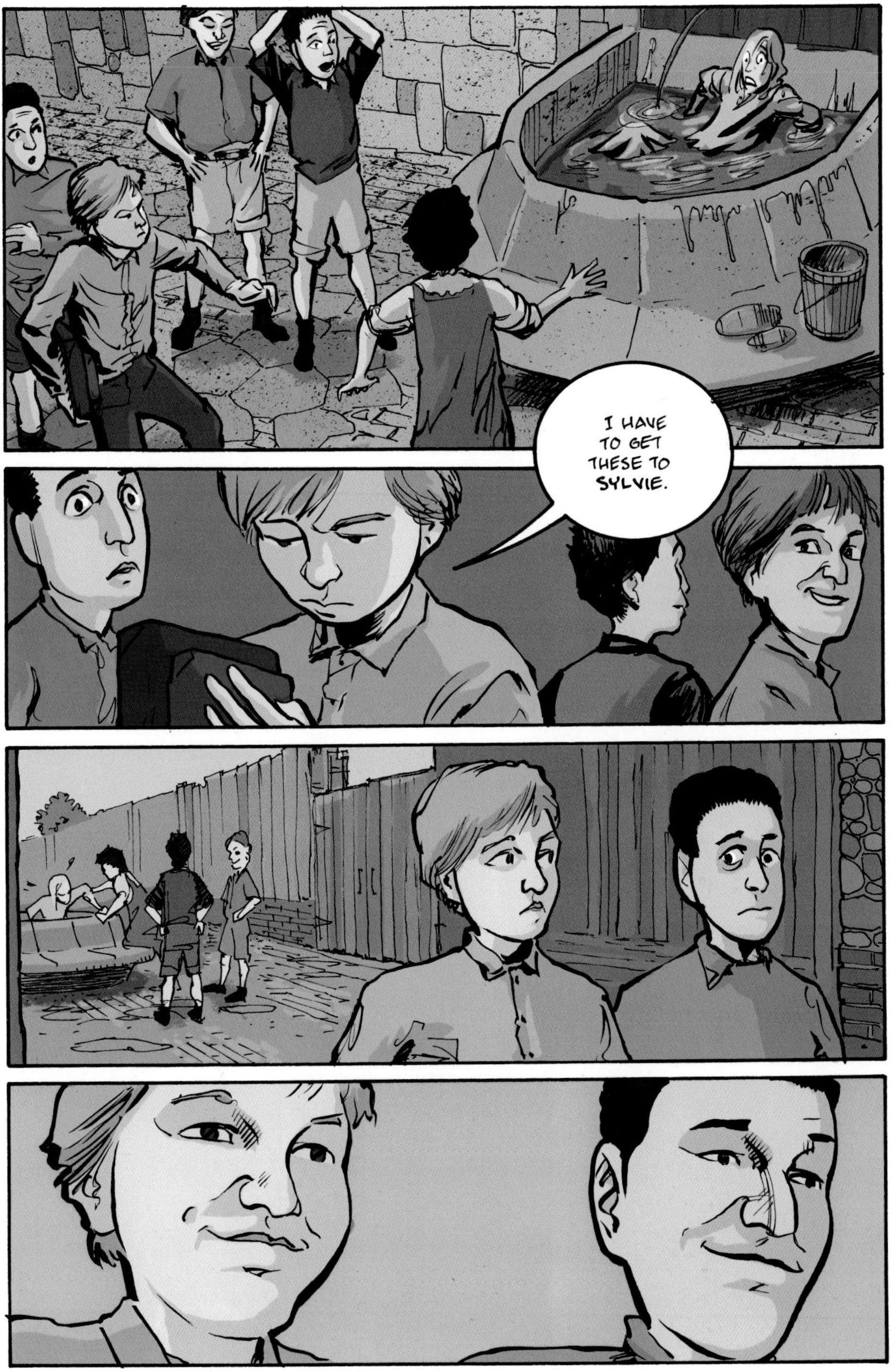
I HAVE TO GET THESE TO SYLVIE.

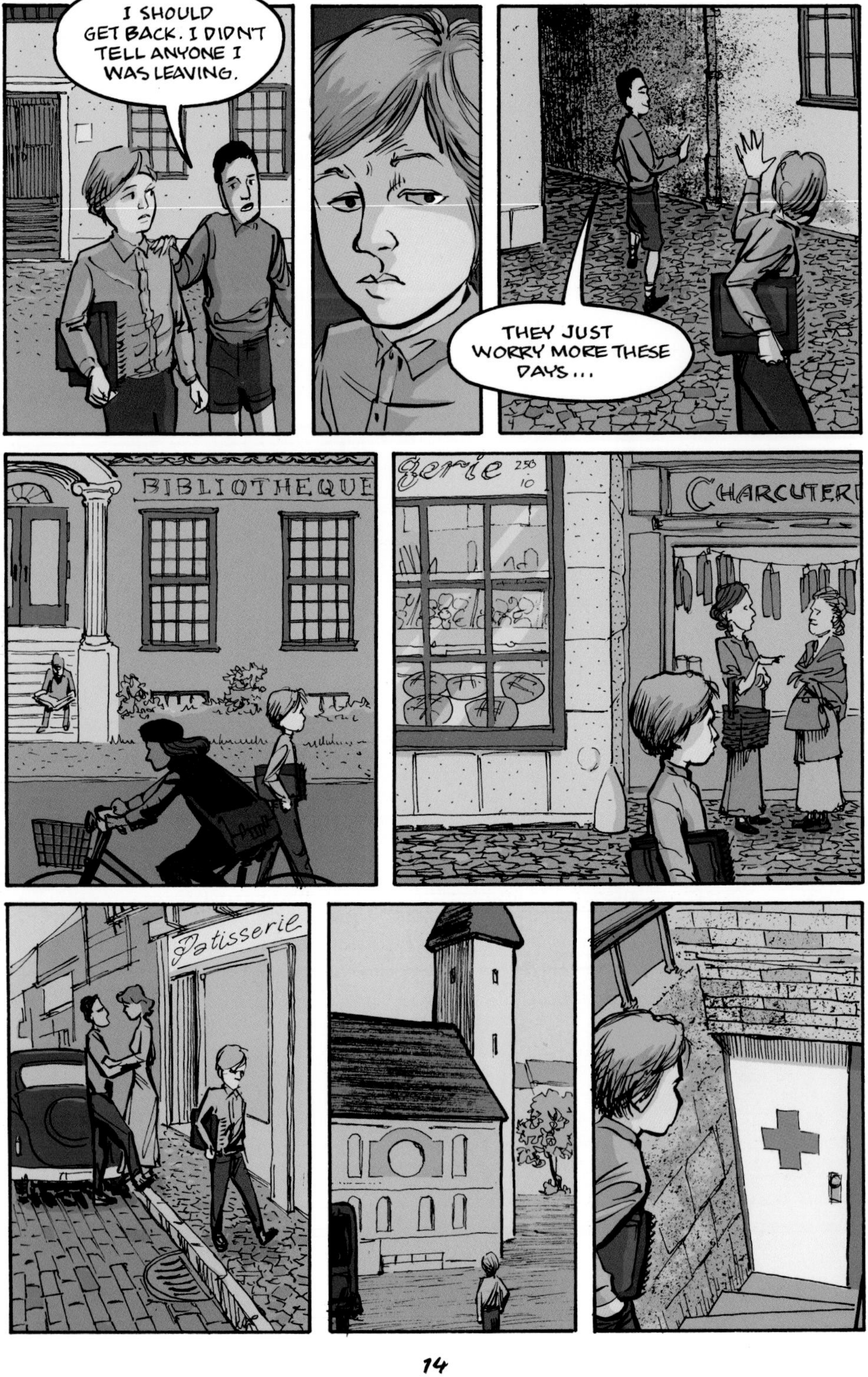
I SHOULD GET BACK. I DIDN'T TELL ANYONE I WAS LEAVING.
THEY JUST WORRY MORE THESE DAYS...
BIBLIOTHEQUE
gerie
250
10
CHARCUTERI
Patisserie

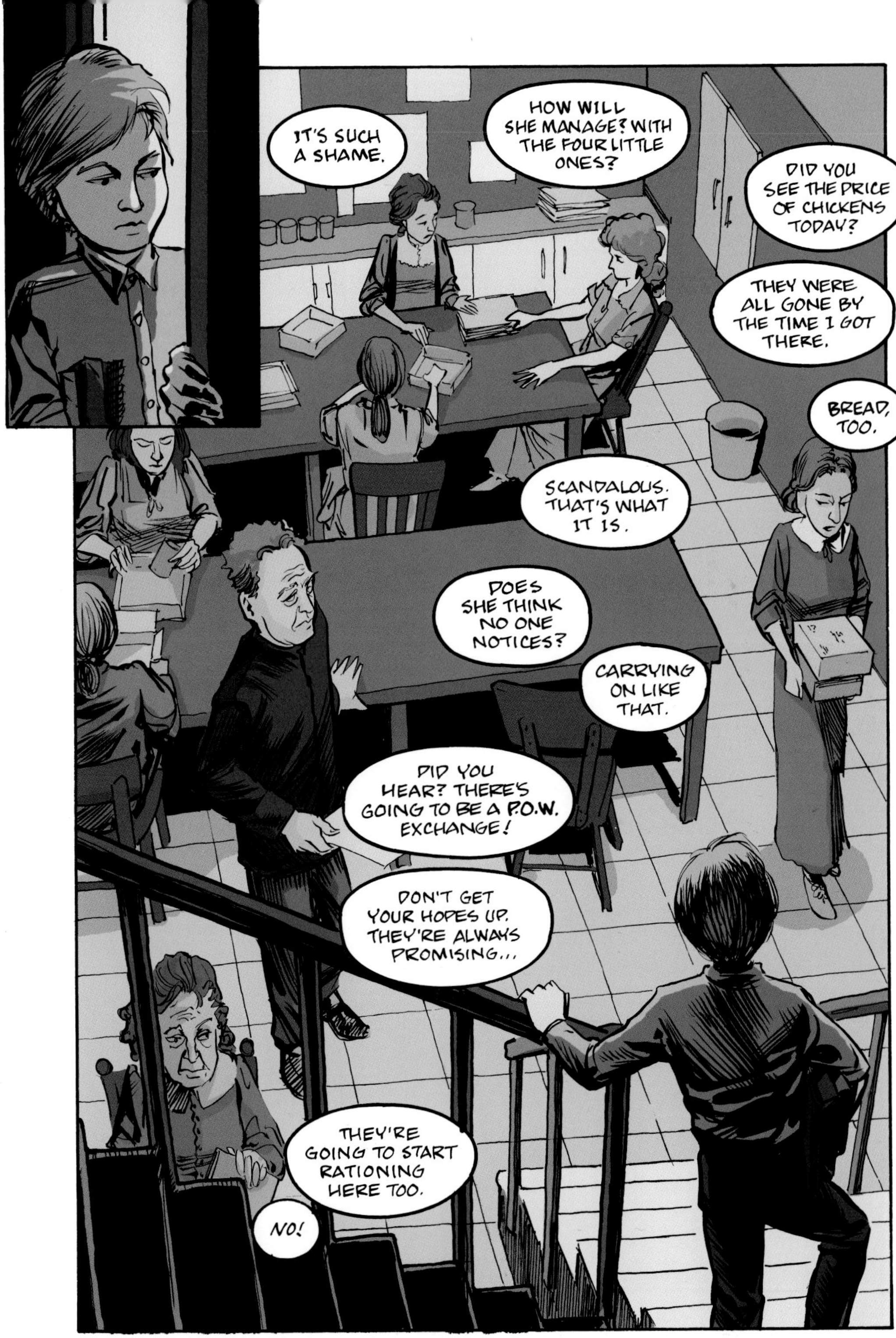
IT'S SUCH A SHAME.
HOW WILL SHE MANAGE? WITH THE FOUR LITTLE ONES?
DID YOU SEE THE PRICE OF CHICKENS TODAY?
THEY WERE ALL GONE BY THE TIME I GOT THERE.
BREAD, TOO.
SCANDALOUS. THAT'S WHAT IT IS.
DOES SHE THINK NO ONE NOTICES?
CARRYING ON LIKE THAT.
DID YOU HEAR? THERE'S GOING TO BE A P.O.W. EXCHANGE!
DON'T GET YOUR HOPES UP. THEY'RE ALWAYS PROMISING...
THEY'RE GOING TO START RATIONING HERE TOO.
NO!

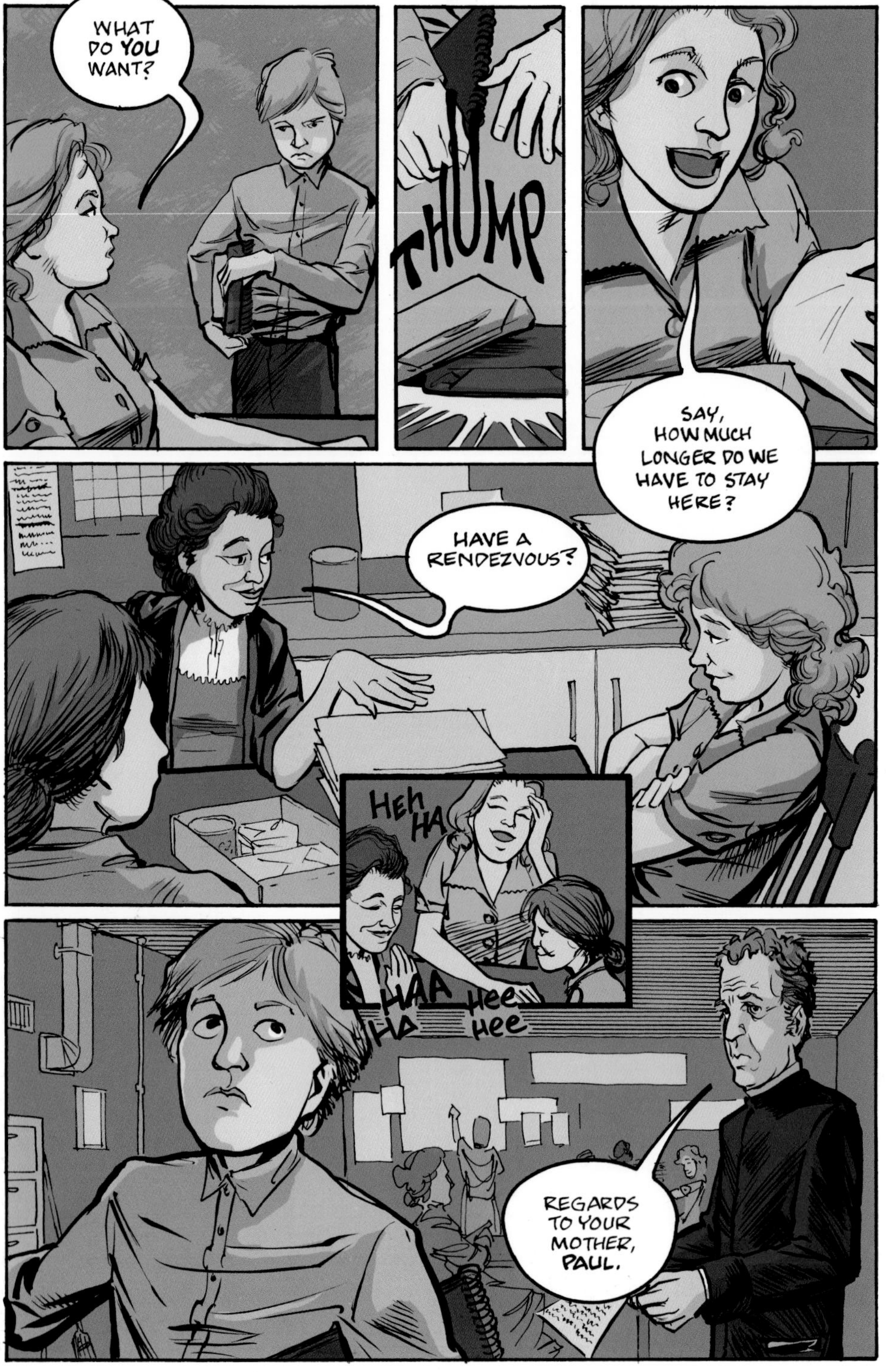
WHAT DO YOU WANT?
THUMP
SAY, HOW MUCH LONGER DO WE HAVE TO STAY HERE?
HAVE A RENDEZVOUS?
Heh HA
HA HA
Hee Hee
REGARDS TO YOUR MOTHER, PAUL.

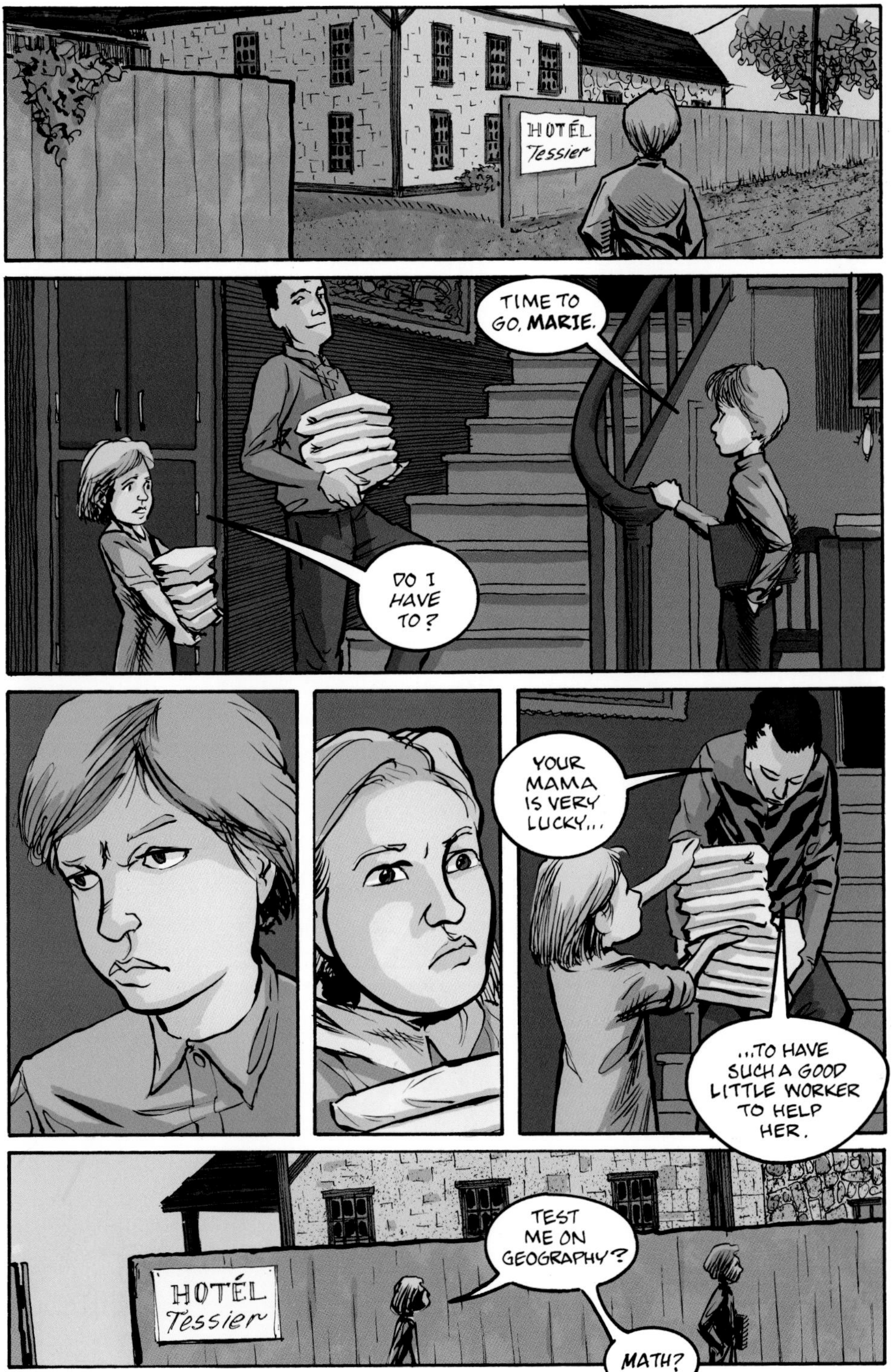
HOTÉL Tessier
TIME TO GO, MARIE.
DO I HAVE TO?
YOUR MAMA IS VERY LUCKY...
...TO HAVE SUCH A GOOD LITTLE WORKER TO HELP HER.
HOTÉL Tessier
TEST ME ON GEOGRAPHY?
MATH?

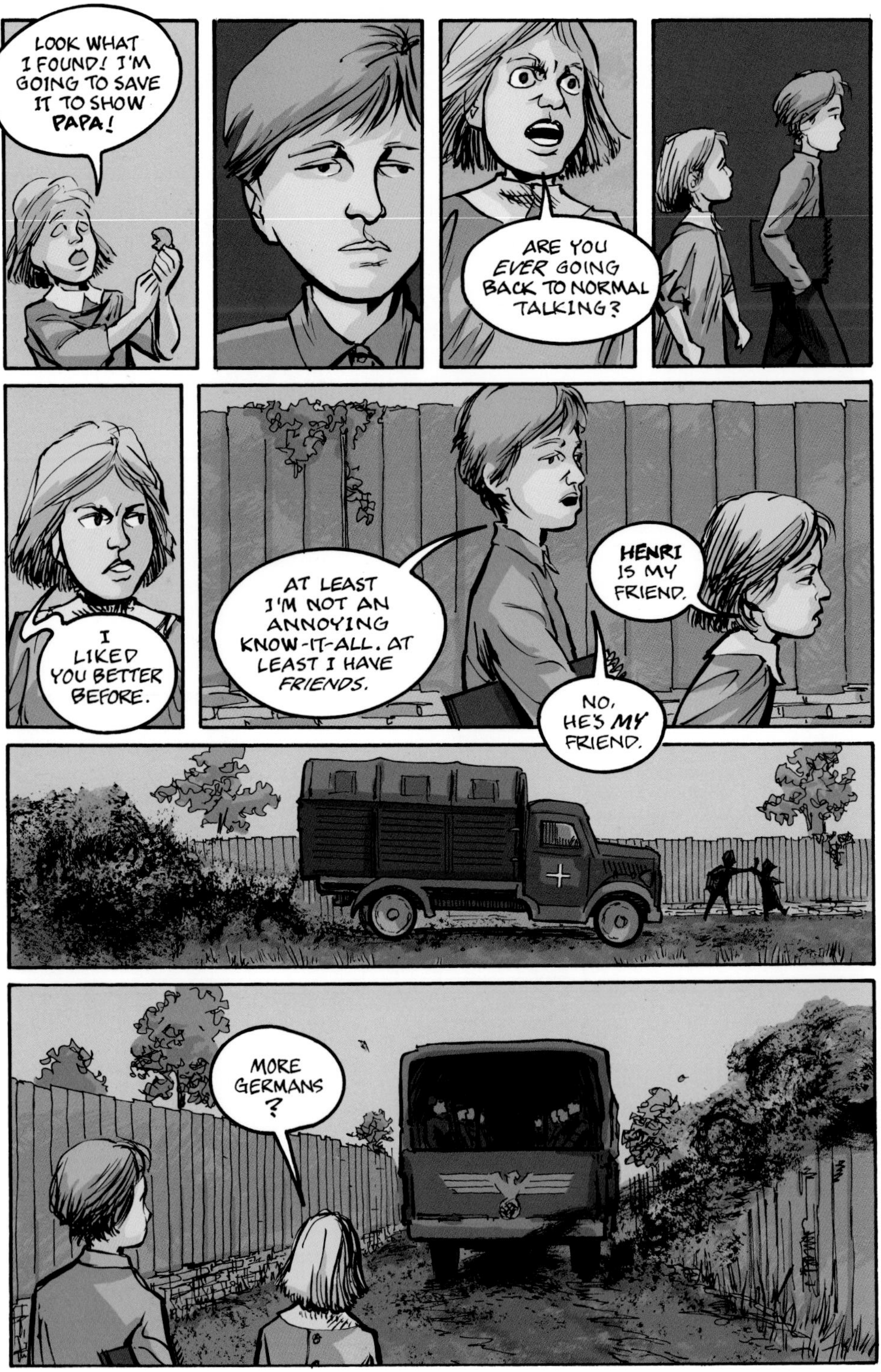
LOOK WHAT I FOUND! I'M GOING TO SAVE IT TO SHOW **PAPA**!
ARE YOU *EVER* GOING BACK TO NORMAL TALKING?
I LIKED YOU BETTER BEFORE.
AT LEAST I'M NOT AN ANNOYING KNOW-IT-ALL. AT LEAST I HAVE *FRIENDS*.
HENRI IS MY FRIEND.
NO, HE'S *MY* FRIEND.
MORE GERMANS?

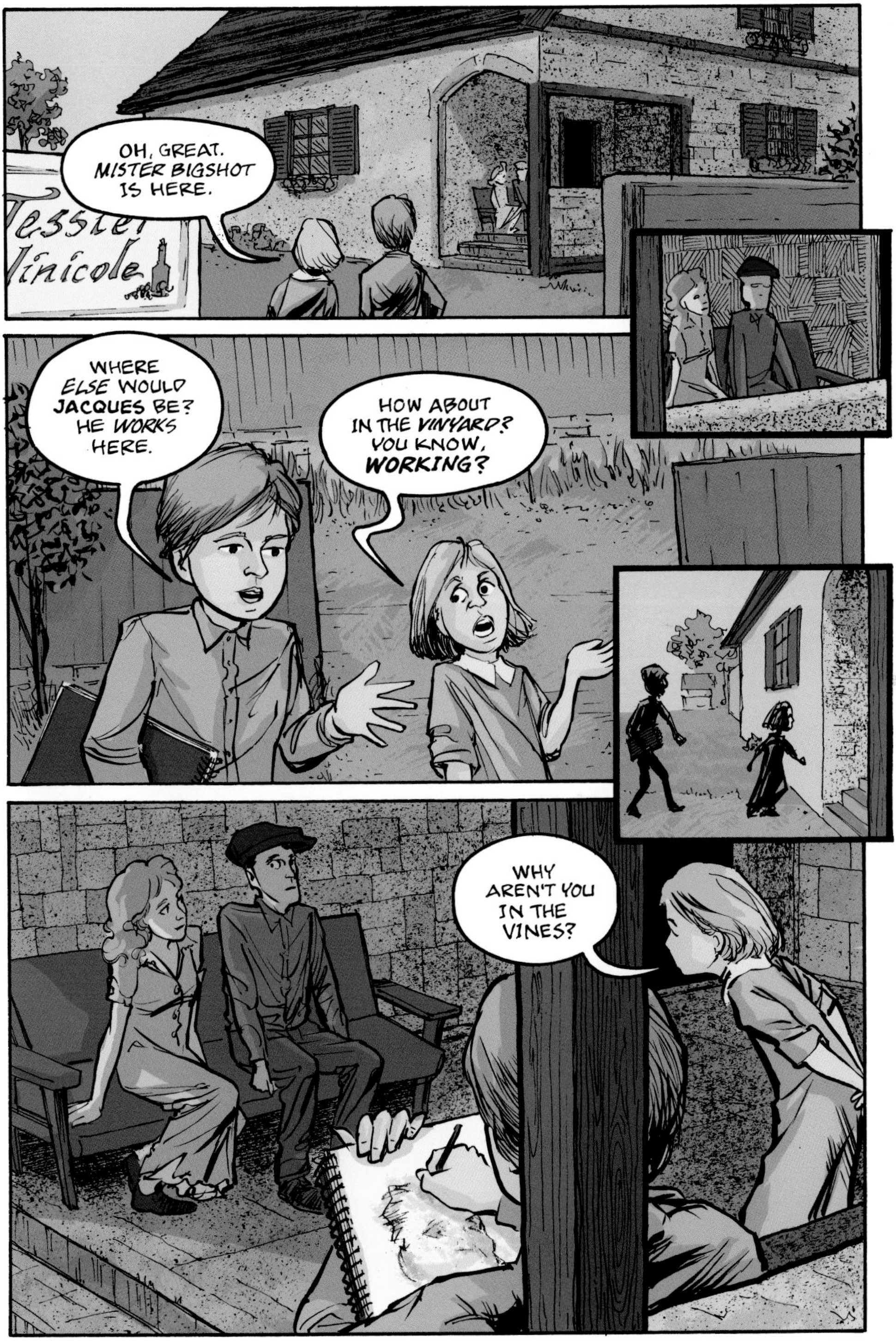
OH, GREAT. MISTER BIGSHOT IS HERE.
Tessier Vinicole
WHERE ELSE WOULD JACQUES BE? HE WORKS HERE.
HOW ABOUT IN THE VINYARD? YOU KNOW, WORKING?
WHY AREN'T YOU IN THE VINES?

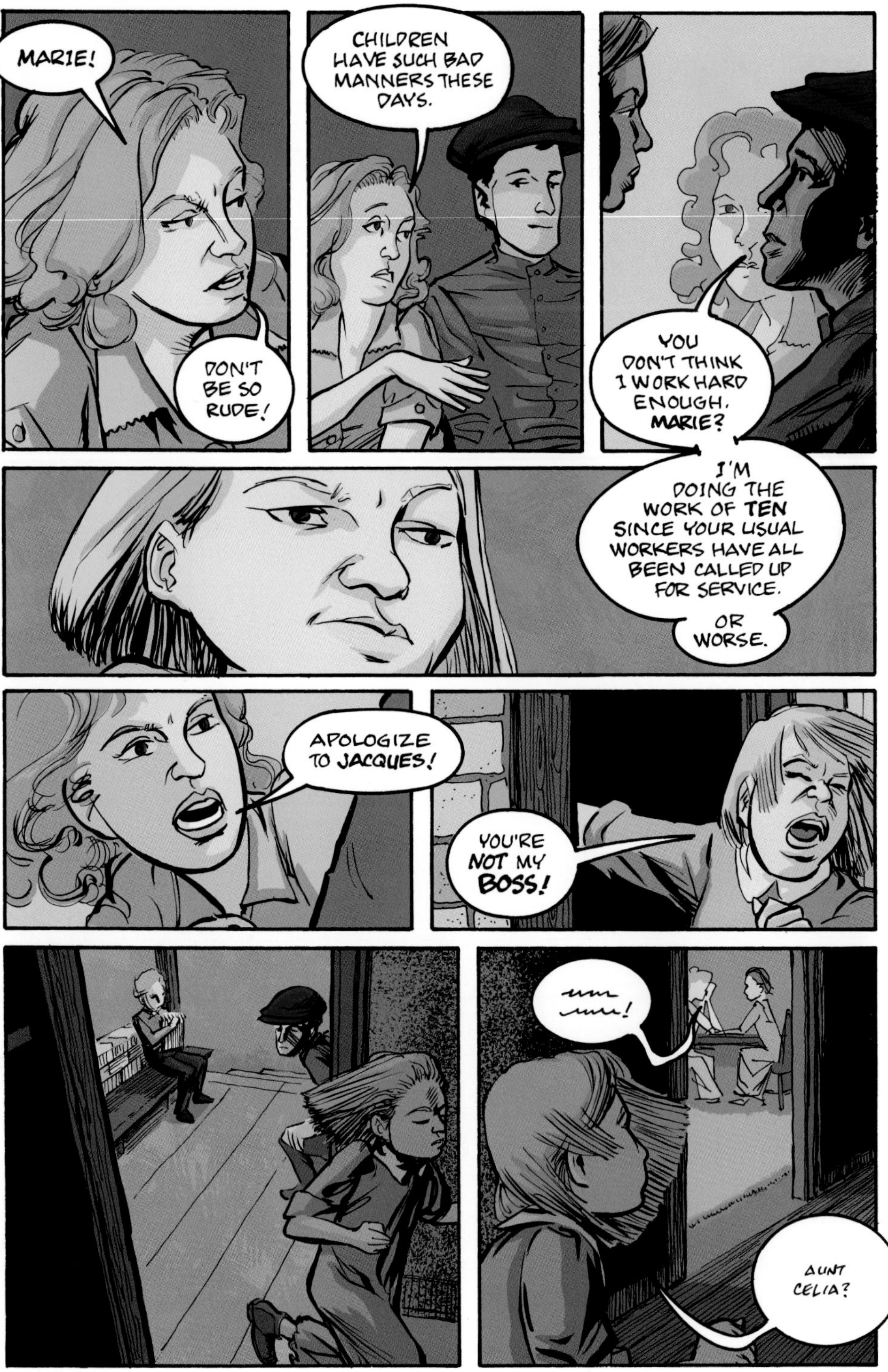
MARIE!
DON'T BE SO RUDE!
CHILDREN HAVE SUCH BAD MANNERS THESE DAYS.
YOU DON'T THINK I WORK HARD ENOUGH, MARIE?
I'M DOING THE WORK OF TEN SINCE YOUR USUAL WORKERS HAVE ALL BEEN CALLED UP FOR SERVICE.
OR WORSE.
APOLOGIZE TO JACQUES!
YOU'RE NOT MY BOSS!
AUNT CELIA?

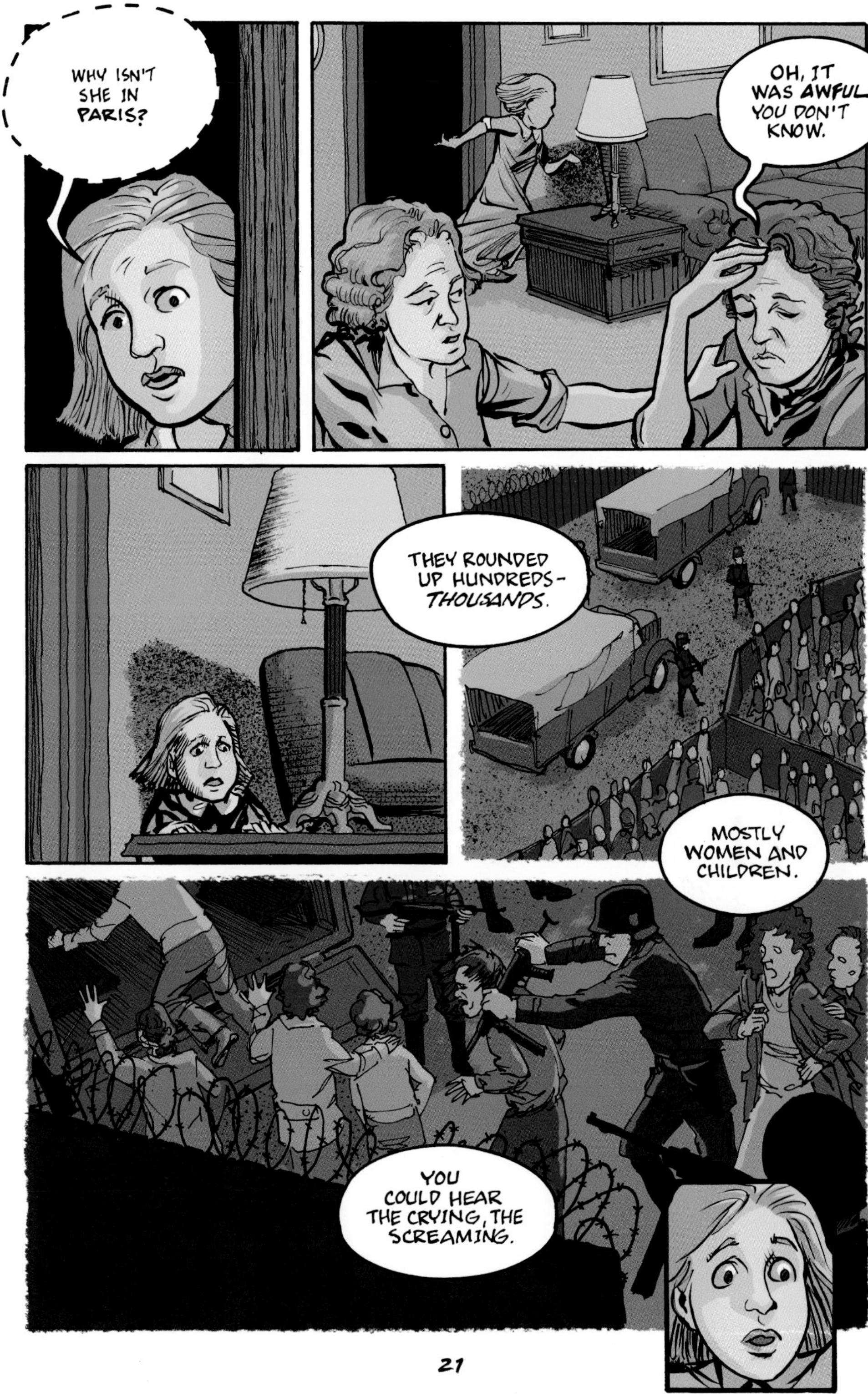
WHY ISN'T SHE IN PARIS?
OH, IT WAS AWFUL. YOU DON'T KNOW.
THEY ROUNDED UP HUNDREDS- THOUSANDS.
MOSTLY WOMEN AND CHILDREN.
YOU COULD HEAR THE CRYING, THE SCREAMING.

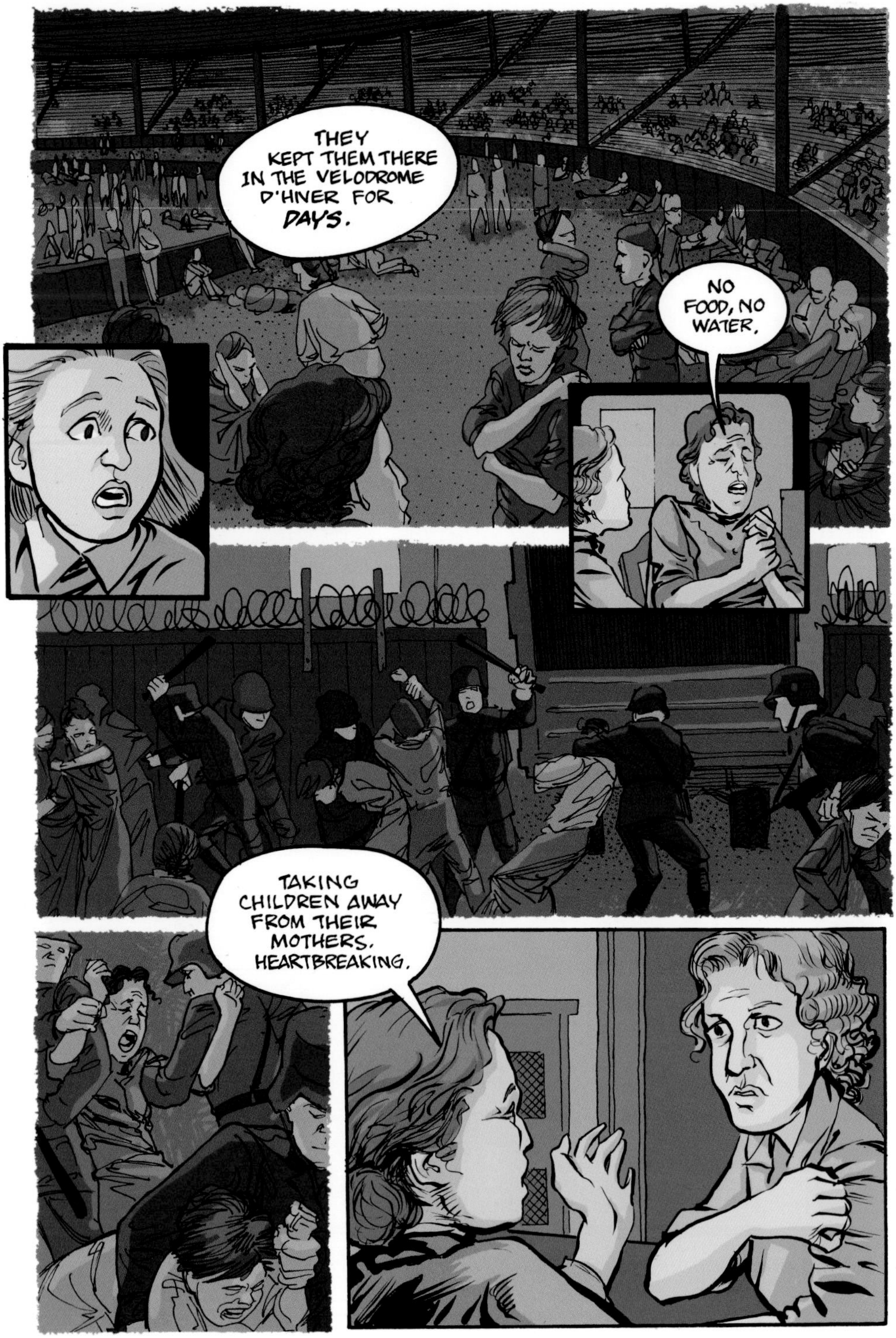
THEY KEPT THEM THERE IN THE VELODROME D'HIVER FOR DAYS.
NO FOOD, NO WATER.
TAKING CHILDREN AWAY FROM THEIR MOTHERS. HEARTBREAKING.

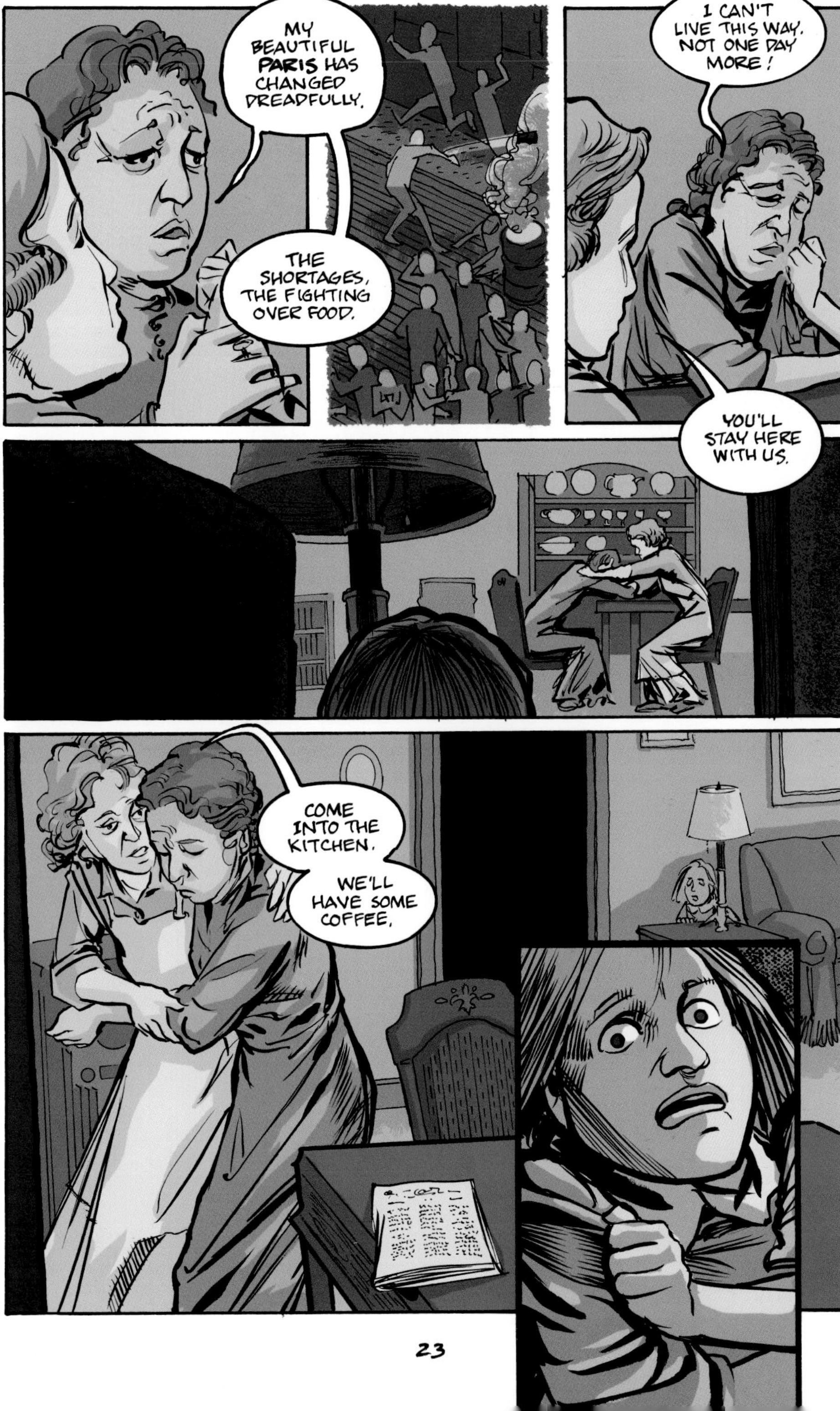
MY BEAUTIFUL PARIS HAS CHANGED DREADFULLY.
THE SHORTAGES, THE FIGHTING OVER FOOD.
I CAN'T LIVE THIS WAY. NOT ONE DAY MORE!
YOU'LL STAY HERE WITH US.
COME INTO THE KITCHEN.
WE'LL HAVE SOME COFFEE.

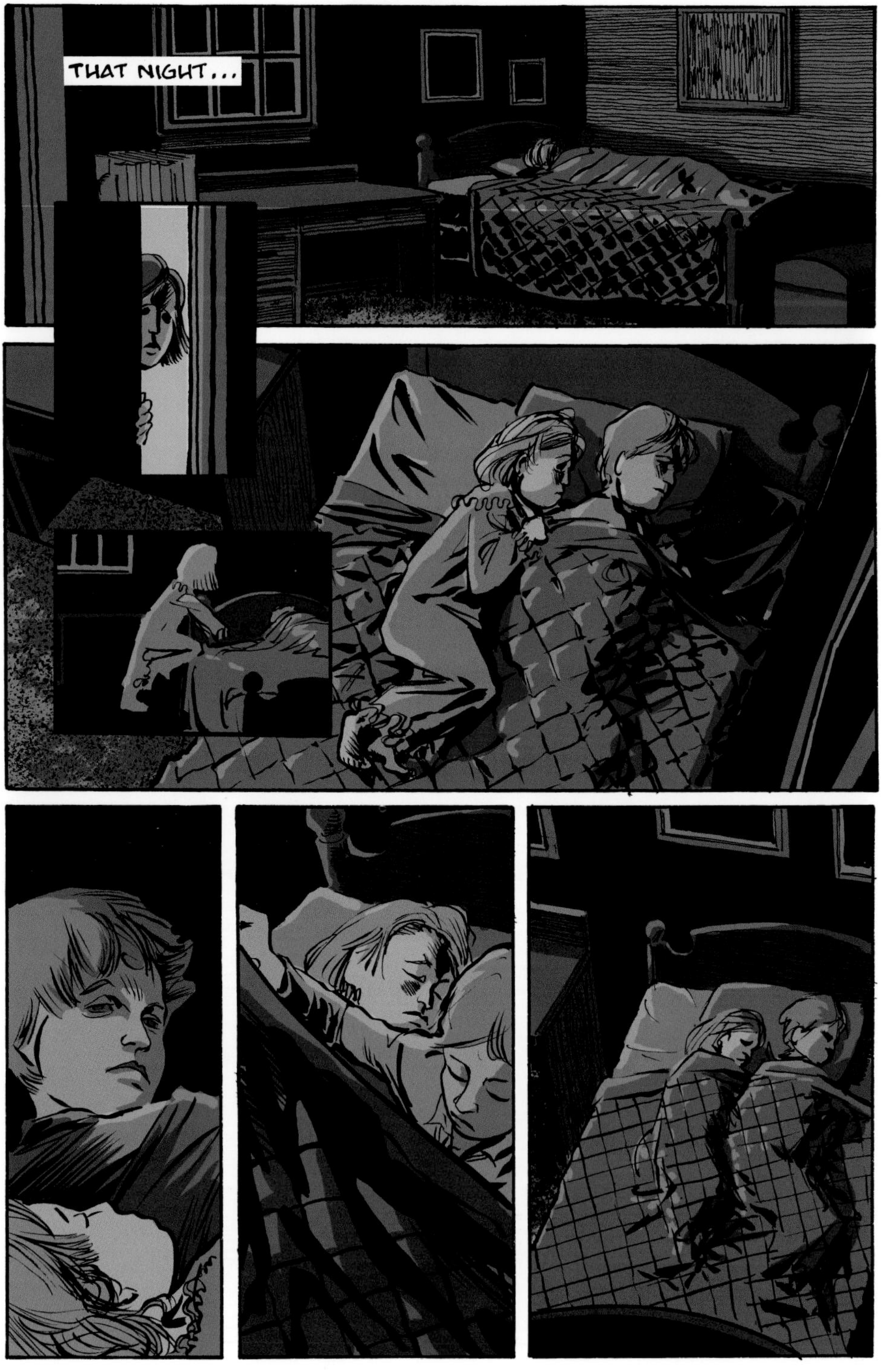
THAT NIGHT...

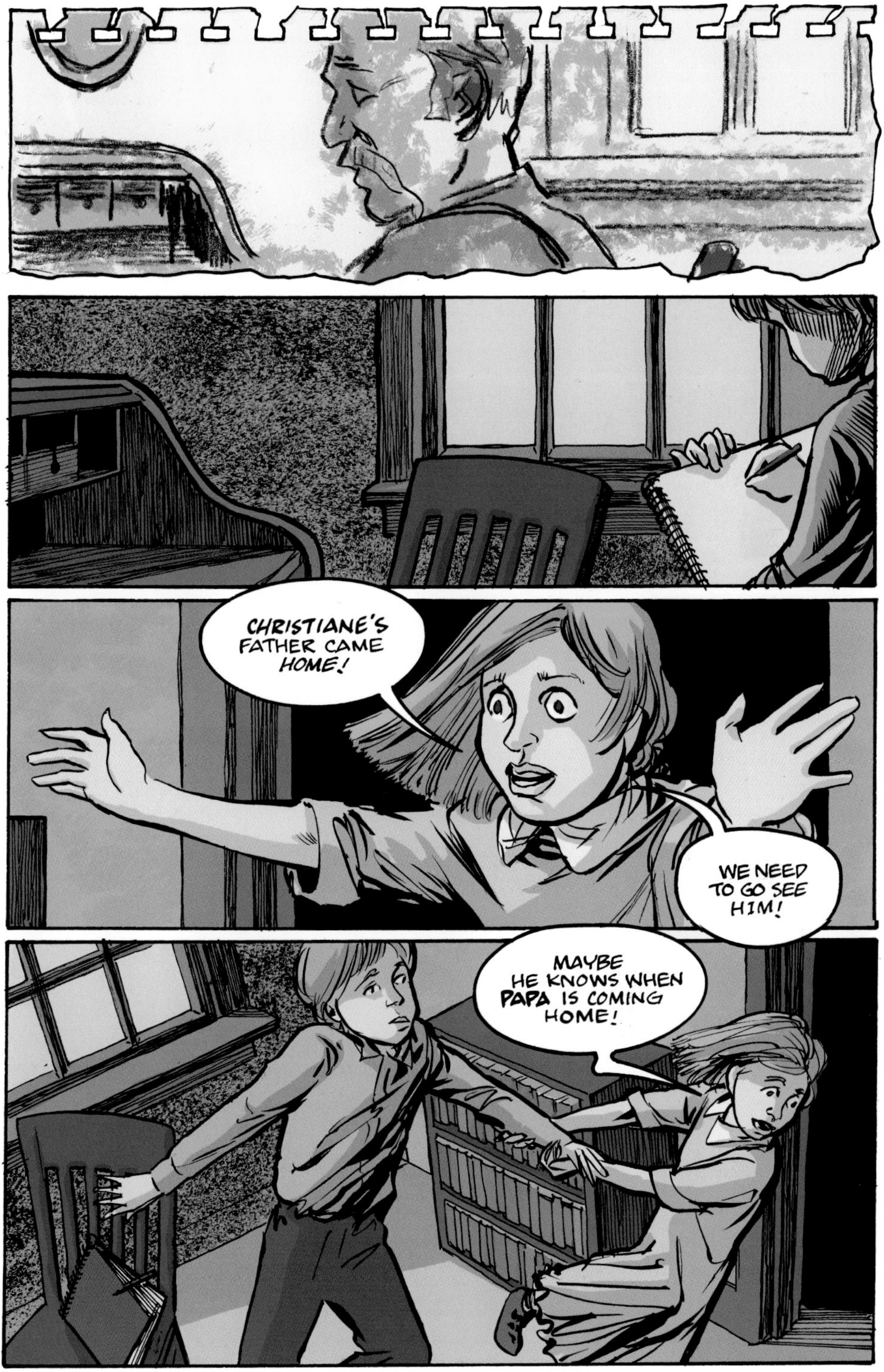
CHRISTIANE'S FATHER CAME HOME!
WE NEED TO GO SEE HIM!
MAYBE HE KNOWS WHEN PAPA IS COMING HOME!

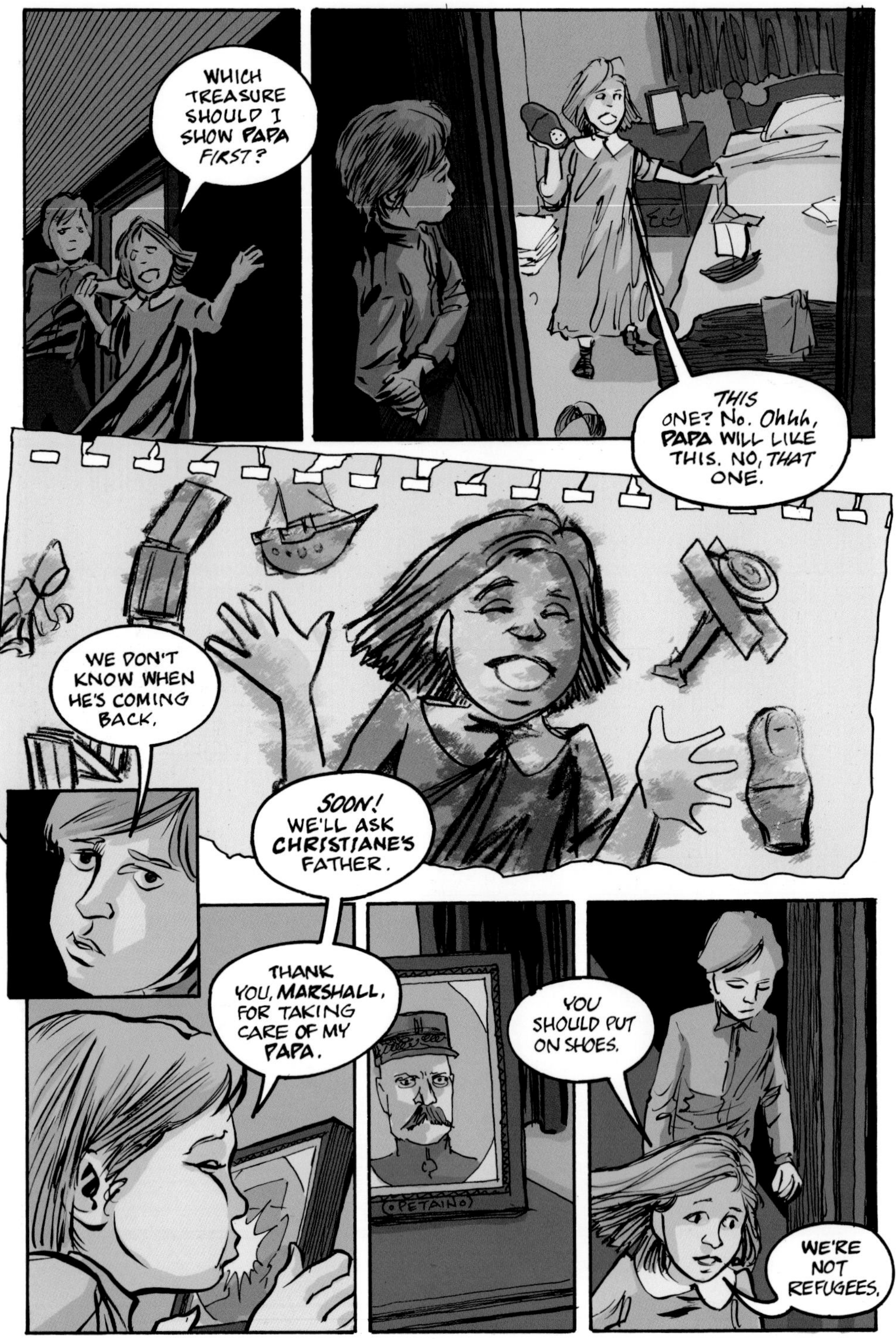
WHICH TREASURE SHOULD I SHOW PAPA FIRST?
THIS ONE? No. Ohhh, PAPA WILL LIKE THIS. NO, THAT ONE.
WE DON'T KNOW WHEN HE'S COMING BACK.
SOON! WE'LL ASK CHRISTIANE'S FATHER.
THANK YOU, MARSHALL, FOR TAKING CARE OF MY PAPA.
PETAIN
YOU SHOULD PUT ON SHOES.
WE'RE NOT REFUGEES.

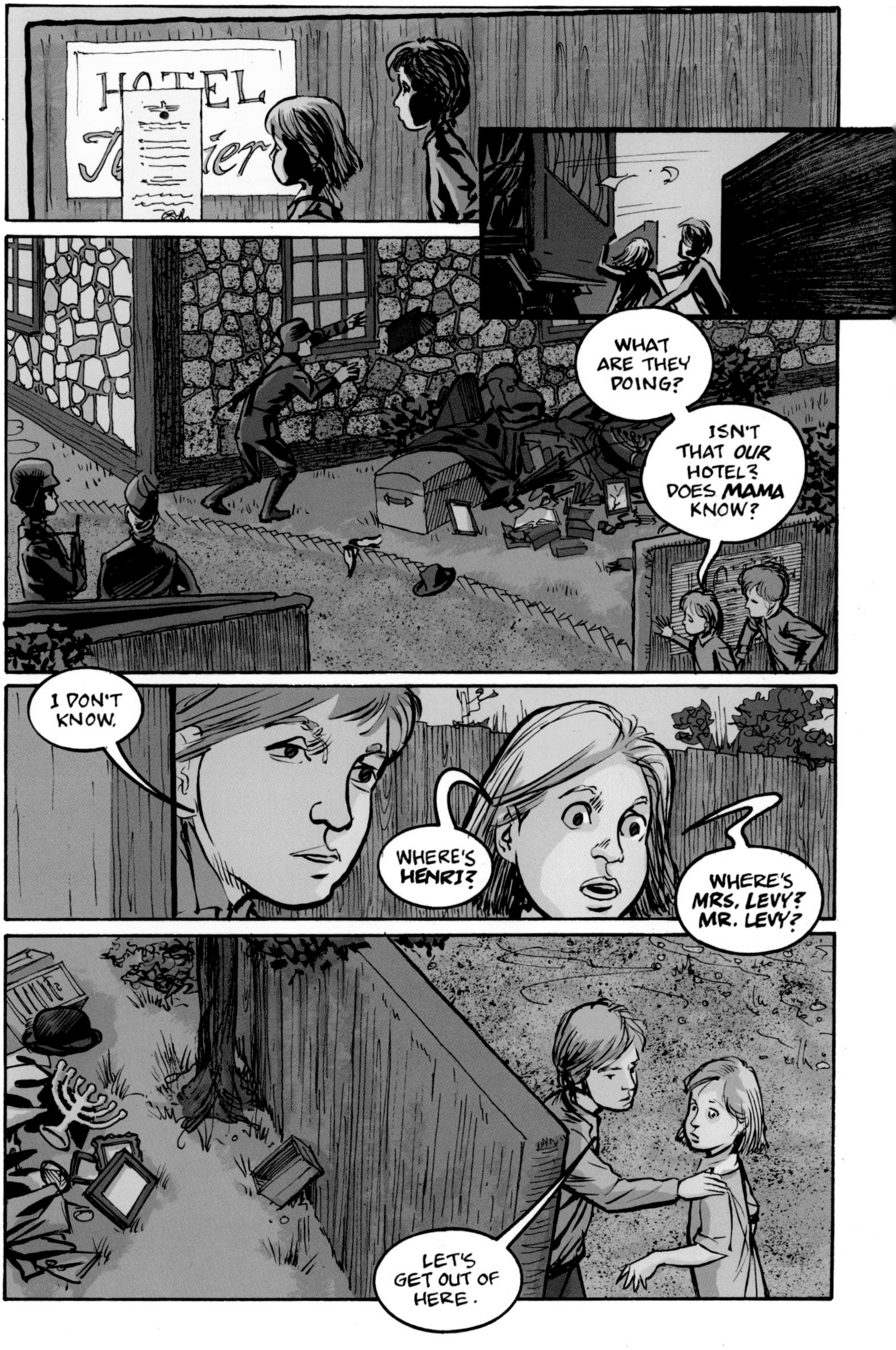
HOTEL
WHAT ARE THEY DOING?
ISN'T THAT *OUR* HOTEL? DOES **MAMA** KNOW?
I DON'T KNOW.
WHERE'S **HENRI**?
WHERE'S **MRS. LEVY? MR. LEVY?**
LET'S GET OUT OF HERE.

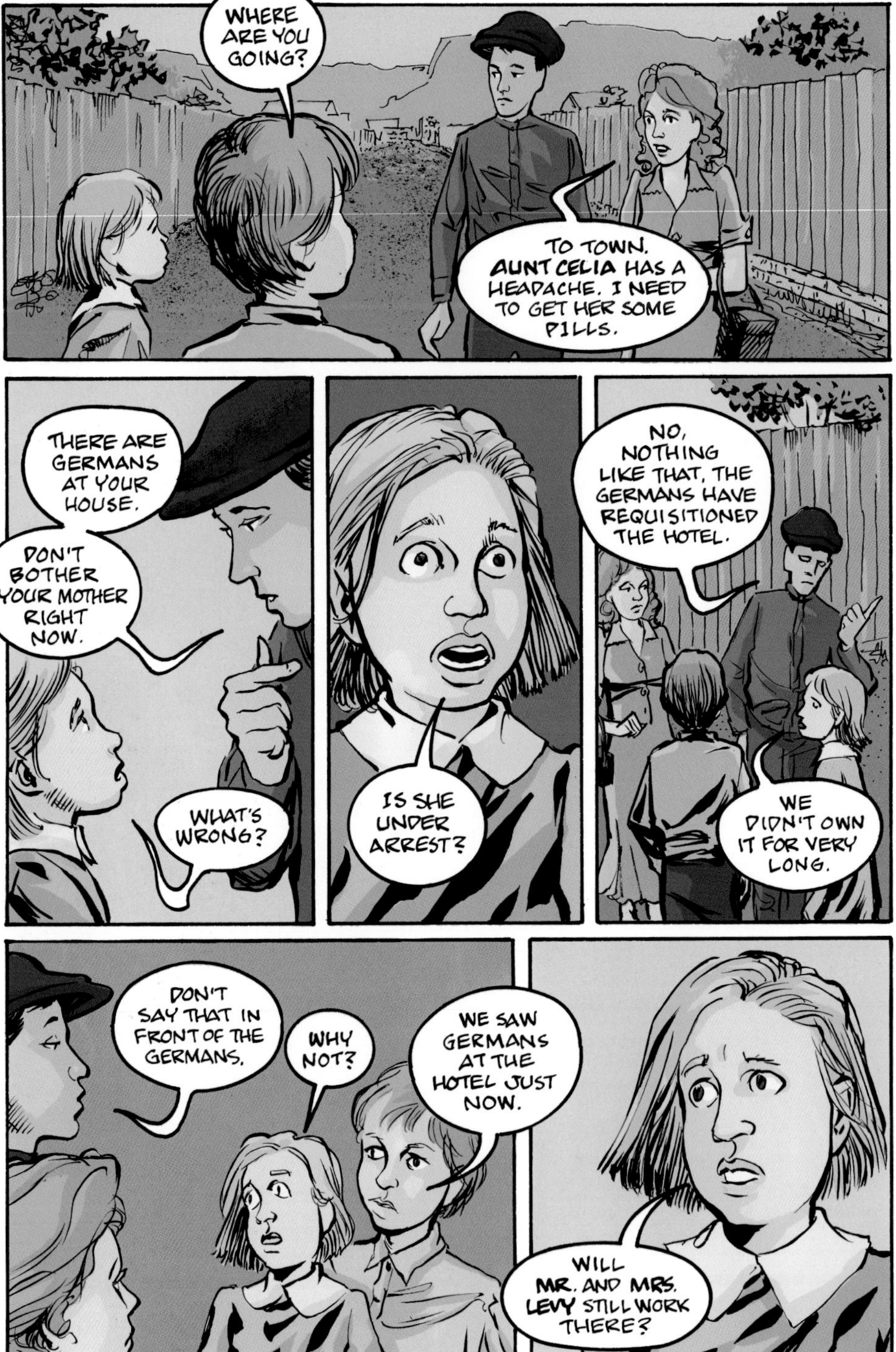
WHERE ARE YOU GOING?
TO TOWN. AUNT CELIA HAS A HEADACHE. I NEED TO GET HER SOME PILLS.
THERE ARE GERMANS AT YOUR HOUSE.
DON'T BOTHER YOUR MOTHER RIGHT NOW.
WHAT'S WRONG?
IS SHE UNDER ARREST?
NO, NOTHING LIKE THAT. THE GERMANS HAVE REQUISITIONED THE HOTEL.
WE DIDN'T OWN IT FOR VERY LONG.
DON'T SAY THAT IN FRONT OF THE GERMANS.
WHY NOT?
WE SAW GERMANS AT THE HOTEL JUST NOW.
WILL MR. AND MRS. LEVY STILL WORK THERE?

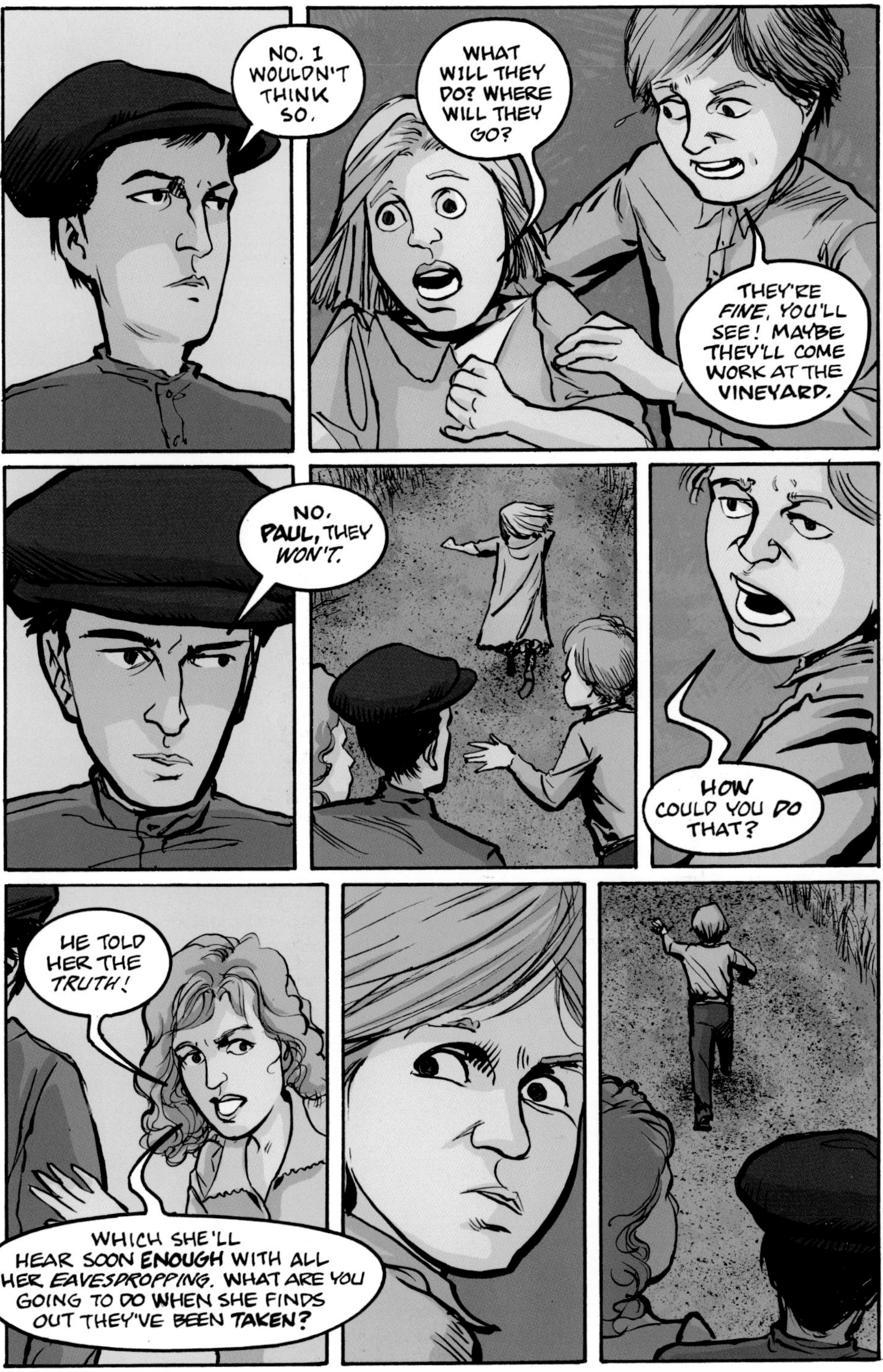
NO. I WOULDN'T THINK SO.
WHAT WILL THEY DO? WHERE WILL THEY GO?
THEY'RE *FINE*, YOU'LL SEE! MAYBE THEY'LL COME WORK AT THE **VINEYARD.**
NO. **PAUL,** THEY *WON'T.*
HOW COULD YOU *DO* THAT?
HE TOLD HER THE *TRUTH!*
WHICH SHE'LL HEAR SOON **ENOUGH** WITH ALL HER *EAVESDROPPING.* WHAT ARE YOU GOING TO **DO WHEN** SHE FINDS OUT THEY'VE BEEN **TAKEN?**

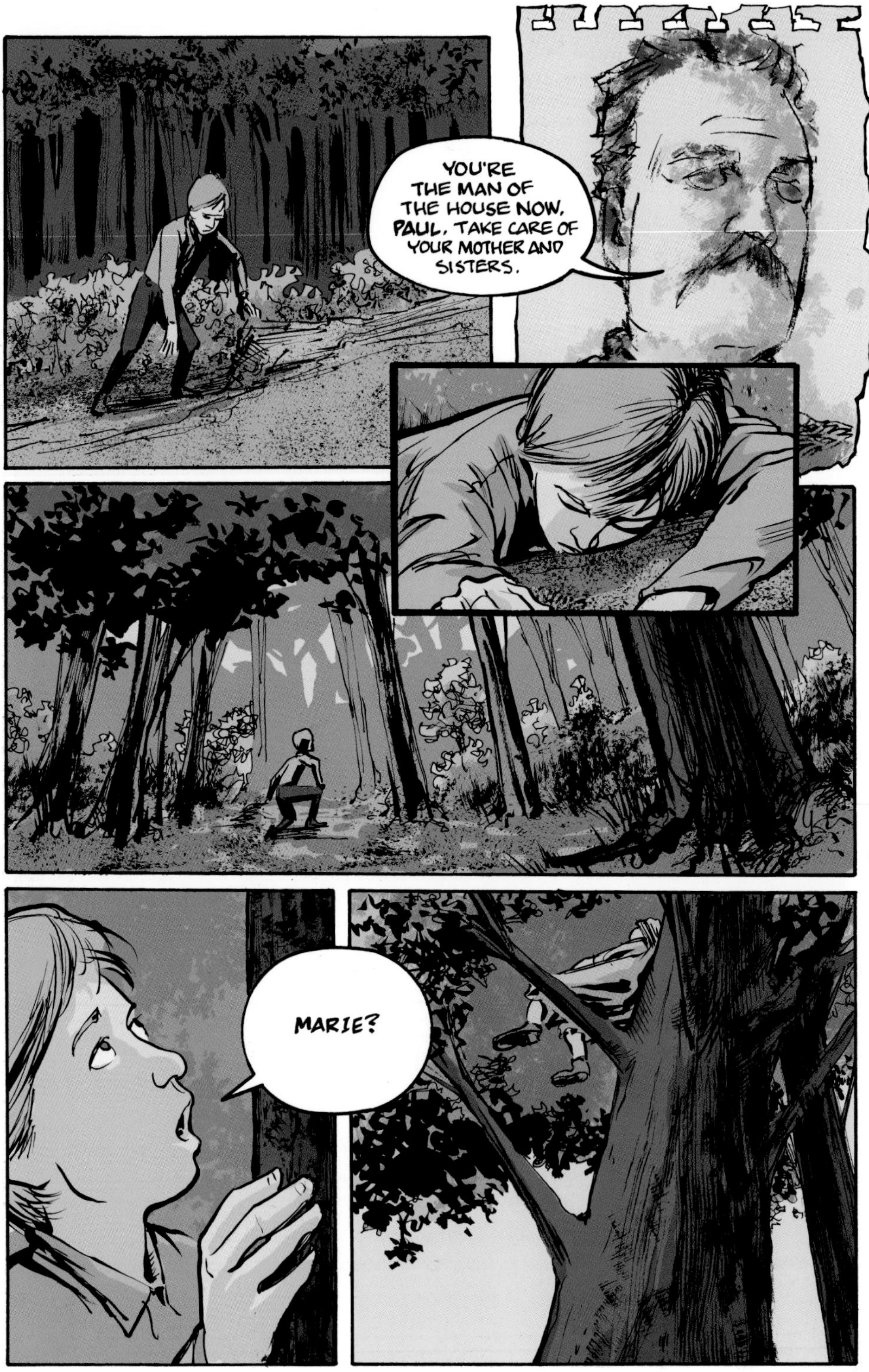
YOU'RE THE MAN OF THE HOUSE NOW, PAUL. TAKE CARE OF YOUR MOTHER AND SISTERS.
MARIE?

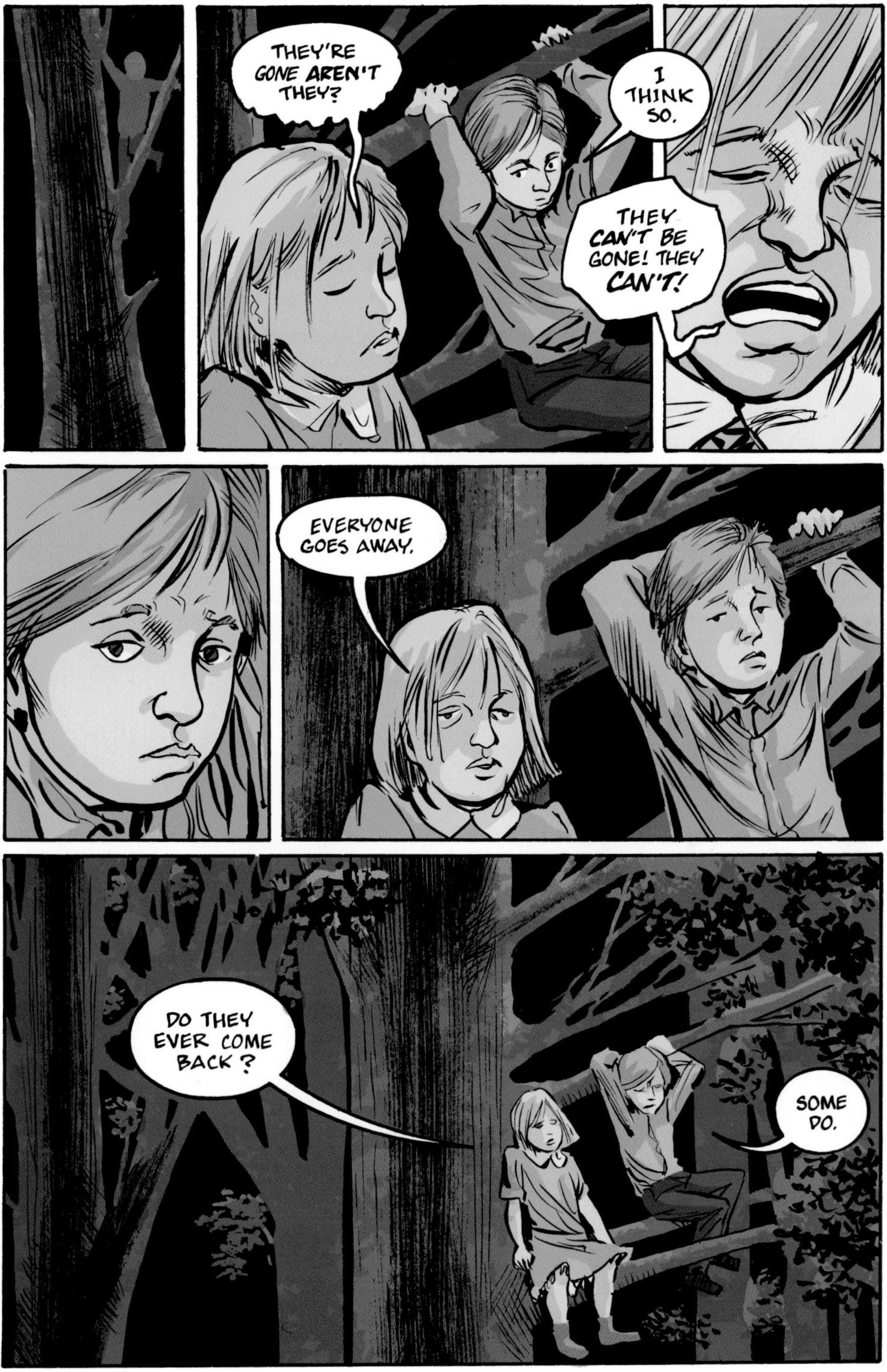
THEY'RE GONE AREN'T THEY?
I THINK SO.
THEY CAN'T BE GONE! THEY CAN'T!
EVERYONE GOES AWAY.
DO THEY EVER COME BACK?
SOME DO.

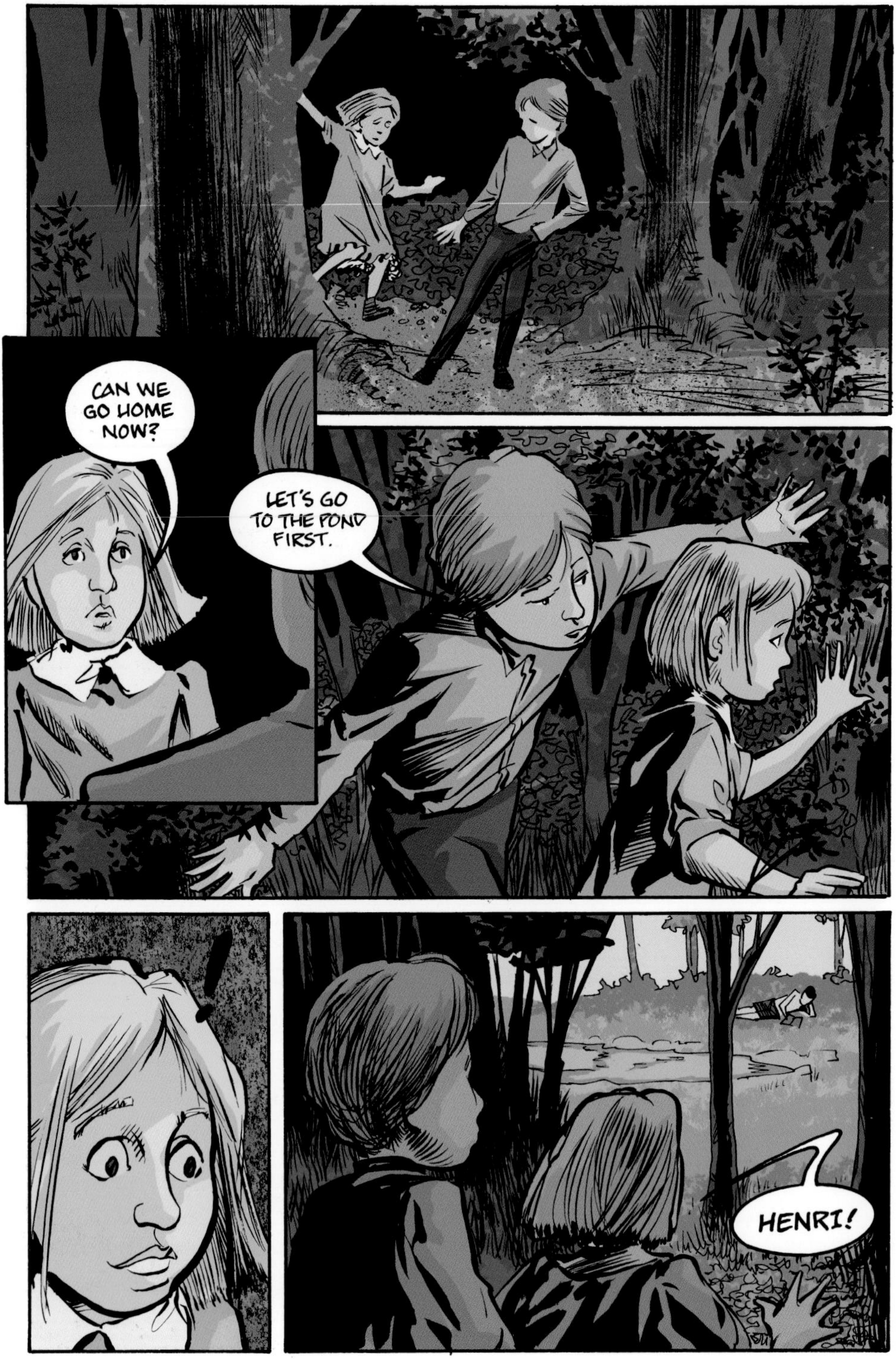
CAN WE GO HOME NOW?
LET'S GO TO THE POND FIRST.
!
HENRI!

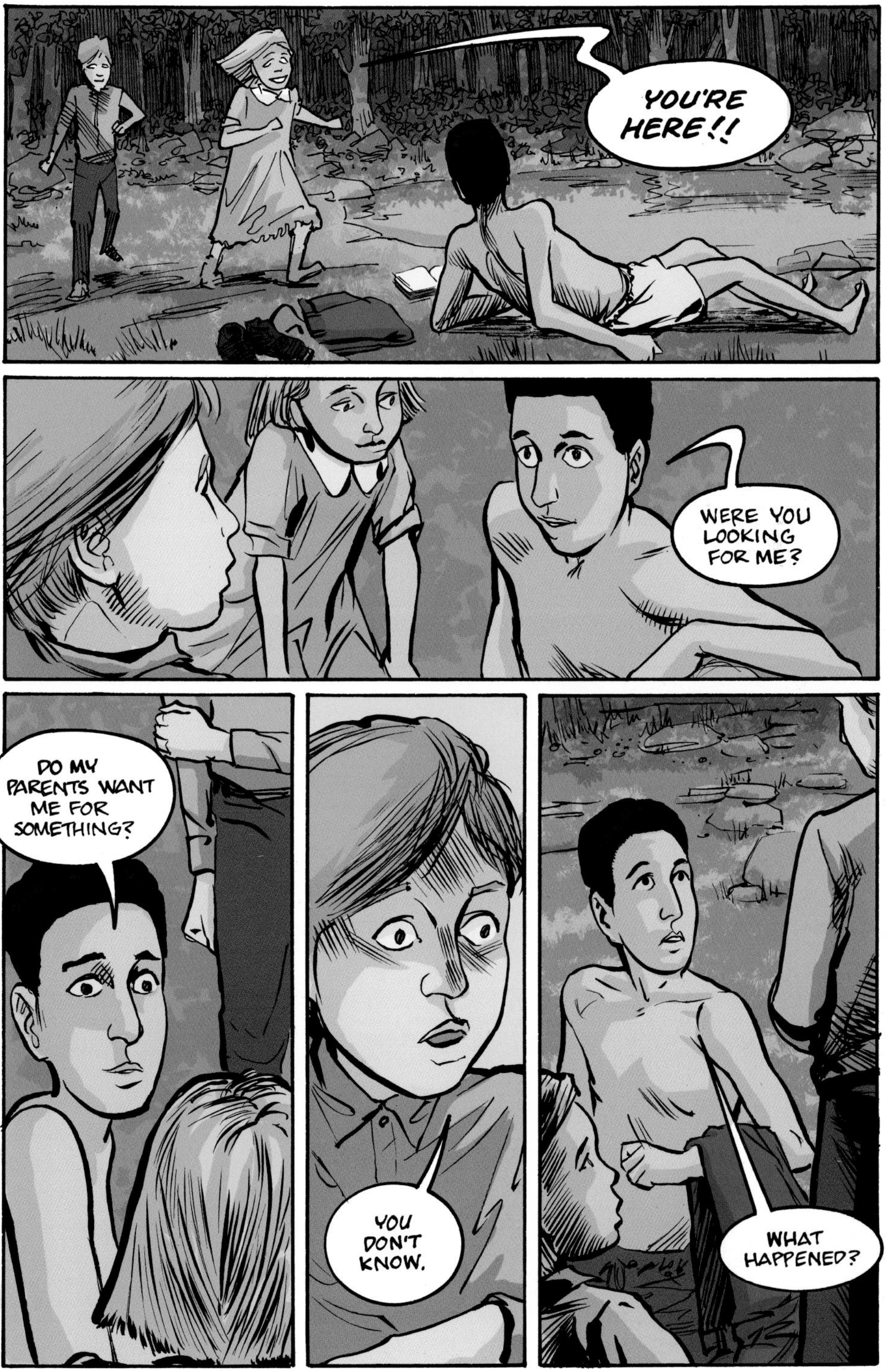
YOU'RE HERE!!
WERE YOU LOOKING FOR ME?
DO MY PARENTS WANT ME FOR SOMETHING?
YOU DON'T KNOW.
WHAT HAPPENED?

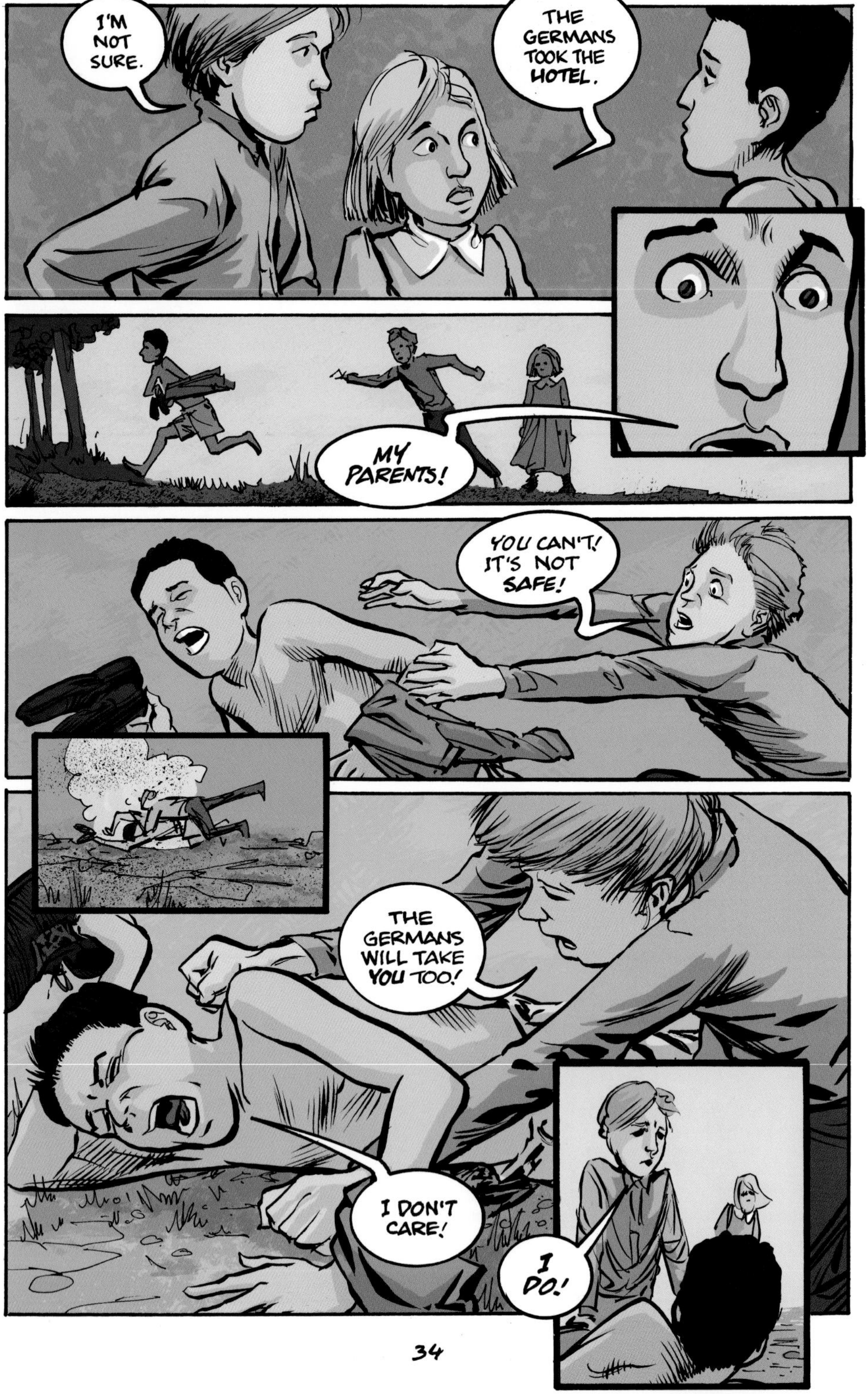
I'M NOT SURE.
THE GERMANS TOOK THE HOTEL.
MY PARENTS!
YOU CAN'T! IT'S NOT SAFE!
THE GERMANS WILL TAKE YOU TOO!
I DON'T CARE!
I DO!

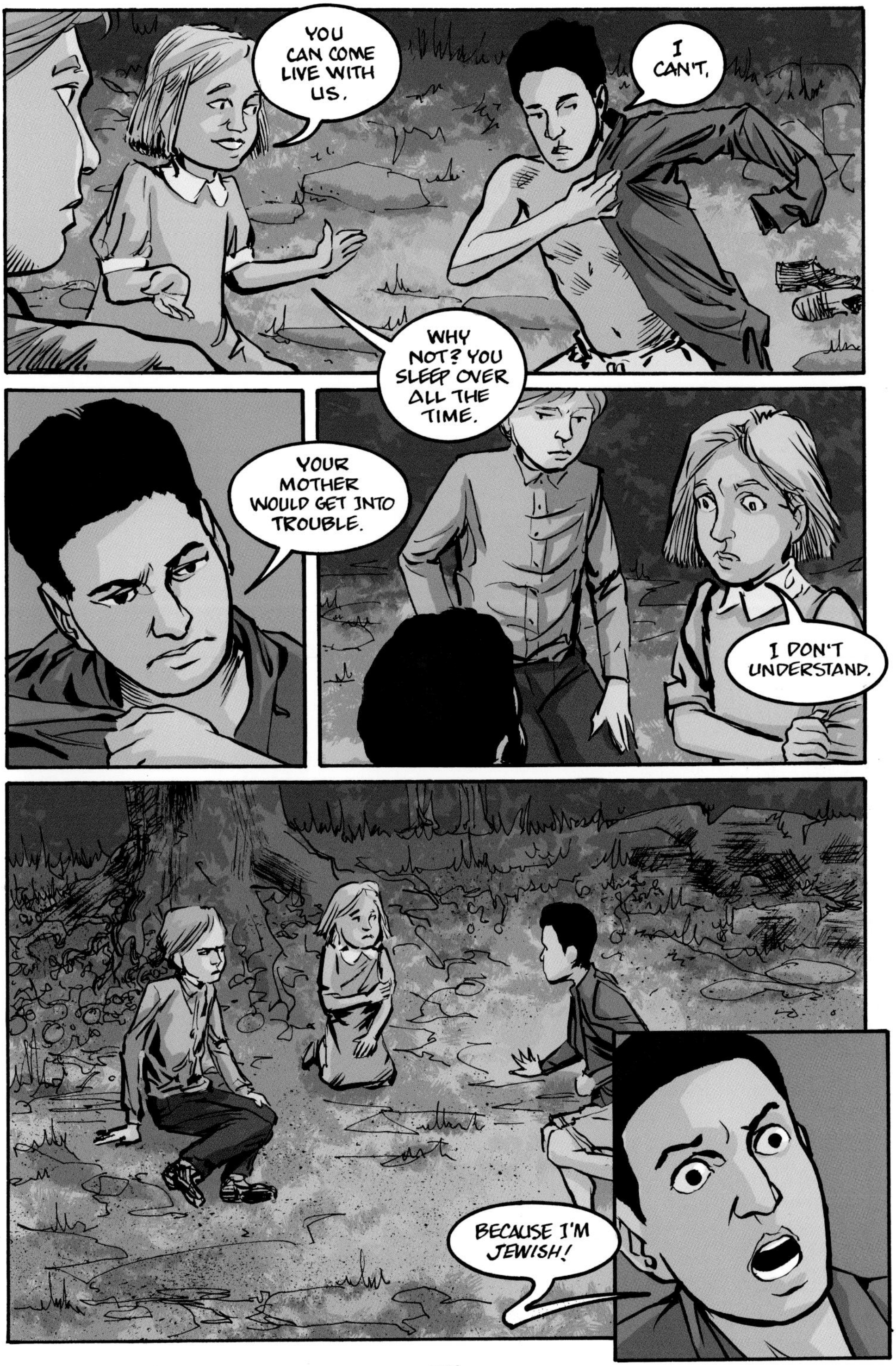
YOU CAN COME LIVE WITH US.
I CAN'T.
WHY NOT? YOU SLEEP OVER ALL THE TIME.
YOUR MOTHER WOULD GET INTO TROUBLE.
I DON'T UNDERSTAND.
BECAUSE I'M JEWISH!

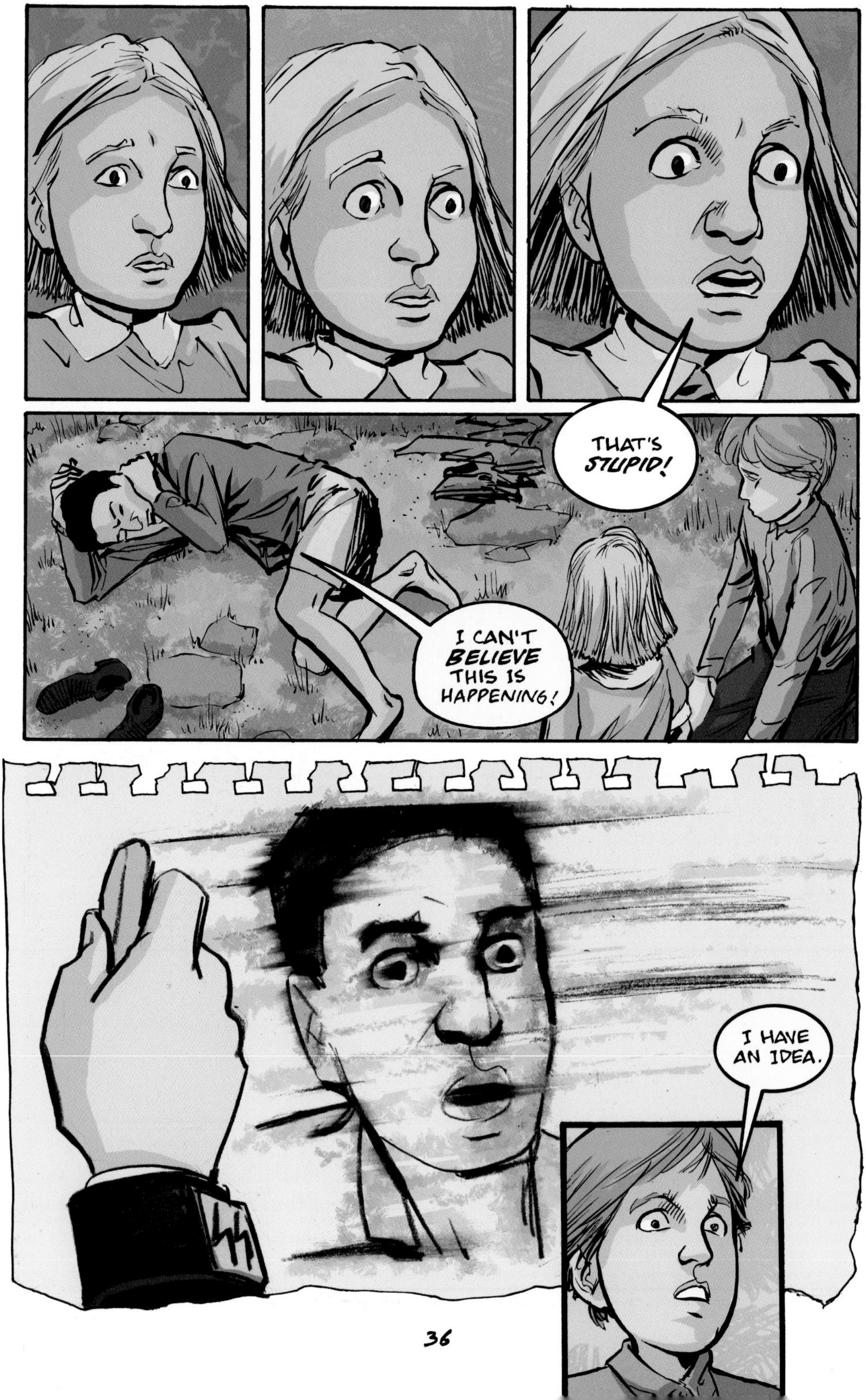
THAT'S *STUPID!*
I CAN'T *BELIEVE* THIS IS HAPPENING!
I HAVE AN IDEA.

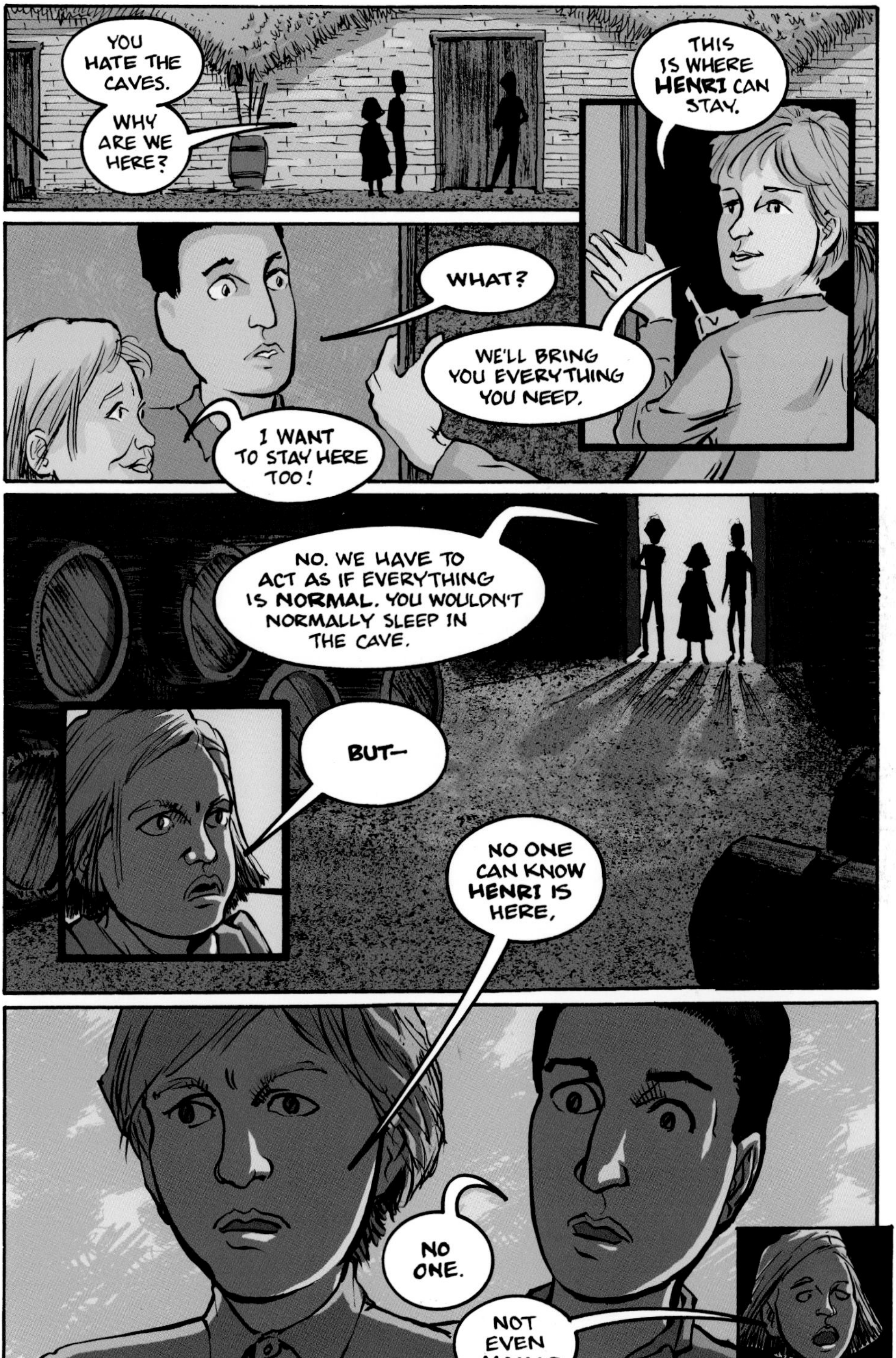
YOU HATE THE CAVES.
WHY ARE WE HERE?
THIS IS WHERE HENRI CAN STAY.
WHAT?
WE'LL BRING YOU EVERYTHING YOU NEED.
I WANT TO STAY HERE TOO!
NO. WE HAVE TO ACT AS IF EVERYTHING IS NORMAL. YOU WOULDN'T NORMALLY SLEEP IN THE CAVE.
BUT—
NO ONE CAN KNOW HENRI IS HERE,
NO ONE.
NOT EVEN MAMA?

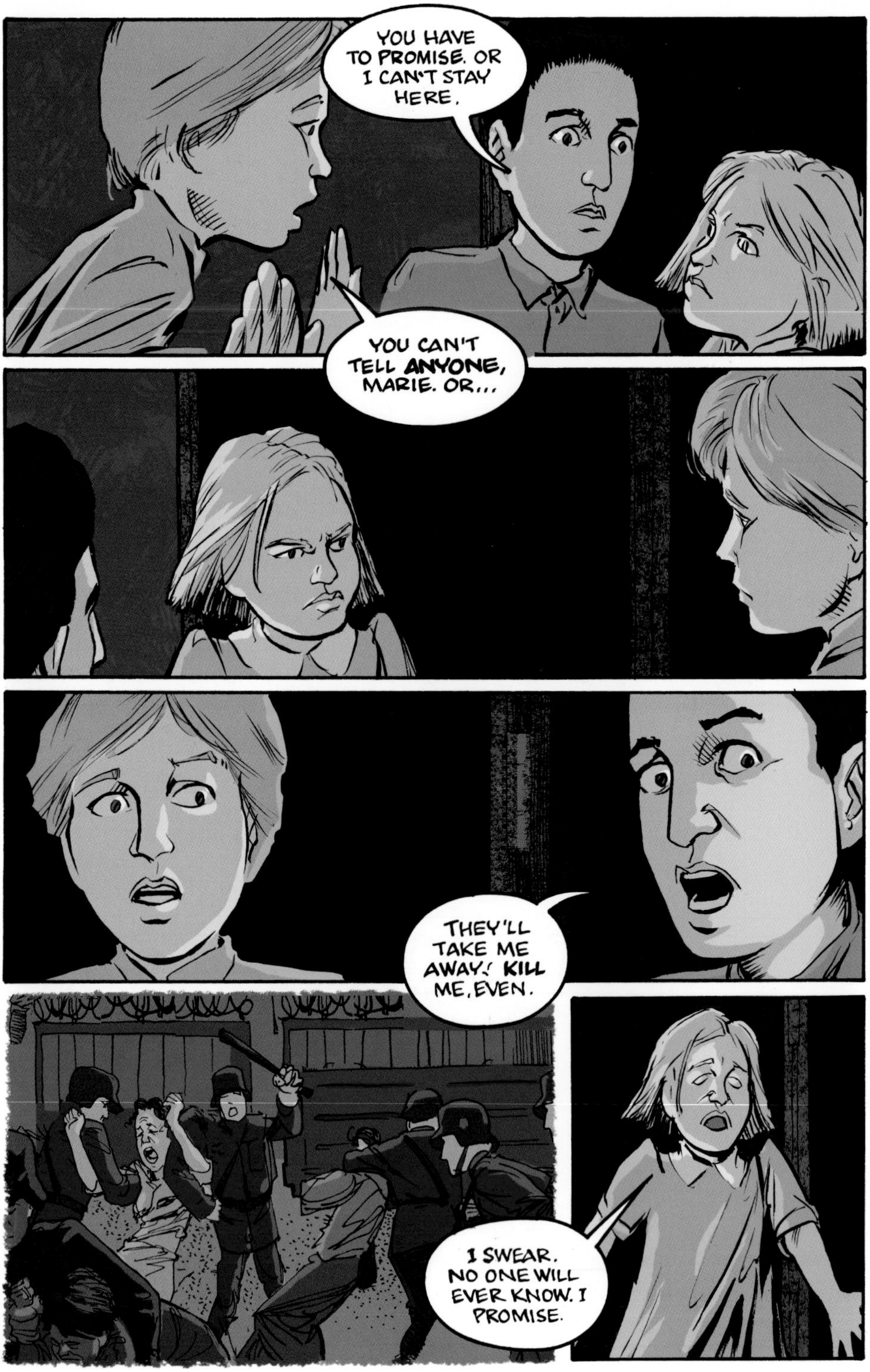
YOU HAVE TO PROMISE. OR I CAN'T STAY HERE.
YOU CAN'T TELL ANYONE, MARIE. OR...
THEY'LL TAKE ME AWAY! KILL ME, EVEN.
I SWEAR. NO ONE WILL EVER KNOW. I PROMISE.

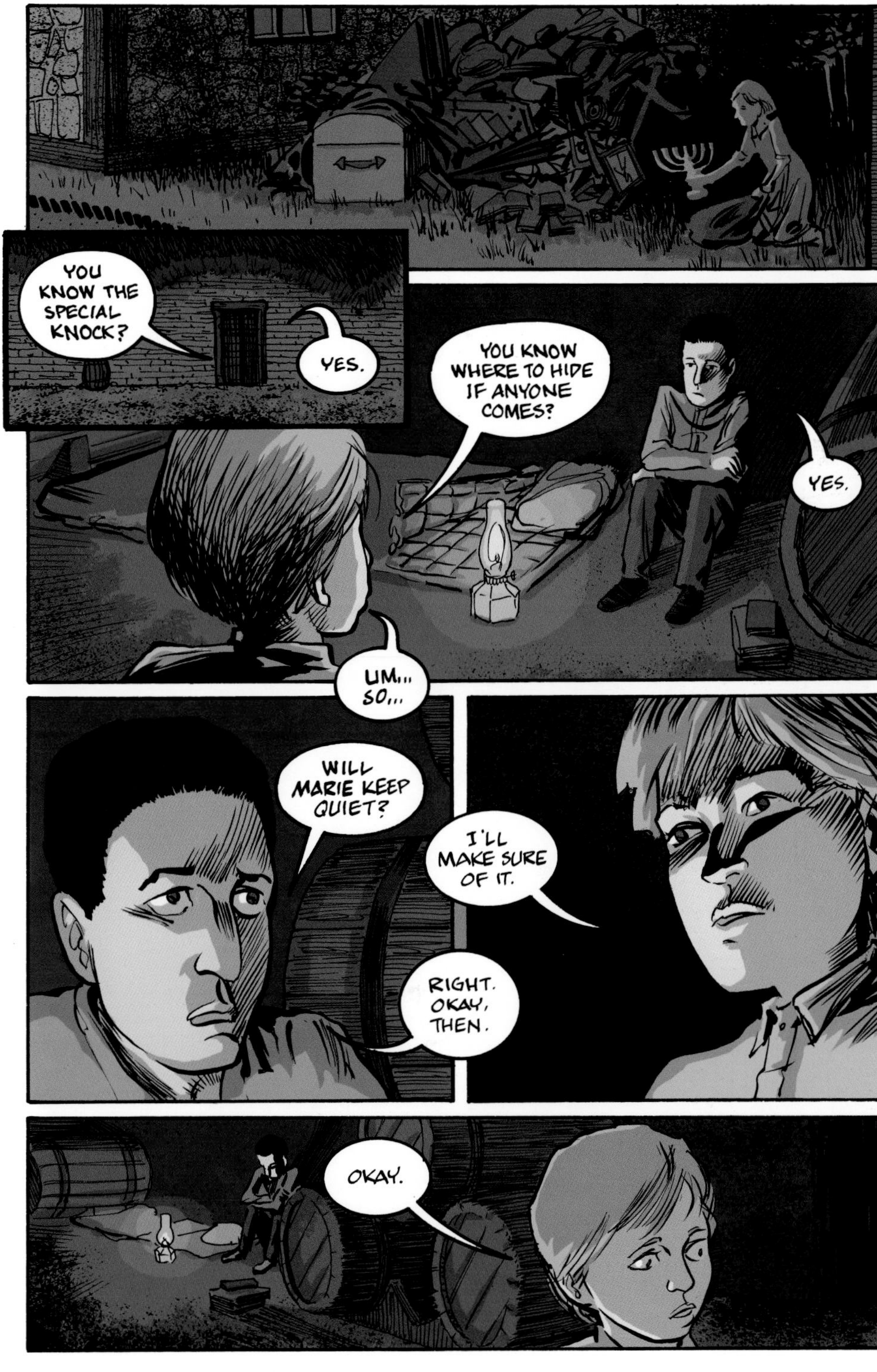
YOU KNOW THE SPECIAL KNOCK?
YES.
YOU KNOW WHERE TO HIDE IF ANYONE COMES?
YES.
UM... SO...
WILL MARIE KEEP QUIET?
I'LL MAKE SURE OF IT.
RIGHT. OKAY, THEN.
OKAY.

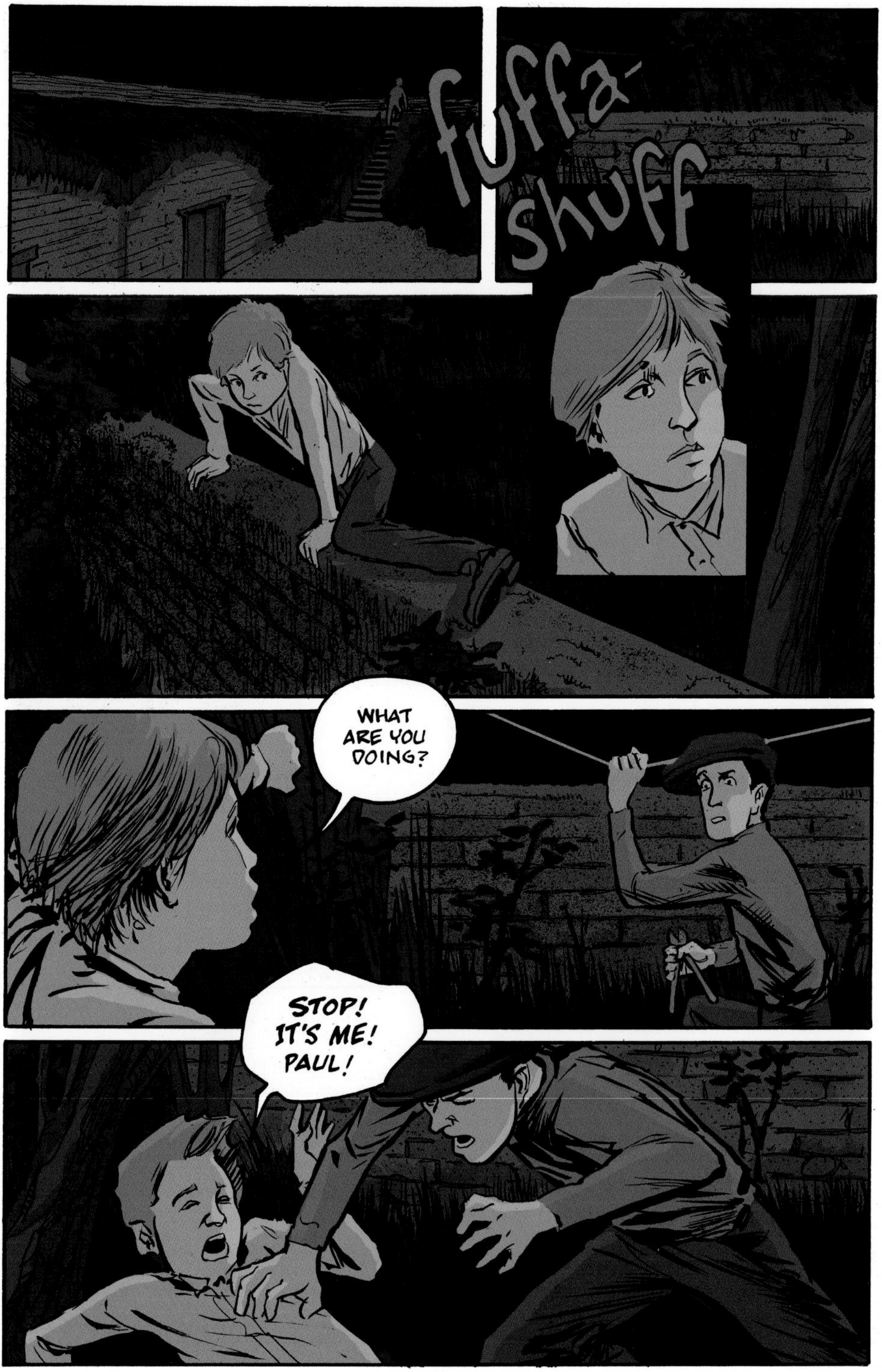
fuffa-shuff
WHAT ARE YOU DOING?
STOP! IT'S ME! PAUL!

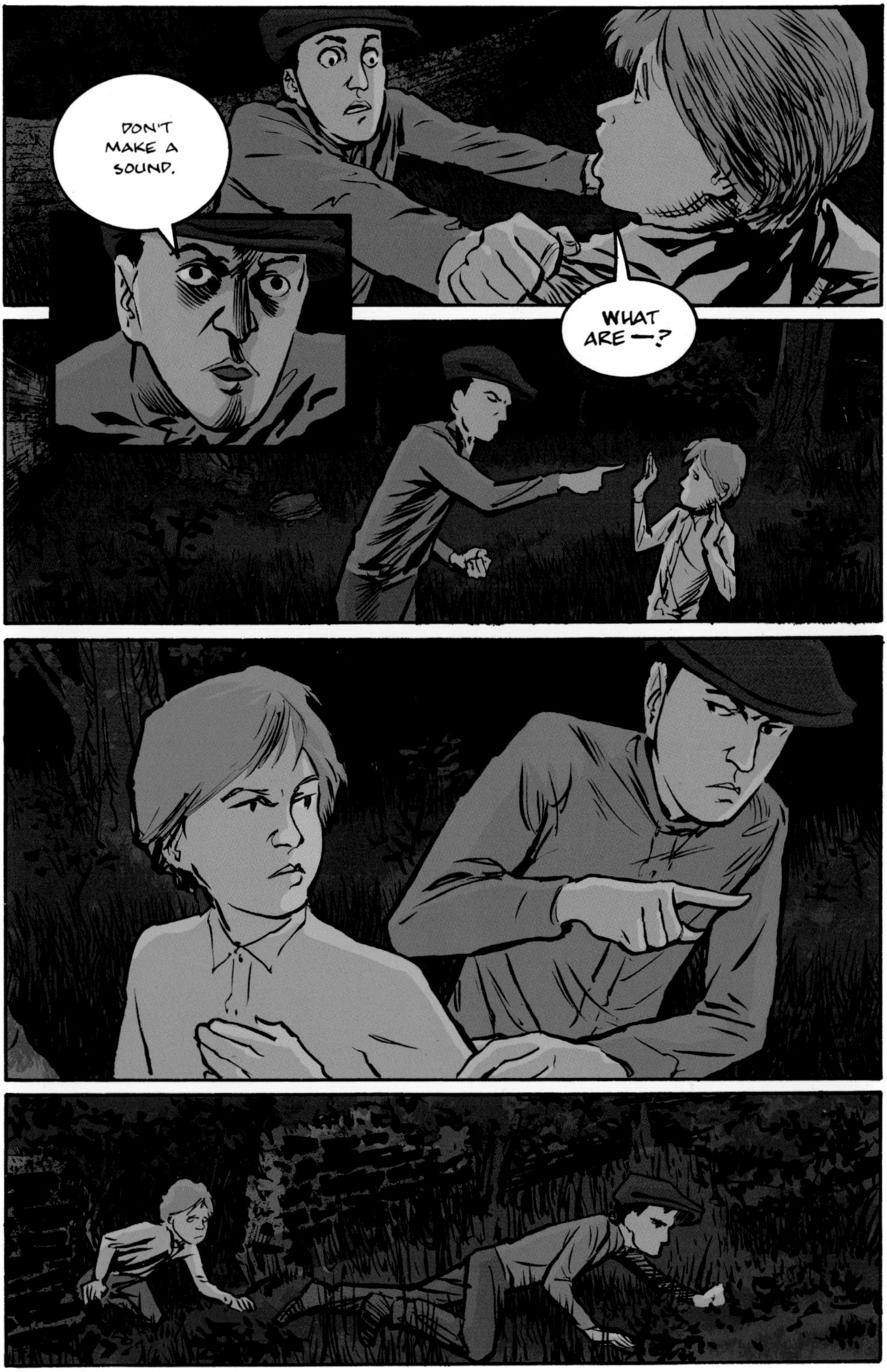
DON'T MAKE A SOUND.
WHAT ARE—?

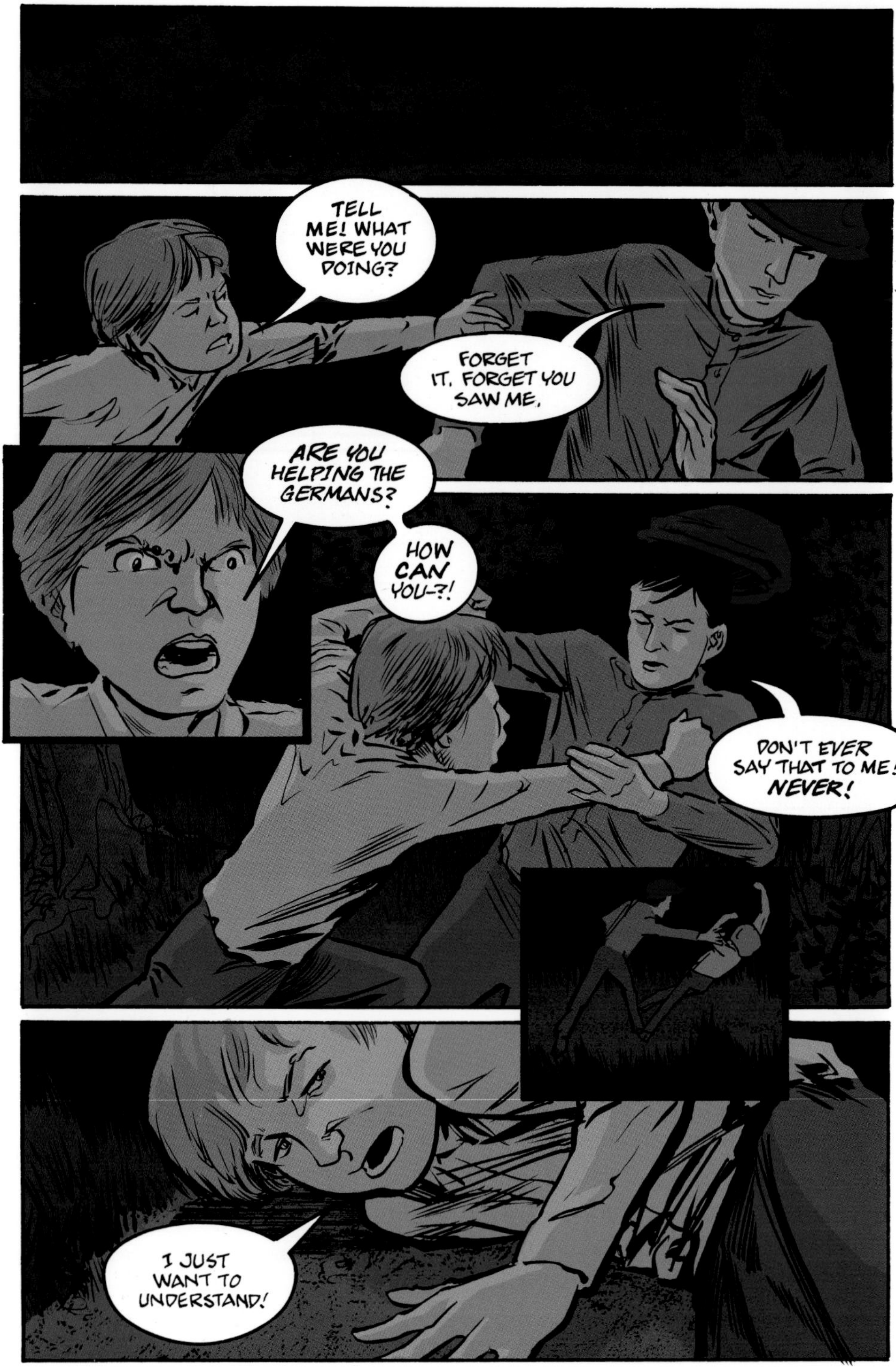
TELL ME! WHAT WERE YOU DOING?
FORGET IT. FORGET YOU SAW ME.
ARE YOU HELPING THE GERMANS?
HOW CAN YOU-?!
DON'T EVER SAY THAT TO ME! NEVER!
I JUST WANT TO UNDERSTAND!

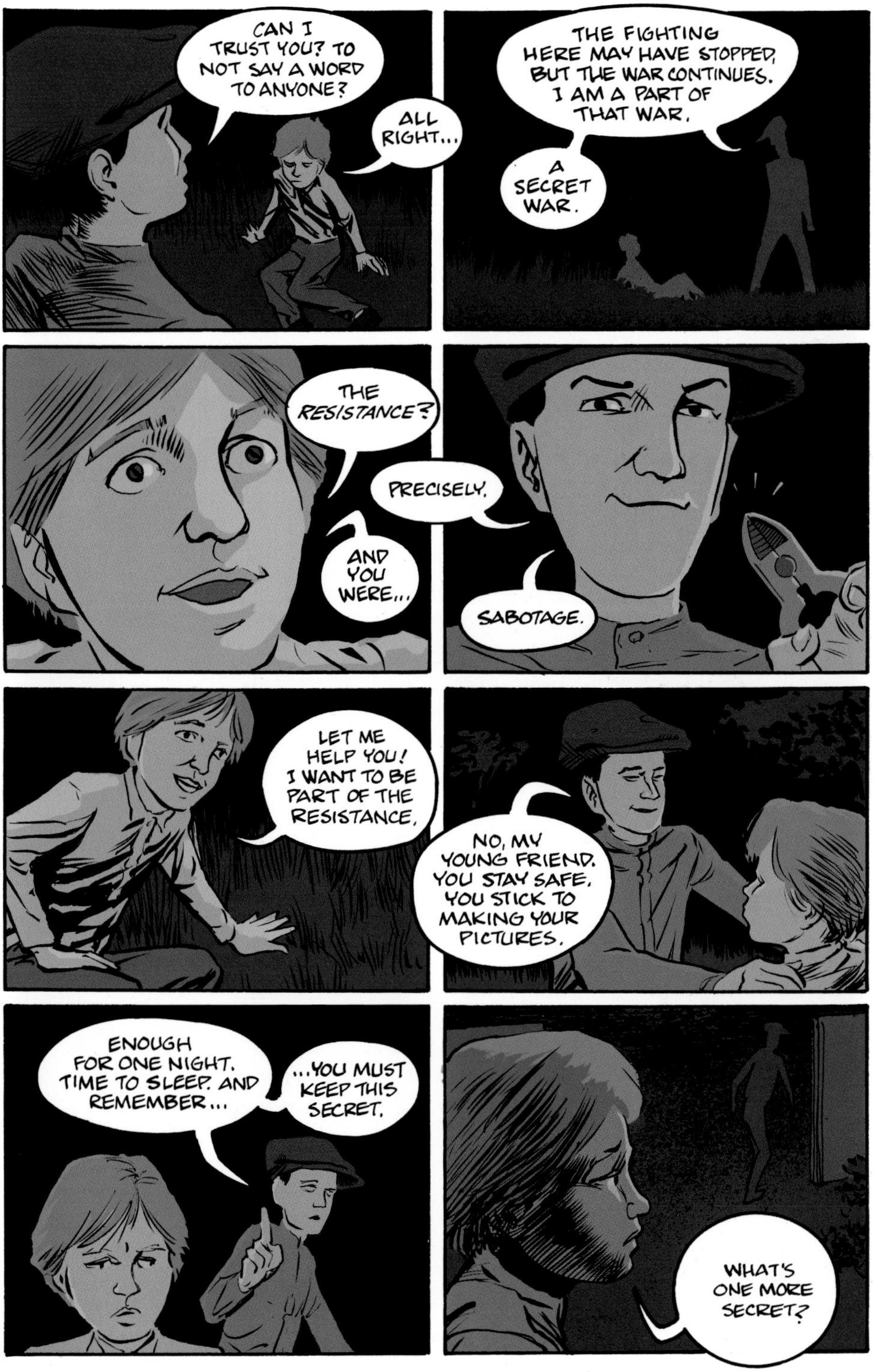
CAN I TRUST YOU? TO NOT SAY A WORD TO ANYONE?
ALL RIGHT...
THE FIGHTING HERE MAY HAVE STOPPED, BUT THE WAR CONTINUES. I AM A PART OF THAT WAR.
A SECRET WAR.
THE *RESISTANCE*?
PRECISELY.
AND YOU WERE...
SABOTAGE.
LET ME HELP YOU! I WANT TO BE PART OF THE RESISTANCE.
NO, MY YOUNG FRIEND. YOU STAY SAFE. YOU STICK TO MAKING YOUR PICTURES.
ENOUGH FOR ONE NIGHT. TIME TO SLEEP. AND REMEMBER...
...YOU MUST KEEP THIS SECRET.
WHAT'S ONE MORE SECRET?

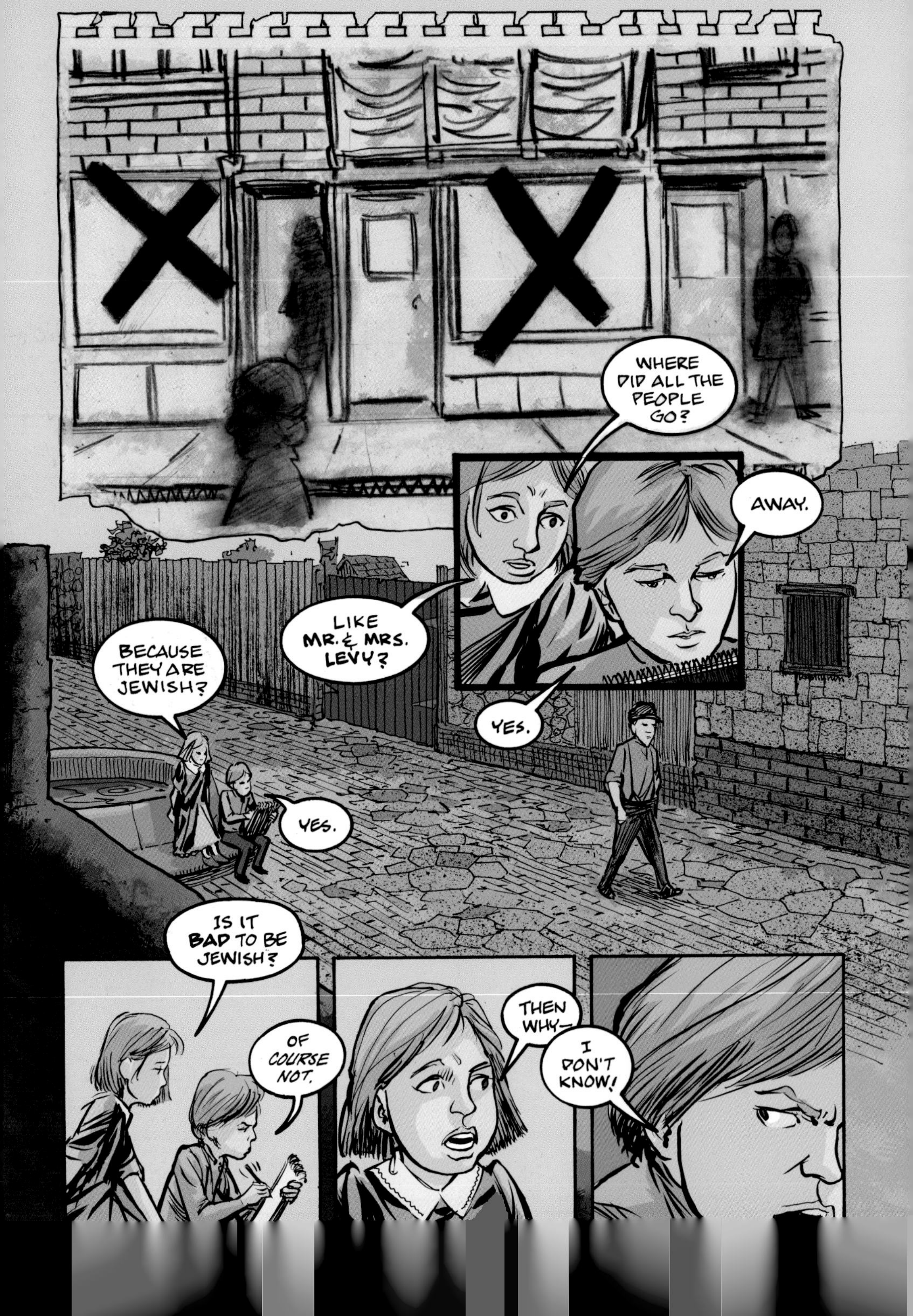
WHERE DID ALL THE PEOPLE GO?
AWAY.
LIKE MR. & MRS. LEVY?
YES.
BECAUSE THEY ARE JEWISH?
YES.
IS IT BAD TO BE JEWISH?
OF COURSE NOT.
THEN WHY—
I DON'T KNOW!

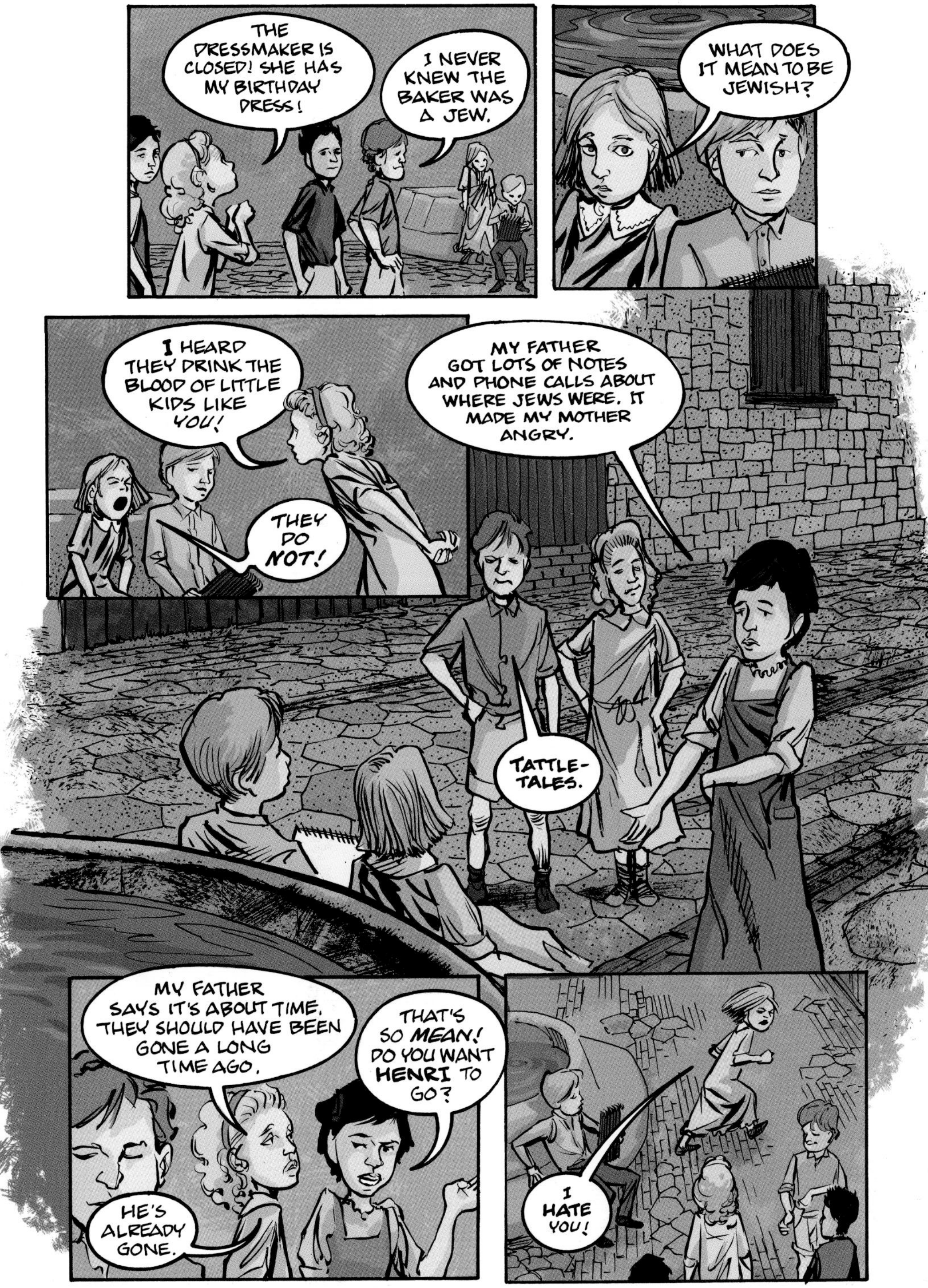
THE DRESSMAKER IS CLOSED! SHE HAS MY BIRTHDAY DRESS!
I NEVER KNEW THE BAKER WAS A JEW.
WHAT DOES IT MEAN TO BE JEWISH?
I HEARD THEY DRINK THE BLOOD OF LITTLE KIDS LIKE YOU!
THEY DO NOT!
MY FATHER GOT LOTS OF NOTES AND PHONE CALLS ABOUT WHERE JEWS WERE. IT MADE MY MOTHER ANGRY.
TATTLE-TALES.
MY FATHER SAYS IT'S ABOUT TIME. THEY SHOULD HAVE BEEN GONE A LONG TIME AGO.
THAT'S SO MEAN! DO YOU WANT HENRI TO GO?
HE'S ALREADY GONE.
I HATE YOU!

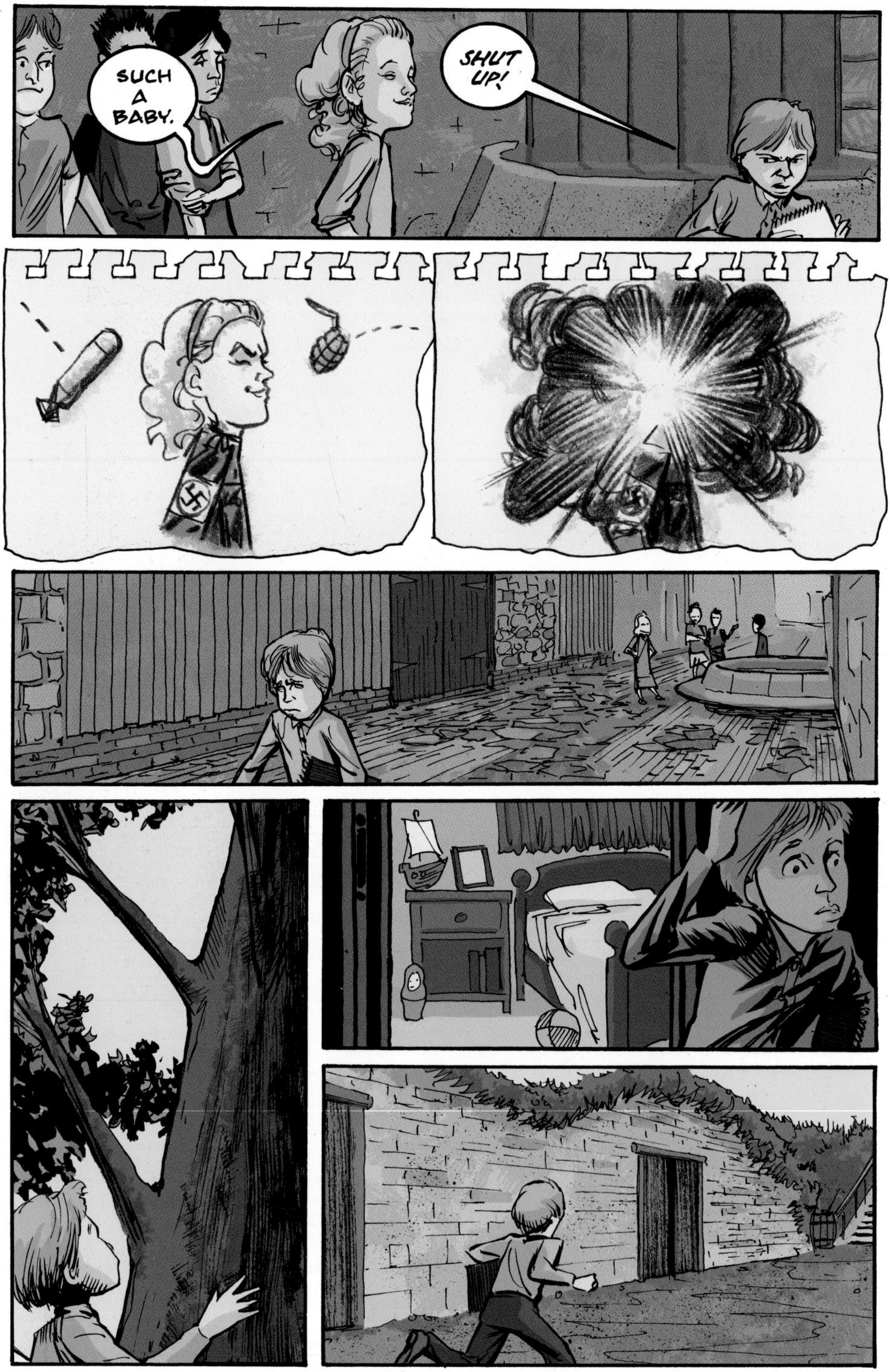
SUCH A BABY.
SHUT UP!

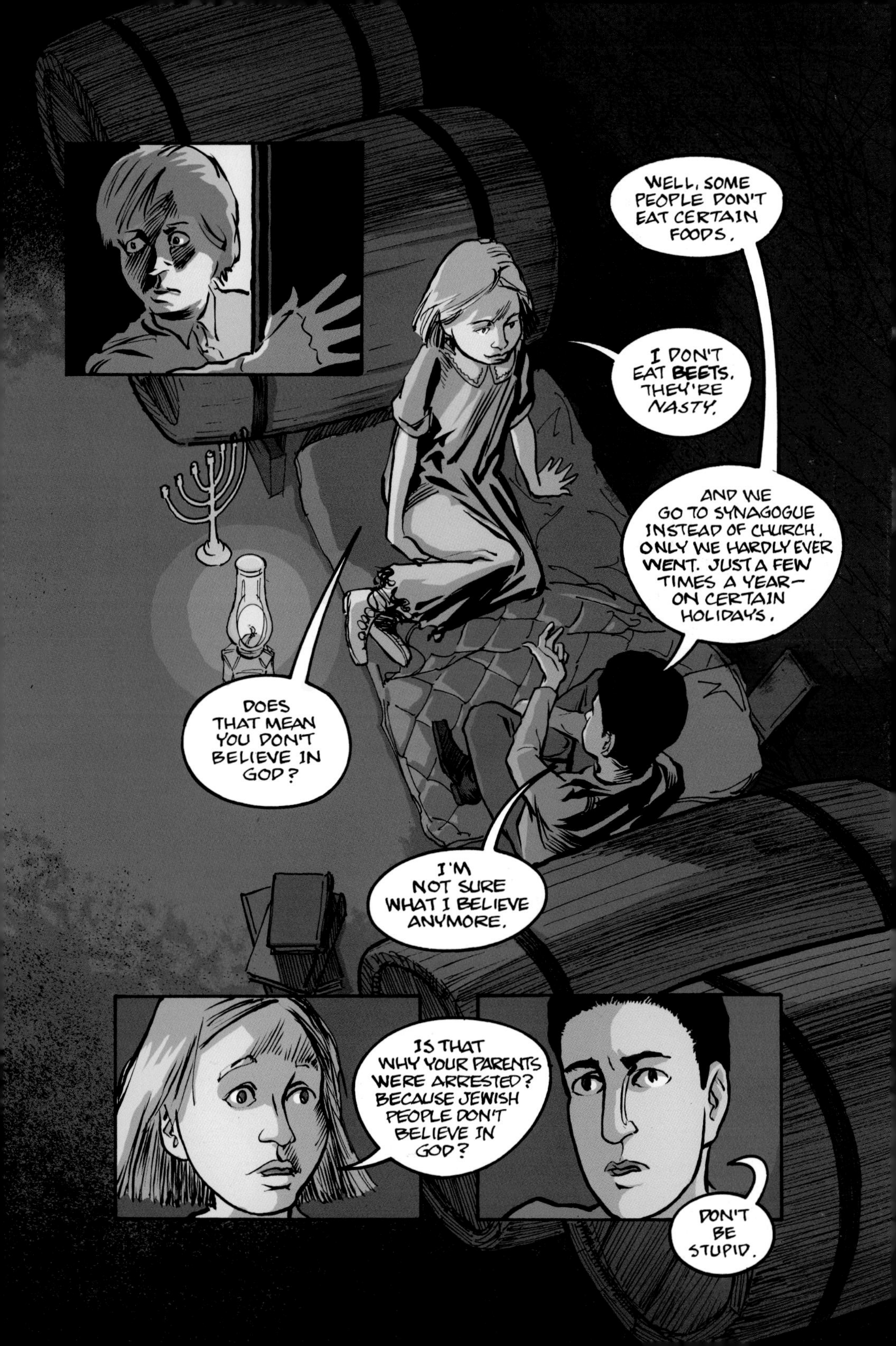
WELL, SOME PEOPLE DON'T EAT CERTAIN FOODS.
I DON'T EAT BEETS. THEY'RE NASTY.
AND WE GO TO SYNAGOGUE INSTEAD OF CHURCH. ONLY WE HARDLY EVER WENT. JUST A FEW TIMES A YEAR— ON CERTAIN HOLIDAYS.
DOES THAT MEAN YOU DON'T BELIEVE IN GOD?
I'M NOT SURE WHAT I BELIEVE ANYMORE.
IS THAT WHY YOUR PARENTS WERE ARRESTED? BECAUSE JEWISH PEOPLE DON'T BELIEVE IN GOD?
DON'T BE STUPID.

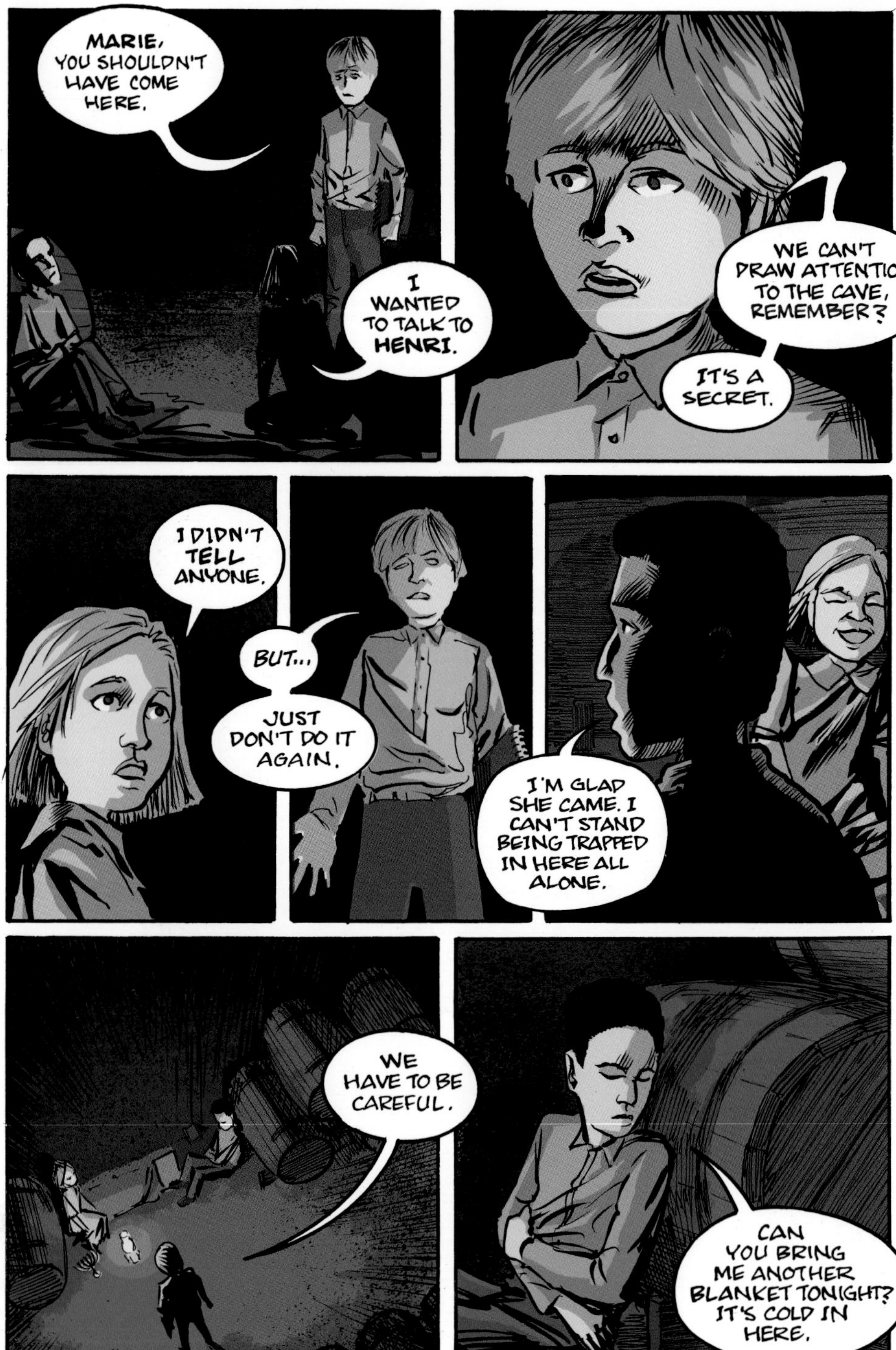
MARIE, YOU SHOULDN'T HAVE COME HERE.
I WANTED TO TALK TO HENRI.
WE CAN'T DRAW ATTENTION TO THE CAVE, REMEMBER?
IT'S A SECRET.
I DIDN'T TELL ANYONE.
BUT...
JUST DON'T DO IT AGAIN.
I'M GLAD SHE CAME. I CAN'T STAND BEING TRAPPED IN HERE ALL ALONE.
WE HAVE TO BE CAREFUL.
CAN YOU BRING ME ANOTHER BLANKET TONIGHT? IT'S COLD IN HERE.

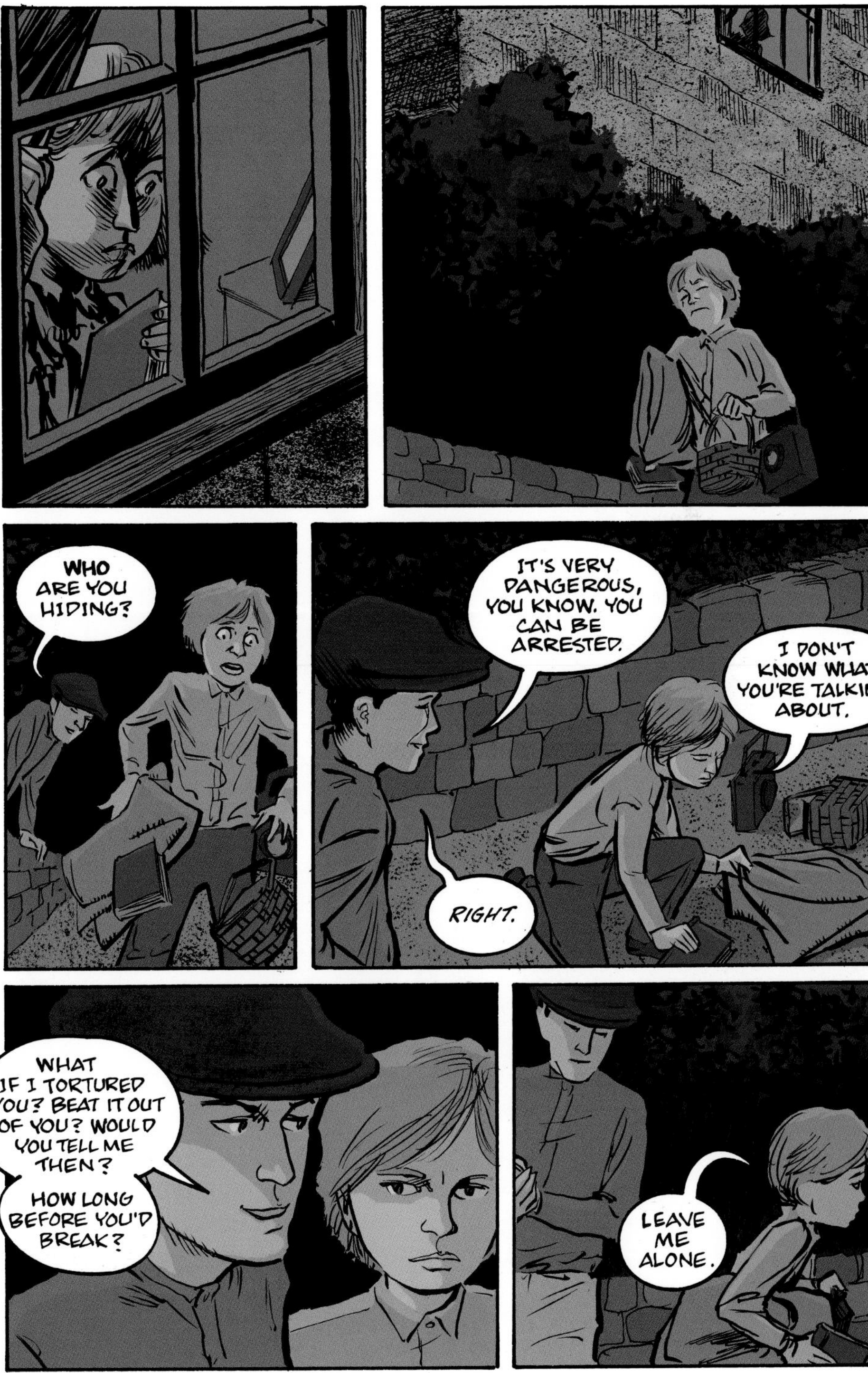
WHO ARE YOU HIDING?
IT'S VERY DANGEROUS, YOU KNOW. YOU CAN BE ARRESTED.
I DON'T KNOW WHAT YOU'RE TALKING ABOUT.
RIGHT.
WHAT IF I TORTURED YOU? BEAT IT OUT OF YOU? WOULD YOU TELL ME THEN?
HOW LONG BEFORE YOU'D BREAK?
LEAVE ME ALONE.

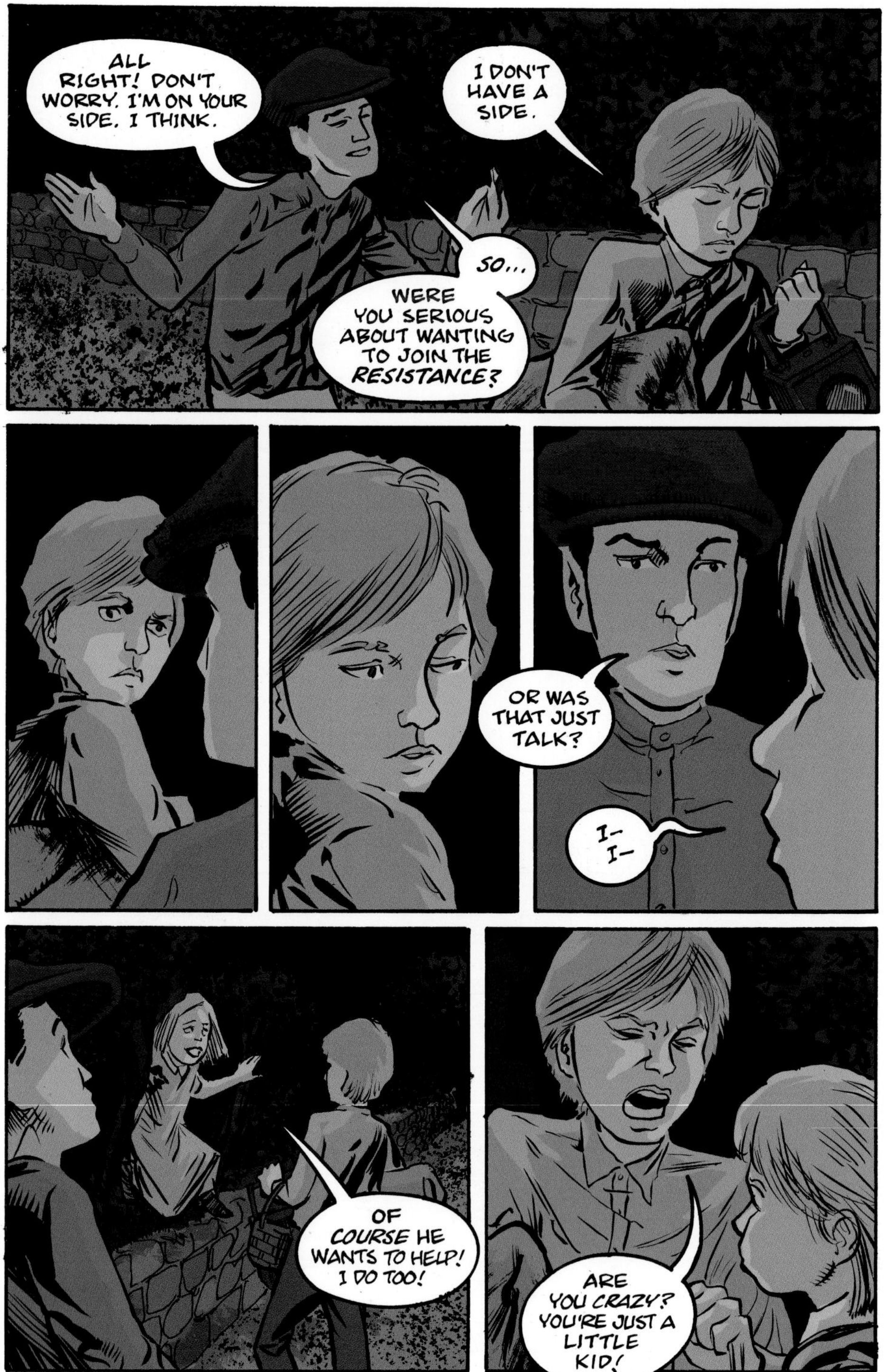
ALL RIGHT! DON'T WORRY. I'M ON YOUR SIDE. I THINK.
I DON'T HAVE A SIDE.
SO...
WERE YOU SERIOUS ABOUT WANTING TO JOIN THE RESISTANCE?
OR WAS THAT JUST TALK?
I- I-
OF COURSE HE WANTS TO HELP! I DO TOO!
ARE YOU CRAZY? YOU'RE JUST A LITTLE KID!

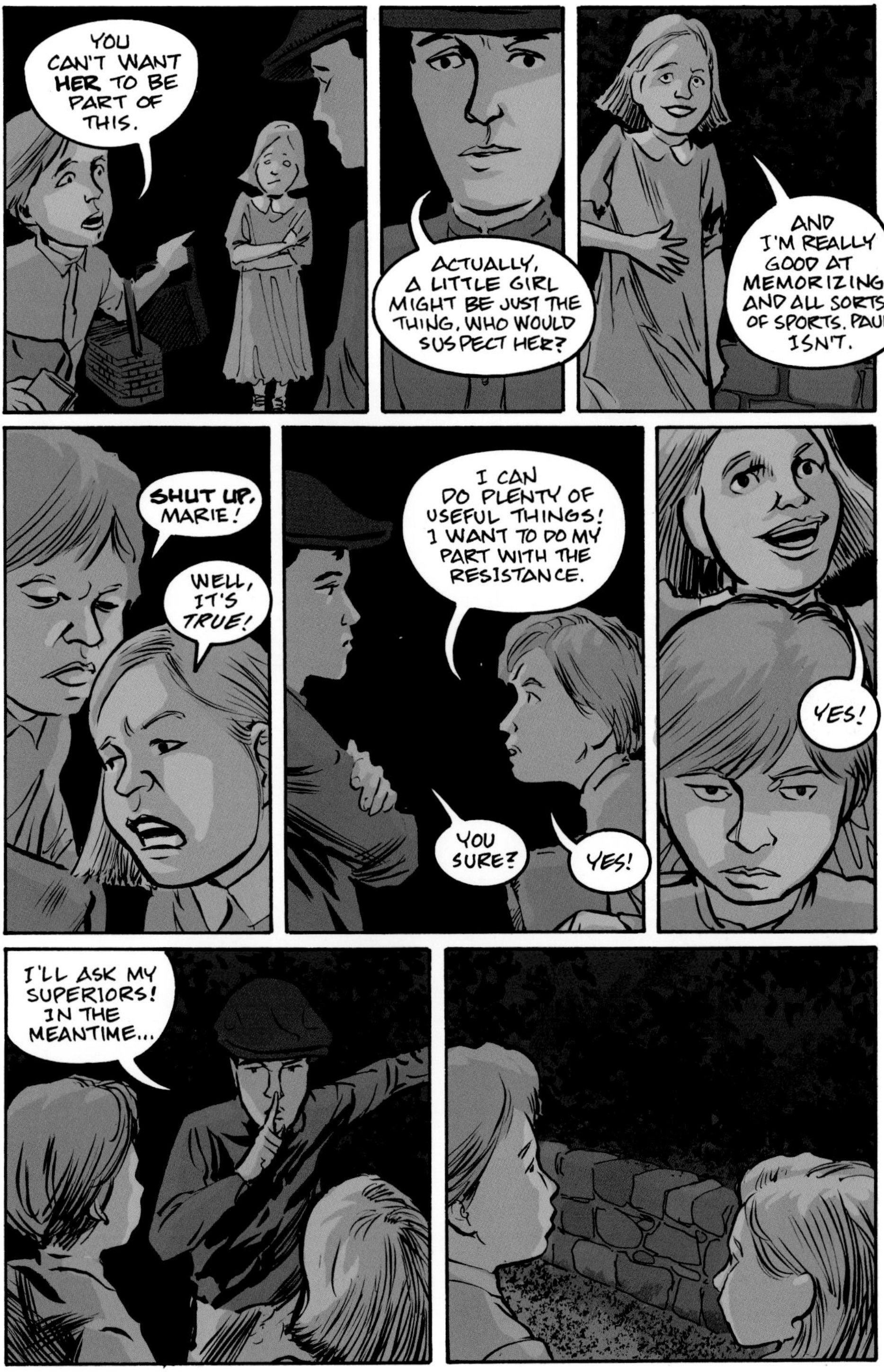
YOU CAN'T WANT HER TO BE PART OF THIS.
ACTUALLY, A LITTLE GIRL MIGHT BE JUST THE THING. WHO WOULD SUSPECT HER?
AND I'M REALLY GOOD AT MEMORIZING AND ALL SORTS OF SPORTS. PAUL ISN'T.
SHUT UP, MARIE!
WELL, IT'S TRUE!
I CAN DO PLENTY OF USEFUL THINGS! I WANT TO DO MY PART WITH THE RESISTANCE.
YOU SURE?
YES!
YES!
I'LL ASK MY SUPERIORS! IN THE MEANTIME...

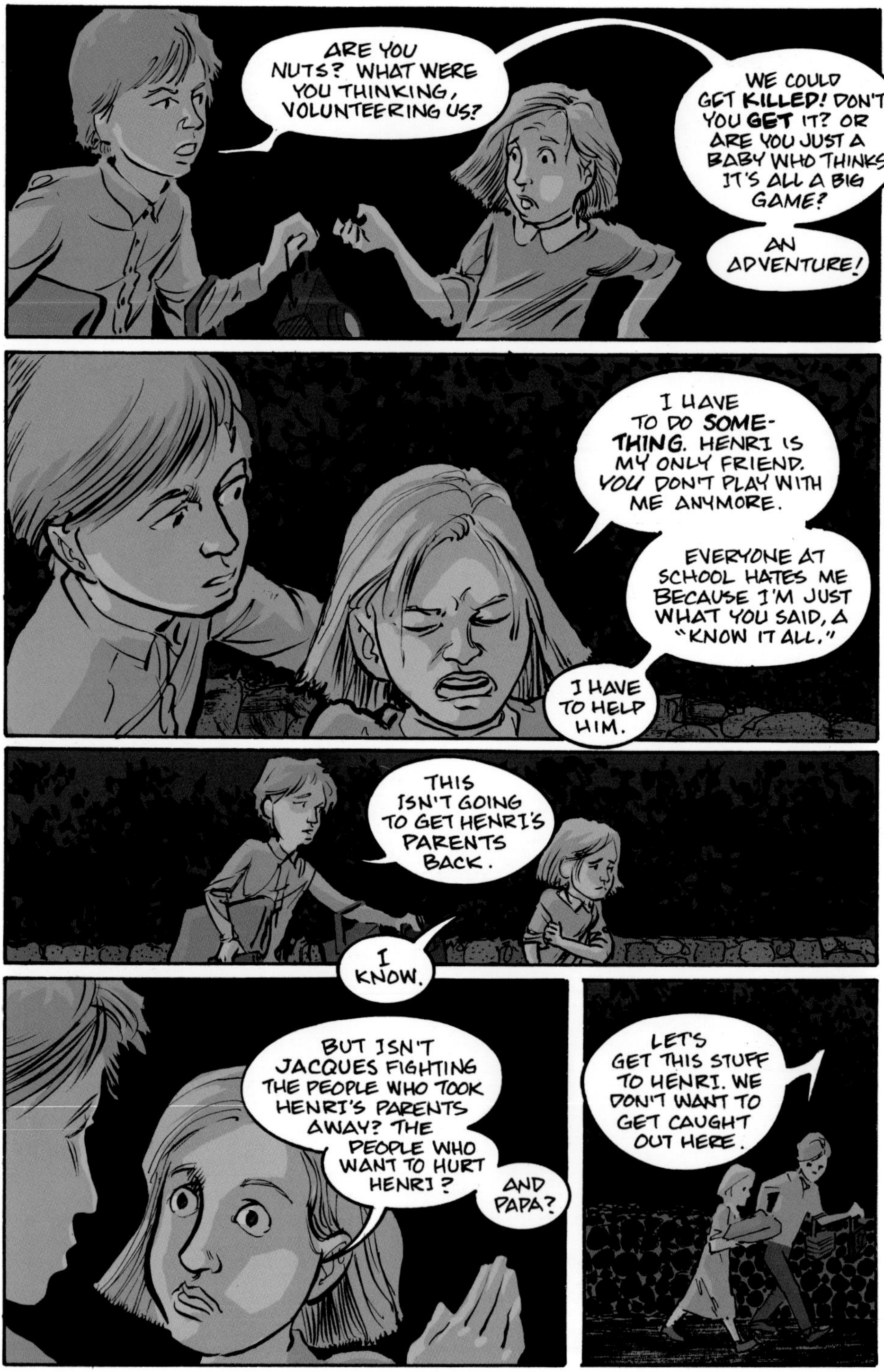
ARE YOU NUTS? WHAT WERE YOU THINKING, VOLUNTEERING US?
WE COULD GET KILLED! DON'T YOU GET IT? OR ARE YOU JUST A BABY WHO THINKS IT'S ALL A BIG GAME?
AN ADVENTURE!
I HAVE TO DO SOME-THING. HENRI IS MY ONLY FRIEND. YOU DON'T PLAY WITH ME ANYMORE.
EVERYONE AT SCHOOL HATES ME BECAUSE I'M JUST WHAT YOU SAID, A "KNOW IT ALL."
I HAVE TO HELP HIM.
THIS ISN'T GOING TO GET HENRI'S PARENTS BACK.
I KNOW.
BUT ISN'T JACQUES FIGHTING THE PEOPLE WHO TOOK HENRI'S PARENTS AWAY? THE PEOPLE WHO WANT TO HURT HENRI?
AND PAPA?
LET'S GET THIS STUFF TO HENRI. WE DON'T WANT TO GET CAUGHT OUT HERE.

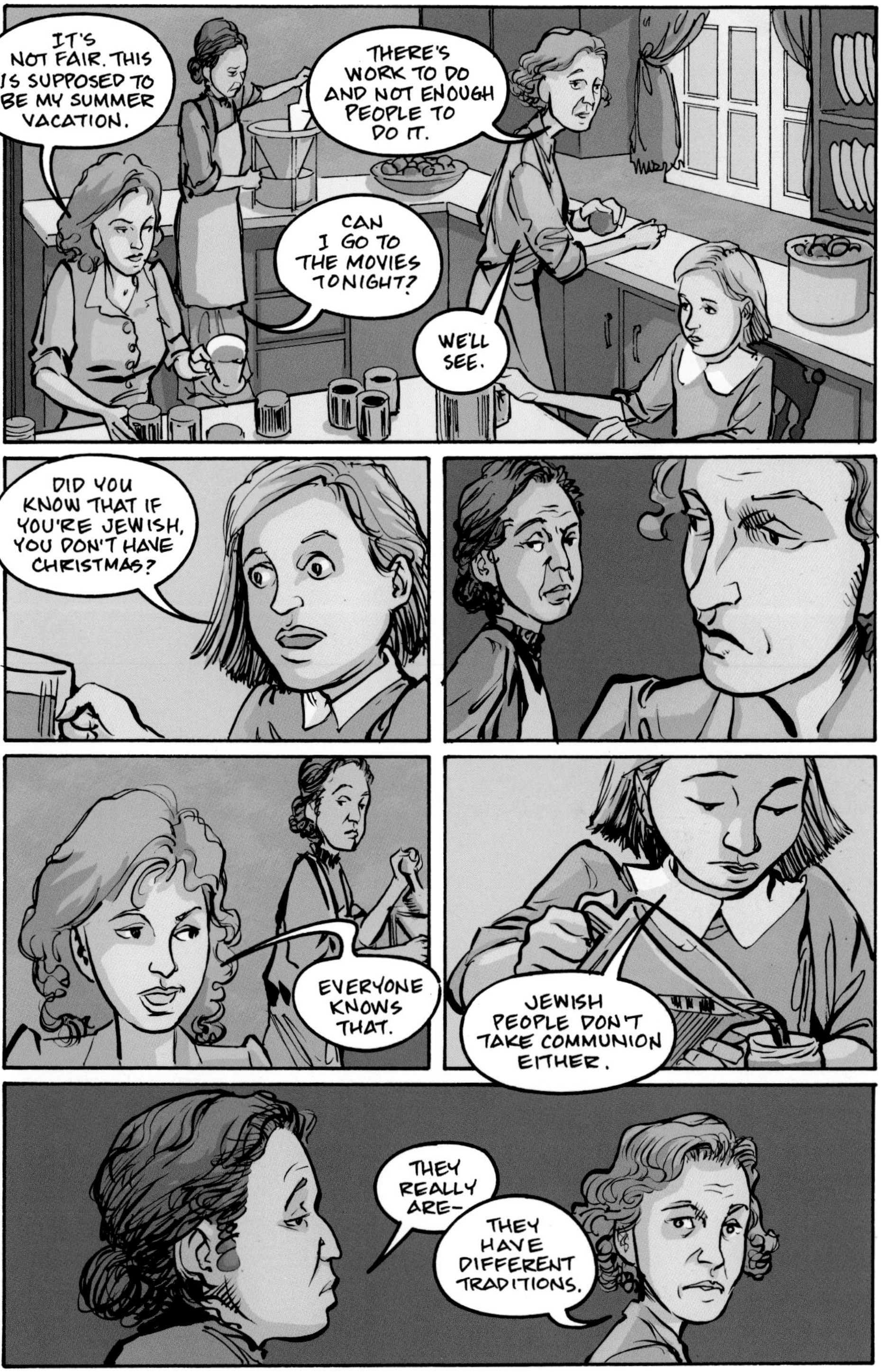
IT'S NOT FAIR. THIS IS SUPPOSED TO BE MY SUMMER VACATION.
THERE'S WORK TO DO AND NOT ENOUGH PEOPLE TO DO IT.
CAN I GO TO THE MOVIES TONIGHT?
WE'LL SEE.
DID YOU KNOW THAT IF YOU'RE JEWISH, YOU DON'T HAVE CHRISTMAS?
EVERYONE KNOWS THAT.
JEWISH PEOPLE DON'T TAKE COMMUNION EITHER.
THEY REALLY ARE-
THEY HAVE DIFFERENT TRADITIONS.

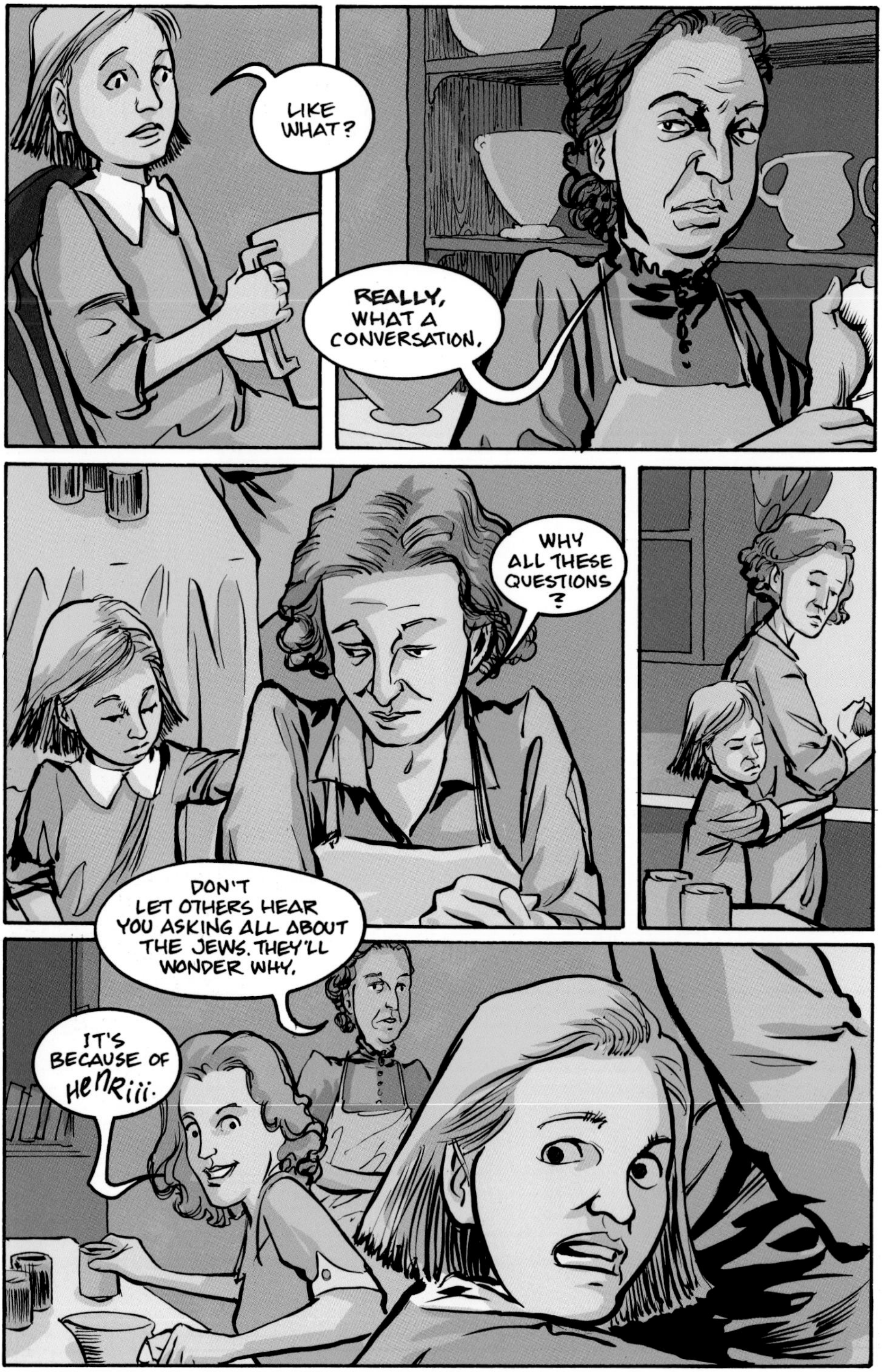
LIKE WHAT?
REALLY, WHAT A CONVERSATION.
WHY ALL THESE QUESTIONS?
DON'T LET OTHERS HEAR YOU ASKING ALL ABOUT THE JEWS. THEY'LL WONDER WHY.
IT'S BECAUSE OF HENRIII.

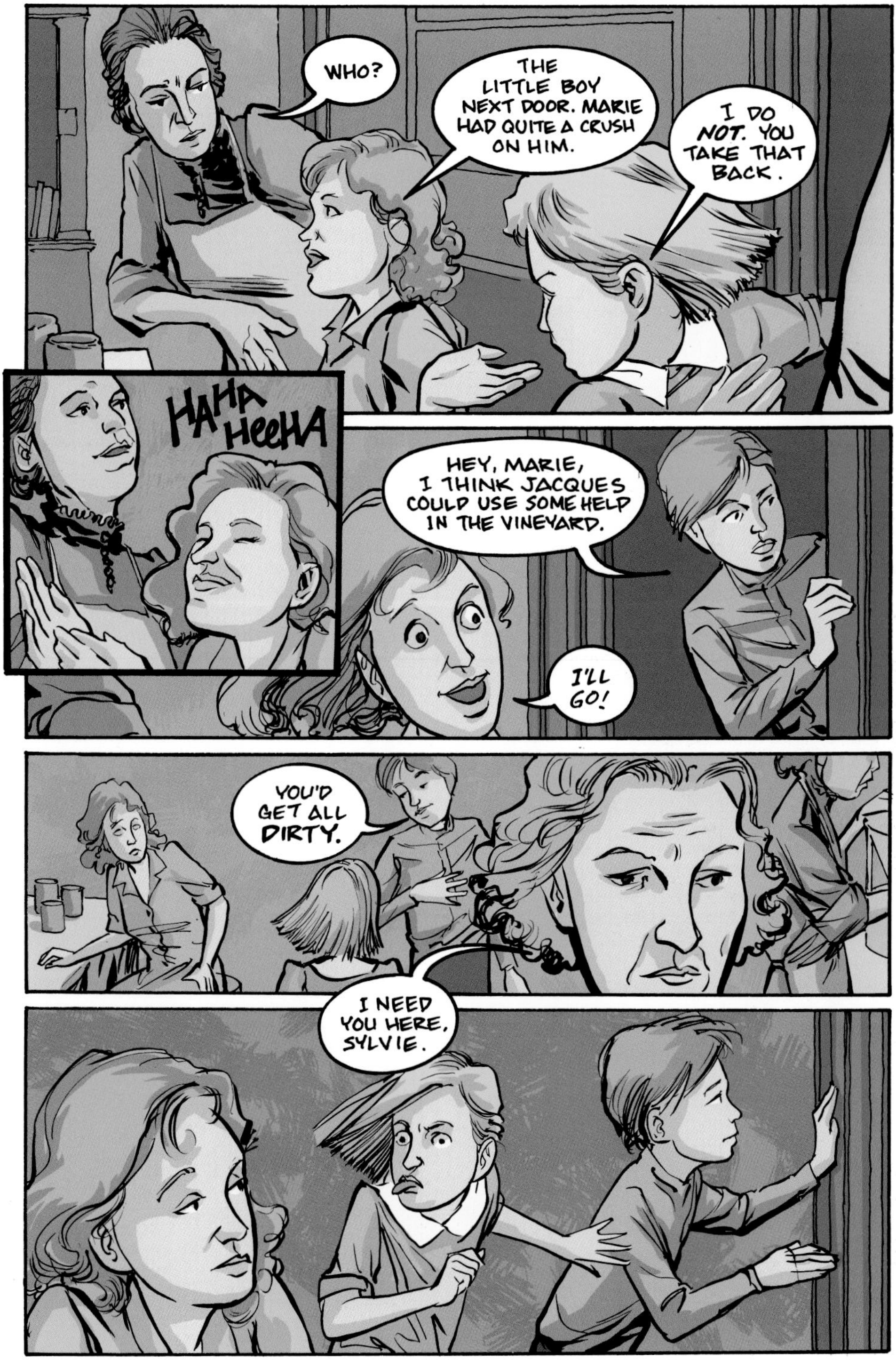
WHO?
THE LITTLE BOY NEXT DOOR. MARIE HAD QUITE A CRUSH ON HIM.
I DO NOT. YOU TAKE THAT BACK.
HAHA HEEHA
HEY, MARIE, I THINK JACQUES COULD USE SOME HELP IN THE VINEYARD.
I'LL GO!
YOU'D GET ALL DIRTY.
I NEED YOU HERE, SYLVIE.

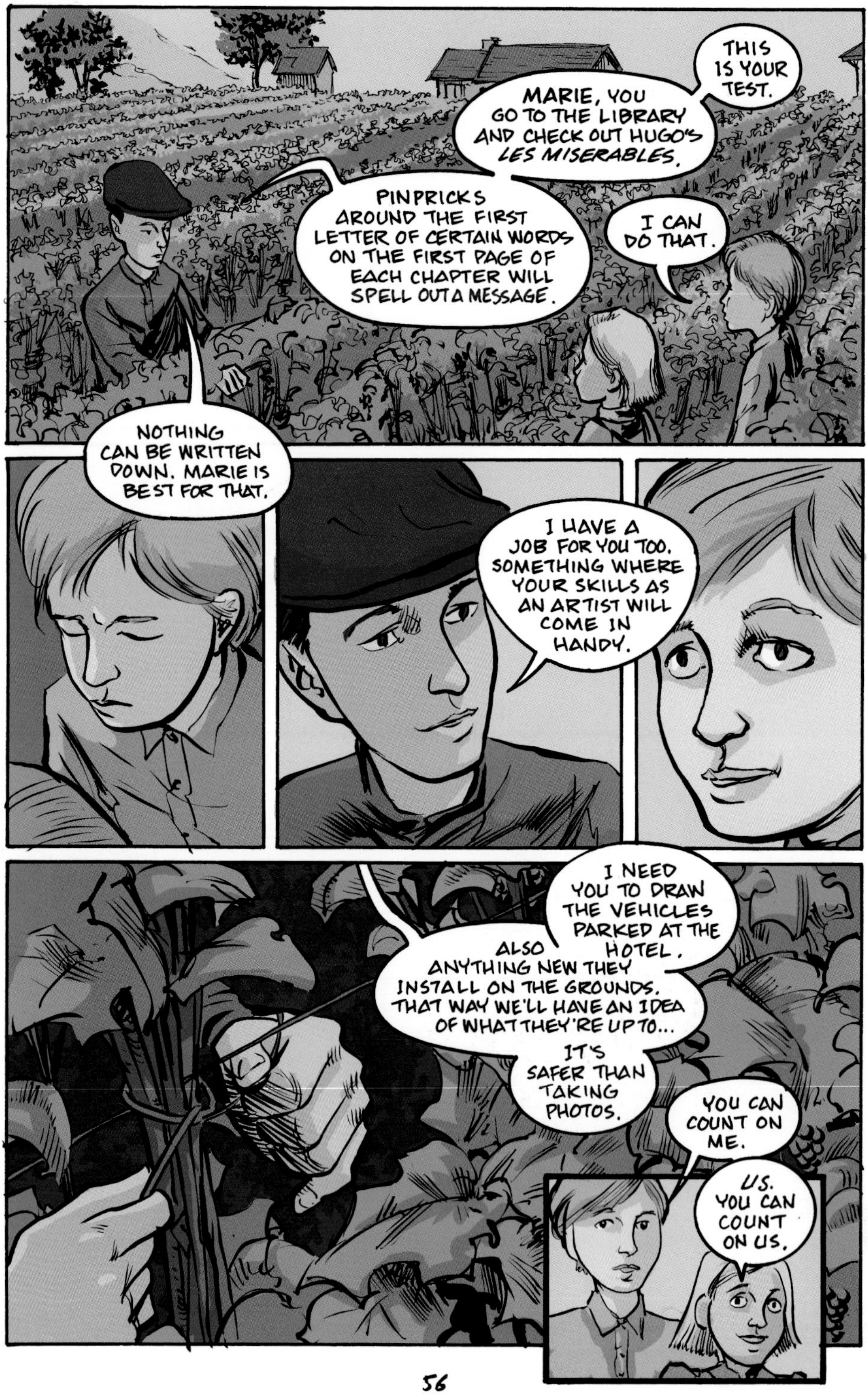
MARIE, YOU GO TO THE LIBRARY AND CHECK OUT HUGO'S *LES MISERABLES*.
THIS IS YOUR TEST.
PINPRICKS AROUND THE FIRST LETTER OF CERTAIN WORDS ON THE FIRST PAGE OF EACH CHAPTER WILL SPELL OUT A MESSAGE.
I CAN DO THAT.
NOTHING CAN BE WRITTEN DOWN. MARIE IS BEST FOR THAT.
I HAVE A JOB FOR YOU TOO. SOMETHING WHERE YOUR SKILLS AS AN ARTIST WILL COME IN HANDY.
I NEED YOU TO DRAW THE VEHICLES PARKED AT THE HOTEL.
ALSO ANYTHING NEW THEY INSTALL ON THE GROUNDS. THAT WAY WE'LL HAVE AN IDEA OF WHAT THEY'RE UP TO...
IT'S SAFER THAN TAKING PHOTOS.
YOU CAN COUNT ON ME.
US. YOU CAN COUNT ON US.

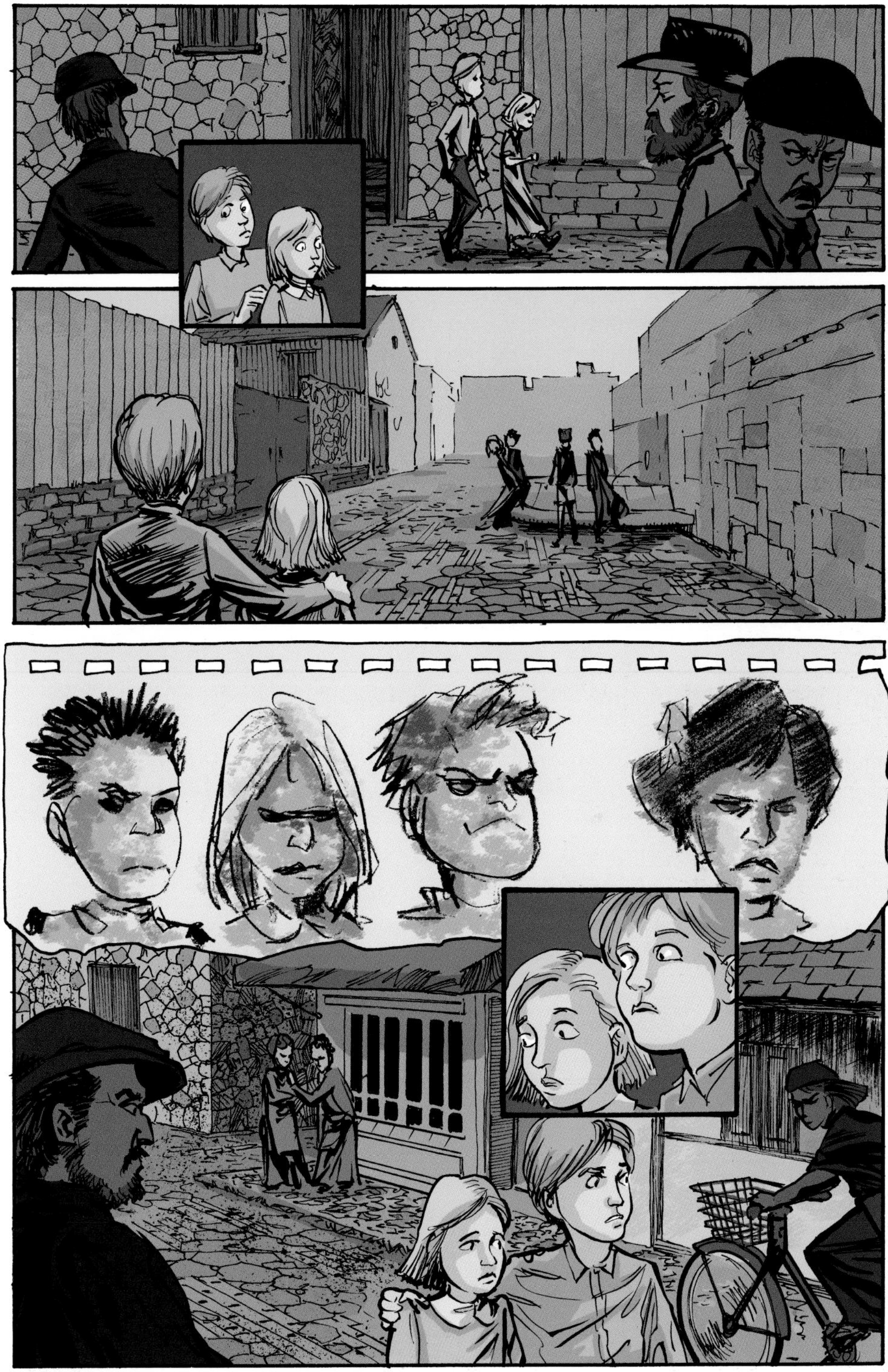

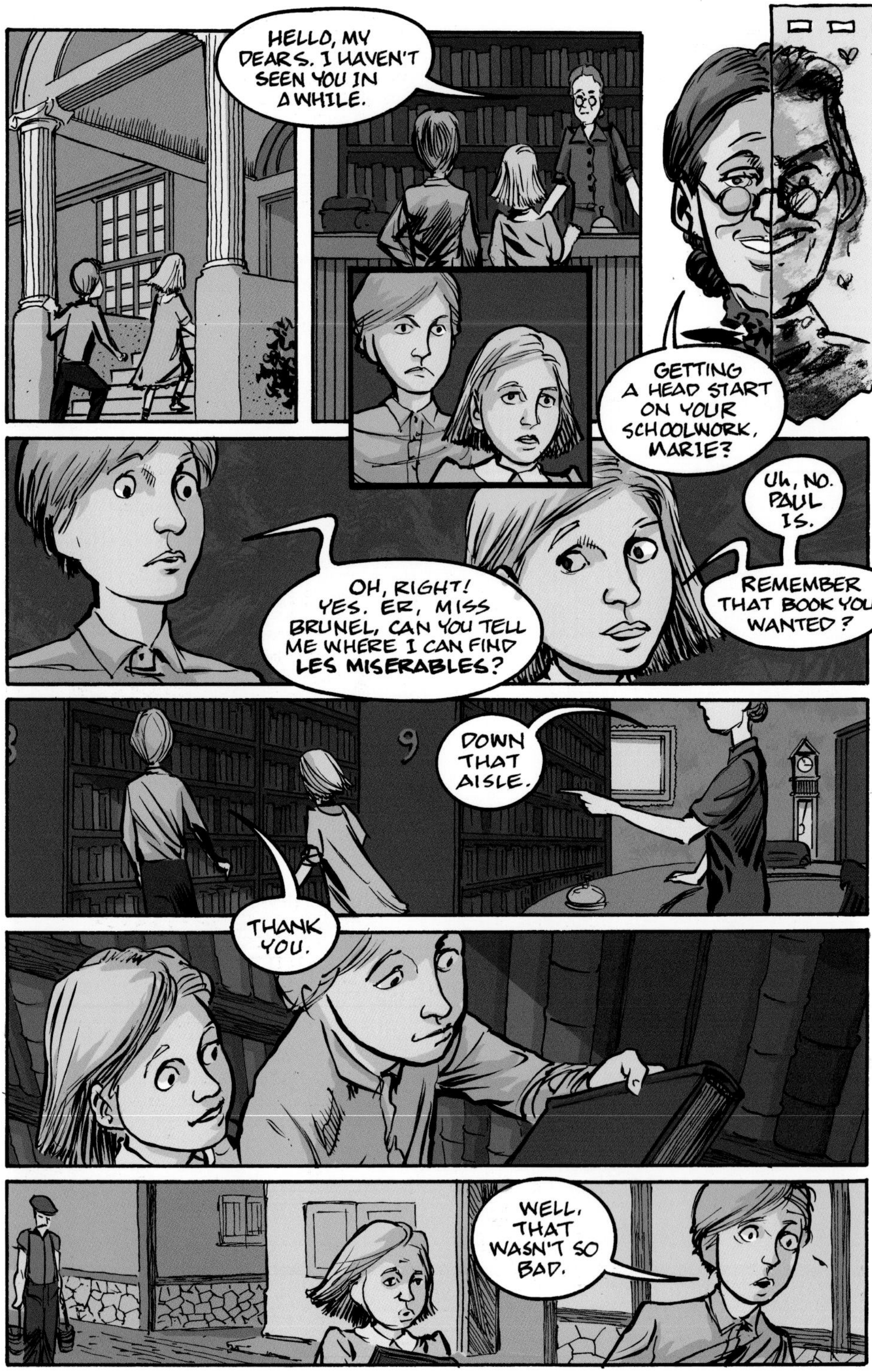
HELLO, MY DEARS. I HAVEN'T SEEN YOU IN A WHILE.
GETTING A HEAD START ON YOUR SCHOOLWORK, MARIE?
UH, NO. PAUL IS.
REMEMBER THAT BOOK YOU WANTED?
OH, RIGHT! YES. ER, MISS BRUNEL, CAN YOU TELL ME WHERE I CAN FIND LES MISERABLES?
DOWN THAT AISLE.
THANK YOU.
WELL, THAT WASN'T SO BAD.

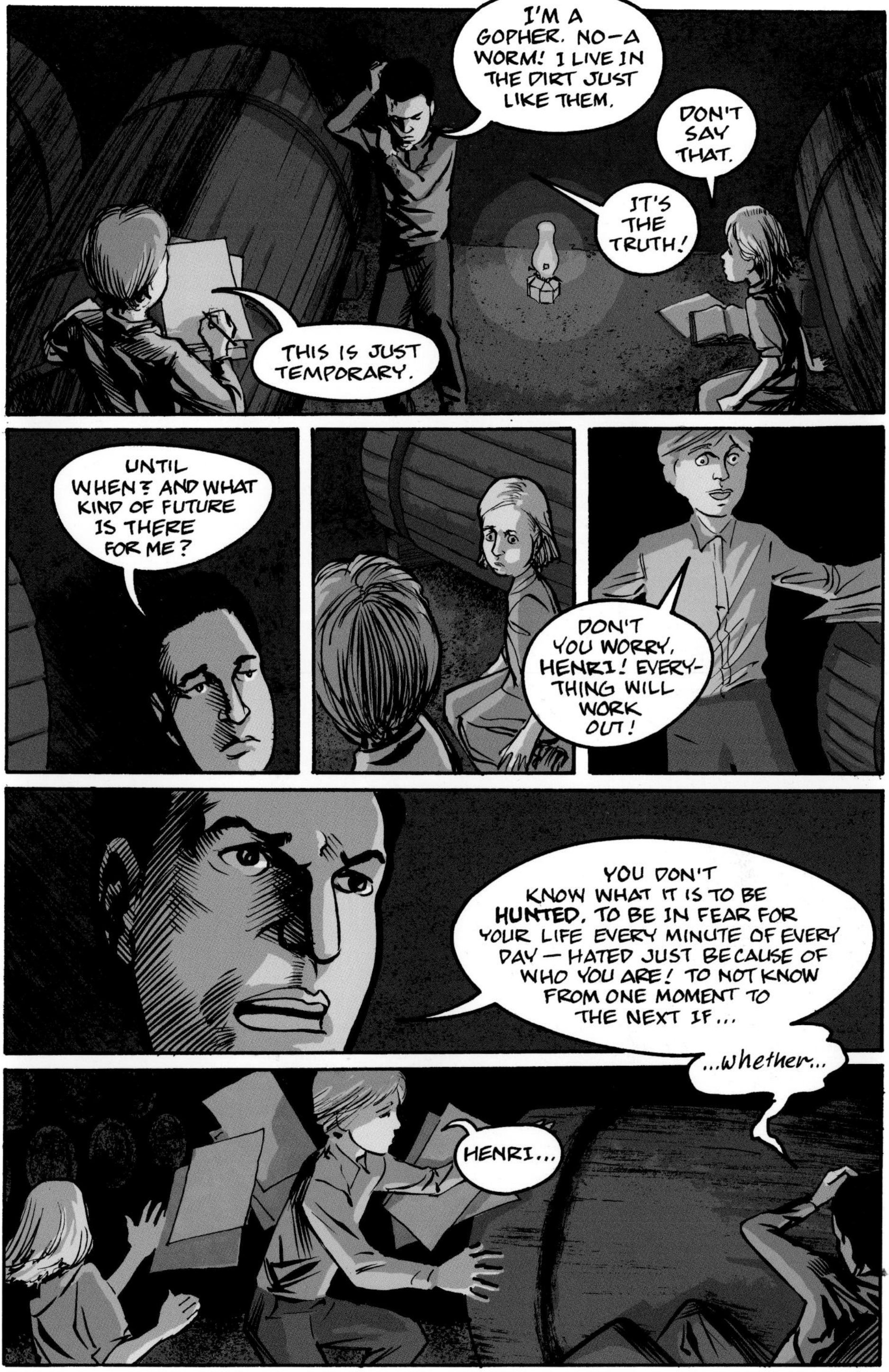
I'M A GOPHER. NO—A WORM! I LIVE IN THE DIRT JUST LIKE THEM.
DON'T SAY THAT.
IT'S THE TRUTH!
THIS IS JUST TEMPORARY.
UNTIL WHEN? AND WHAT KIND OF FUTURE IS THERE FOR ME?
DON'T YOU WORRY, HENRI! EVERY-THING WILL WORK OUT!
YOU DON'T KNOW WHAT IT IS TO BE HUNTED. TO BE IN FEAR FOR YOUR LIFE EVERY MINUTE OF EVERY DAY—HATED JUST BECAUSE OF WHO YOU ARE! TO NOT KNOW FROM ONE MOMENT TO THE NEXT IF...
...whether...
HENRI...

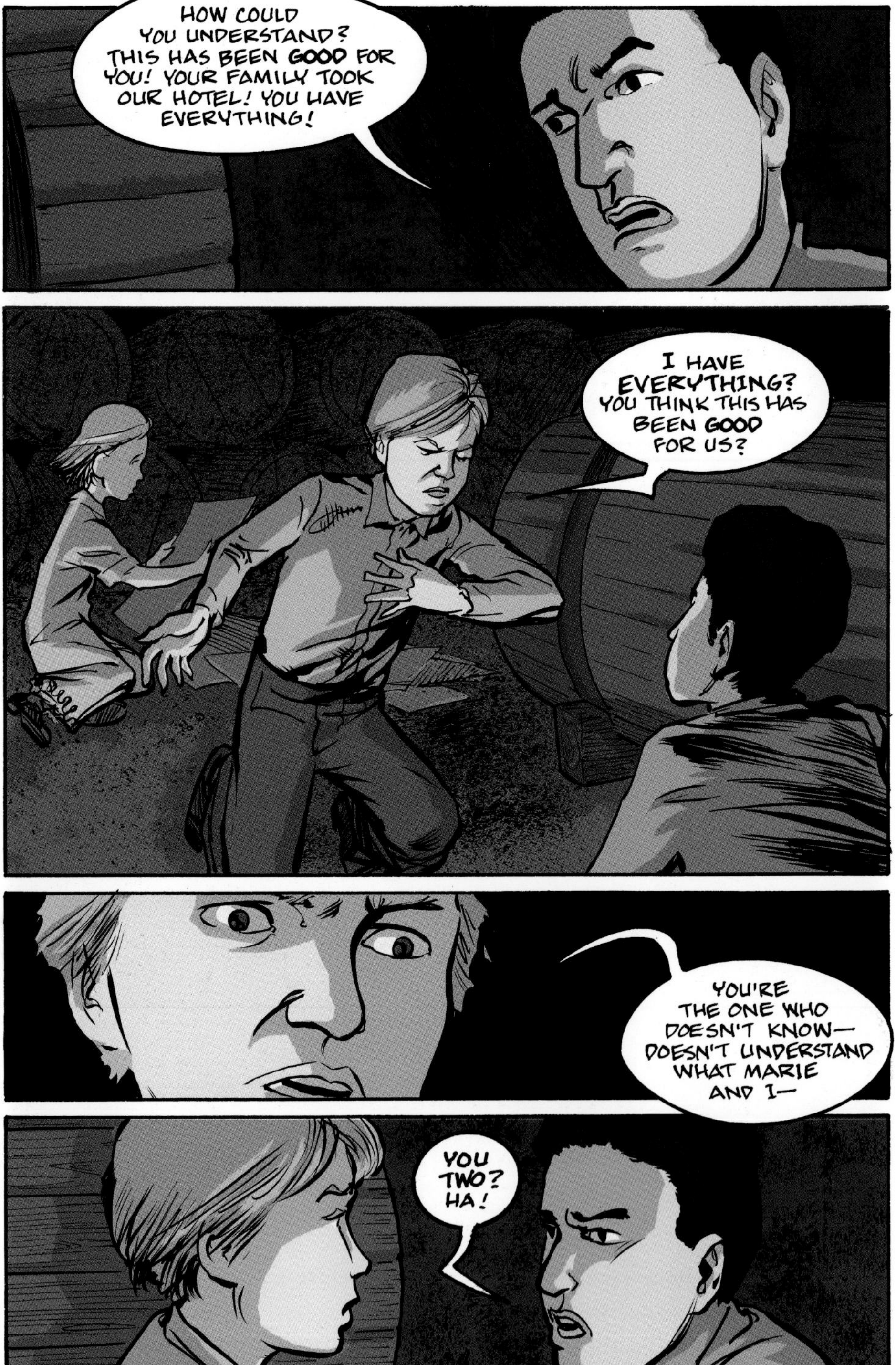
HOW COULD YOU UNDERSTAND? THIS HAS BEEN GOOD FOR YOU! YOUR FAMILY TOOK OUR HOTEL! YOU HAVE EVERYTHING!
I HAVE EVERYTHING? YOU THINK THIS HAS BEEN GOOD FOR US?
YOU'RE THE ONE WHO DOESN'T KNOW— DOESN'T UNDERSTAND WHAT MARIE AND I—
YOU TWO? HA!

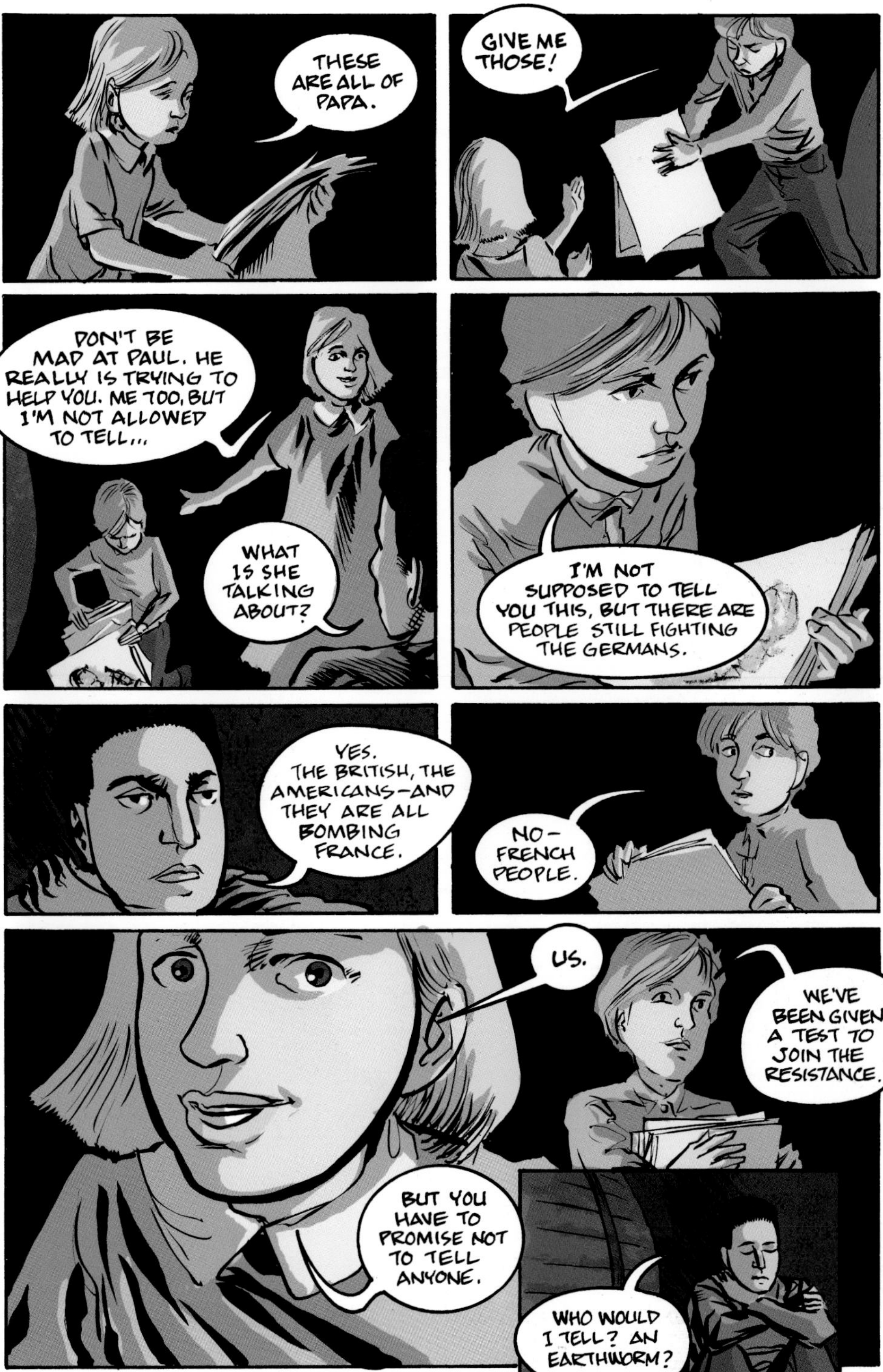
THESE ARE ALL OF PAPA.
GIVE ME THOSE!
DON'T BE MAD AT PAUL. HE REALLY IS TRYING TO HELP YOU. ME TOO, BUT I'M NOT ALLOWED TO TELL...
WHAT IS SHE TALKING ABOUT?
I'M NOT SUPPOSED TO TELL YOU THIS, BUT THERE ARE PEOPLE STILL FIGHTING THE GERMANS.
YES. THE BRITISH, THE AMERICANS—AND THEY ARE ALL BOMBING FRANCE.
NO—FRENCH PEOPLE.
US.
WE'VE BEEN GIVEN A TEST TO JOIN THE RESISTANCE.
BUT YOU HAVE TO PROMISE NOT TO TELL ANYONE.
WHO WOULD I TELL? AN EARTHWORM?

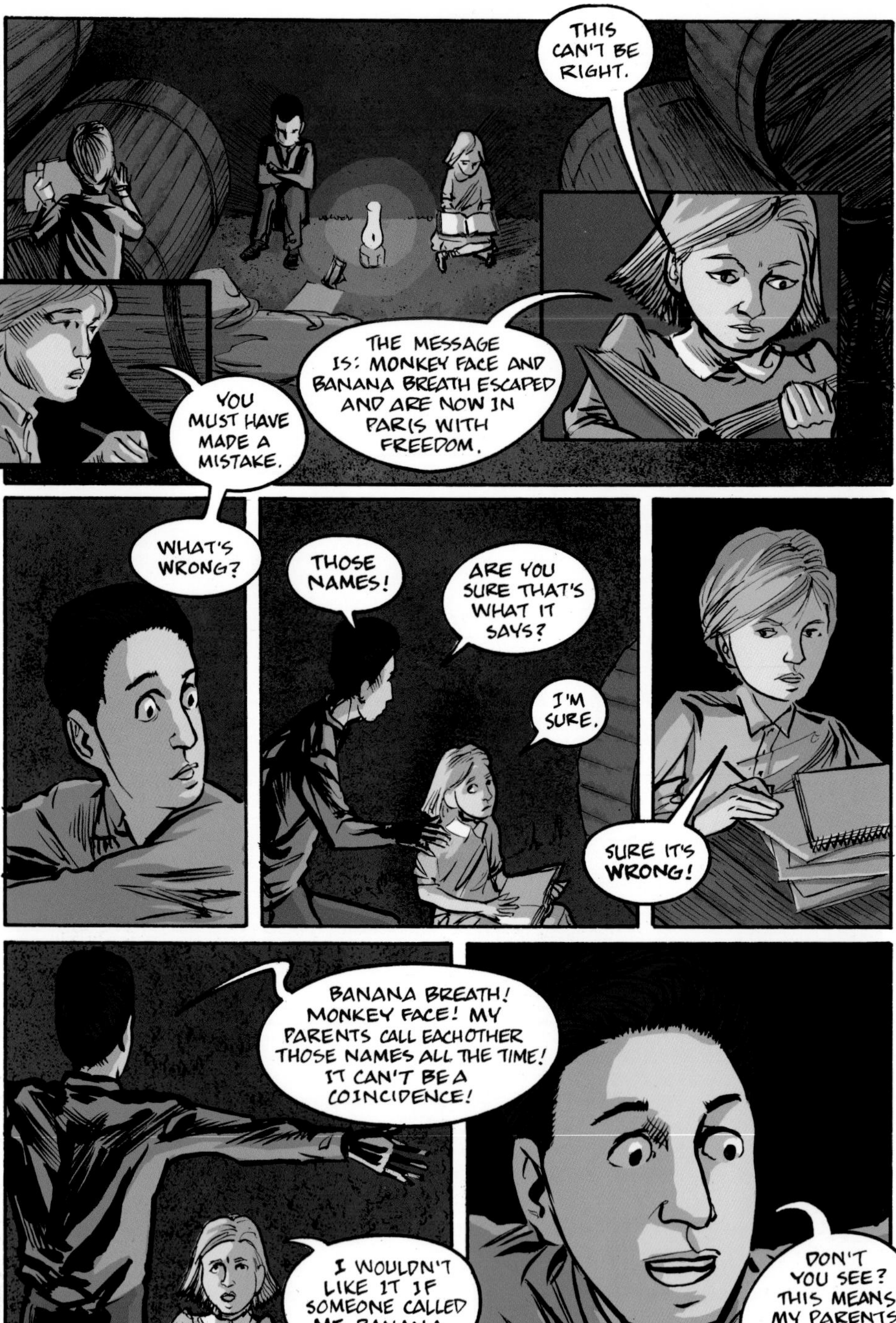
THIS CAN'T BE RIGHT.
THE MESSAGE IS: MONKEY FACE AND BANANA BREATH ESCAPED AND ARE NOW IN PARIS WITH FREEDOM.
YOU MUST HAVE MADE A MISTAKE.
WHAT'S WRONG?
THOSE NAMES!
ARE YOU SURE THAT'S WHAT IT SAYS?
I'M SURE.
SURE IT'S WRONG!
BANANA BREATH! MONKEY FACE! MY PARENTS CALL EACHOTHER THOSE NAMES ALL THE TIME! IT CAN'T BE A COINCIDENCE!
I WOULDN'T LIKE IT IF SOMEONE CALLED ME BANANA BREATH. OR MONKEY FACE.
DON'T YOU SEE? THIS MEANS MY PARENTS ARE ALIVE AND IN PARIS!

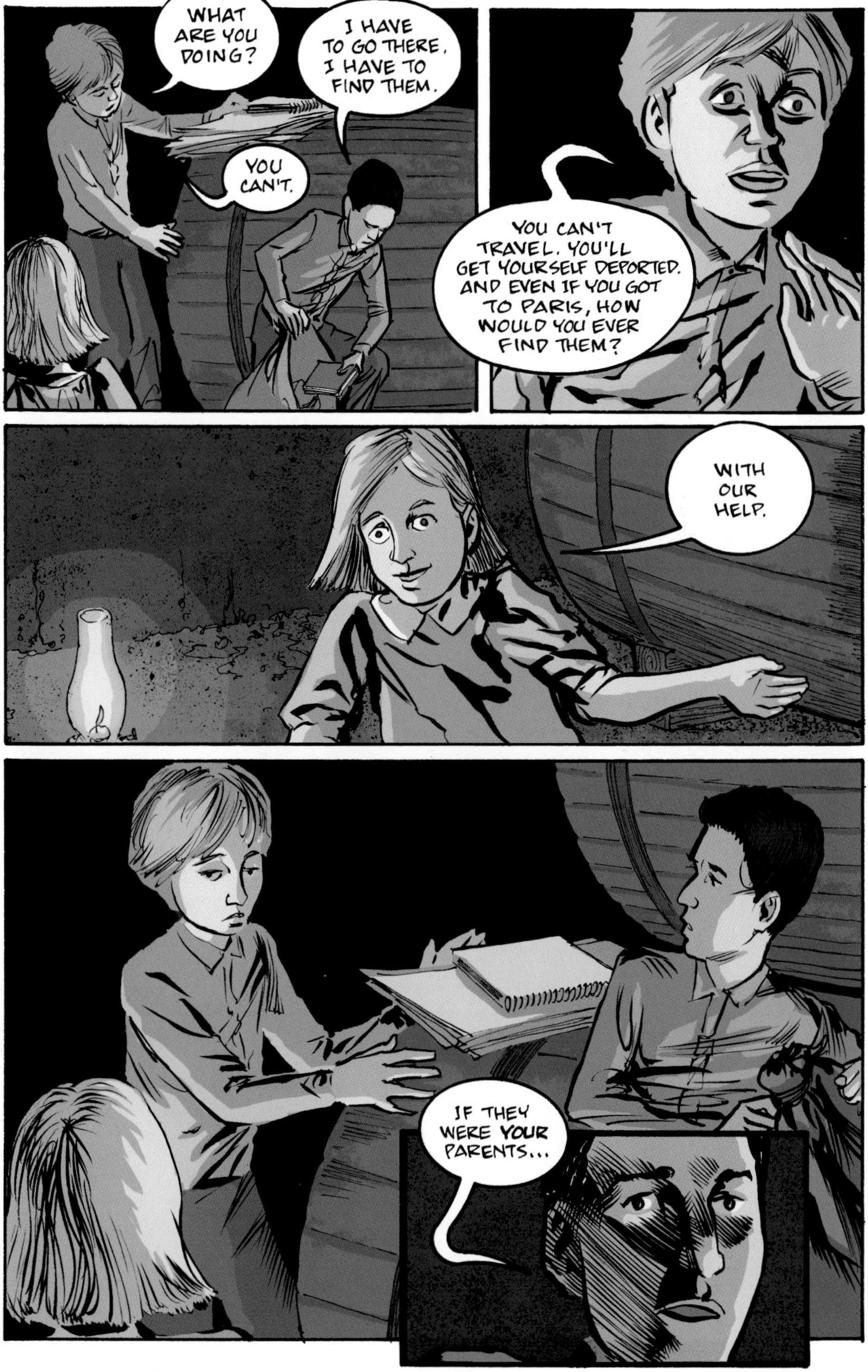

WHAT ARE YOU DOING?
I HAVE TO GO THERE, I HAVE TO FIND THEM.
YOU CAN'T.
YOU CAN'T TRAVEL. YOU'LL GET YOURSELF DEPORTED. AND EVEN IF YOU GOT TO PARIS, HOW WOULD YOU EVER FIND THEM?
WITH OUR HELP.
IF THEY WERE YOUR PARENTS...

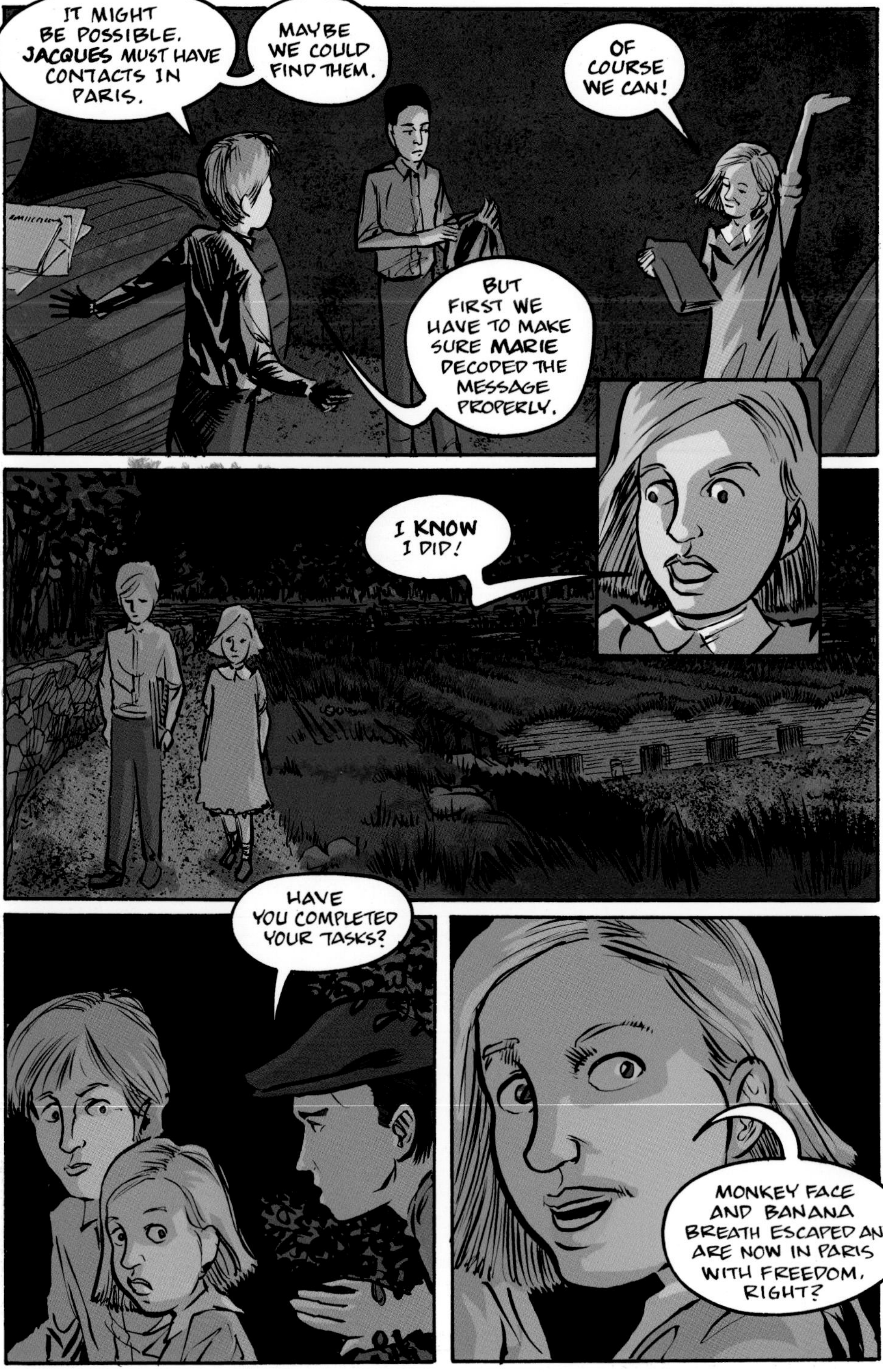
IT MIGHT BE POSSIBLE. JACQUES MUST HAVE CONTACTS IN PARIS.
MAYBE WE COULD FIND THEM.
OF COURSE WE CAN!
BUT FIRST WE HAVE TO MAKE SURE MARIE DECODED THE MESSAGE PROPERLY.
I KNOW I DID!
HAVE YOU COMPLETED YOUR TASKS?
MONKEY FACE AND BANANA BREATH ESCAPED AND ARE NOW IN PARIS WITH FREEDOM, RIGHT?

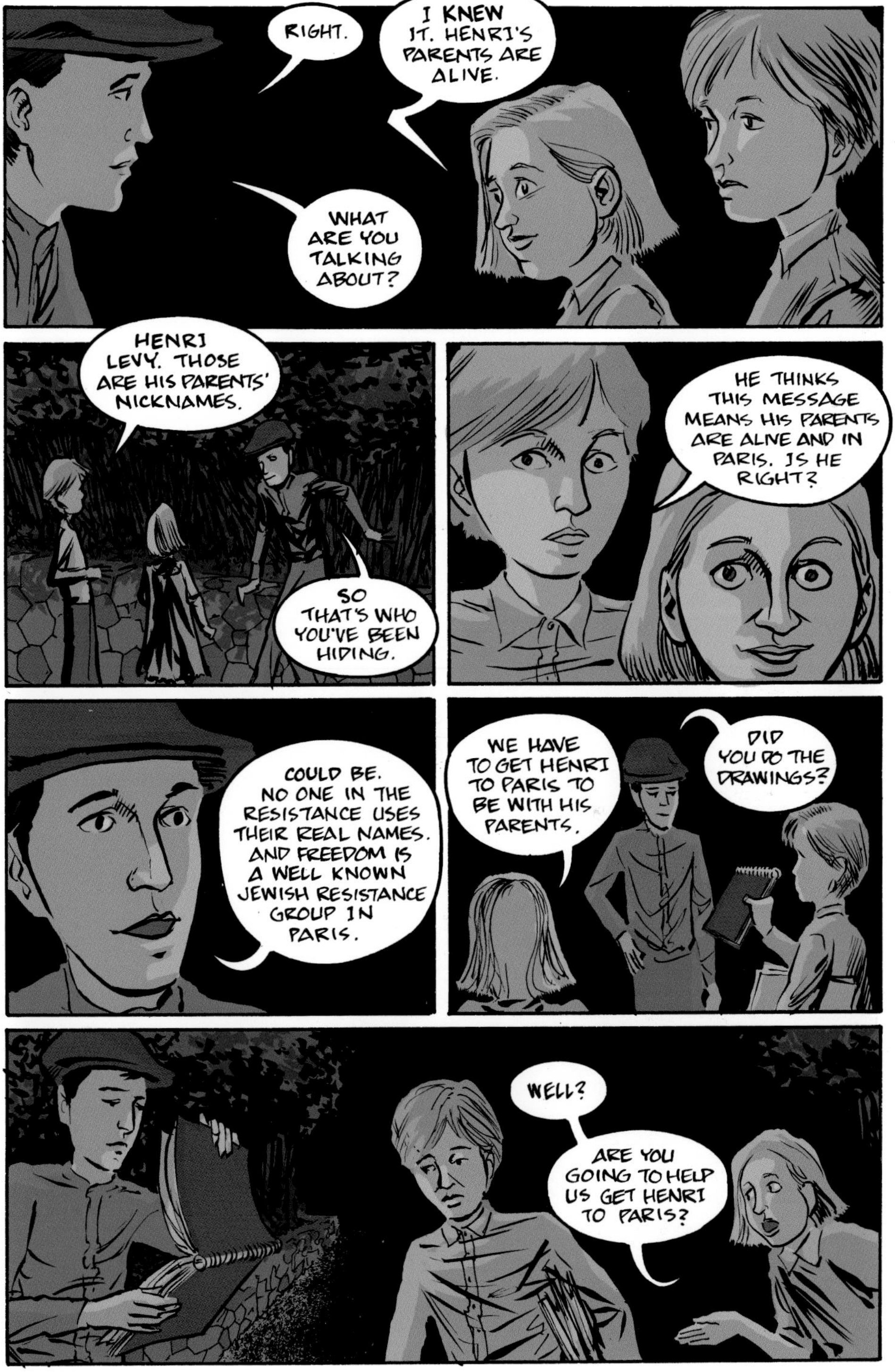

RIGHT.
I KNEW IT. HENRI'S PARENTS ARE ALIVE.
WHAT ARE YOU TALKING ABOUT?
HENRI LEVY. THOSE ARE HIS PARENTS' NICKNAMES.
SO THAT'S WHO YOU'VE BEEN HIDING.
HE THINKS THIS MESSAGE MEANS HIS PARENTS ARE ALIVE AND IN PARIS. IS HE RIGHT?
COULD BE. NO ONE IN THE RESISTANCE USES THEIR REAL NAMES. AND FREEDOM IS A WELL KNOWN JEWISH RESISTANCE GROUP IN PARIS.
WE HAVE TO GET HENRI TO PARIS TO BE WITH HIS PARENTS.
DID YOU DO THE DRAWINGS?
WELL?
ARE YOU GOING TO HELP US GET HENRI TO PARIS?

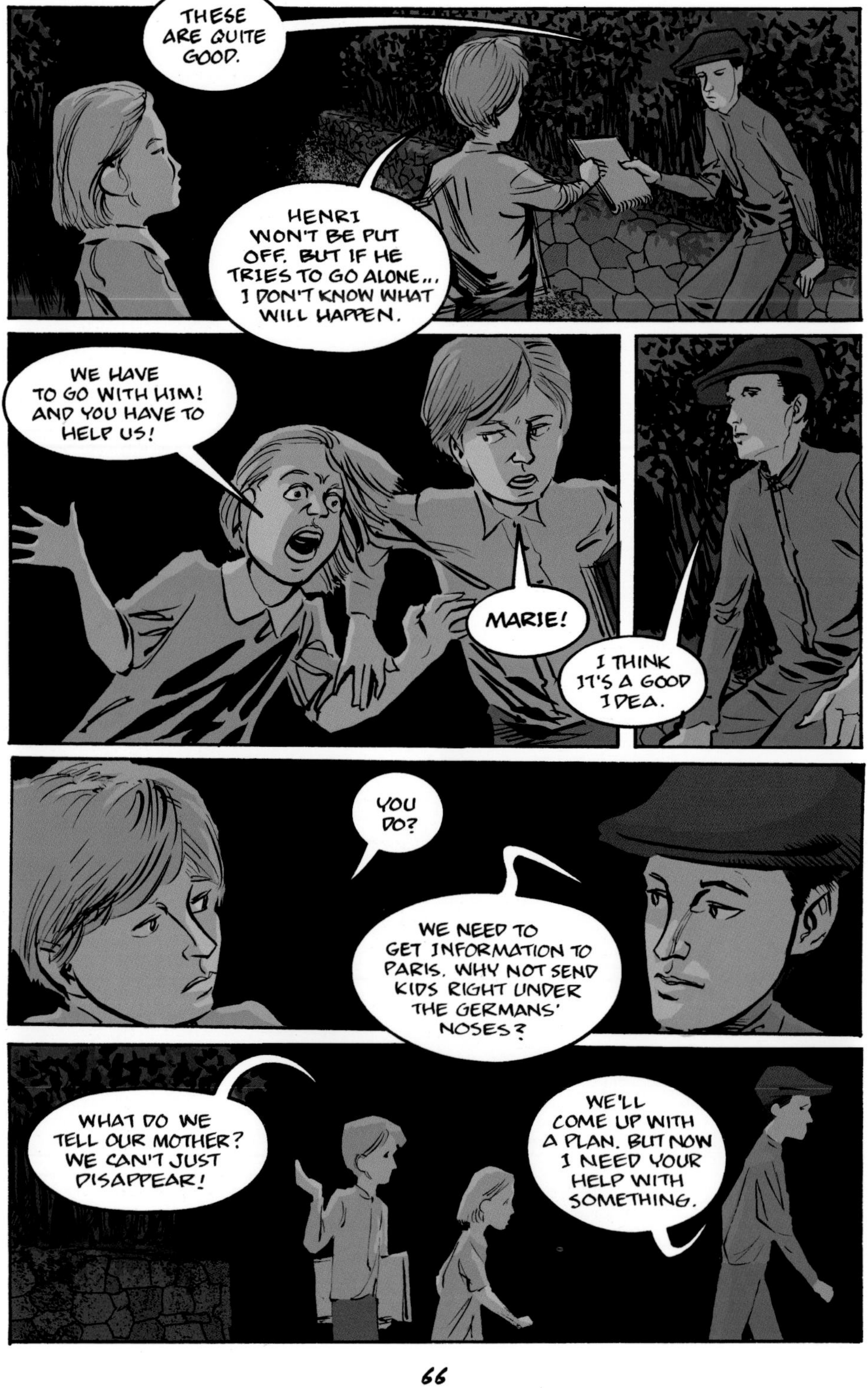
THESE ARE QUITE GOOD.
HENRI WON'T BE PUT OFF. BUT IF HE TRIES TO GO ALONE... I DON'T KNOW WHAT WILL HAPPEN.
WE HAVE TO GO WITH HIM! AND YOU HAVE TO HELP US!
MARIE!
I THINK IT'S A GOOD IDEA.
YOU DO?
WE NEED TO GET INFORMATION TO PARIS. WHY NOT SEND KIDS RIGHT UNDER THE GERMANS' NOSES?
WHAT DO WE TELL OUR MOTHER? WE CAN'T JUST DISAPPEAR!
WE'LL COME UP WITH A PLAN. BUT NOW I NEED YOUR HELP WITH SOMETHING.

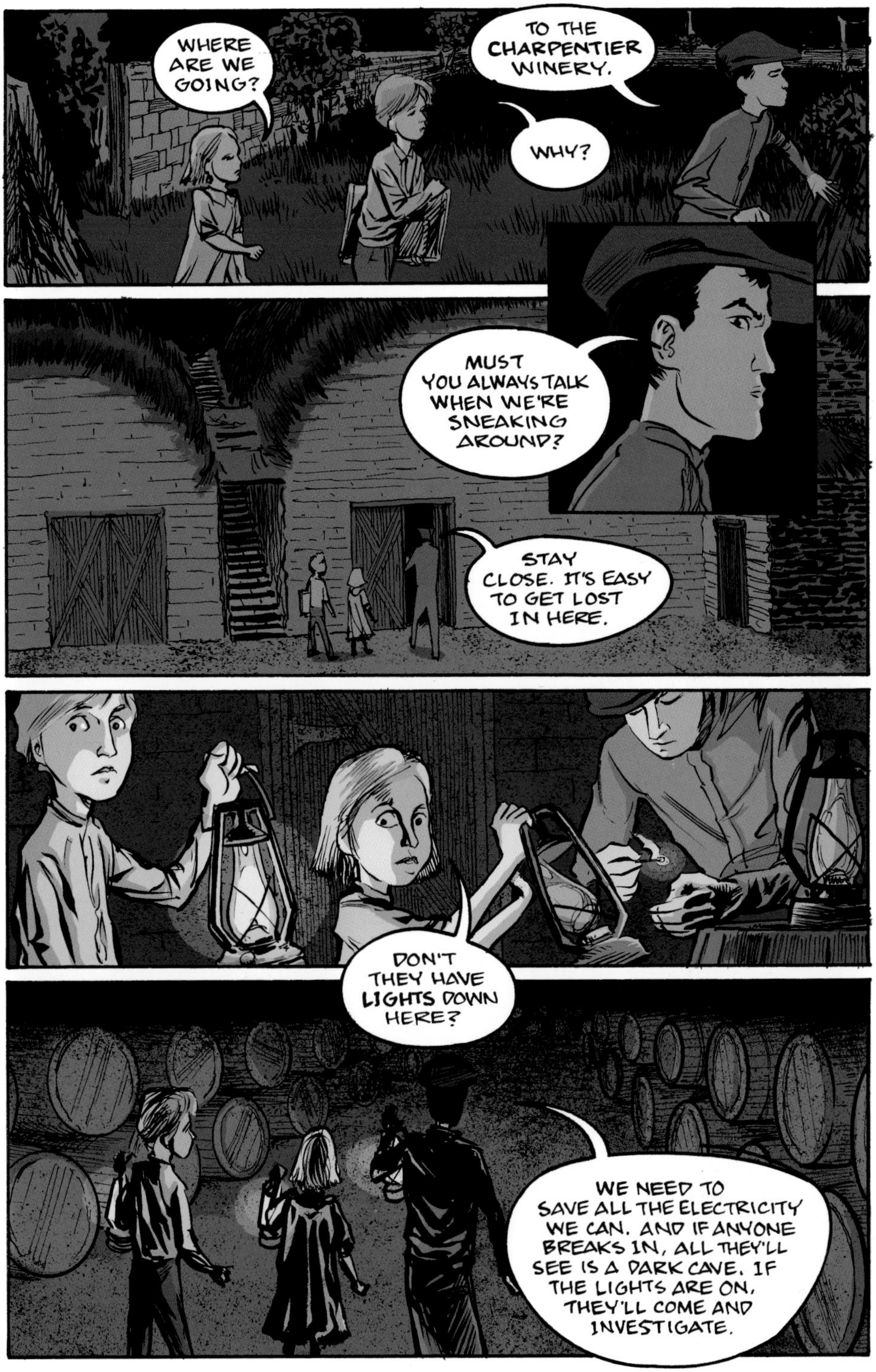
WHERE ARE WE GOING?
TO THE CHARPENTIER WINERY.
WHY?
MUST YOU ALWAYS TALK WHEN WE'RE SNEAKING AROUND?
STAY CLOSE. IT'S EASY TO GET LOST IN HERE.
DON'T THEY HAVE LIGHTS DOWN HERE?
WE NEED TO SAVE ALL THE ELECTRICITY WE CAN. AND IF ANYONE BREAKS IN, ALL THEY'LL SEE IS A DARK CAVE. IF THE LIGHTS ARE ON, THEY'LL COME AND INVESTIGATE.

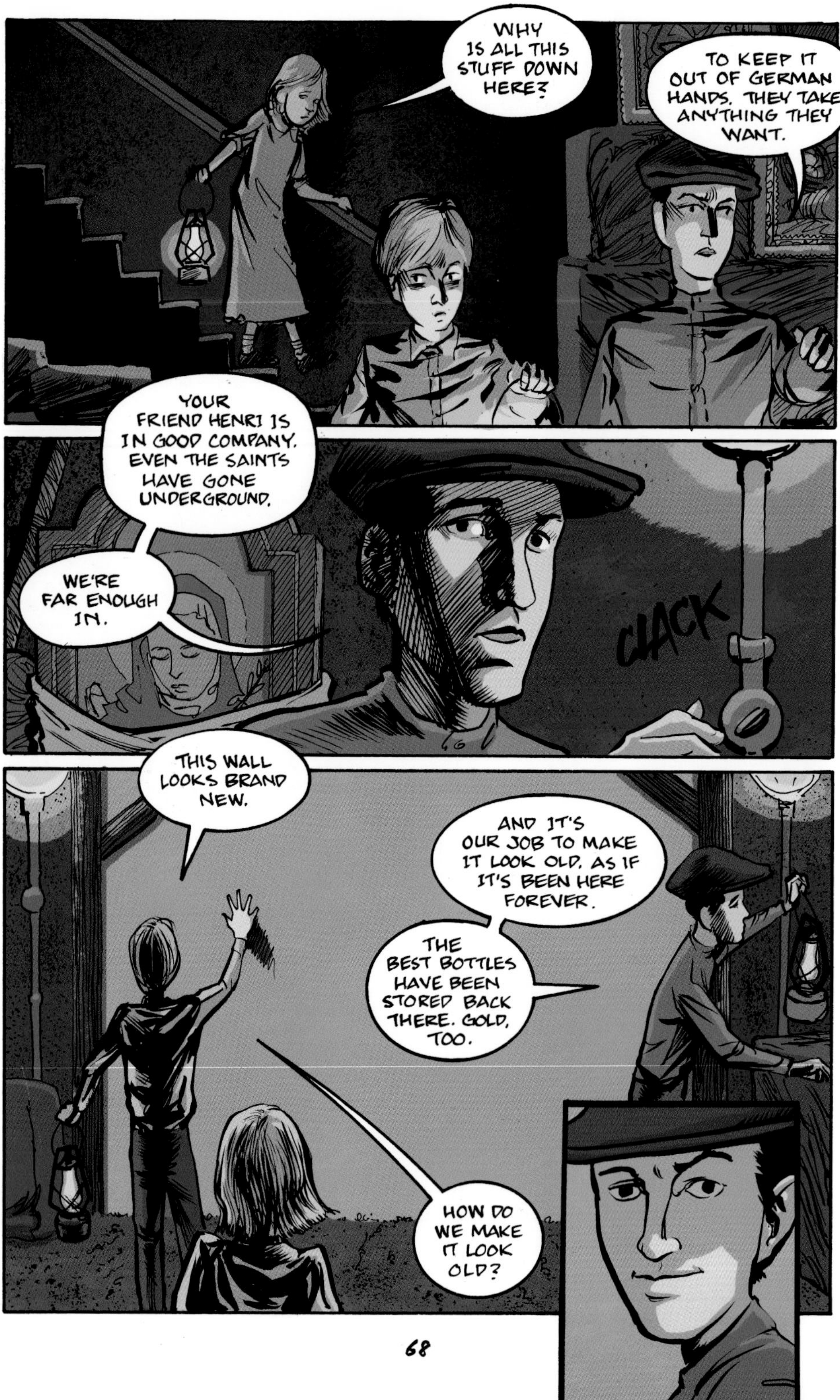

WHY IS ALL THIS STUFF DOWN HERE?
TO KEEP IT OUT OF GERMAN HANDS. THEY TAKE ANYTHING THEY WANT.
YOUR FRIEND HENRI IS IN GOOD COMPANY. EVEN THE SAINTS HAVE GONE UNDERGROUND.
WE'RE FAR ENOUGH IN.
CLACK
THIS WALL LOOKS BRAND NEW.
AND IT'S OUR JOB TO MAKE IT LOOK OLD, AS IF IT'S BEEN HERE FOREVER.
THE BEST BOTTLES HAVE BEEN STORED BACK THERE. GOLD, TOO.
HOW DO WE MAKE IT LOOK OLD?

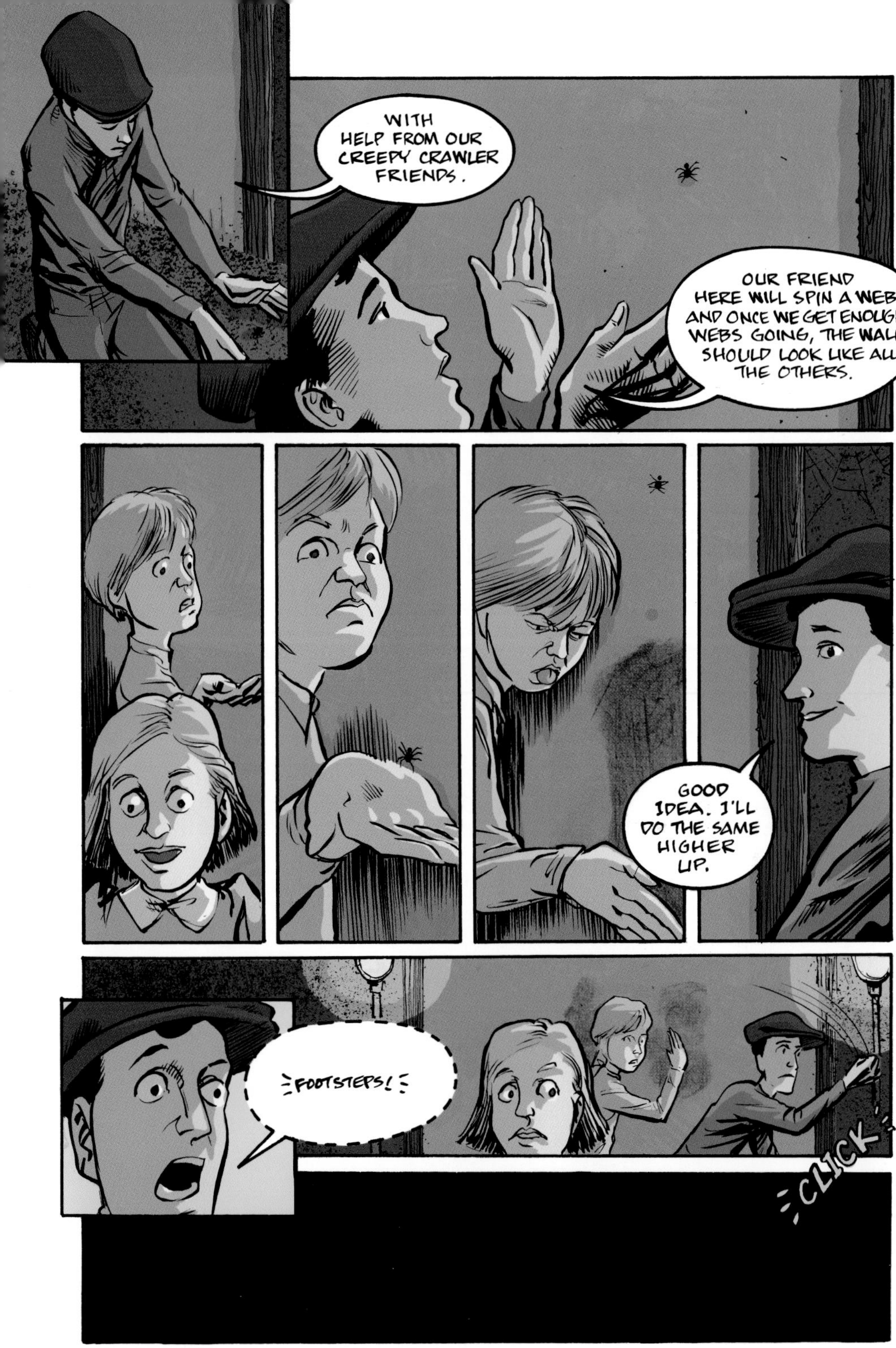
WITH HELP FROM OUR CREEPY CRAWLER FRIENDS.
OUR FRIEND HERE WILL SPIN A WEB. AND ONCE WE GET ENOUGH WEBS GOING, THE WALL SHOULD LOOK LIKE ALL THE OTHERS.
GOOD IDEA. I'LL DO THE SAME HIGHER UP.
FOOTSTEPS!
CLICK

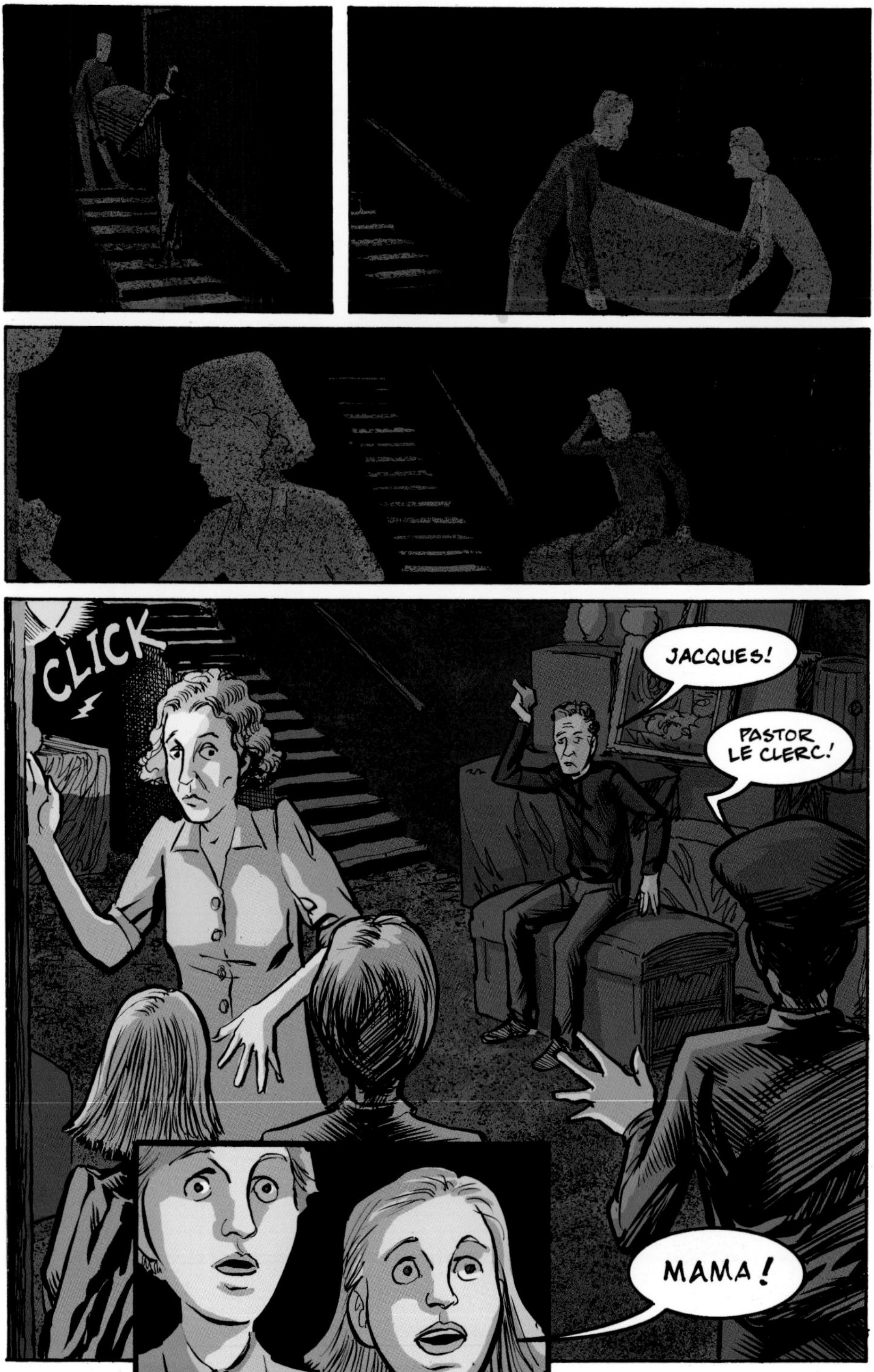
CLICK
JACQUES!
PASTOR LE CLERC!
MAMA!

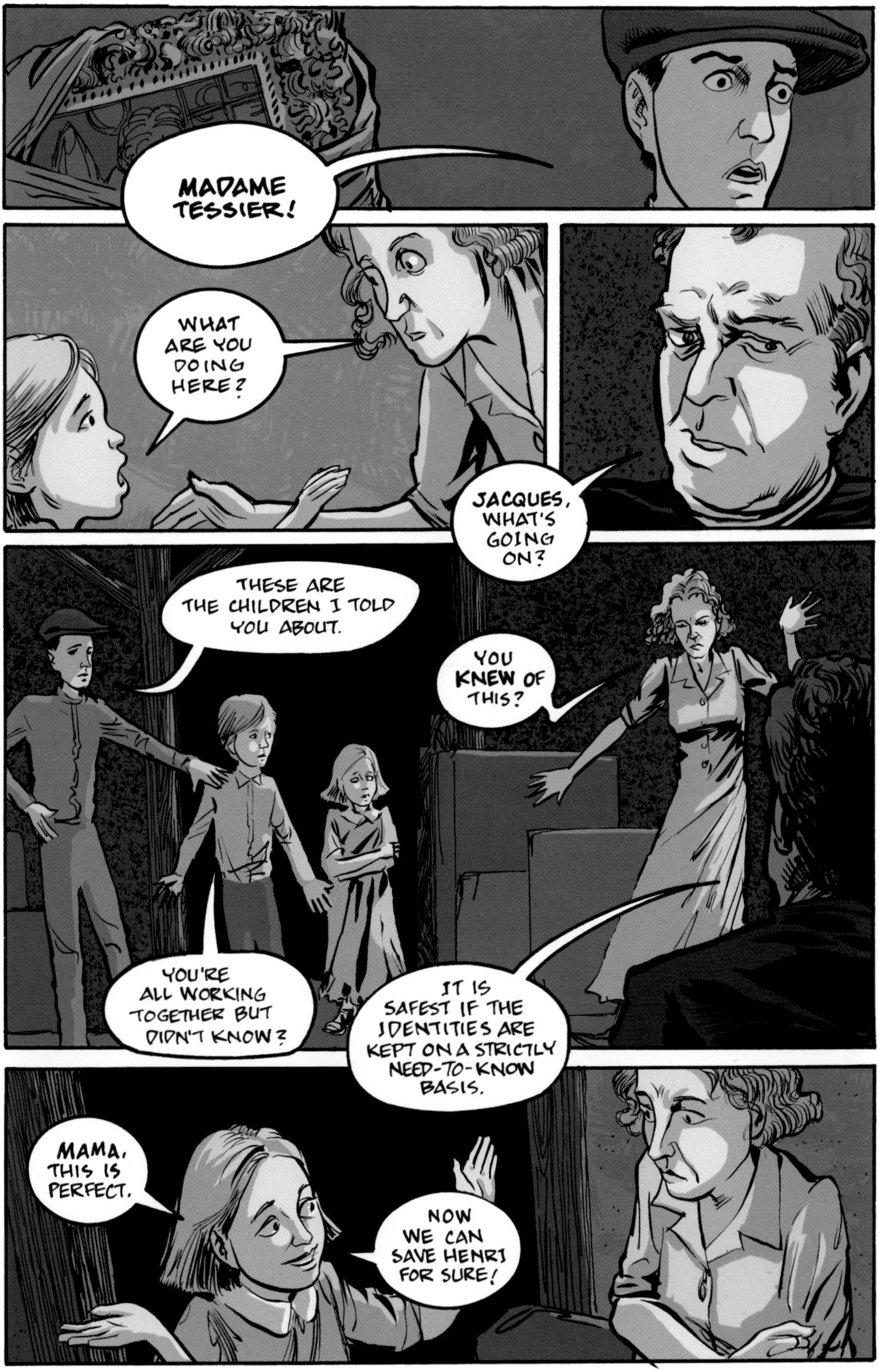
MADAME TESSIER!
WHAT ARE YOU DOING HERE?
JACQUES, WHAT'S GOING ON?
THESE ARE THE CHILDREN I TOLD YOU ABOUT.
YOU KNEW OF THIS?
YOU'RE ALL WORKING TOGETHER BUT DIDN'T KNOW?
IT IS SAFEST IF THE IDENTITIES ARE KEPT ON A STRICTLY NEED-TO-KNOW BASIS.
MAMA, THIS IS PERFECT.
NOW WE CAN SAVE HENRI FOR SURE!

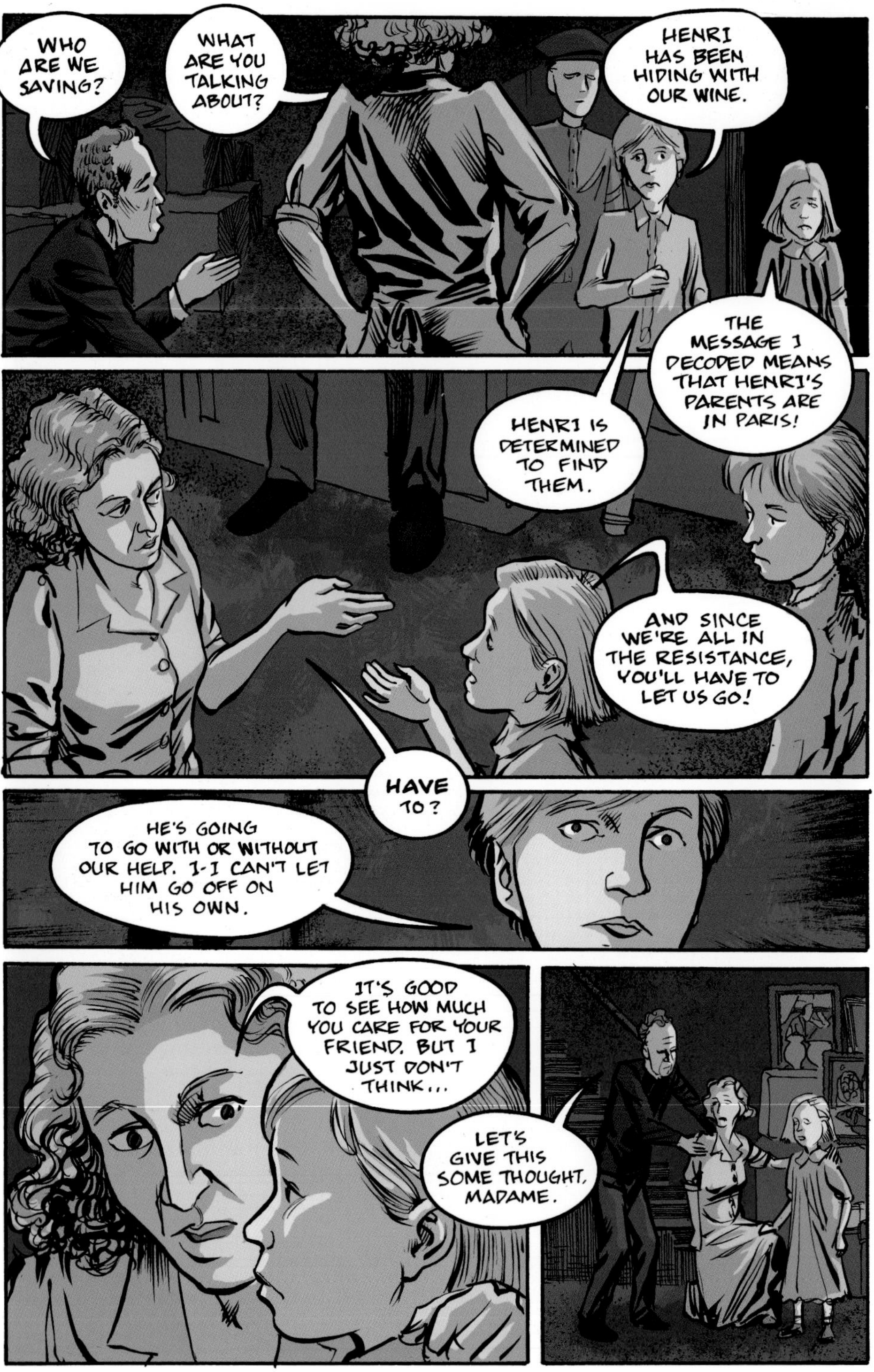
WHO ARE WE SAVING?
WHAT ARE YOU TALKING ABOUT?
HENRI HAS BEEN HIDING WITH OUR WINE.
THE MESSAGE I DECODED MEANS THAT HENRI'S PARENTS ARE IN PARIS!
HENRI IS DETERMINED TO FIND THEM.
AND SINCE WE'RE ALL IN THE RESISTANCE, YOU'LL HAVE TO LET US GO!
HAVE TO?
HE'S GOING TO GO WITH OR WITHOUT OUR HELP. I-I CAN'T LET HIM GO OFF ON HIS OWN.
IT'S GOOD TO SEE HOW MUCH YOU CARE FOR YOUR FRIEND. BUT I JUST DON'T THINK...
LET'S GIVE THIS SOME THOUGHT, MADAME.

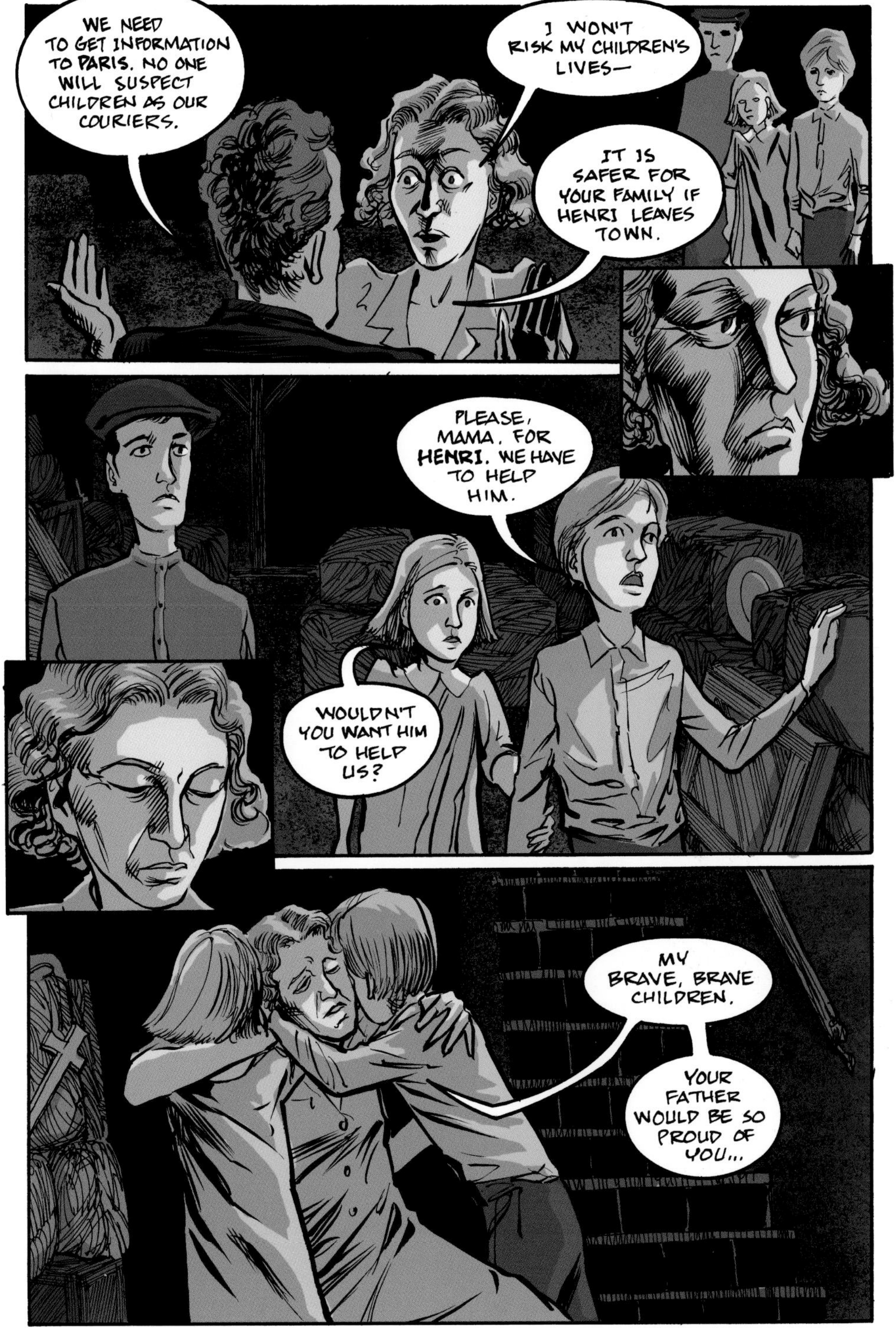
WE NEED TO GET INFORMATION TO PARIS. NO ONE WILL SUSPECT CHILDREN AS OUR COURIERS.
I WON'T RISK MY CHILDREN'S LIVES—
IT IS SAFER FOR YOUR FAMILY IF HENRI LEAVES TOWN.
PLEASE, MAMA. FOR HENRI. WE HAVE TO HELP HIM.
WOULDN'T YOU WANT HIM TO HELP US?
MY BRAVE, BRAVE CHILDREN.
YOUR FATHER WOULD BE SO PROUD OF YOU...

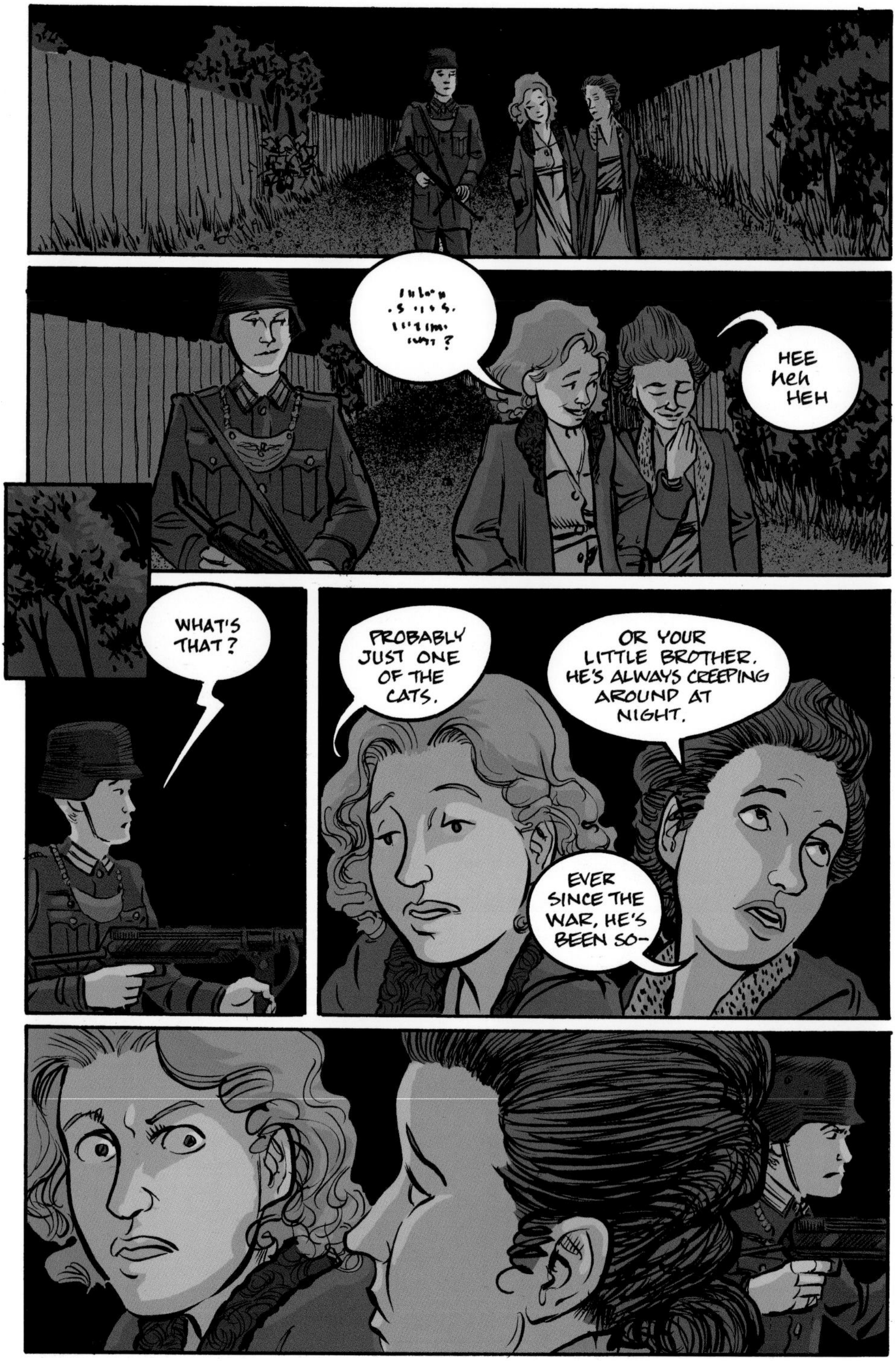
HEE heh HEH
WHAT'S THAT?
PROBABLY JUST ONE OF THE CATS.
OR YOUR LITTLE BROTHER. HE'S ALWAYS CREEPING AROUND AT NIGHT.
EVER SINCE THE WAR, HE'S BEEN SO-

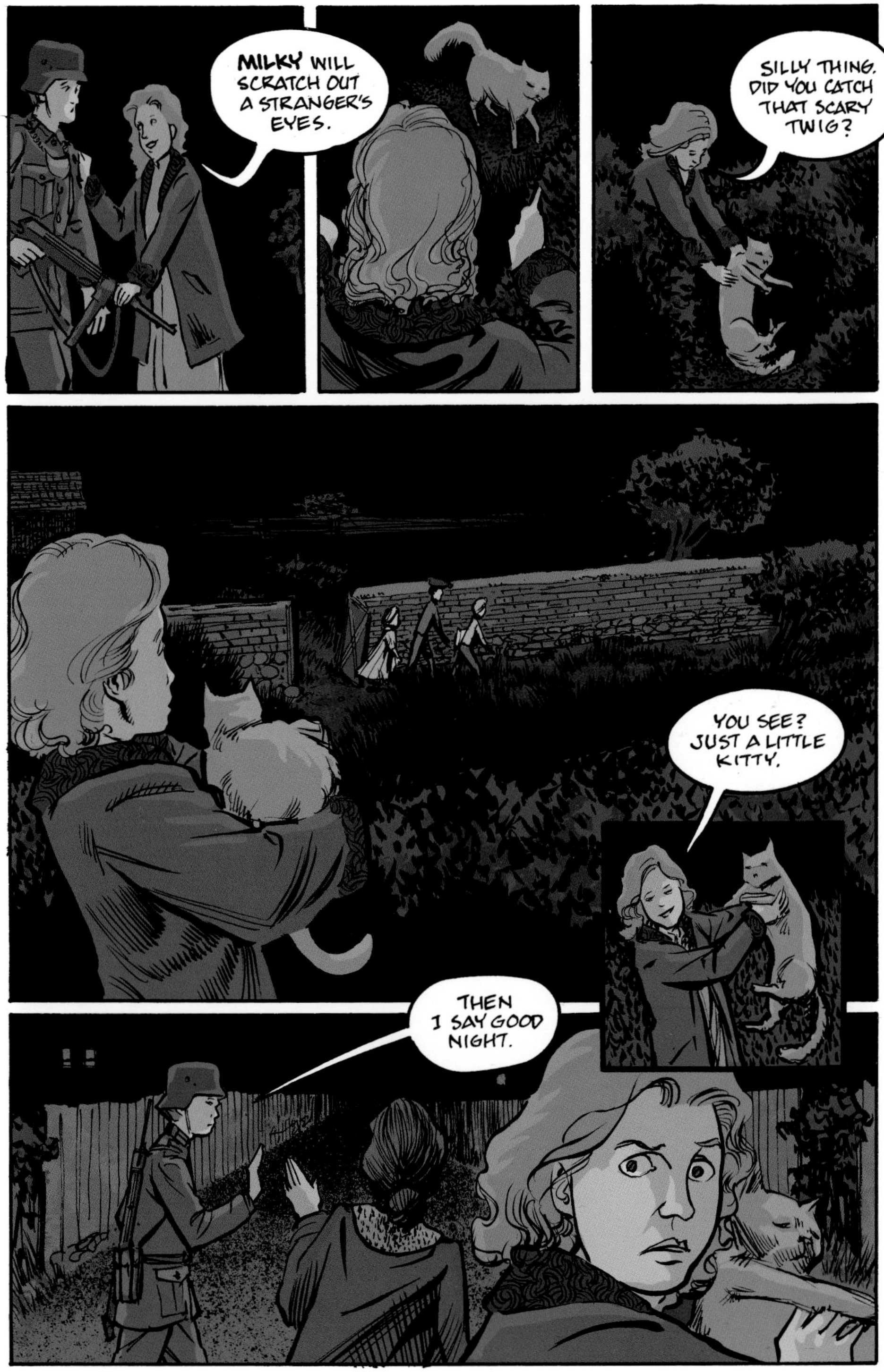
MILKY WILL SCRATCH OUT A STRANGER'S EYES.
SILLY THING. DID YOU CATCH THAT SCARY TWIG?
YOU SEE? JUST A LITTLE KITTY.
THEN I SAY GOOD NIGHT.

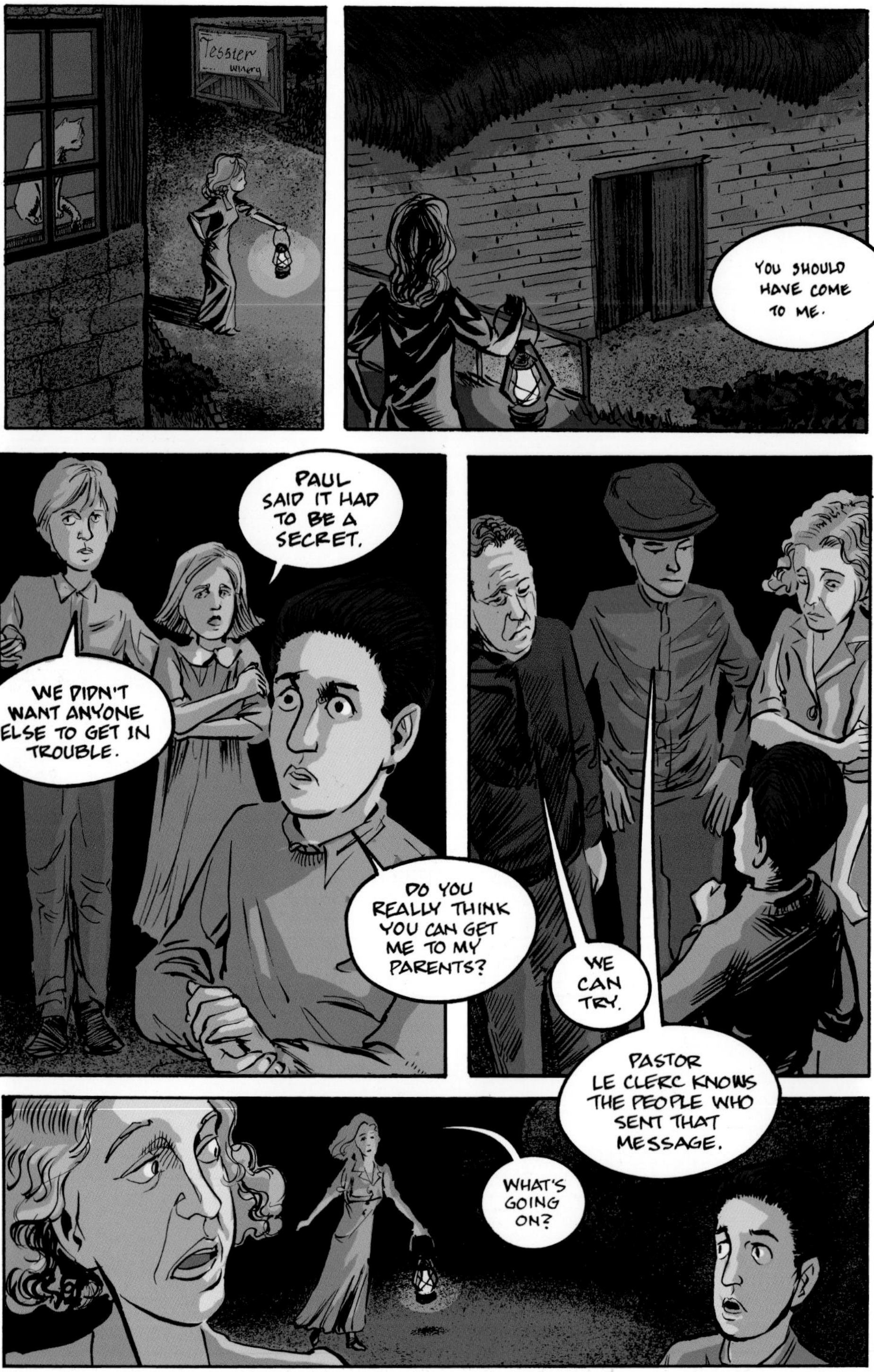
Tessier
winery
YOU SHOULD HAVE COME TO ME.
PAUL SAID IT HAD TO BE A SECRET.
WE DIDN'T WANT ANYONE ELSE TO GET IN TROUBLE.
DO YOU REALLY THINK YOU CAN GET ME TO MY PARENTS?
WE CAN TRY.
PASTOR LE CLERC KNOWS THE PEOPLE WHO SENT THAT MESSAGE.
WHAT'S GOING ON?

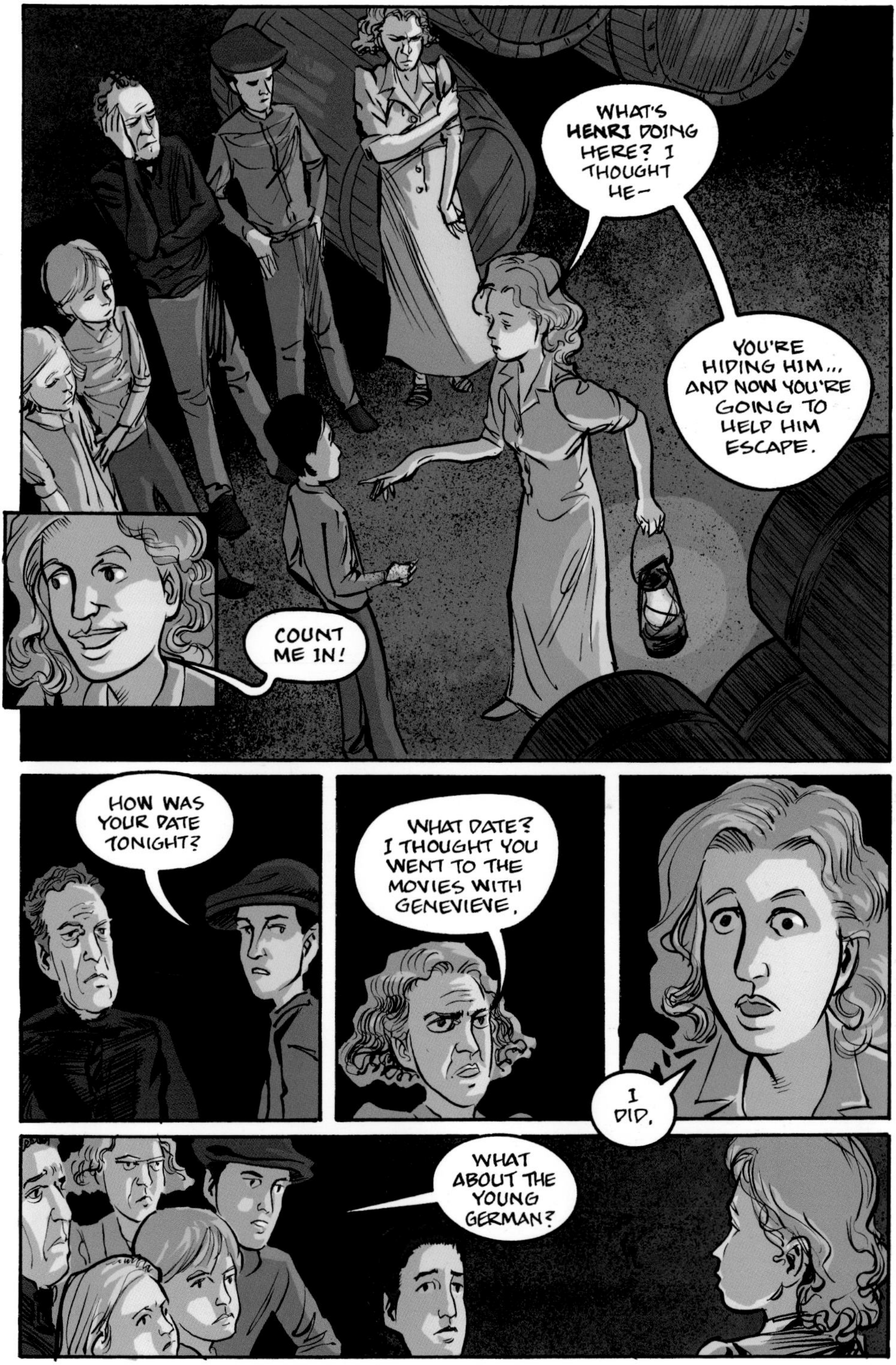
WHAT'S HENRI DOING HERE? I THOUGHT HE–
YOU'RE HIDING HIM... AND NOW YOU'RE GOING TO HELP HIM ESCAPE.
COUNT ME IN!
HOW WAS YOUR DATE TONIGHT?
WHAT DATE? I THOUGHT YOU WENT TO THE MOVIES WITH GENEVIEVE.
I DID.
WHAT ABOUT THE YOUNG GERMAN?

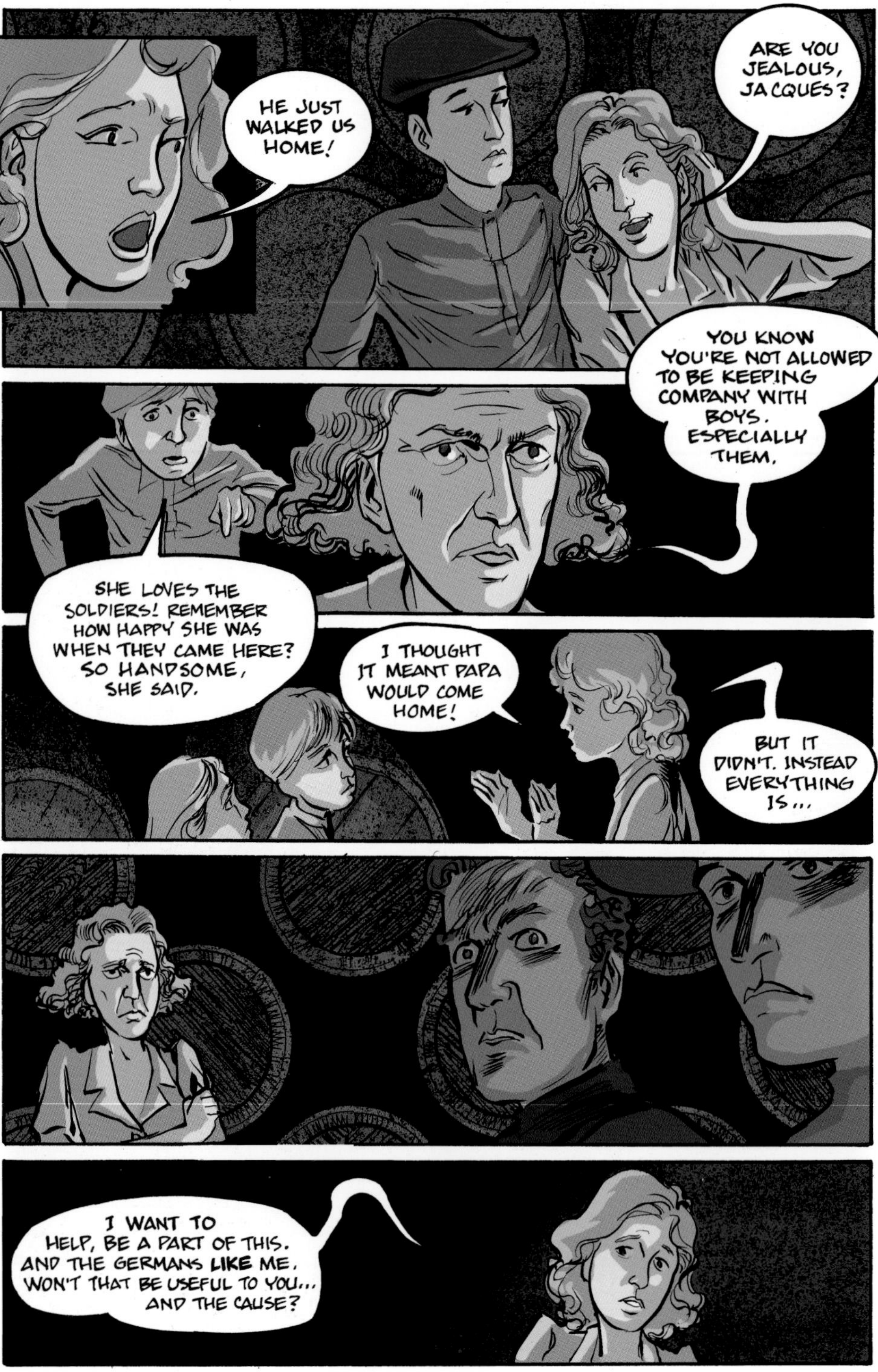
HE JUST WALKED US HOME!
ARE YOU JEALOUS, JACQUES?
YOU KNOW YOU'RE NOT ALLOWED TO BE KEEPING COMPANY WITH BOYS. ESPECIALLY THEM.
SHE LOVES THE SOLDIERS! REMEMBER HOW HAPPY SHE WAS WHEN THEY CAME HERE? SO HANDSOME, SHE SAID.
I THOUGHT IT MEANT PAPA WOULD COME HOME!
BUT IT DIDN'T. INSTEAD EVERYTHING IS...
I WANT TO HELP, BE A PART OF THIS. AND THE GERMANS **LIKE** ME. WON'T THAT BE USEFUL TO YOU... AND THE CAUSE?

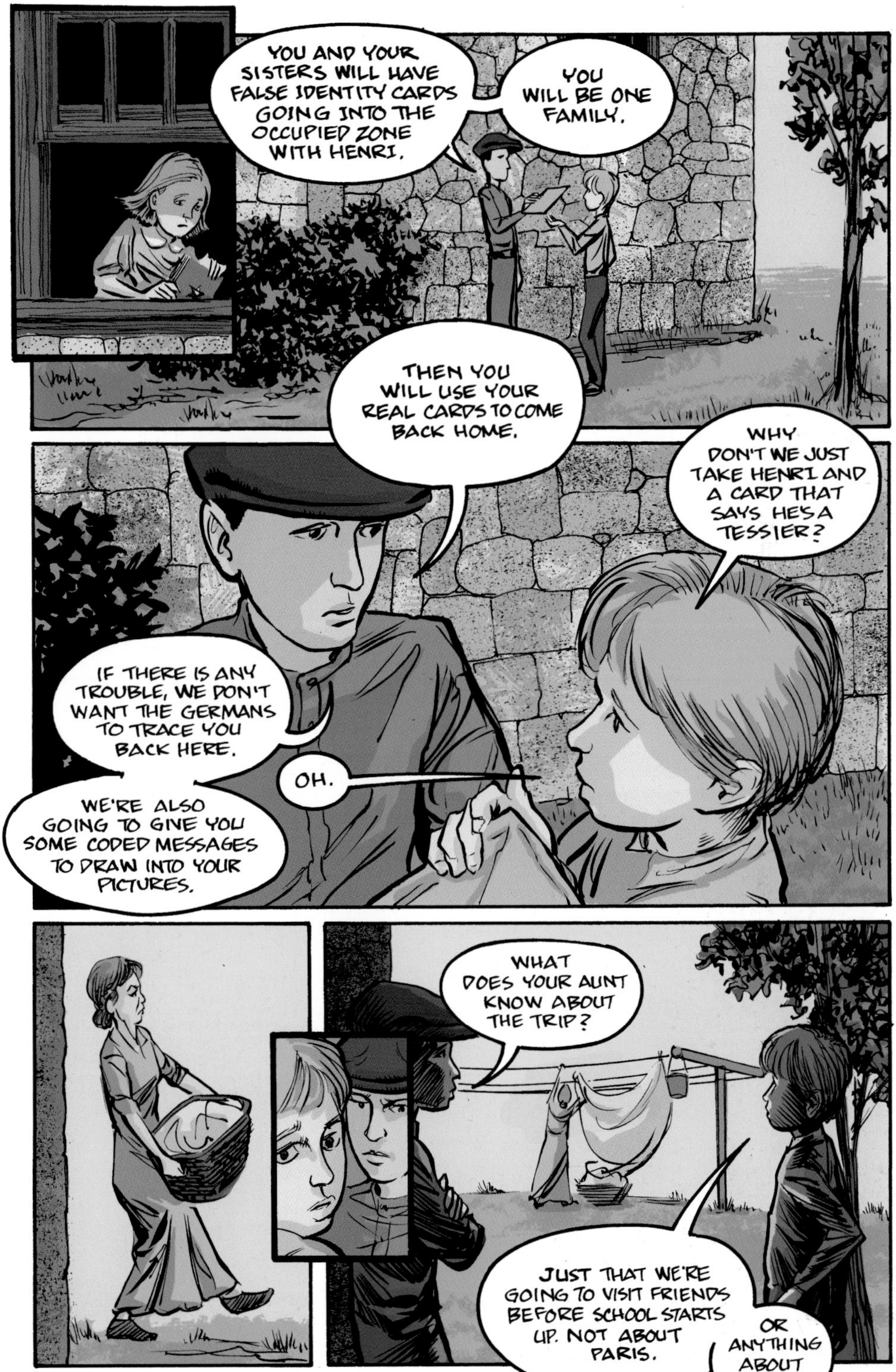
YOU AND YOUR SISTERS WILL HAVE FALSE IDENTITY CARDS GOING INTO THE OCCUPIED ZONE WITH HENRI.
YOU WILL BE ONE FAMILY.
THEN YOU WILL USE YOUR REAL CARDS TO COME BACK HOME.
WHY DON'T WE JUST TAKE HENRI AND A CARD THAT SAYS HE'S A TESSIER?
IF THERE IS ANY TROUBLE, WE DON'T WANT THE GERMANS TO TRACE YOU BACK HERE.
OH.
WE'RE ALSO GOING TO GIVE YOU SOME CODED MESSAGES TO DRAW INTO YOUR PICTURES.
WHAT DOES YOUR AUNT KNOW ABOUT THE TRIP?
JUST THAT WE'RE GOING TO VISIT FRIENDS BEFORE SCHOOL STARTS UP. NOT ABOUT PARIS.
OR ANYTHING ABOUT HENRI.

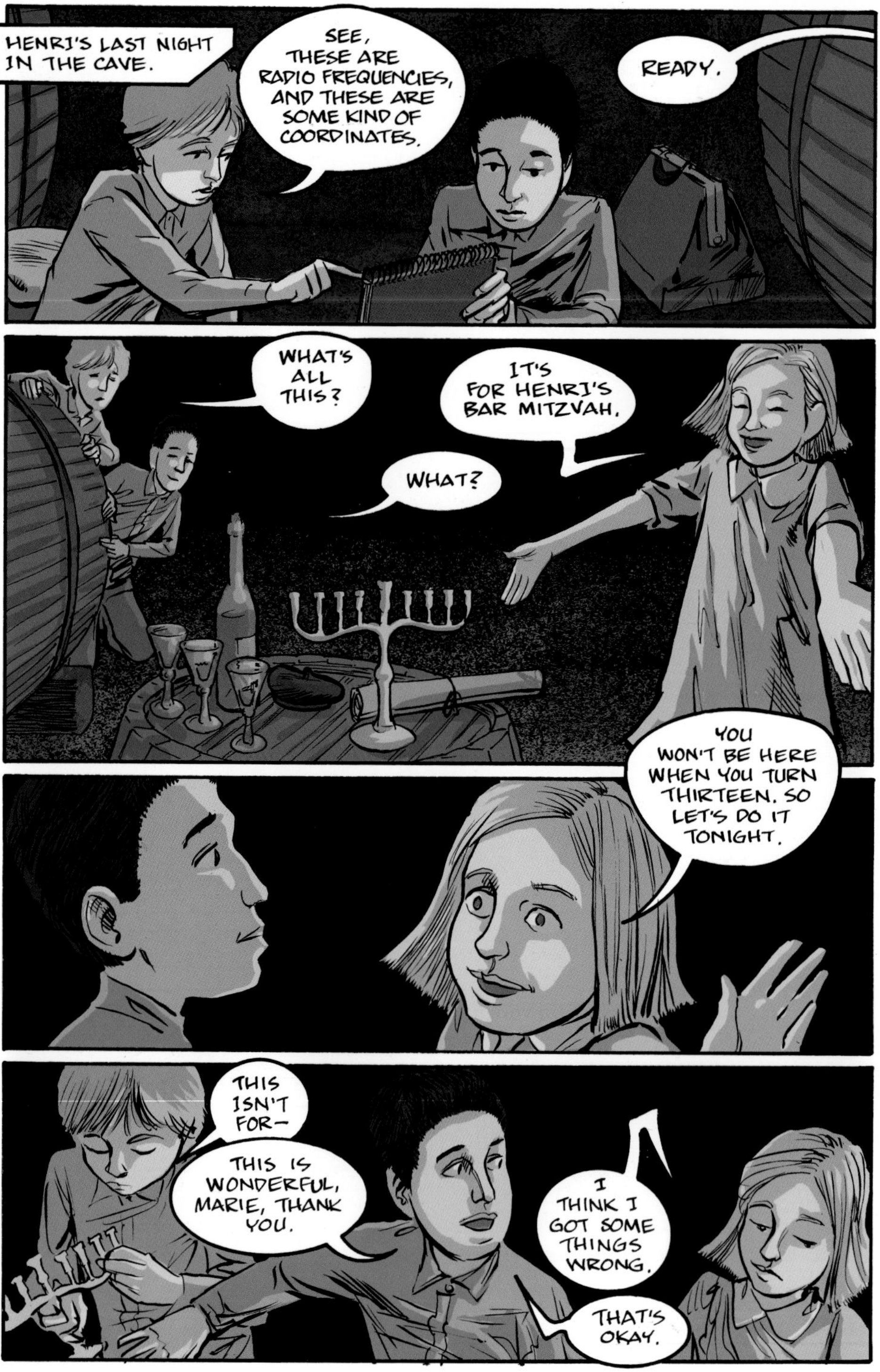
HENRI'S LAST NIGHT IN THE CAVE.
SEE, THESE ARE RADIO FREQUENCIES, AND THESE ARE SOME KIND OF COORDINATES.
READY.
WHAT'S ALL THIS?
IT'S FOR HENRI'S BAR MITZVAH.
WHAT?
YOU WON'T BE HERE WHEN YOU TURN THIRTEEN. SO LET'S DO IT TONIGHT.
THIS ISN'T FOR—
THIS IS WONDERFUL, MARIE, THANK YOU.
I THINK I GOT SOME THINGS WRONG.
THAT'S OKAY.

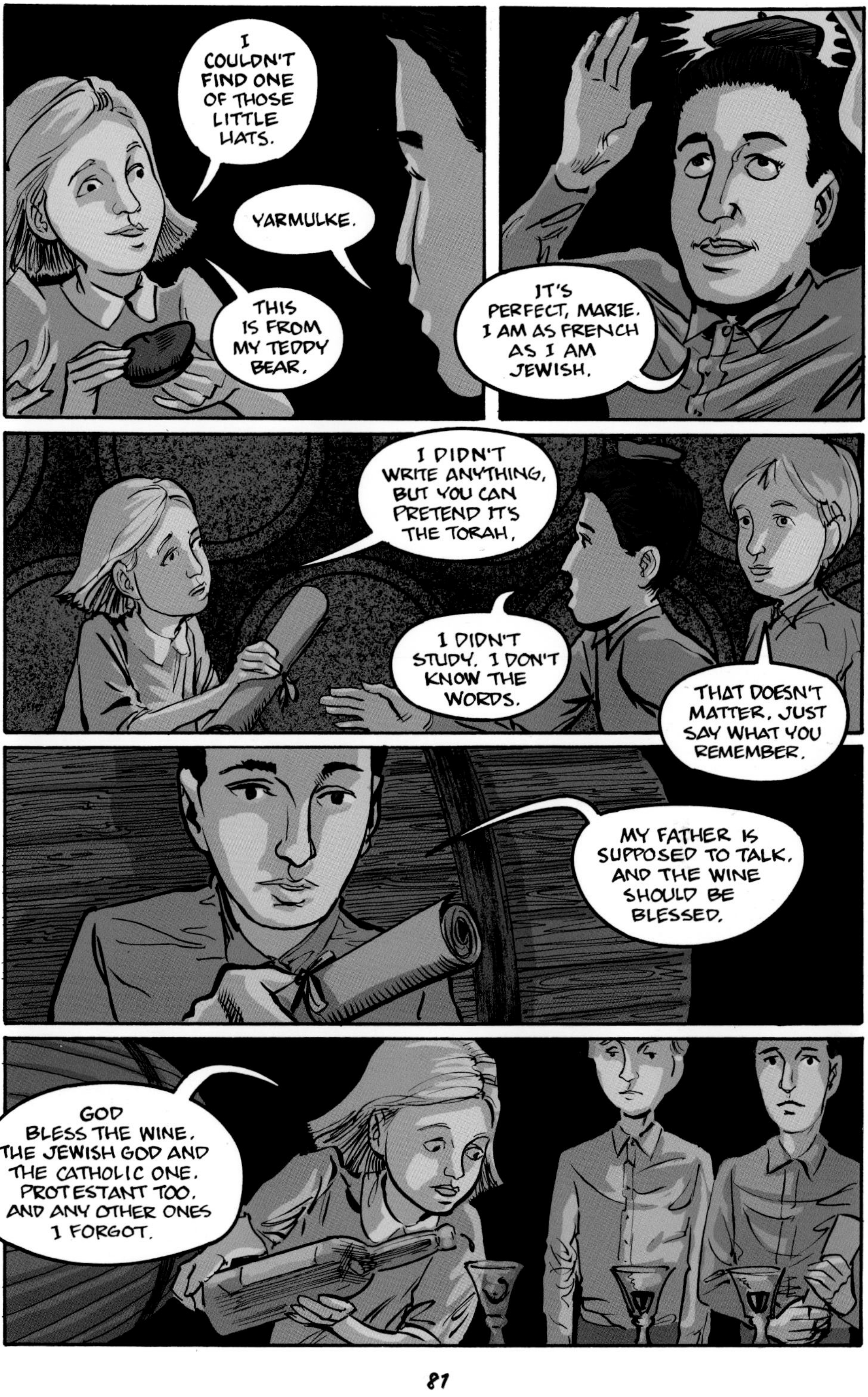
I COULDN'T FIND ONE OF THOSE LITTLE HATS.
YARMULKE.
THIS IS FROM MY TEDDY BEAR.
IT'S PERFECT, MARIE. I AM AS FRENCH AS I AM JEWISH.
I DIDN'T WRITE ANYTHING, BUT YOU CAN PRETEND IT'S THE TORAH.
I DIDN'T STUDY. I DON'T KNOW THE WORDS.
THAT DOESN'T MATTER. JUST SAY WHAT YOU REMEMBER.
MY FATHER IS SUPPOSED TO TALK, AND THE WINE SHOULD BE BLESSED.
GOD BLESS THE WINE. THE JEWISH GOD AND THE CATHOLIC ONE. PROTESTANT TOO. AND ANY OTHER ONES I FORGOT.

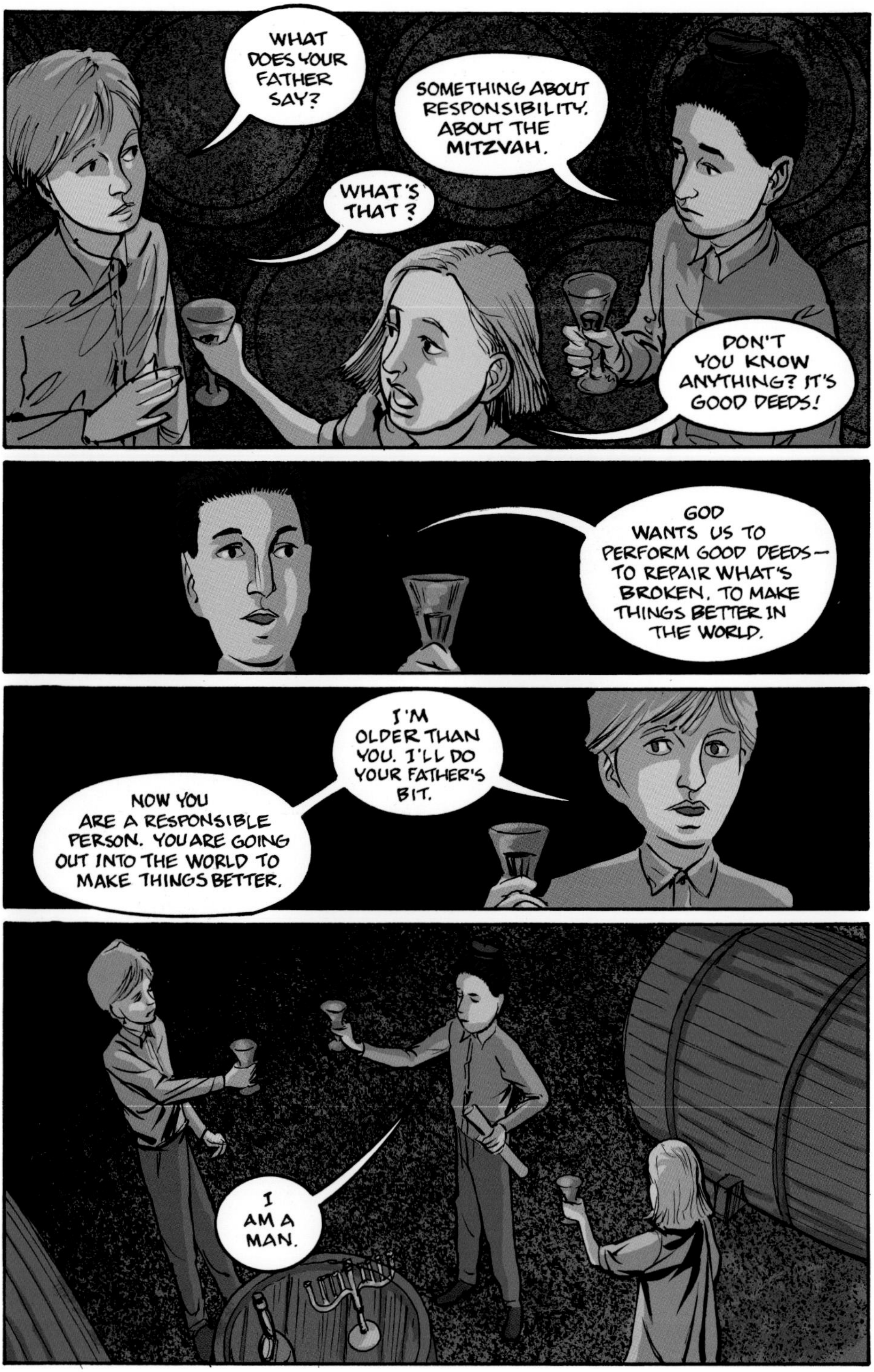
WHAT DOES YOUR FATHER SAY?
SOMETHING ABOUT RESPONSIBILITY. ABOUT THE MITZVAH.
WHAT'S THAT?
DON'T YOU KNOW ANYTHING? IT'S GOOD DEEDS!
GOD WANTS US TO PERFORM GOOD DEEDS— TO REPAIR WHAT'S BROKEN. TO MAKE THINGS BETTER IN THE WORLD.
I'M OLDER THAN YOU. I'LL DO YOUR FATHER'S BIT.
NOW YOU ARE A RESPONSIBLE PERSON. YOU ARE GOING OUT INTO THE WORLD TO MAKE THINGS BETTER.
I AM A MAN.

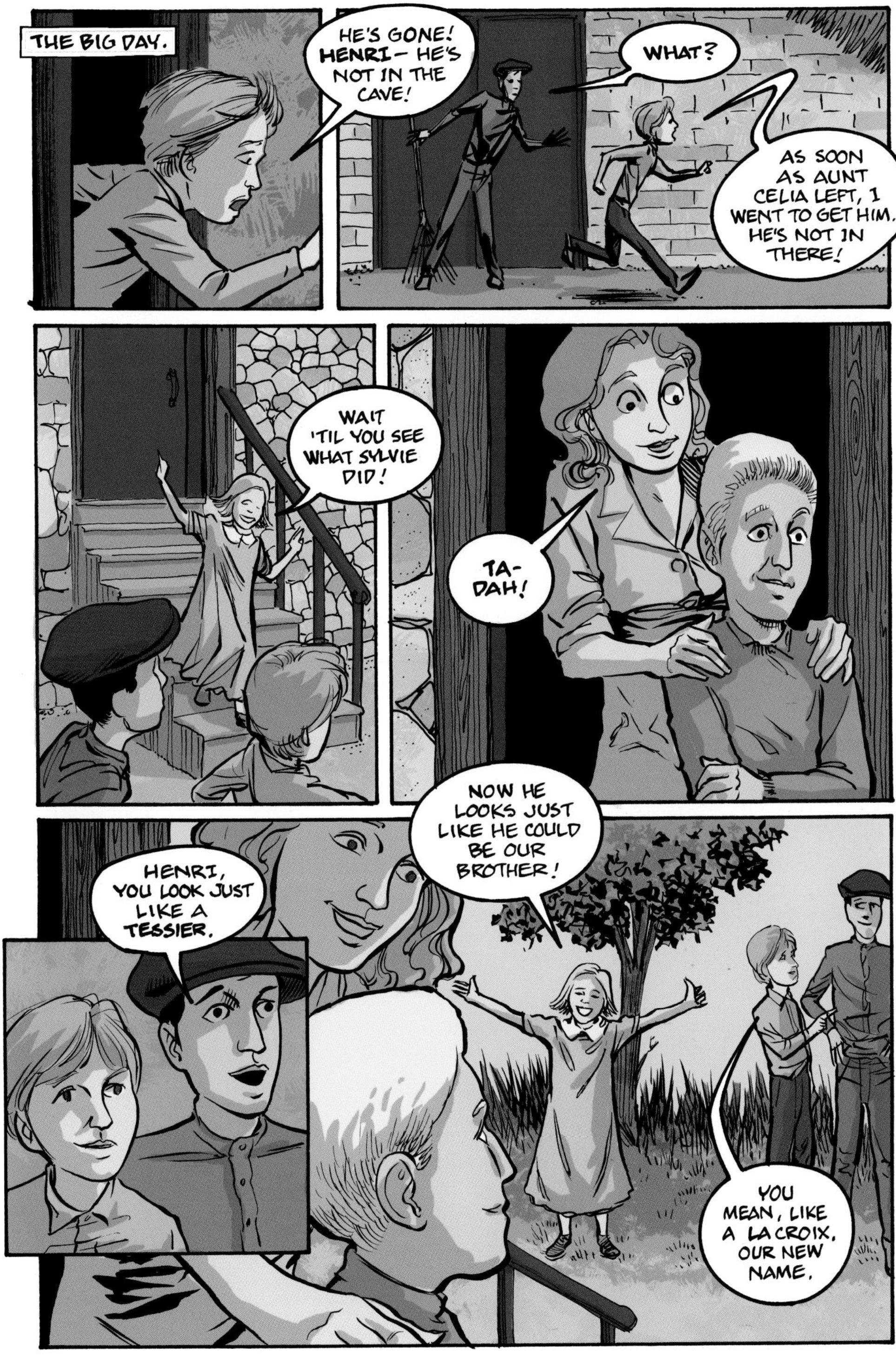
THE BIG DAY.
HE'S GONE! HENRI— HE'S NOT IN THE CAVE!
WHAT?
AS SOON AS AUNT CELIA LEFT, I WENT TO GET HIM. HE'S NOT IN THERE!
WAIT 'TIL YOU SEE WHAT SYLVIE DID!
TA-DAH!
HENRI, YOU LOOK JUST LIKE A TESSIER.
NOW HE LOOKS JUST LIKE HE COULD BE OUR BROTHER!
YOU MEAN, LIKE A LACROIX, OUR NEW NAME.

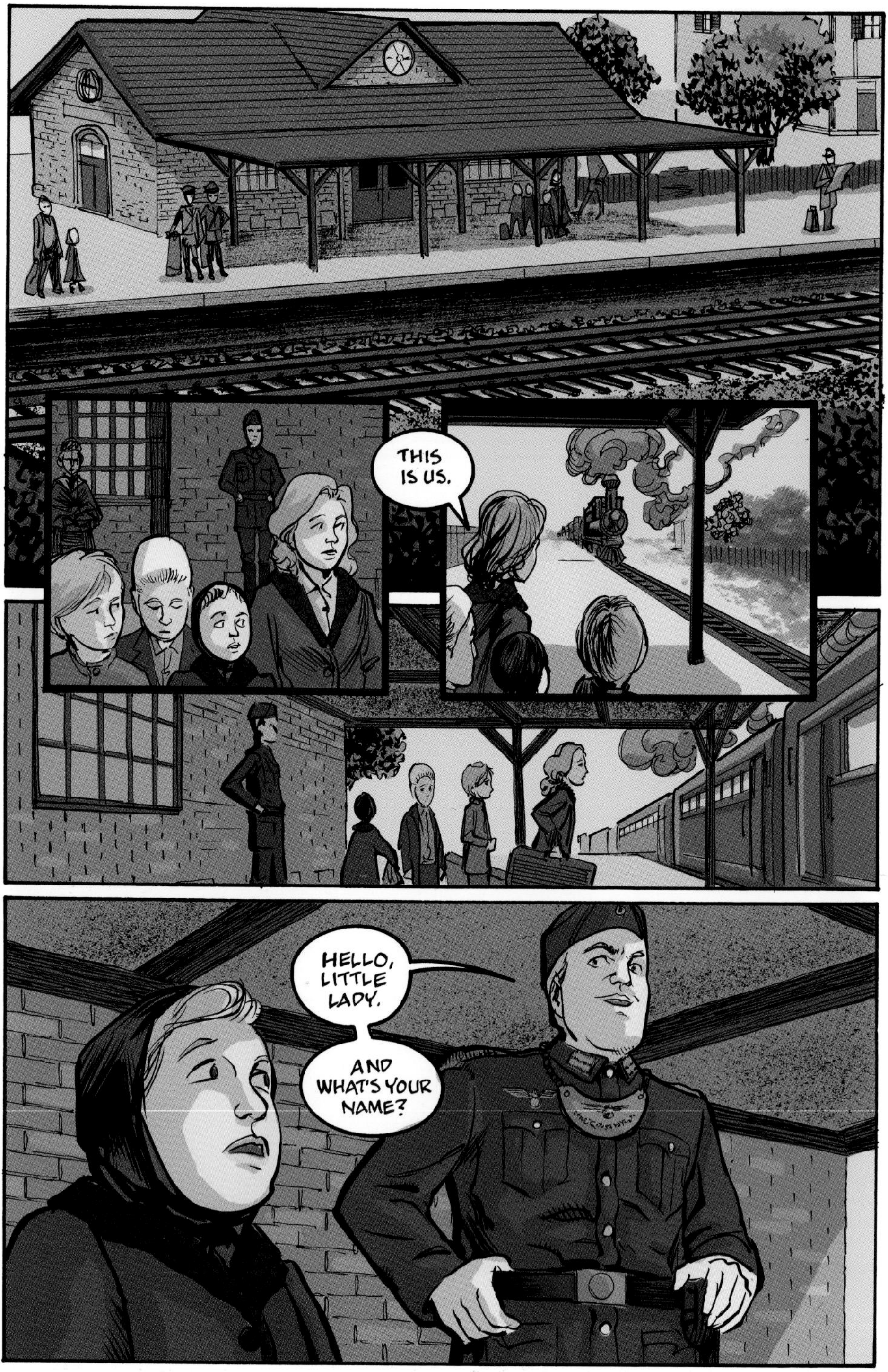
THIS IS US.
HELLO, LITTLE LADY.
AND WHAT'S YOUR NAME?

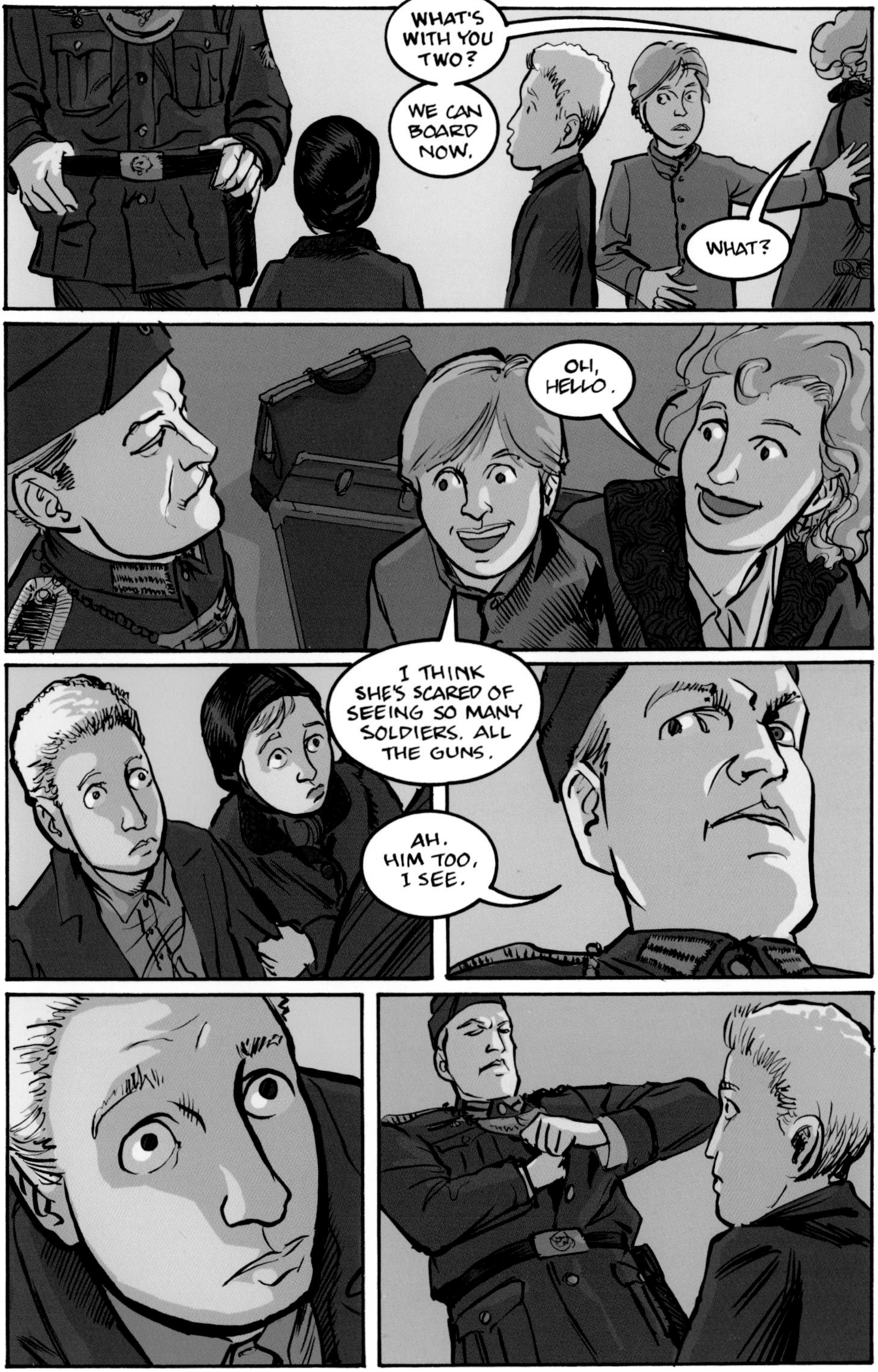
WHAT'S WITH YOU TWO?
WE CAN BOARD NOW.
WHAT?
OH, HELLO.
I THINK SHE'S SCARED OF SEEING SO MANY SOLDIERS. ALL THE GUNS.
AH. HIM TOO, I SEE.

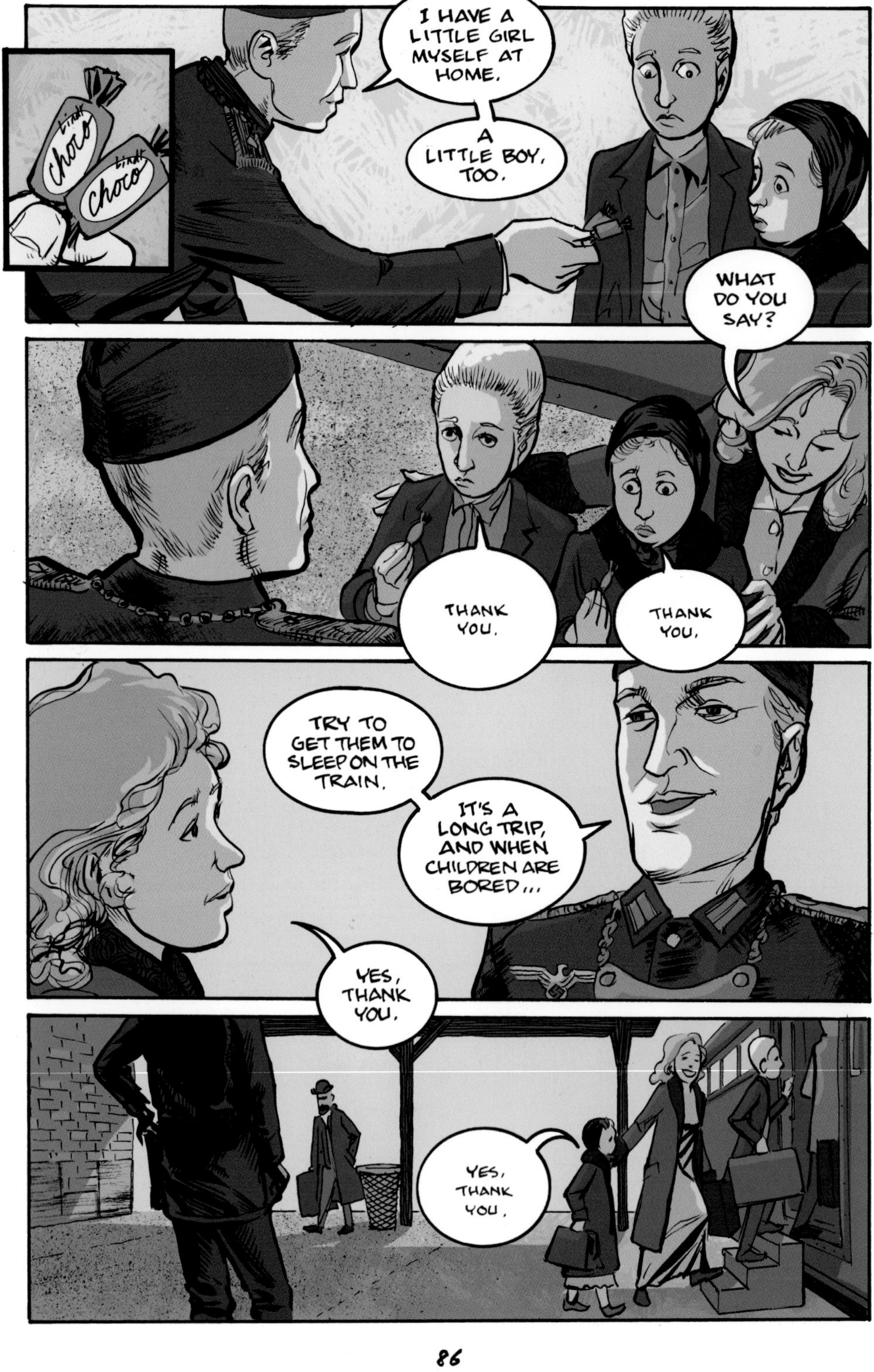
Lindt
Choco
Lindt
Choco
I HAVE A LITTLE GIRL MYSELF AT HOME.
A LITTLE BOY, TOO.
WHAT DO YOU SAY?
THANK YOU.
THANK YOU.
TRY TO GET THEM TO SLEEP ON THE TRAIN.
IT'S A LONG TRIP, AND WHEN CHILDREN ARE BORED...
YES, THANK YOU.
YES, THANK YOU.

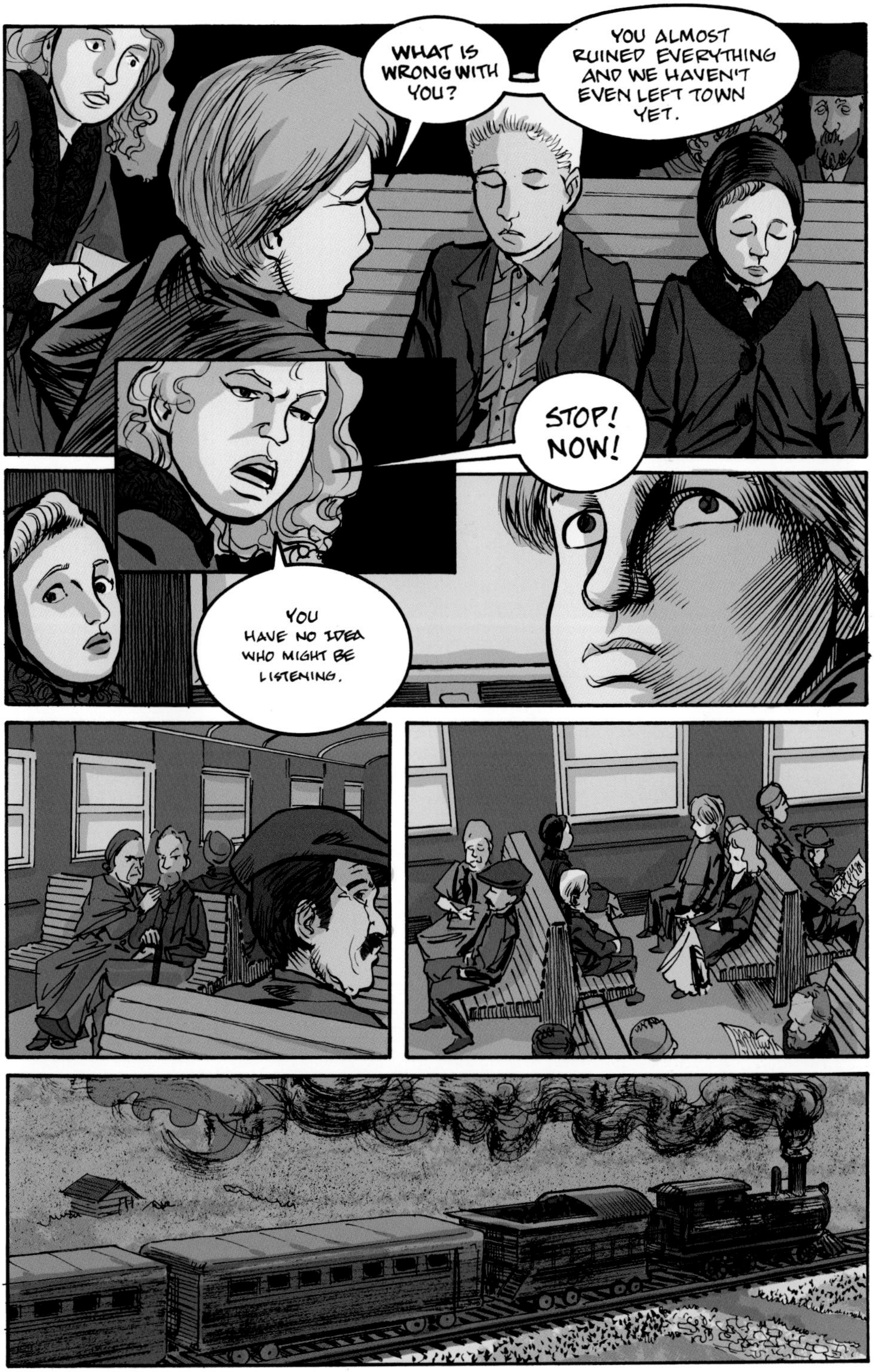
WHAT IS WRONG WITH YOU?
YOU ALMOST RUINED EVERYTHING AND WE HAVEN'T EVEN LEFT TOWN YET.
STOP! NOW!
YOU HAVE NO IDEA WHO MIGHT BE LISTENING.

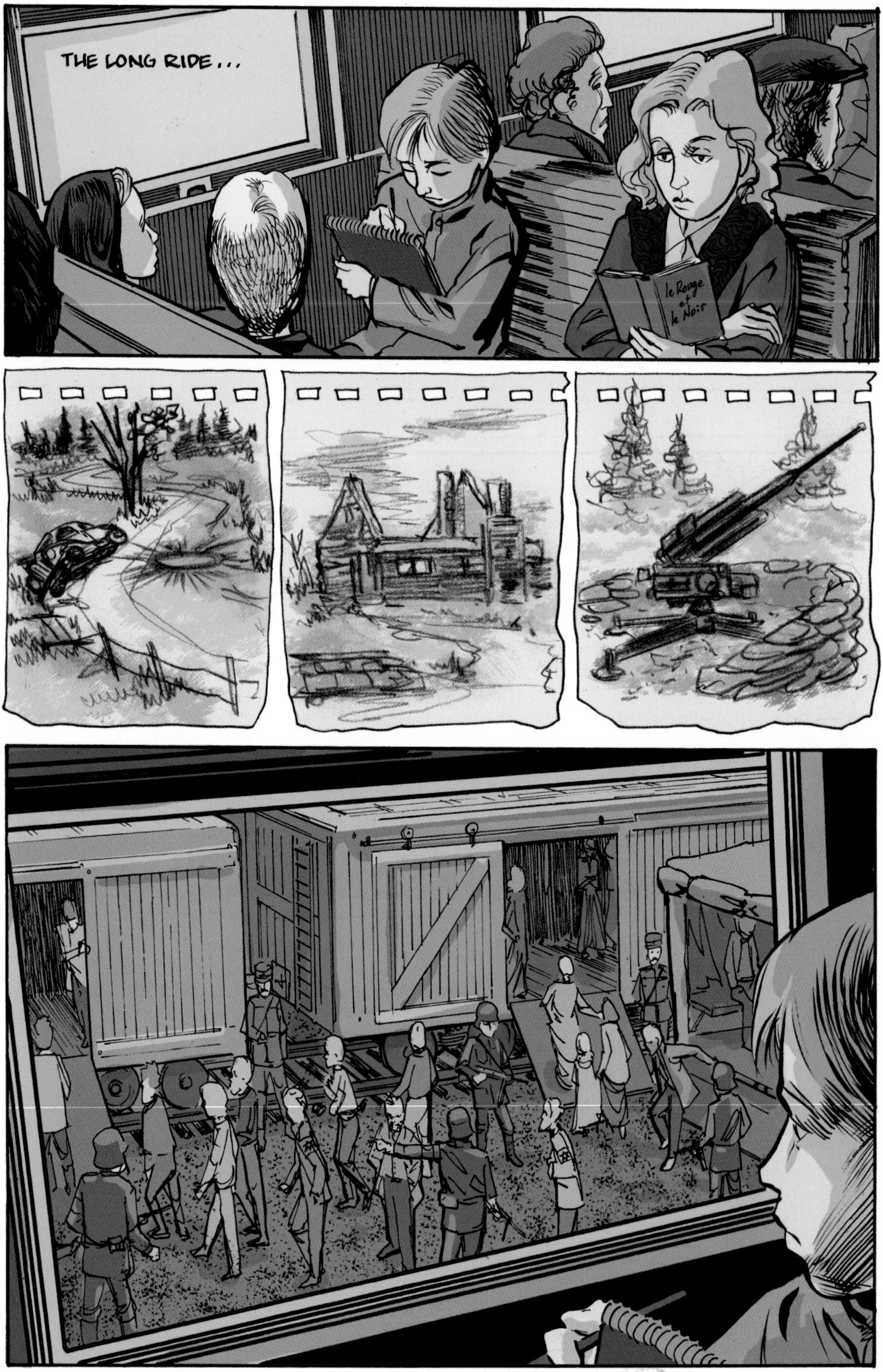
THE LONG RIDE . . .
le Rouge et le Noir

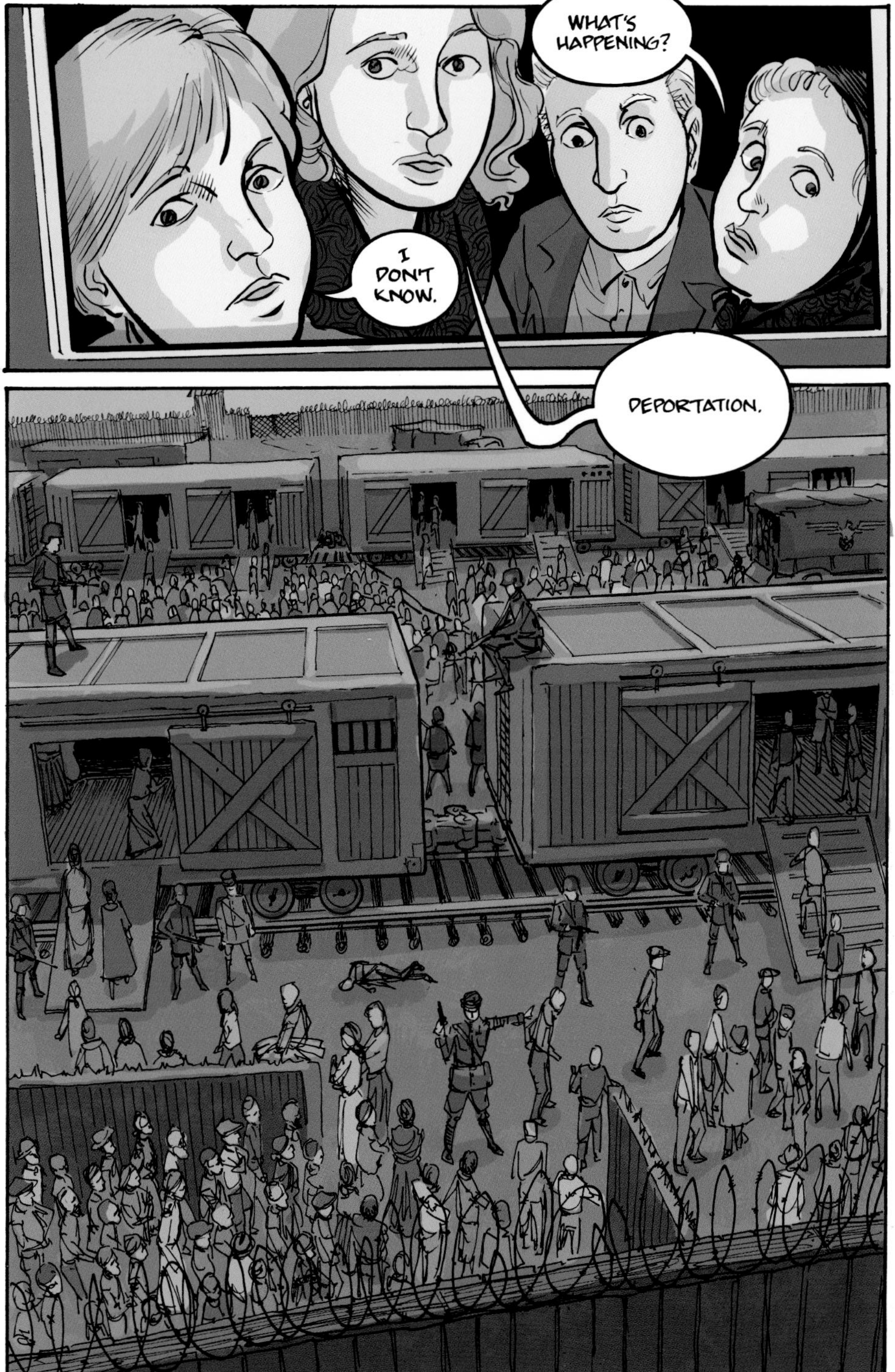
WHAT'S HAPPENING?
I DON'T KNOW.
DEPORTATION.

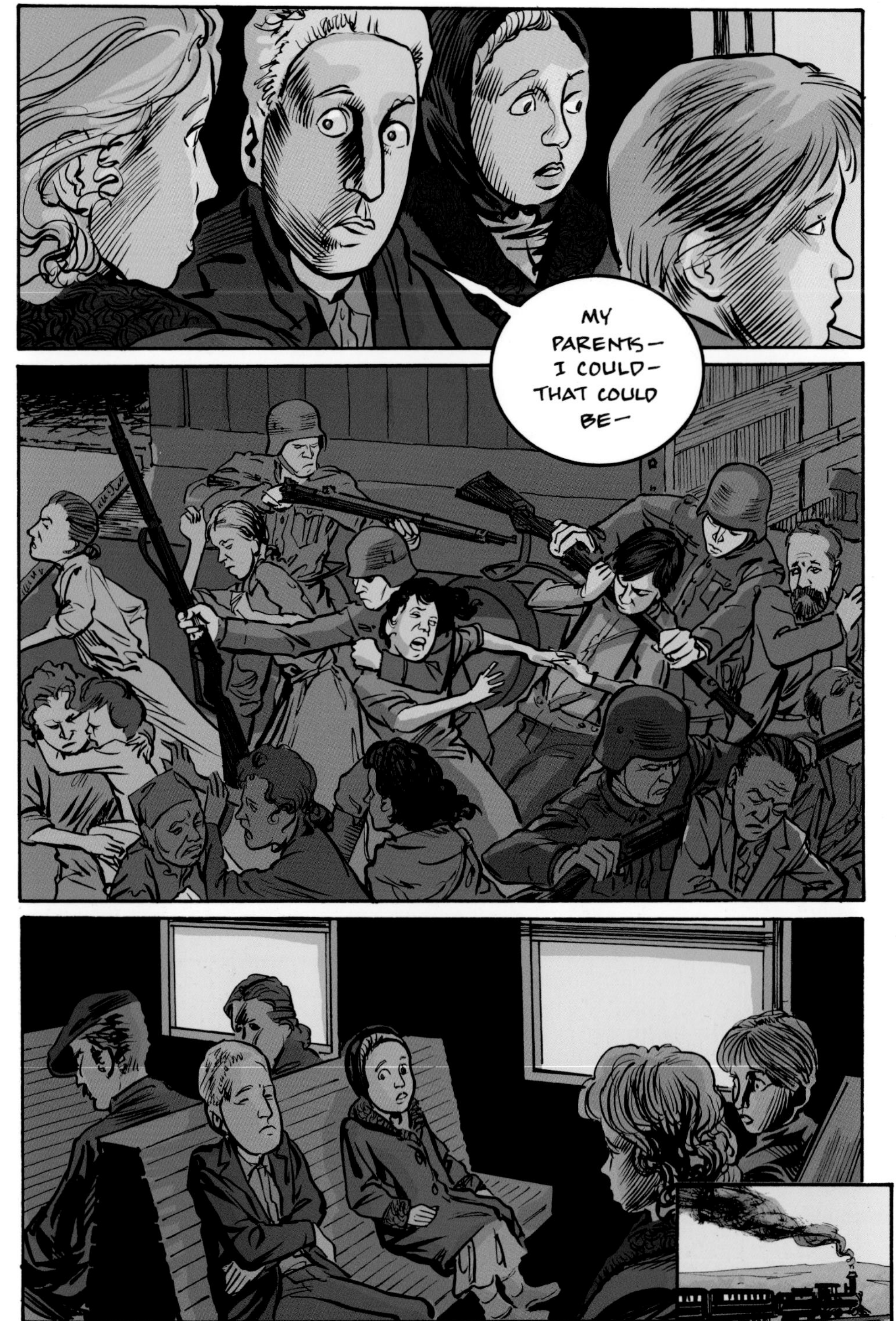
MY PARENTS— I COULD— THAT COULD BE—

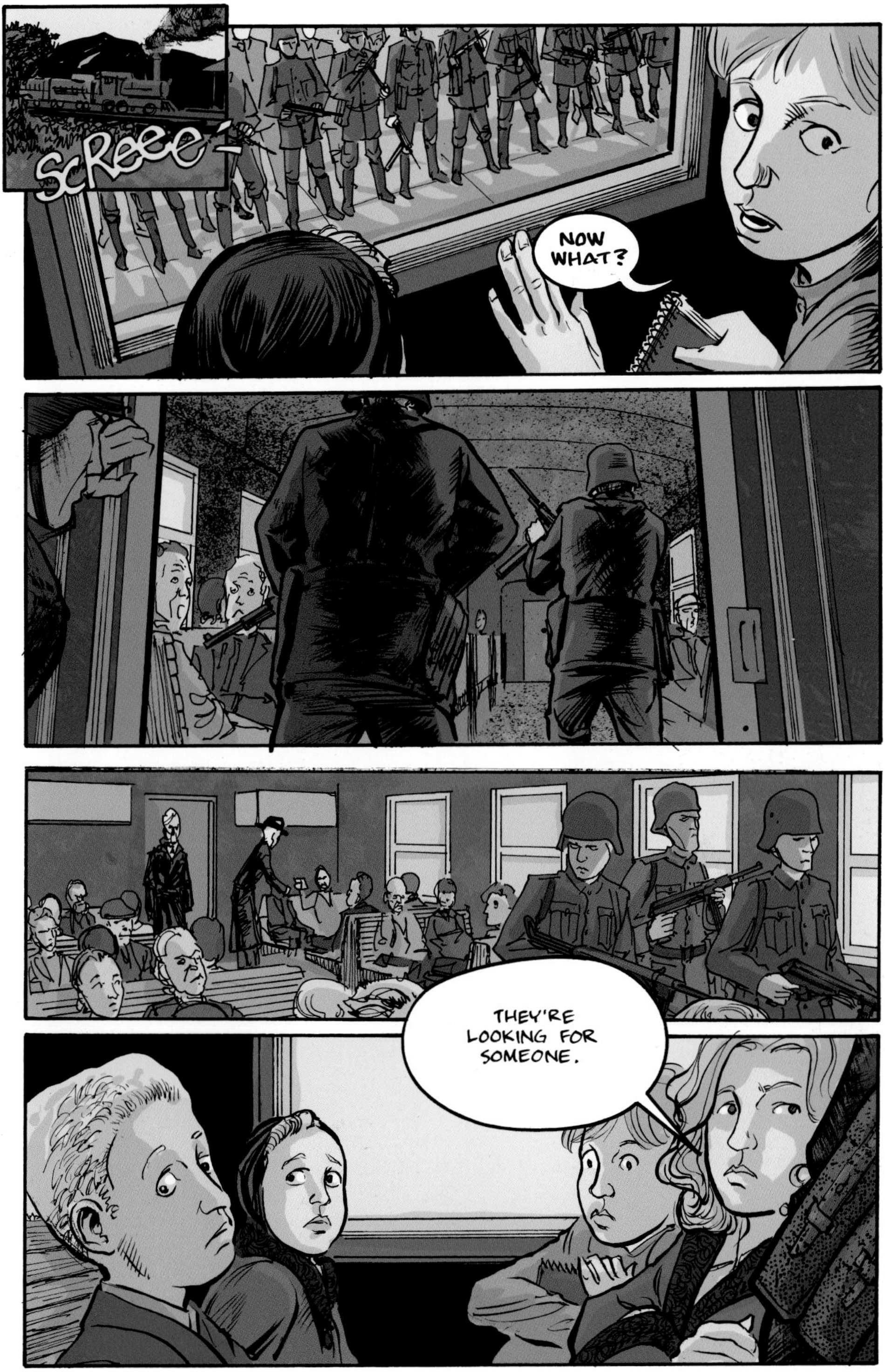
SCREEE
NOW WHAT?
THEY'RE LOOKING FOR SOMEONE.

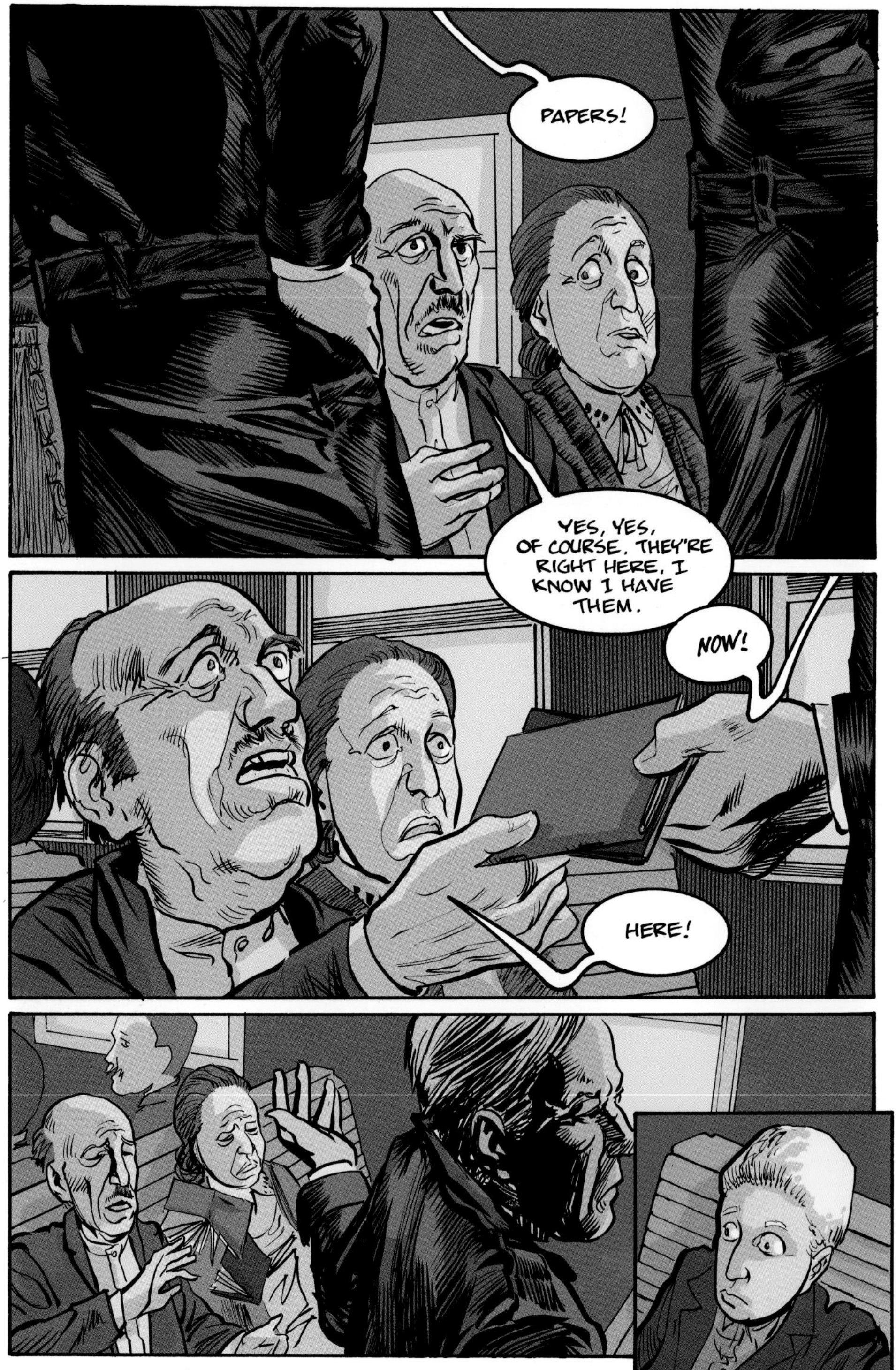
PAPERS!
YES, YES, OF COURSE. THEY'RE RIGHT HERE. I KNOW I HAVE THEM.
NOW!
HERE!

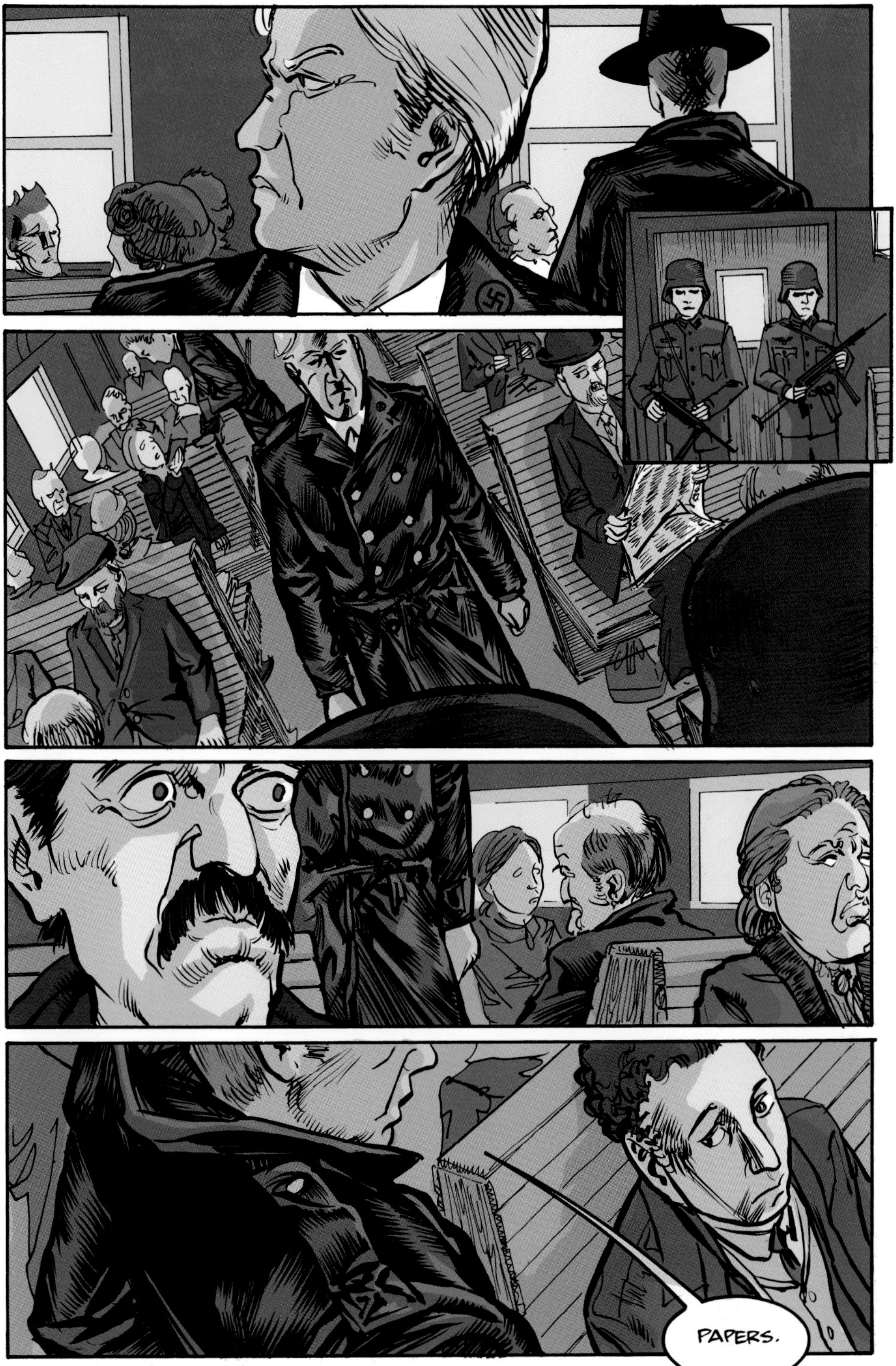
PAPERS.

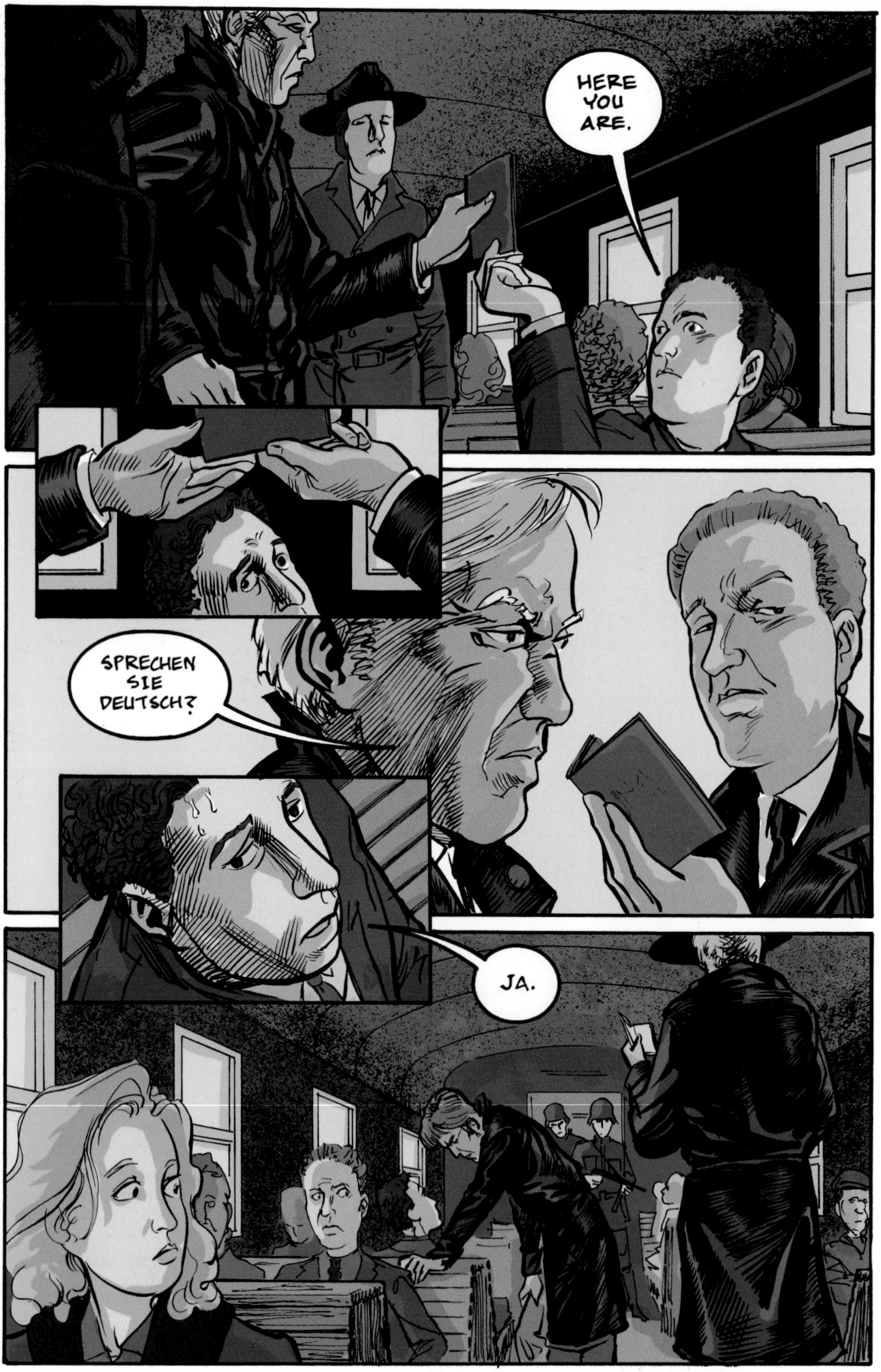
HERE YOU ARE.
SPRECHEN SIE DEUTSCH?
JA.

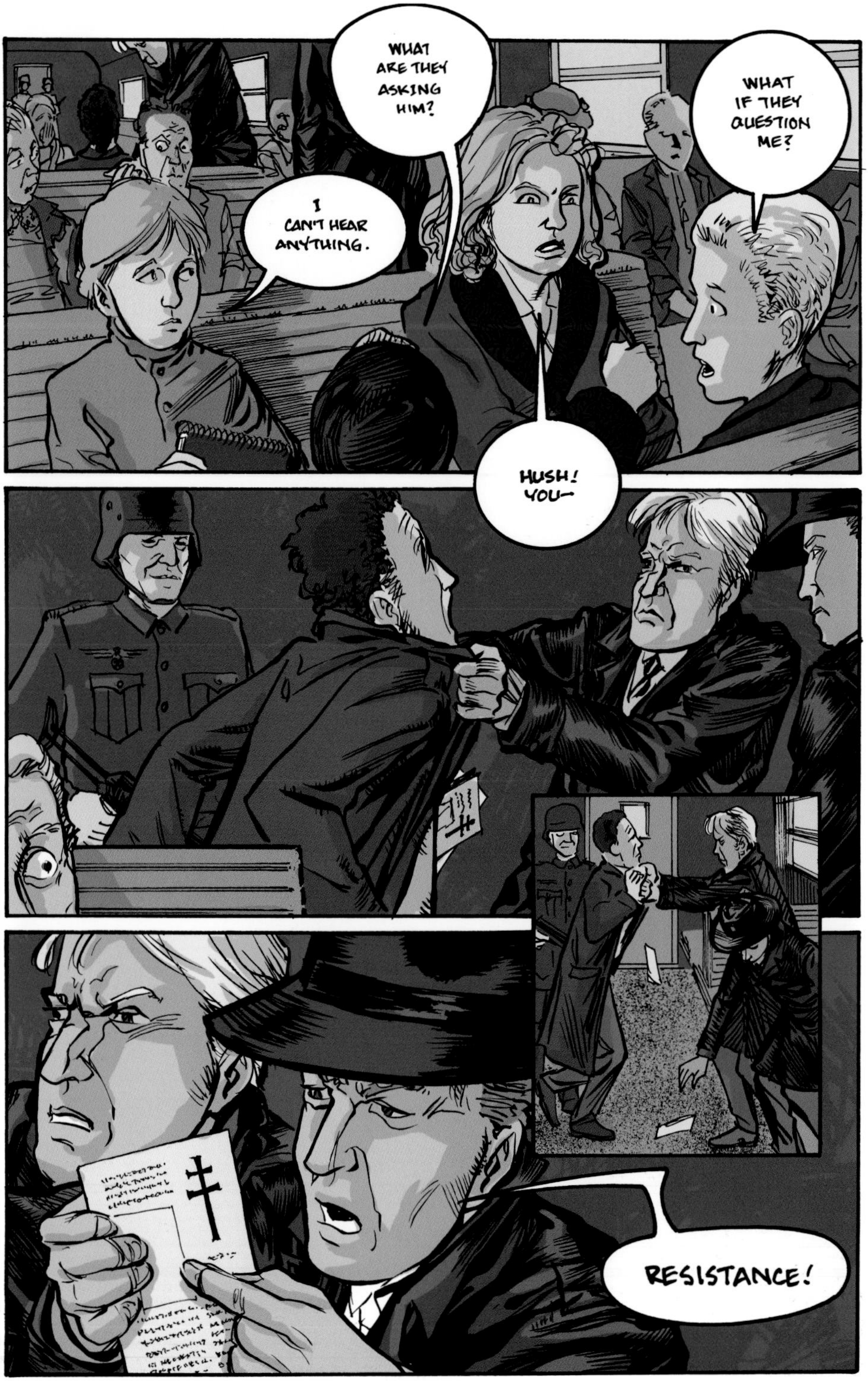
WHAT ARE THEY ASKING HIM?
I CAN'T HEAR ANYTHING.
WHAT IF THEY QUESTION ME?
HUSH! YOU—
RESISTANCE!

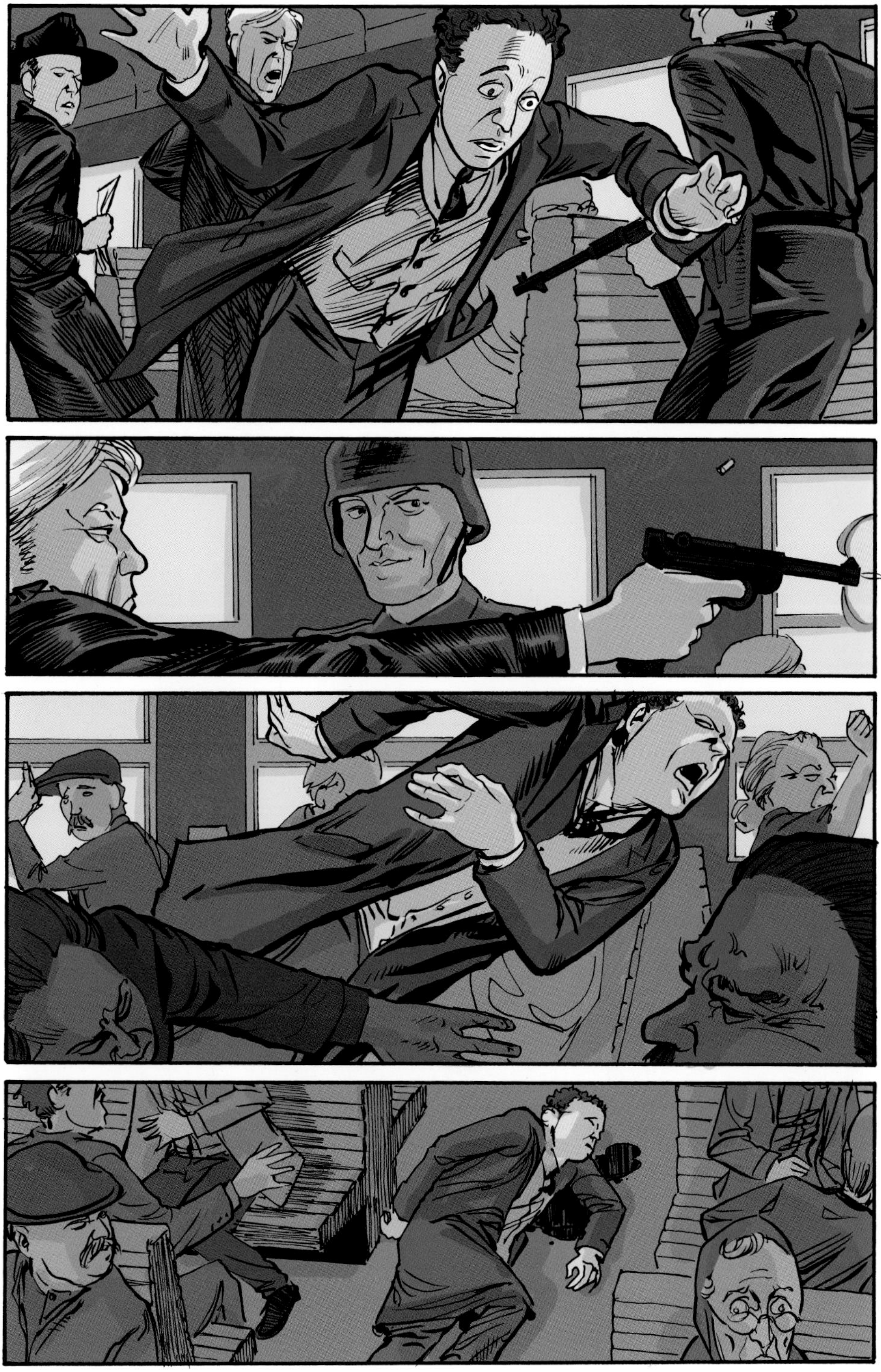

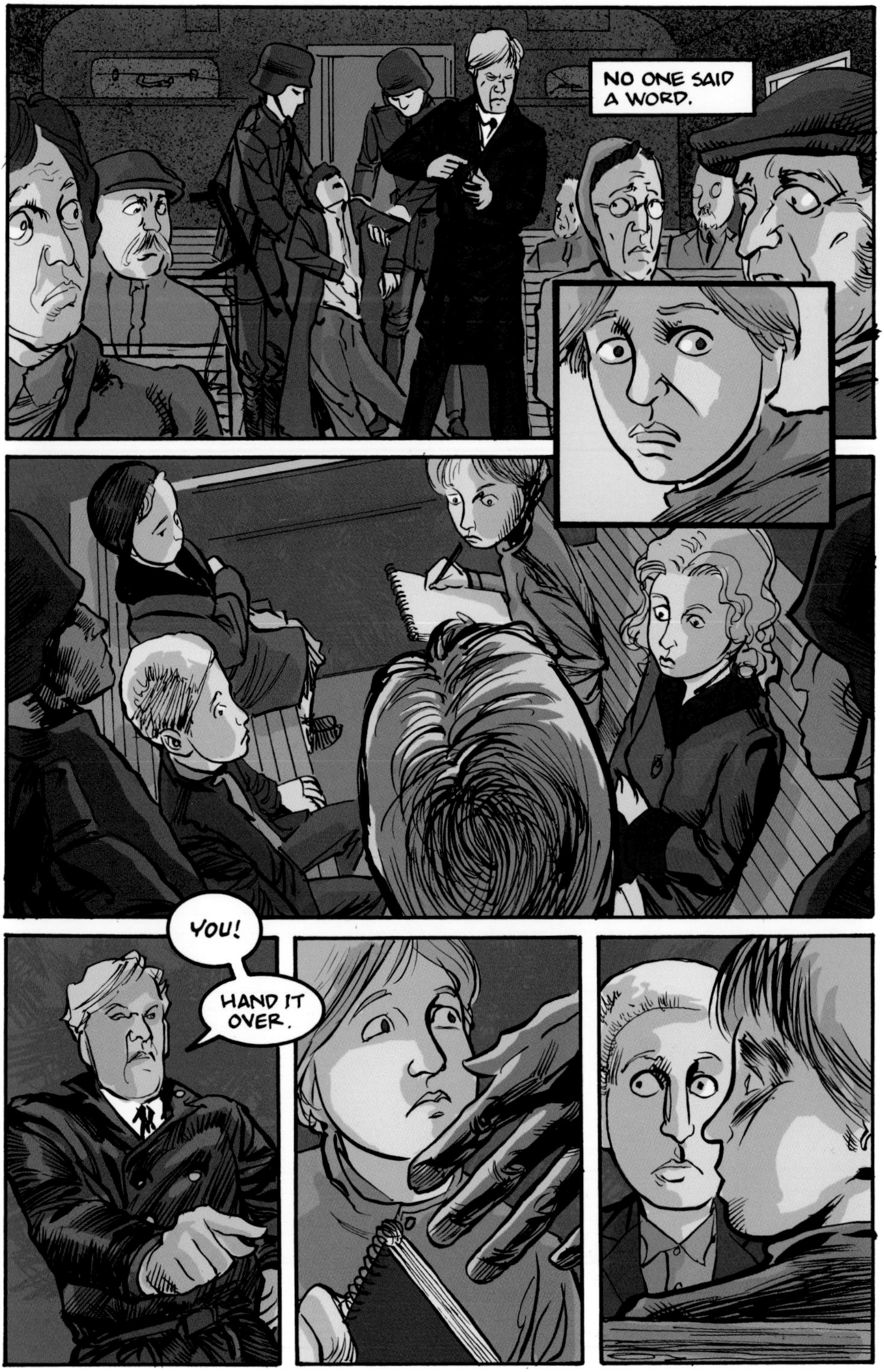
NO ONE SAID A WORD.
YOU!
HAND IT OVER.

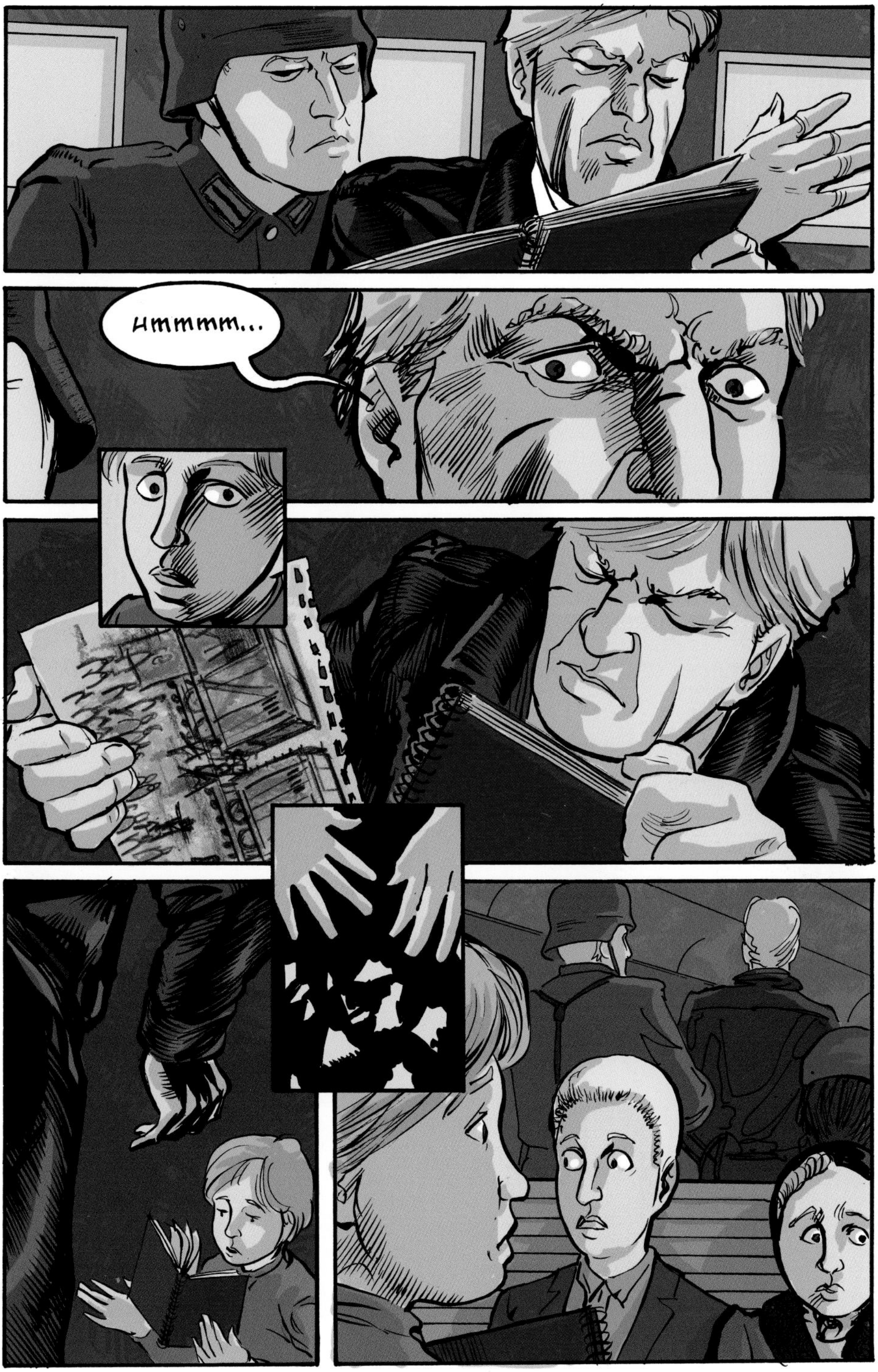
Hmmmm...

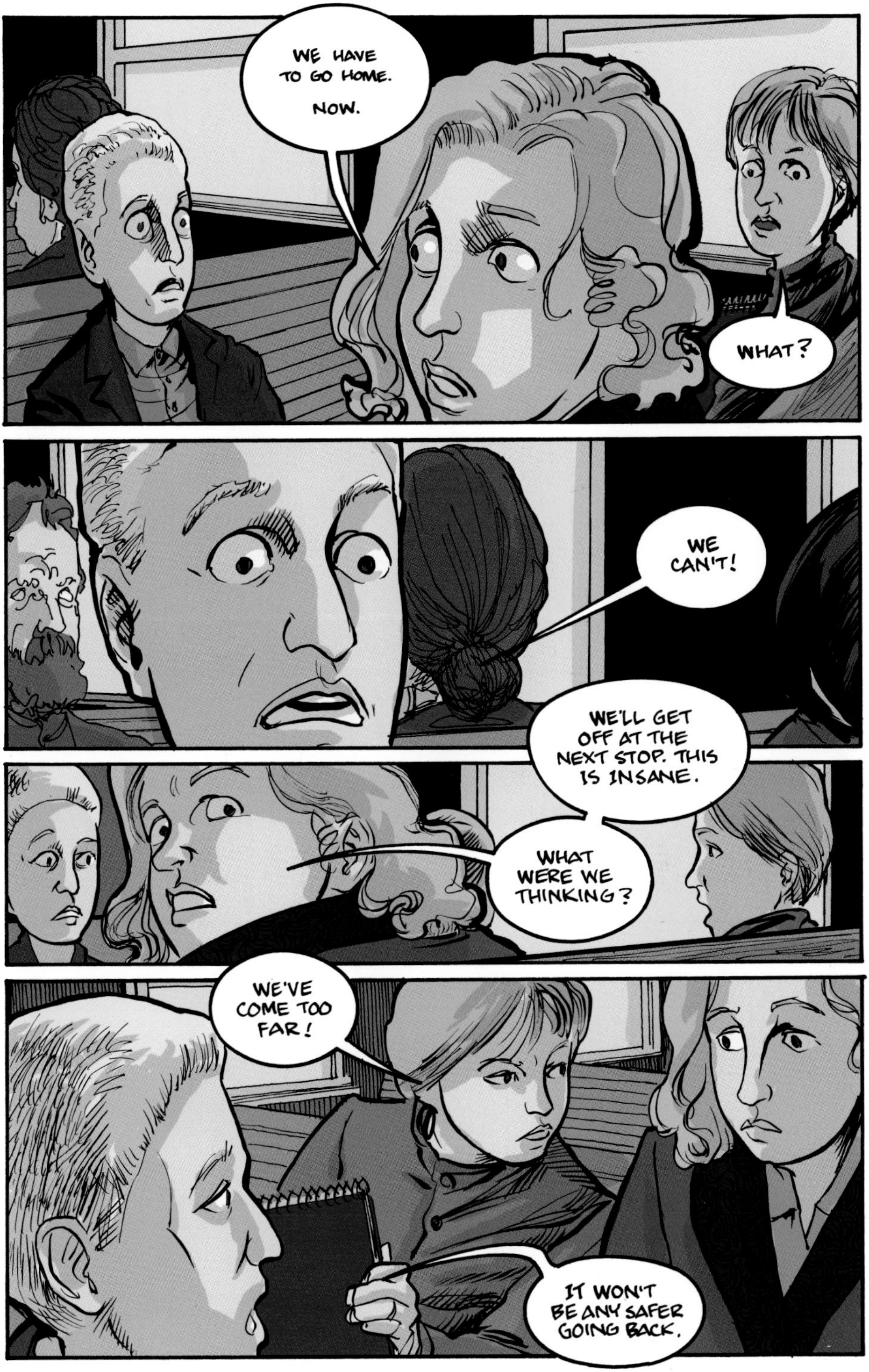
WE HAVE TO GO HOME.
NOW.
WHAT?
WE CAN'T!
WE'LL GET OFF AT THE NEXT STOP. THIS IS INSANE.
WHAT WERE WE THINKING?
WE'VE COME TOO FAR!
IT WON'T BE ANY SAFER GOING BACK.

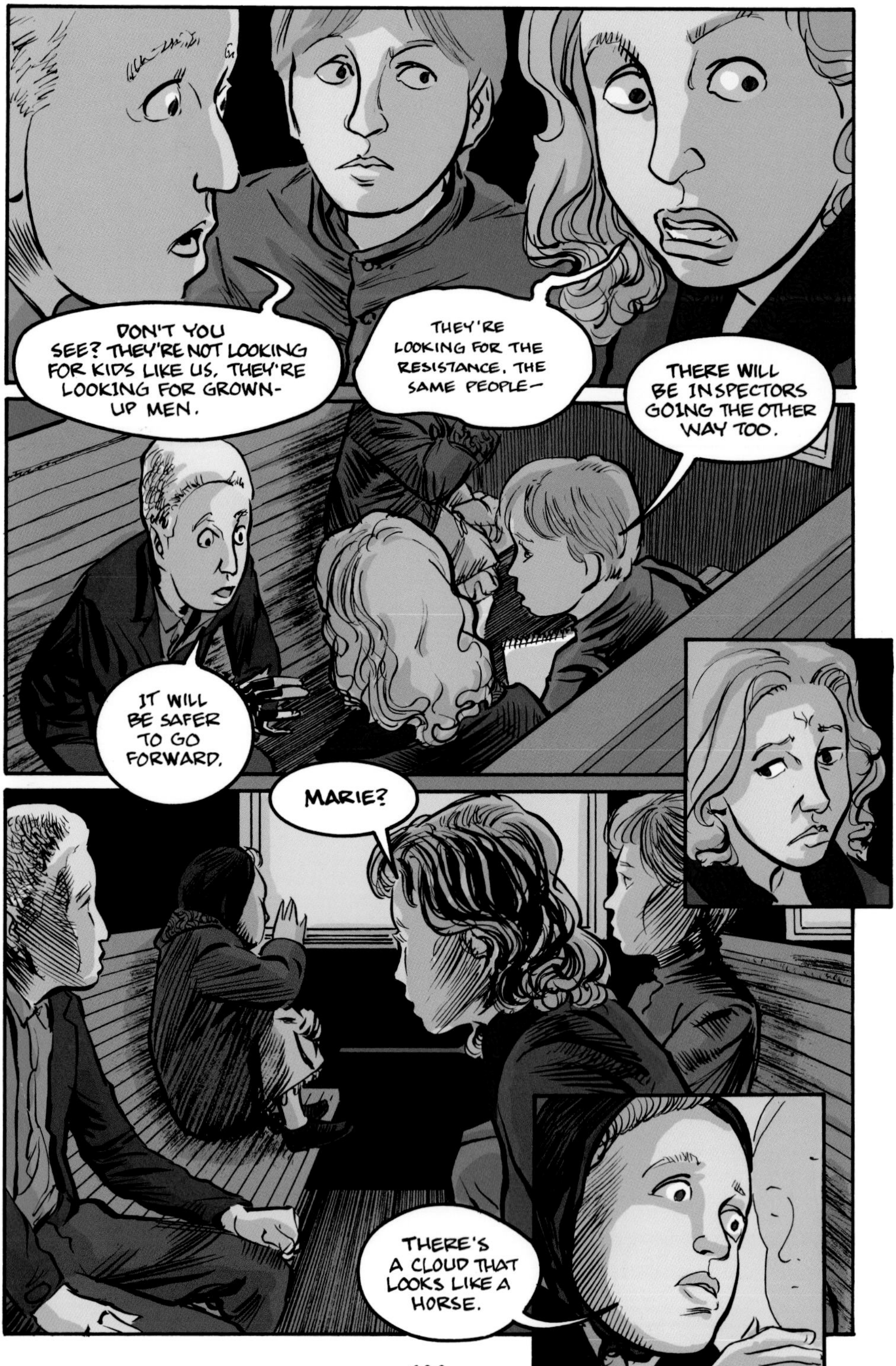
DON'T YOU SEE? THEY'RE NOT LOOKING FOR KIDS LIKE US. THEY'RE LOOKING FOR GROWN-UP MEN.
THEY'RE LOOKING FOR THE RESISTANCE. THE SAME PEOPLE—
THERE WILL BE INSPECTORS GOING THE OTHER WAY TOO.
IT WILL BE SAFER TO GO FORWARD.
MARIE?
THERE'S A CLOUD THAT LOOKS LIKE A HORSE.

PARIS
Gare l'Est
GET YOUR PAPERS READY. I WANT TO GET OUT OF HERE FAST.
JASPER LA CROIX. JASPER LA CROIX.
OH NO!

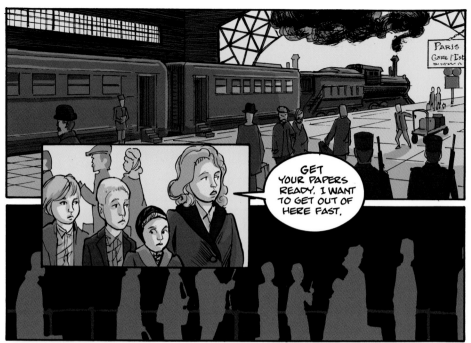

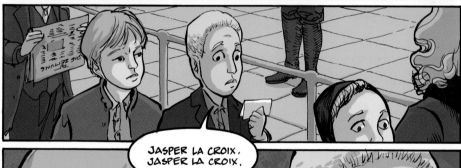

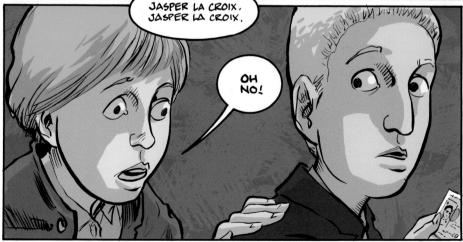

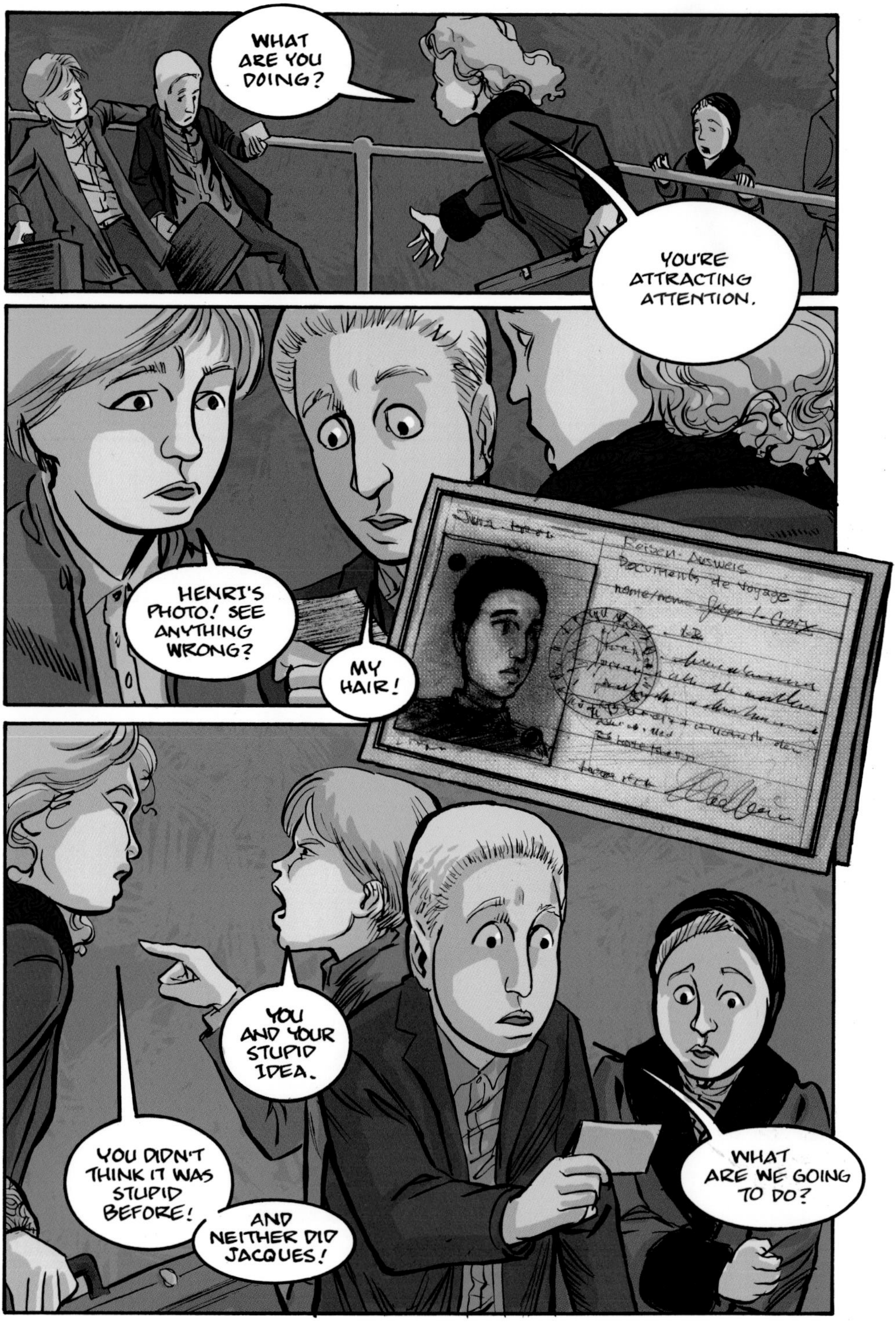
WHAT ARE YOU DOING?
YOU'RE ATTRACTING ATTENTION.
HENRI'S PHOTO! SEE ANYTHING WRONG?
MY HAIR!
YOU AND YOUR STUPID IDEA.
YOU DIDN'T THINK IT WAS STUPID BEFORE!
AND NEITHER DID JACQUES!
WHAT ARE WE GOING TO DO?

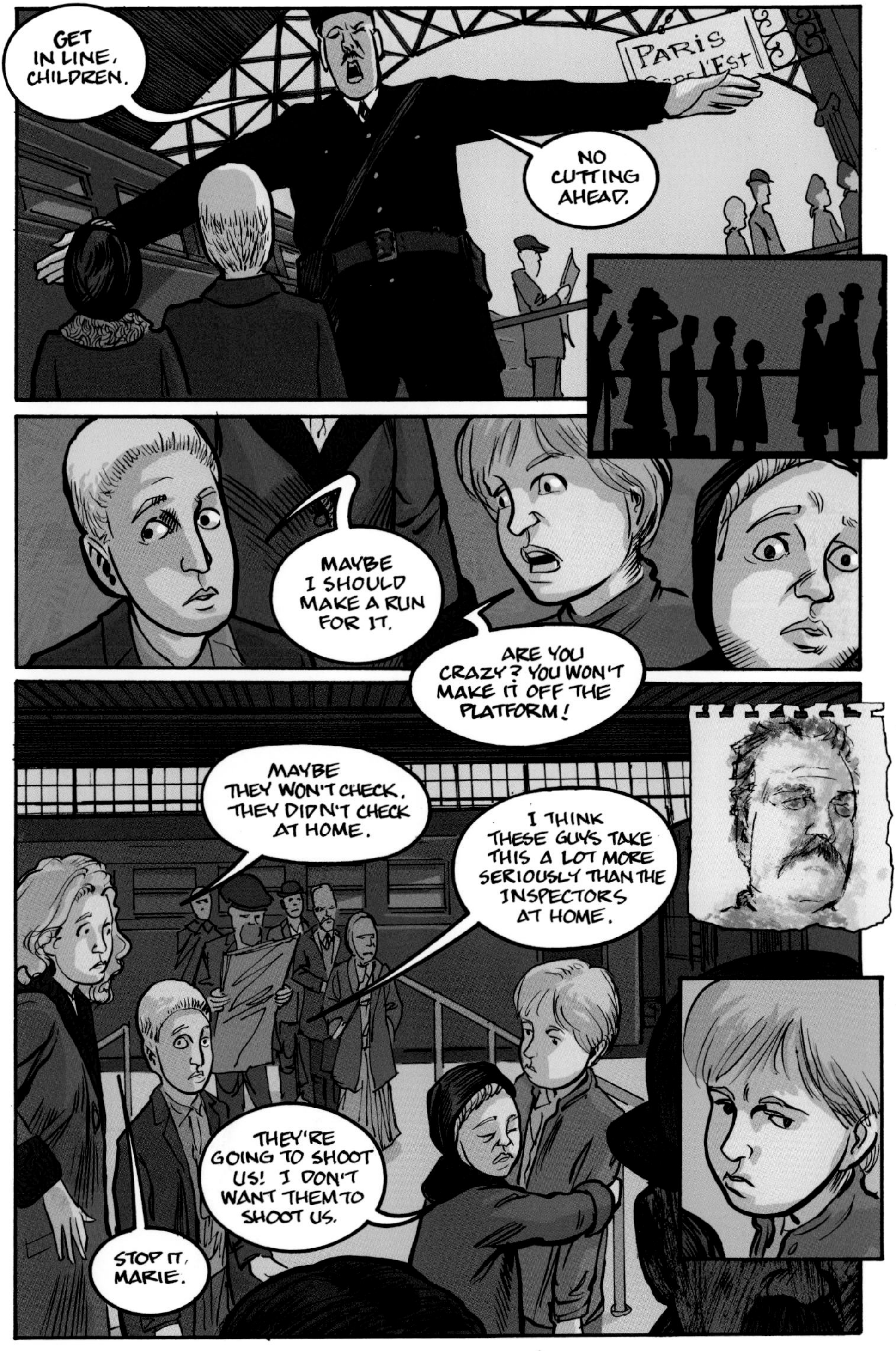
PARIS
L'Est
GET IN LINE, CHILDREN.
NO CUTTING AHEAD.
MAYBE I SHOULD MAKE A RUN FOR IT.
ARE YOU CRAZY? YOU WON'T MAKE IT OFF THE PLATFORM!
MAYBE THEY WON'T CHECK. THEY DIDN'T CHECK AT HOME.
I THINK THESE GUYS TAKE THIS A LOT MORE SERIOUSLY THAN THE INSPECTORS AT HOME.
THEY'RE GOING TO SHOOT US! I DON'T WANT THEM TO SHOOT US.
STOP IT, MARIE.

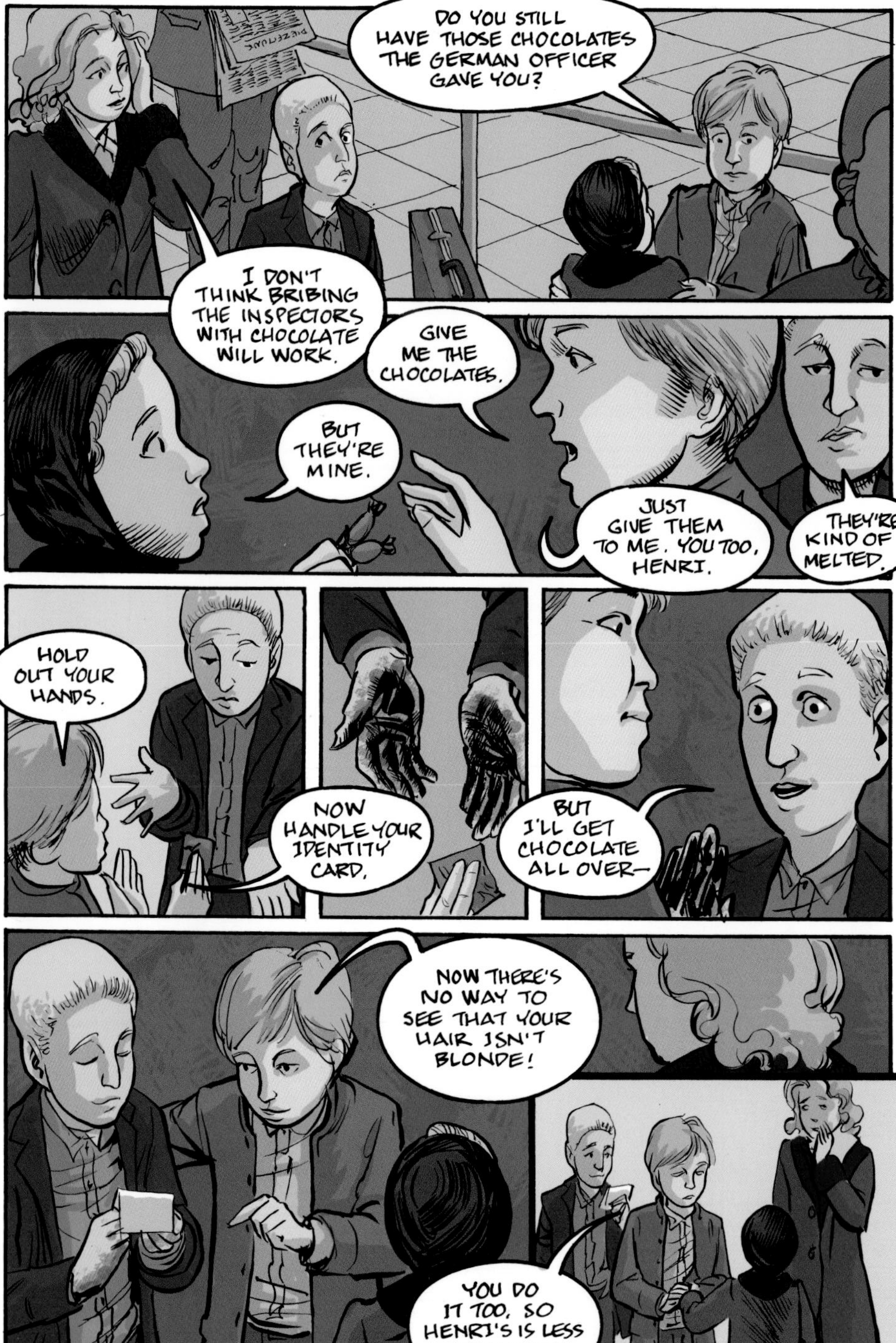
DO YOU STILL HAVE THOSE CHOCOLATES THE GERMAN OFFICER GAVE YOU?
I DON'T THINK BRIBING THE INSPECTORS WITH CHOCOLATE WILL WORK.
GIVE ME THE CHOCOLATES.
BUT THEY'RE MINE.
JUST GIVE THEM TO ME. YOU TOO, HENRI.
THEY'RE KIND OF MELTED.
HOLD OUT YOUR HANDS.
NOW HANDLE YOUR IDENTITY CARD.
BUT I'LL GET CHOCOLATE ALL OVER—
NOW THERE'S NO WAY TO SEE THAT YOUR HAIR ISN'T BLONDE!
YOU DO IT TOO, SO HENRI'S IS LESS SUSPICIOUS.

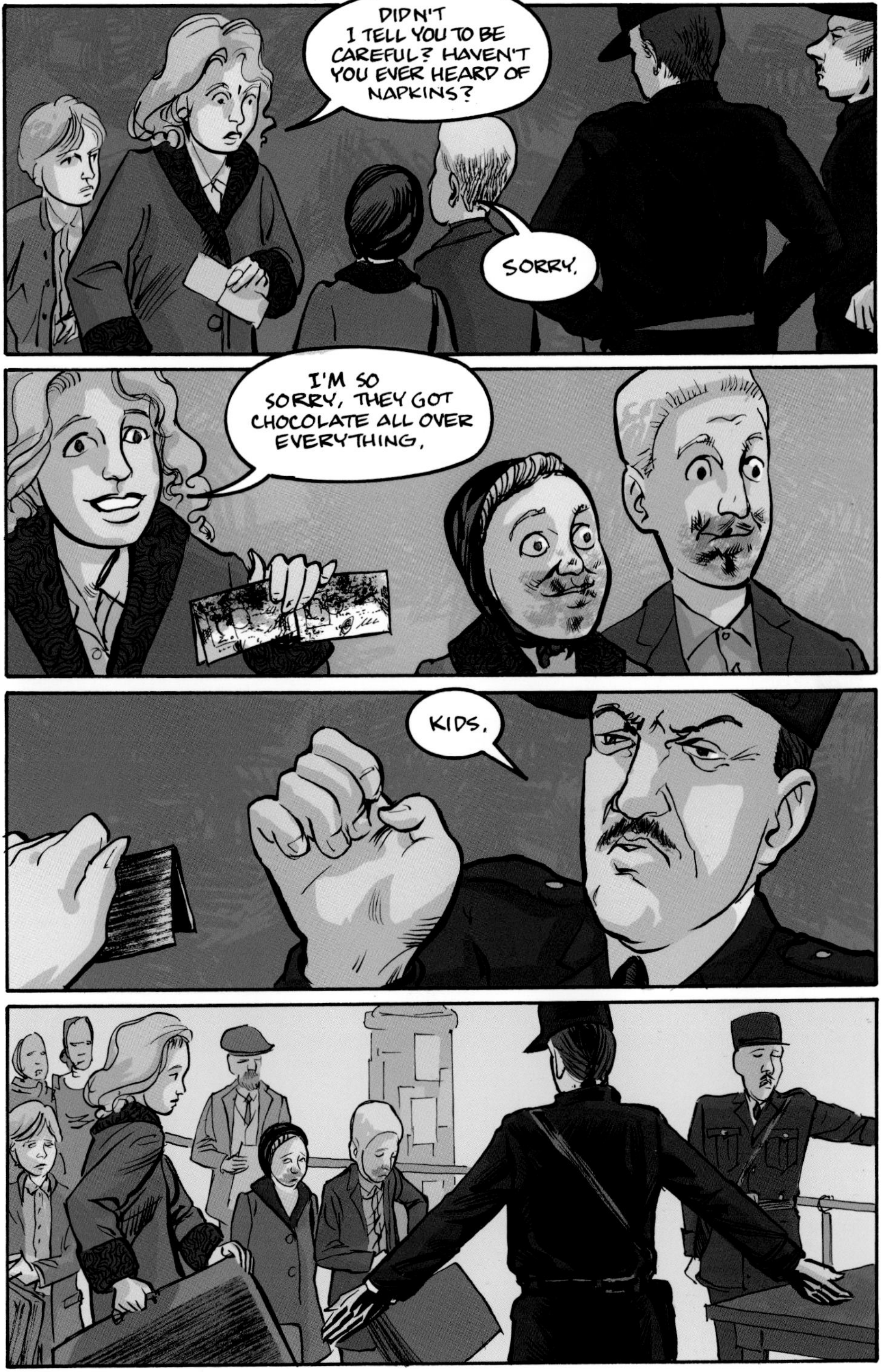
DIDN'T I TELL YOU TO BE CAREFUL? HAVEN'T YOU EVER HEARD OF NAPKINS?
SORRY.
I'M SO SORRY, THEY GOT CHOCOLATE ALL OVER EVERYTHING.
KIDS.

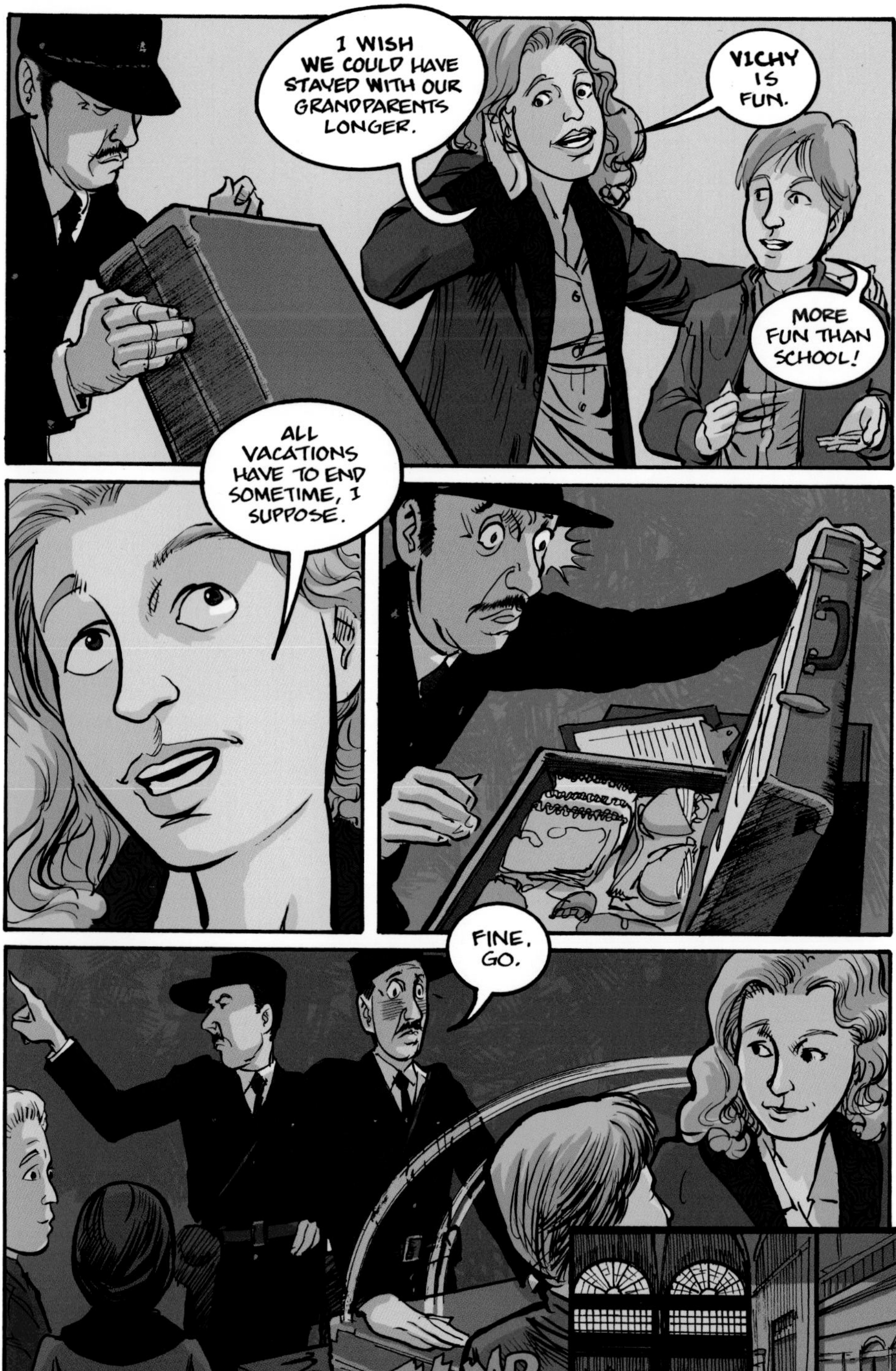
I WISH WE COULD HAVE STAYED WITH OUR GRANDPARENTS LONGER.
VICHY IS FUN.
MORE FUN THAN SCHOOL!
ALL VACATIONS HAVE TO END SOMETIME, I SUPPOSE.
FINE. GO.
THUMP

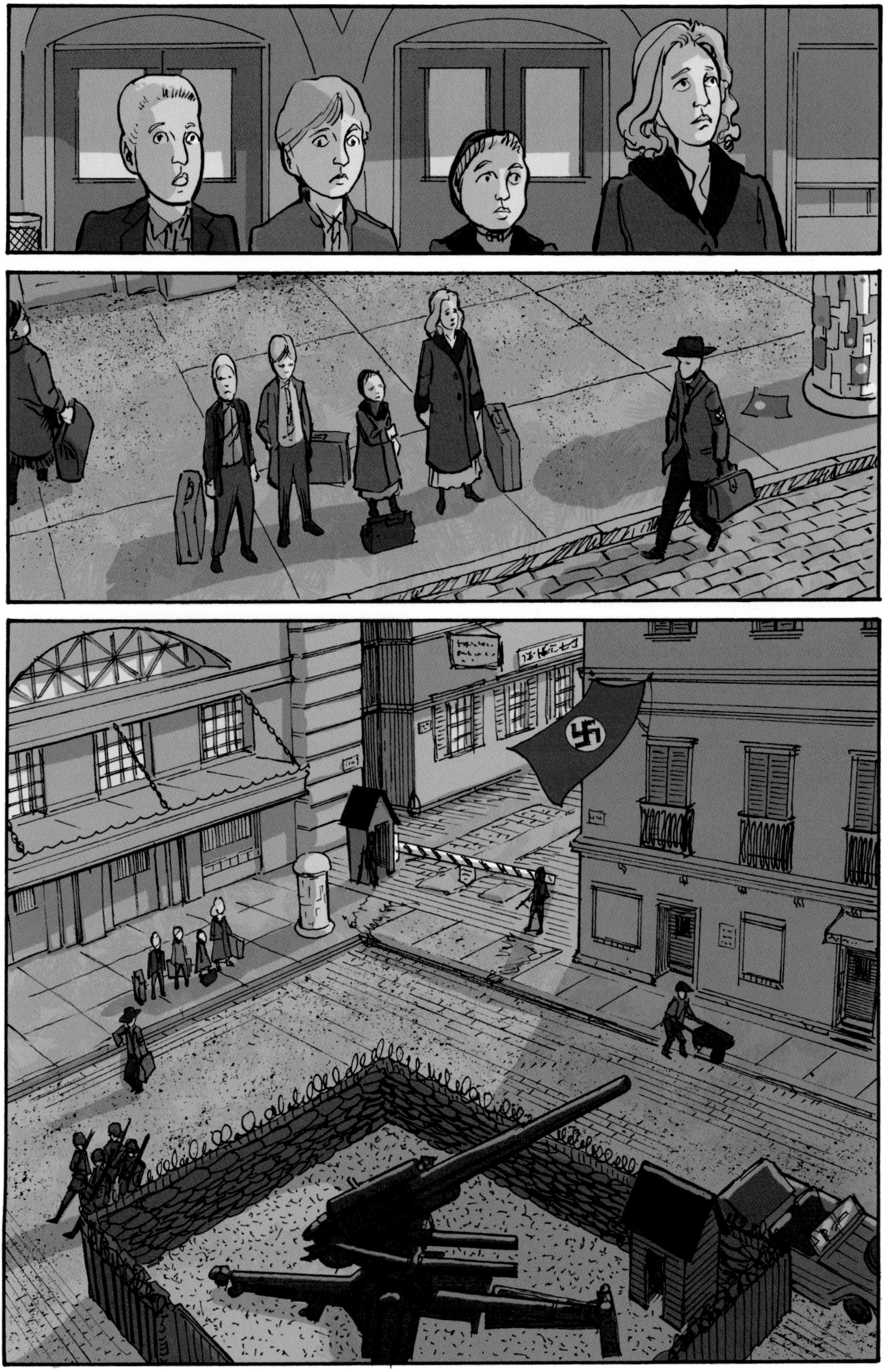

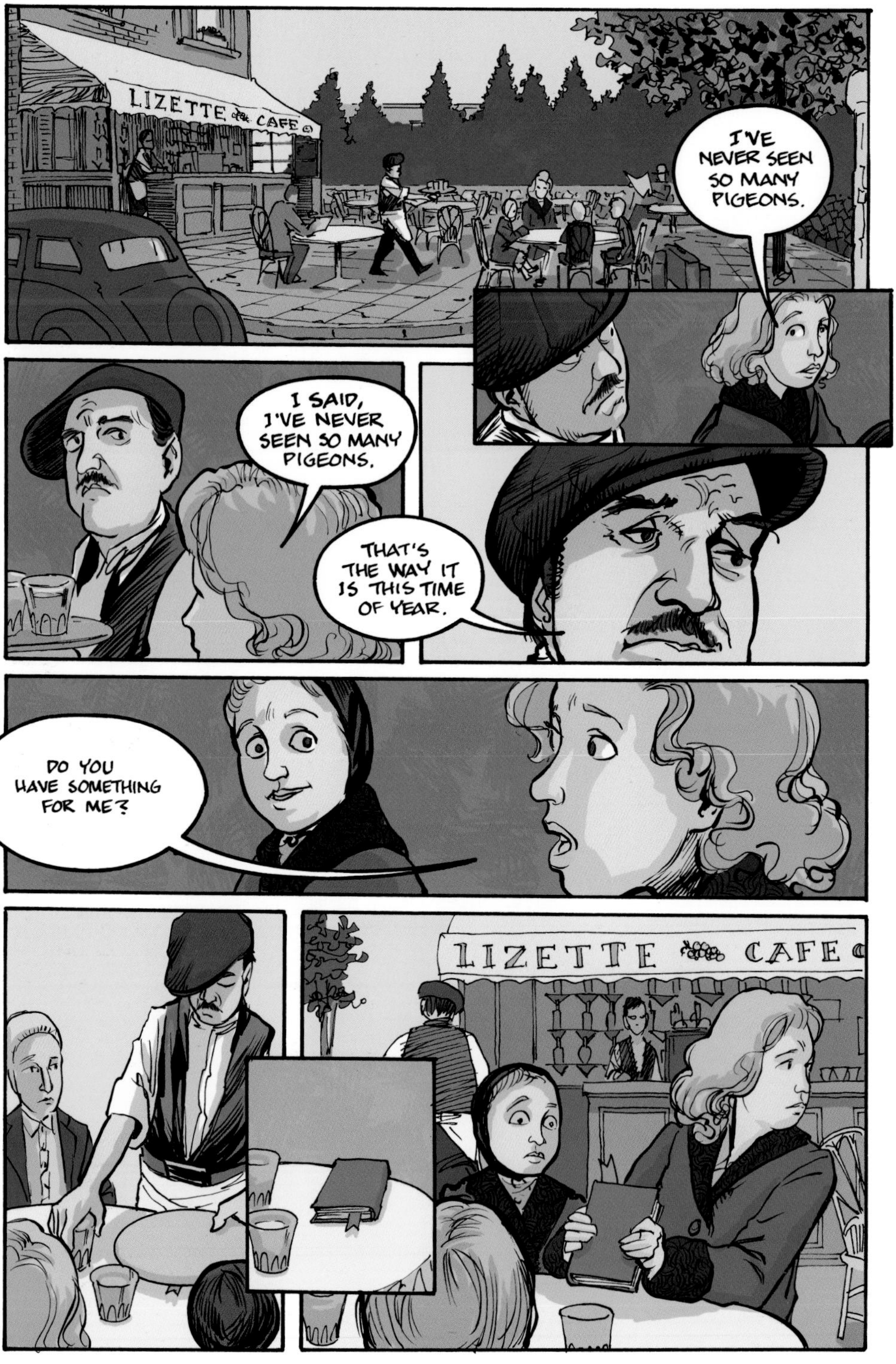
LIZETTE CAFE
I'VE NEVER SEEN SO MANY PIGEONS.
I SAID, I'VE NEVER SEEN SO MANY PIGEONS.
THAT'S THE WAY IT IS THIS TIME OF YEAR.
DO YOU HAVE SOMETHING FOR ME?
LIZETTE CAFE

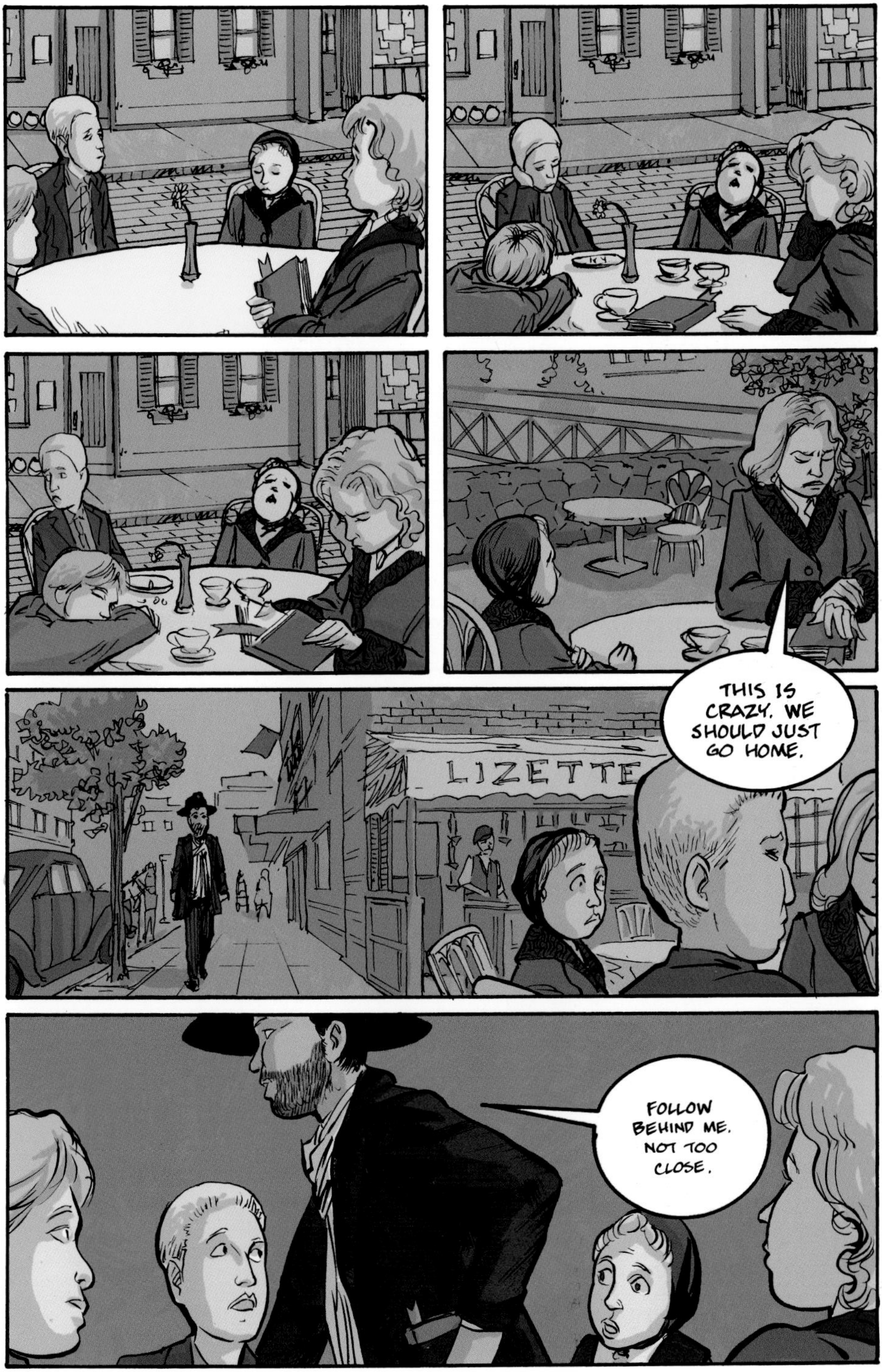
LIZETTE
THIS IS CRAZY. WE SHOULD JUST GO HOME.
FOLLOW BEHIND ME. NOT TOO CLOSE.

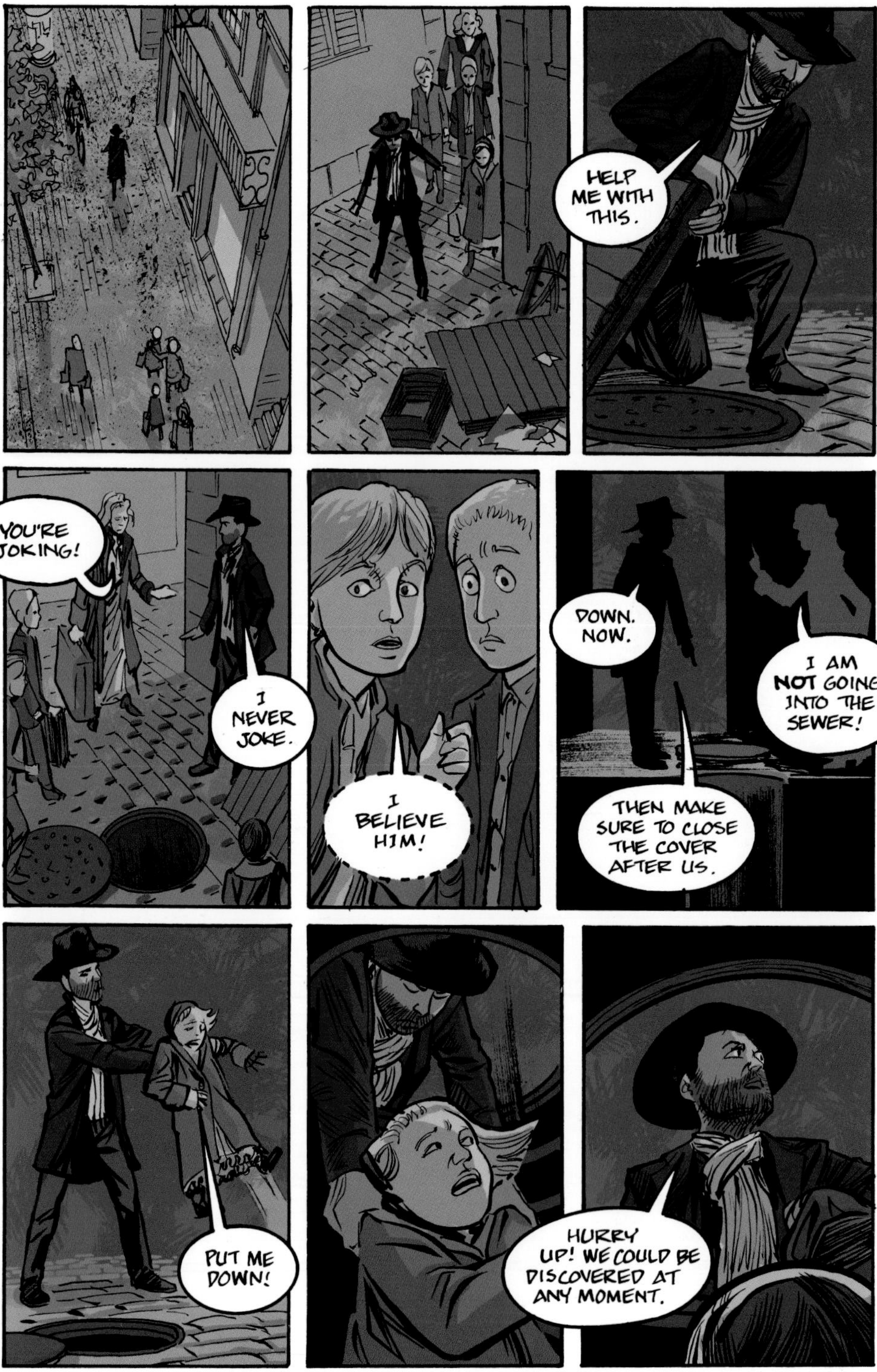
HELP ME WITH THIS.
YOU'RE JOKING!
I NEVER JOKE.
I BELIEVE HIM!
DOWN. NOW.
I AM NOT GOING INTO THE SEWER!
THEN MAKE SURE TO CLOSE THE COVER AFTER US.
PUT ME DOWN!
HURRY UP! WE COULD BE DISCOVERED AT ANY MOMENT.

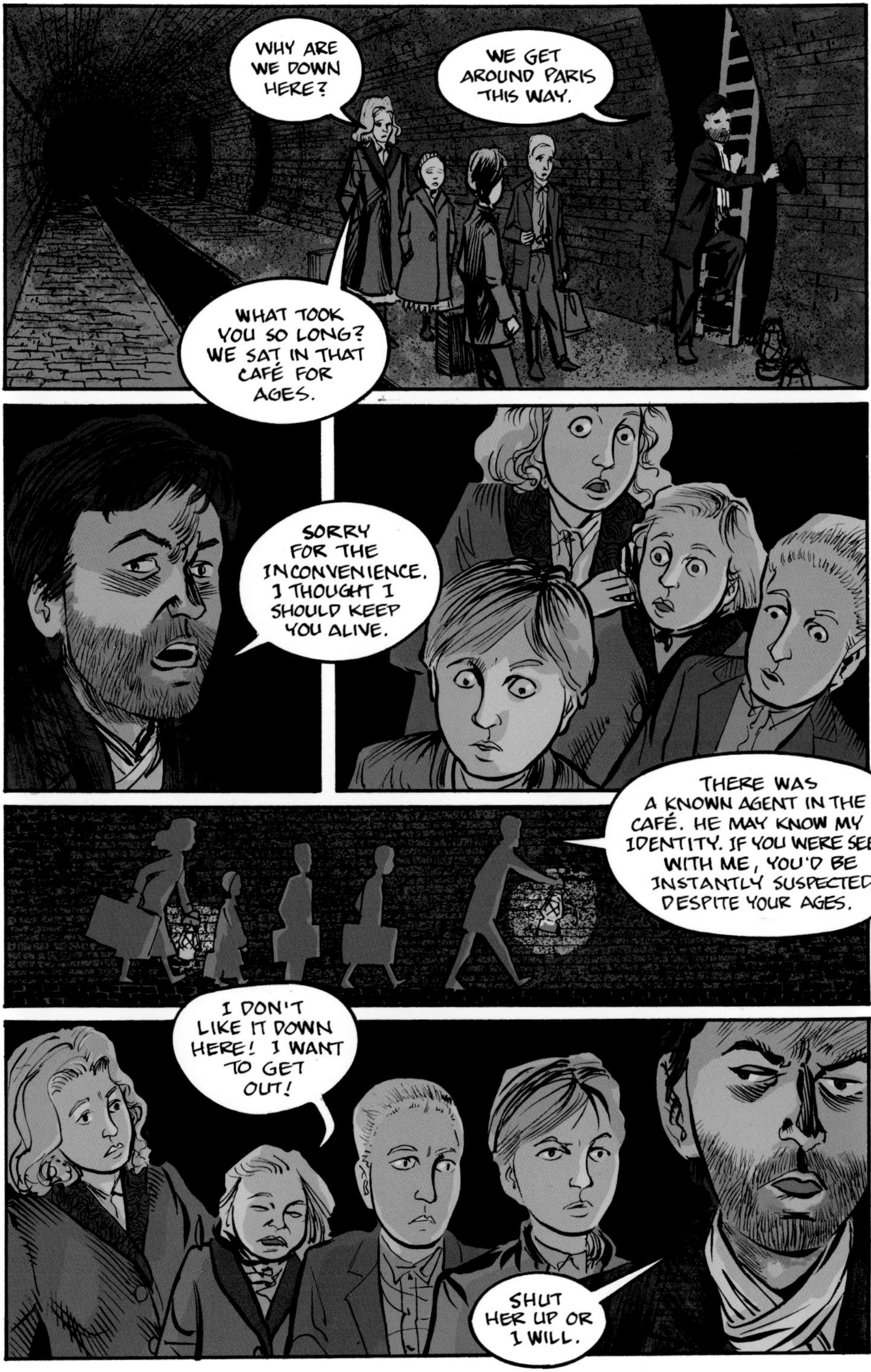
WHY ARE WE DOWN HERE?
WE GET AROUND PARIS THIS WAY.
WHAT TOOK YOU SO LONG? WE SAT IN THAT CAFÉ FOR AGES.
SORRY FOR THE INCONVENIENCE. I THOUGHT I SHOULD KEEP YOU ALIVE.
THERE WAS A KNOWN AGENT IN THE CAFÉ. HE MAY KNOW MY IDENTITY. IF YOU WERE SEEN WITH ME, YOU'D BE INSTANTLY SUSPECTED, DESPITE YOUR AGES.
I DON'T LIKE IT DOWN HERE! I WANT TO GET OUT!
SHUT HER UP OR I WILL.

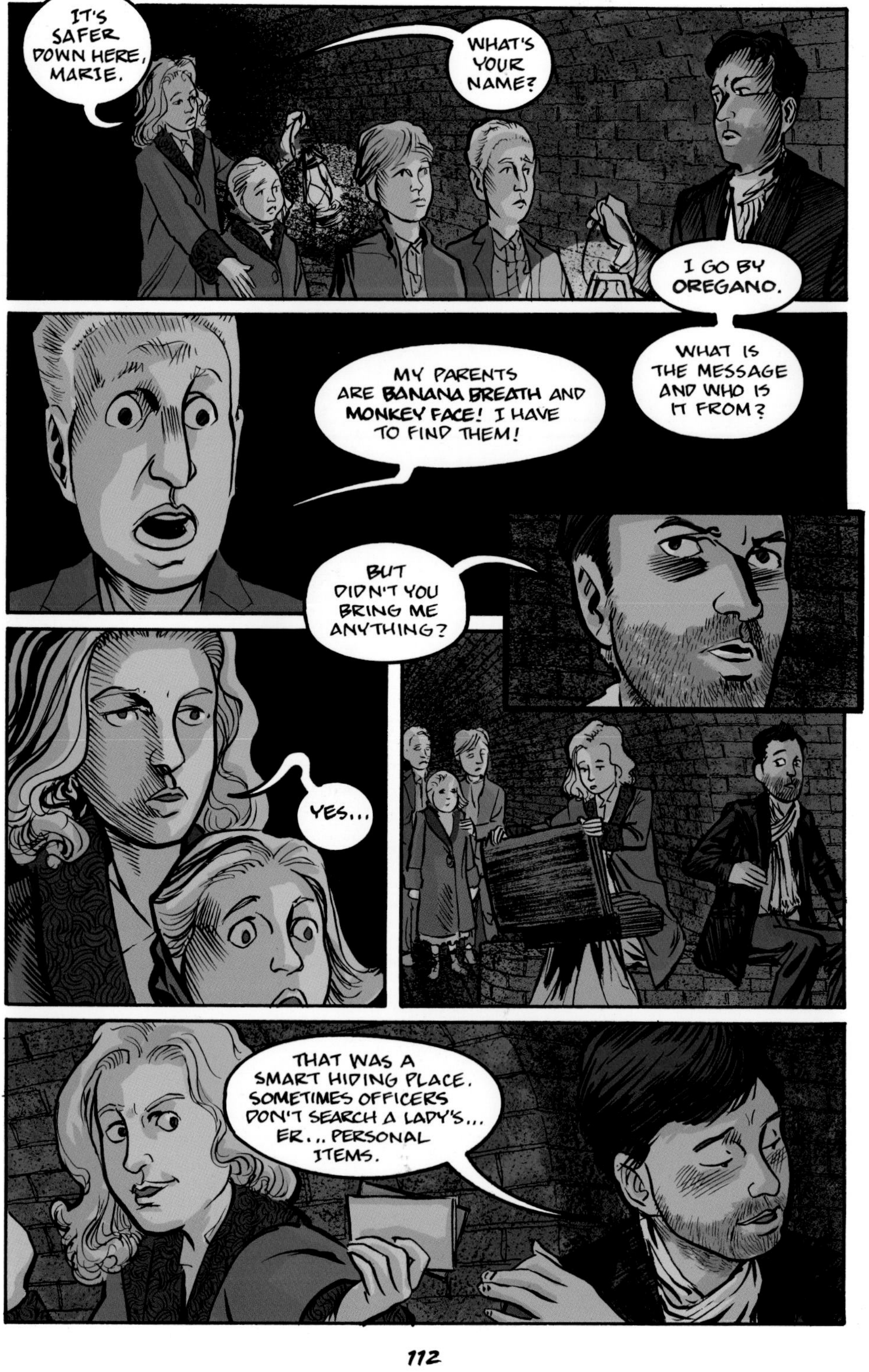
IT'S SAFER DOWN HERE, MARIE.
WHAT'S YOUR NAME?
I GO BY OREGANO.
WHAT IS THE MESSAGE AND WHO IS IT FROM?
MY PARENTS ARE BANANA BREATH AND MONKEY FACE! I HAVE TO FIND THEM!
BUT DIDN'T YOU BRING ME ANYTHING?
YES...
THAT WAS A SMART HIDING PLACE. SOMETIMES OFFICERS DON'T SEARCH A LADY'S... ER... PERSONAL ITEMS.

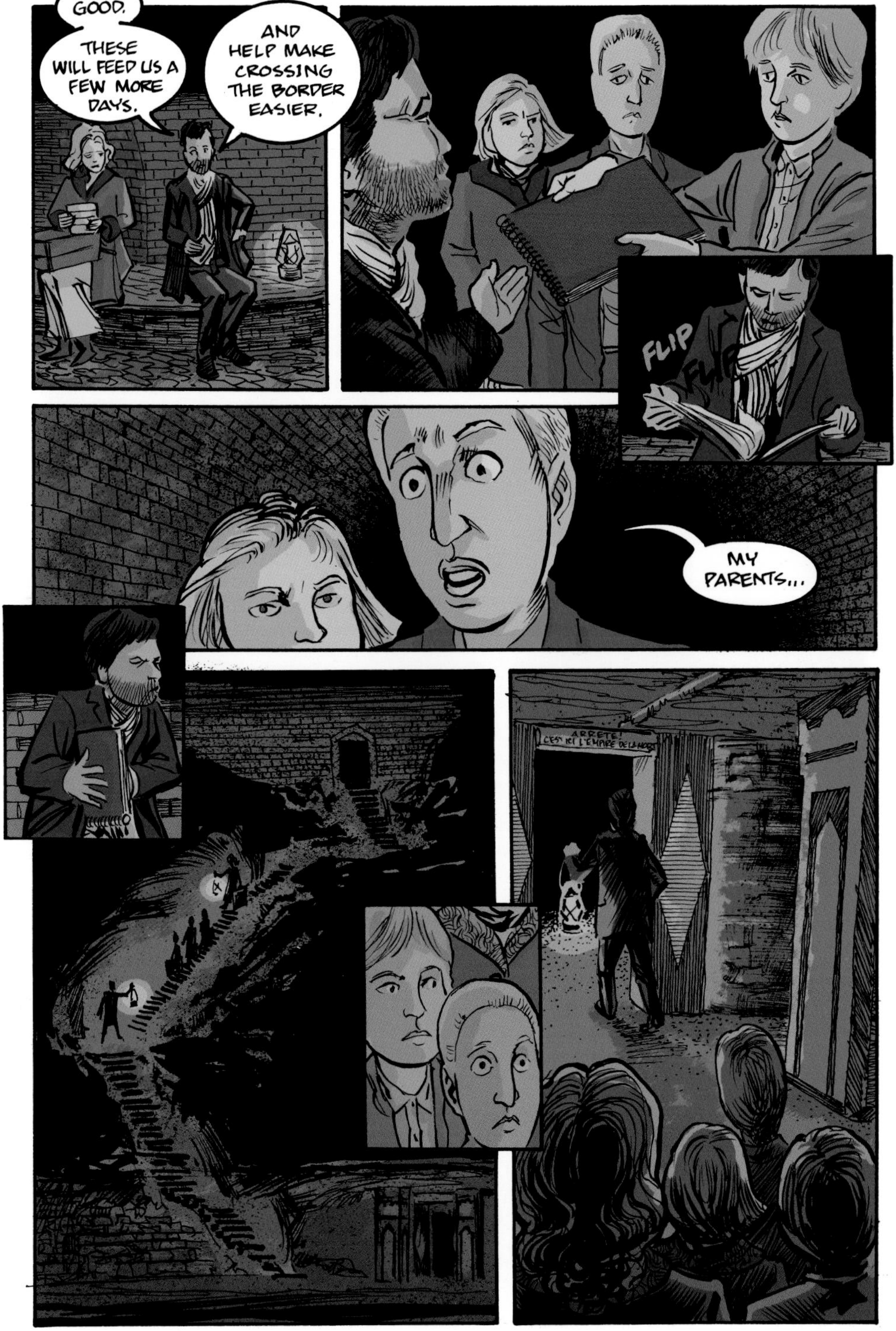
GOOD.
THESE WILL FEED US A FEW MORE DAYS.
AND HELP MAKE CROSSING THE BORDER EASIER.
FLIP FLIP
MY PARENTS...
ARRETE! C'EST ICI L'EMPIRE DE LA MORT

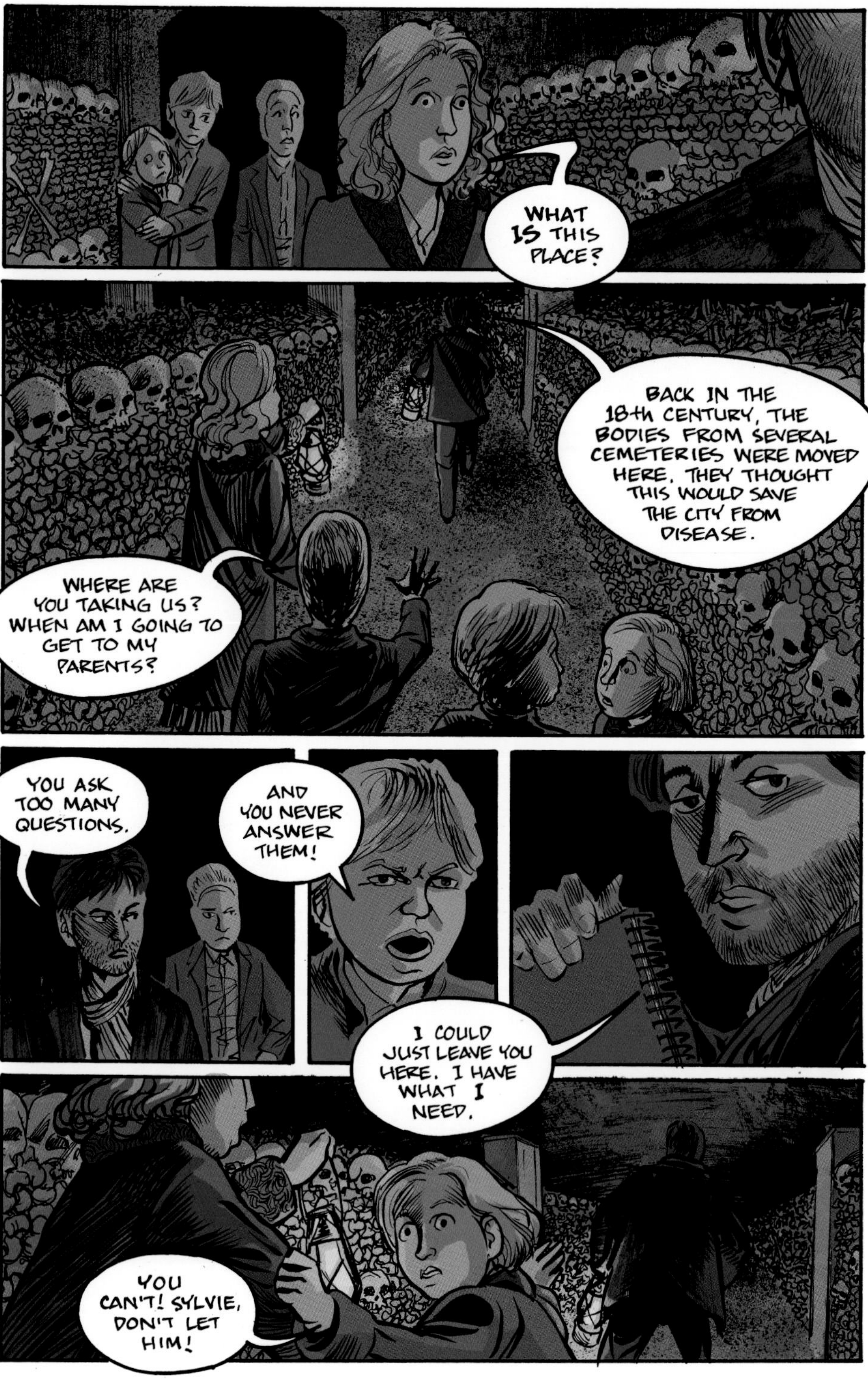
WHAT IS THIS PLACE?
BACK IN THE 18th CENTURY, THE BODIES FROM SEVERAL CEMETERIES WERE MOVED HERE. THEY THOUGHT THIS WOULD SAVE THE CITY FROM DISEASE.
WHERE ARE YOU TAKING US? WHEN AM I GOING TO GET TO MY PARENTS?
YOU ASK TOO MANY QUESTIONS.
AND YOU NEVER ANSWER THEM!
I COULD JUST LEAVE YOU HERE. I HAVE WHAT I NEED.
YOU CAN'T! SYLVIE, DON'T LET HIM!

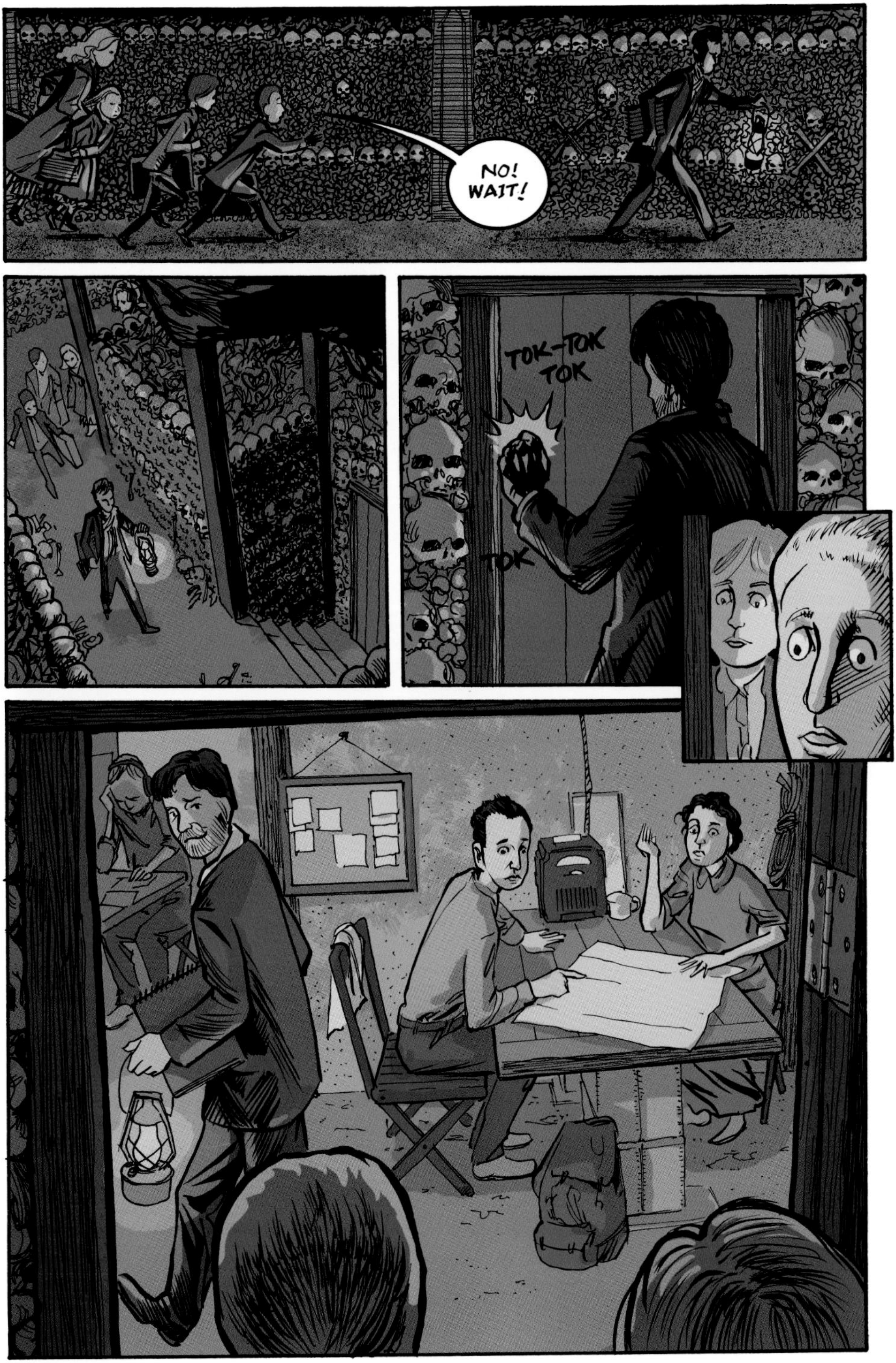
NO! WAIT!
TOK-TOK TOK
TOK

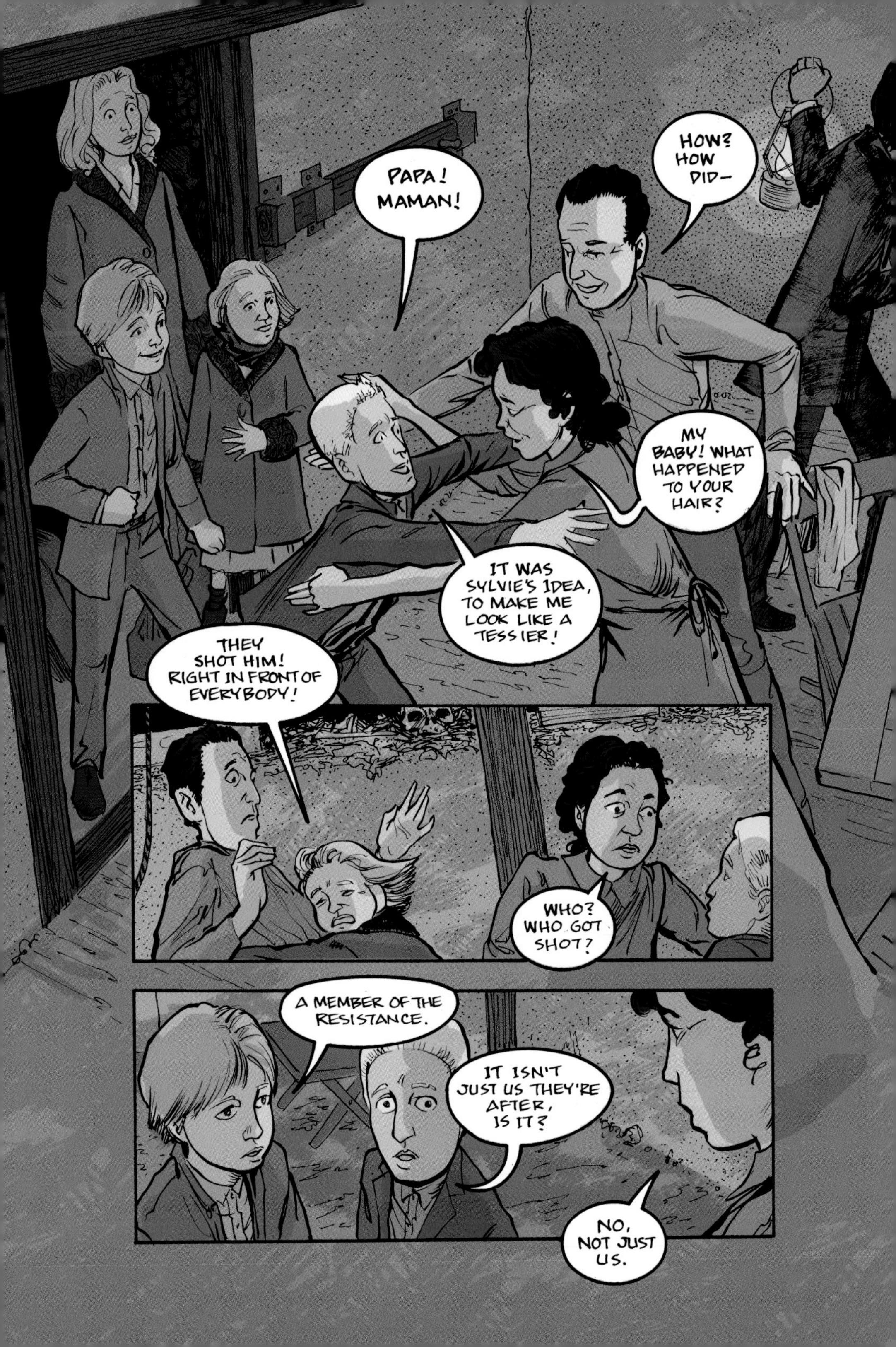
PAPA! MAMAN!
HOW? HOW DID—
MY BABY! WHAT HAPPENED TO YOUR HAIR?
IT WAS SYLVIE'S IDEA, TO MAKE ME LOOK LIKE A TESSIER!
THEY SHOT HIM! RIGHT IN FRONT OF EVERYBODY!
WHO? WHO GOT SHOT?
A MEMBER OF THE RESISTANCE.
IT ISN'T JUST US THEY'RE AFTER, IS IT?
NO, NOT JUST US.

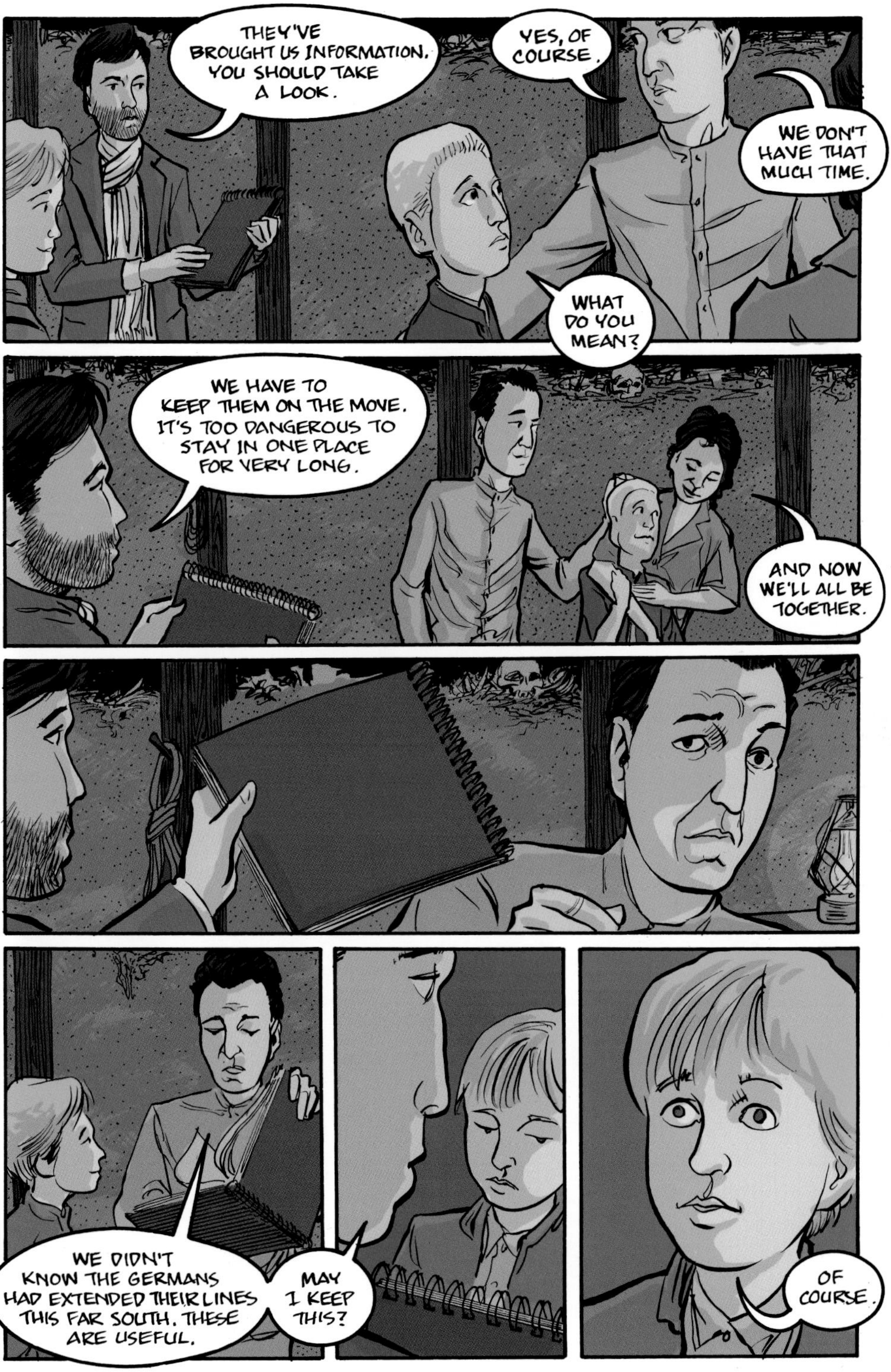
THEY'VE BROUGHT US INFORMATION. YOU SHOULD TAKE A LOOK.
YES, OF COURSE.
WE DON'T HAVE THAT MUCH TIME.
WHAT DO YOU MEAN?
WE HAVE TO KEEP THEM ON THE MOVE. IT'S TOO DANGEROUS TO STAY IN ONE PLACE FOR VERY LONG.
AND NOW WE'LL ALL BE TOGETHER.
WE DIDN'T KNOW THE GERMANS HAD EXTENDED THEIR LINES THIS FAR SOUTH. THESE ARE USEFUL.
MAY I KEEP THIS?
OF COURSE.

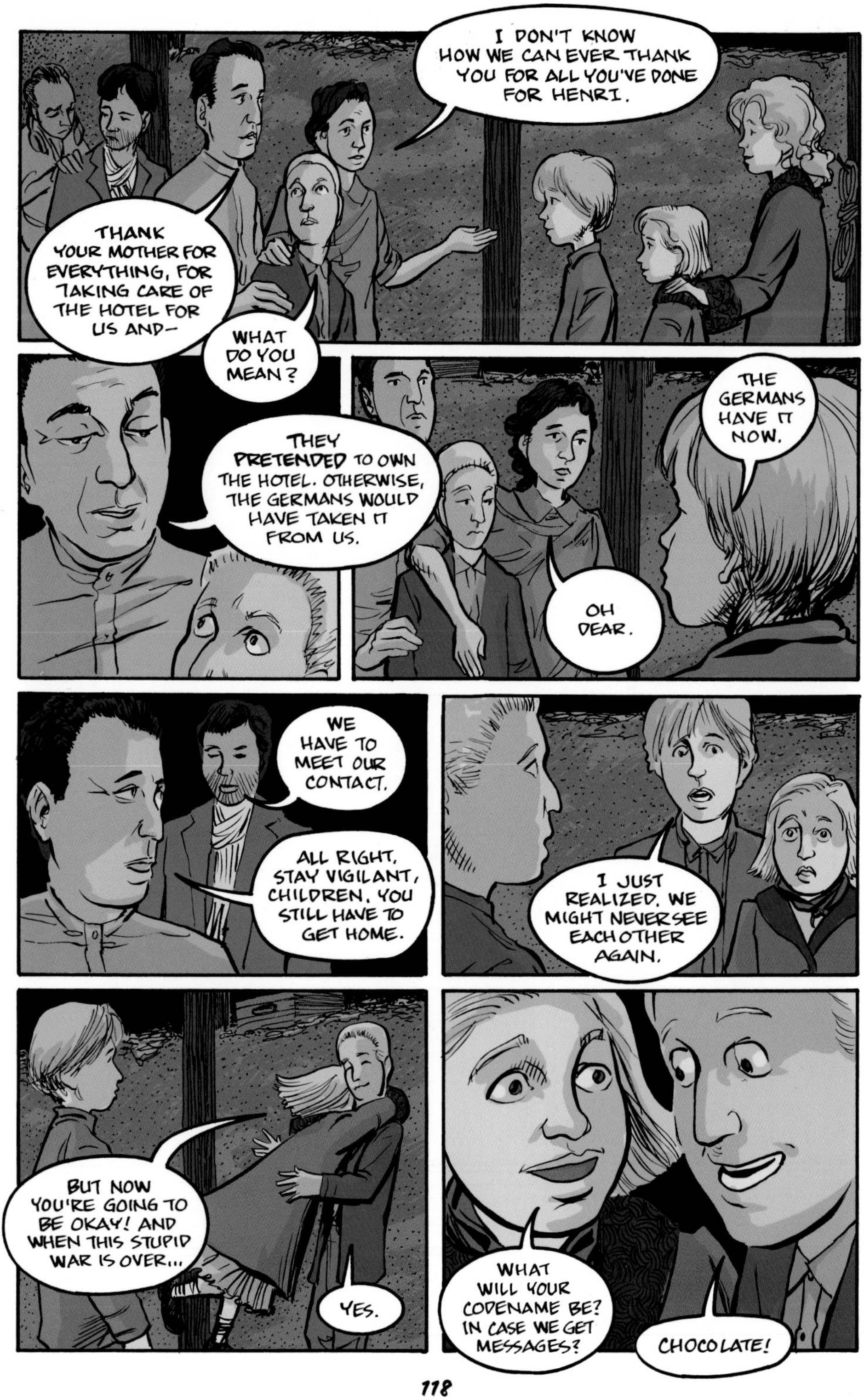
I DON'T KNOW HOW WE CAN EVER THANK YOU FOR ALL YOU'VE DONE FOR HENRI.
THANK YOUR MOTHER FOR EVERYTHING, FOR TAKING CARE OF THE HOTEL FOR US AND–
WHAT DO YOU MEAN?
THEY PRETENDED TO OWN THE HOTEL. OTHERWISE, THE GERMANS WOULD HAVE TAKEN IT FROM US.
THE GERMANS HAVE IT NOW.
OH DEAR.
WE HAVE TO MEET OUR CONTACT.
ALL RIGHT. STAY VIGILANT, CHILDREN. YOU STILL HAVE TO GET HOME.
I JUST REALIZED. WE MIGHT NEVER SEE EACH OTHER AGAIN.
BUT NOW YOU'RE GOING TO BE OKAY! AND WHEN THIS STUPID WAR IS OVER...
YES.
WHAT WILL YOUR CODENAME BE? IN CASE WE GET MESSAGES?
CHOCOLATE!

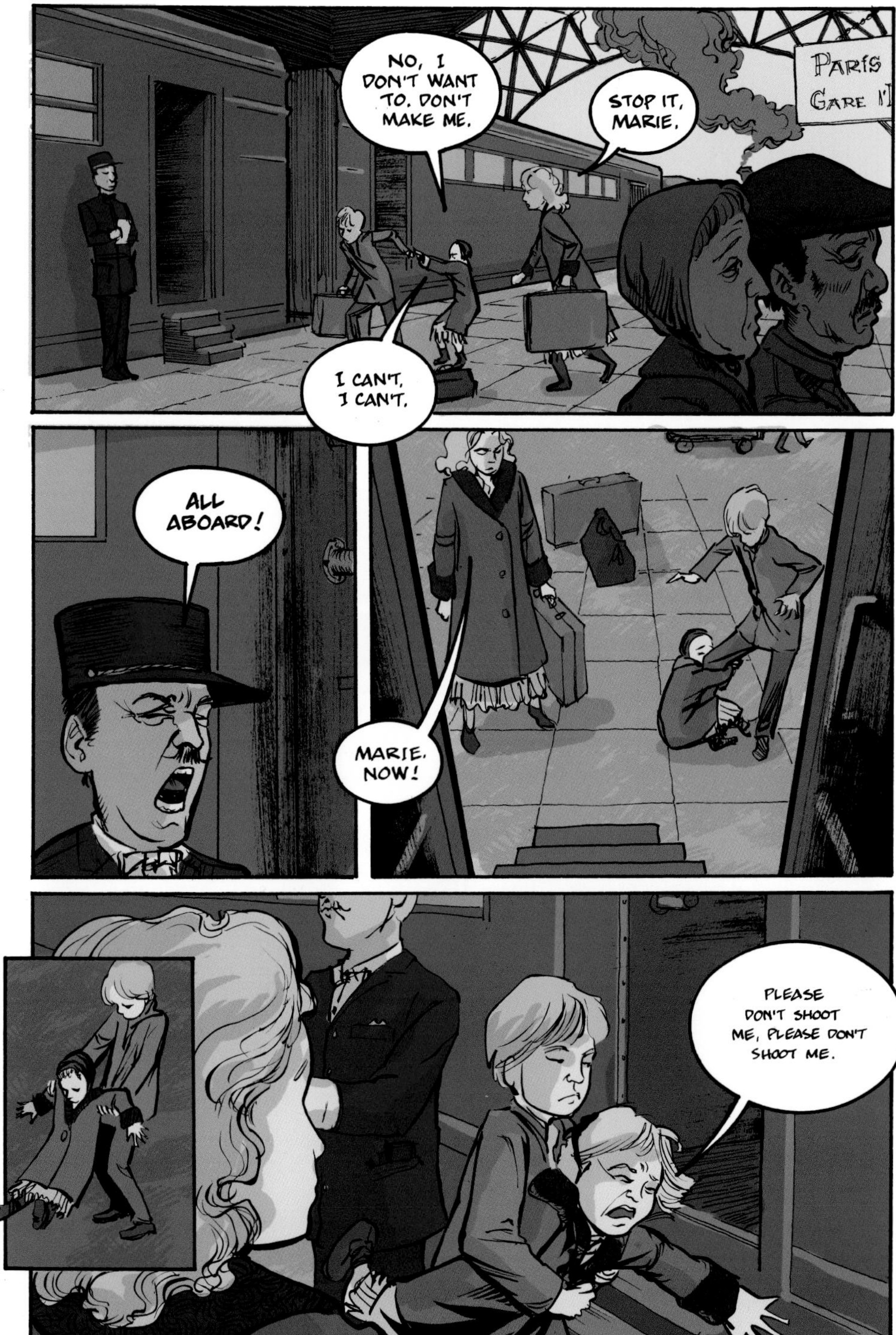
Paris
Gare l'
NO, I DON'T WANT TO. DON'T MAKE ME.
STOP IT, MARIE.
I CAN'T, I CAN'T.
ALL ABOARD!
MARIE, NOW!
PLEASE DON'T SHOOT ME, PLEASE DON'T SHOOT ME.

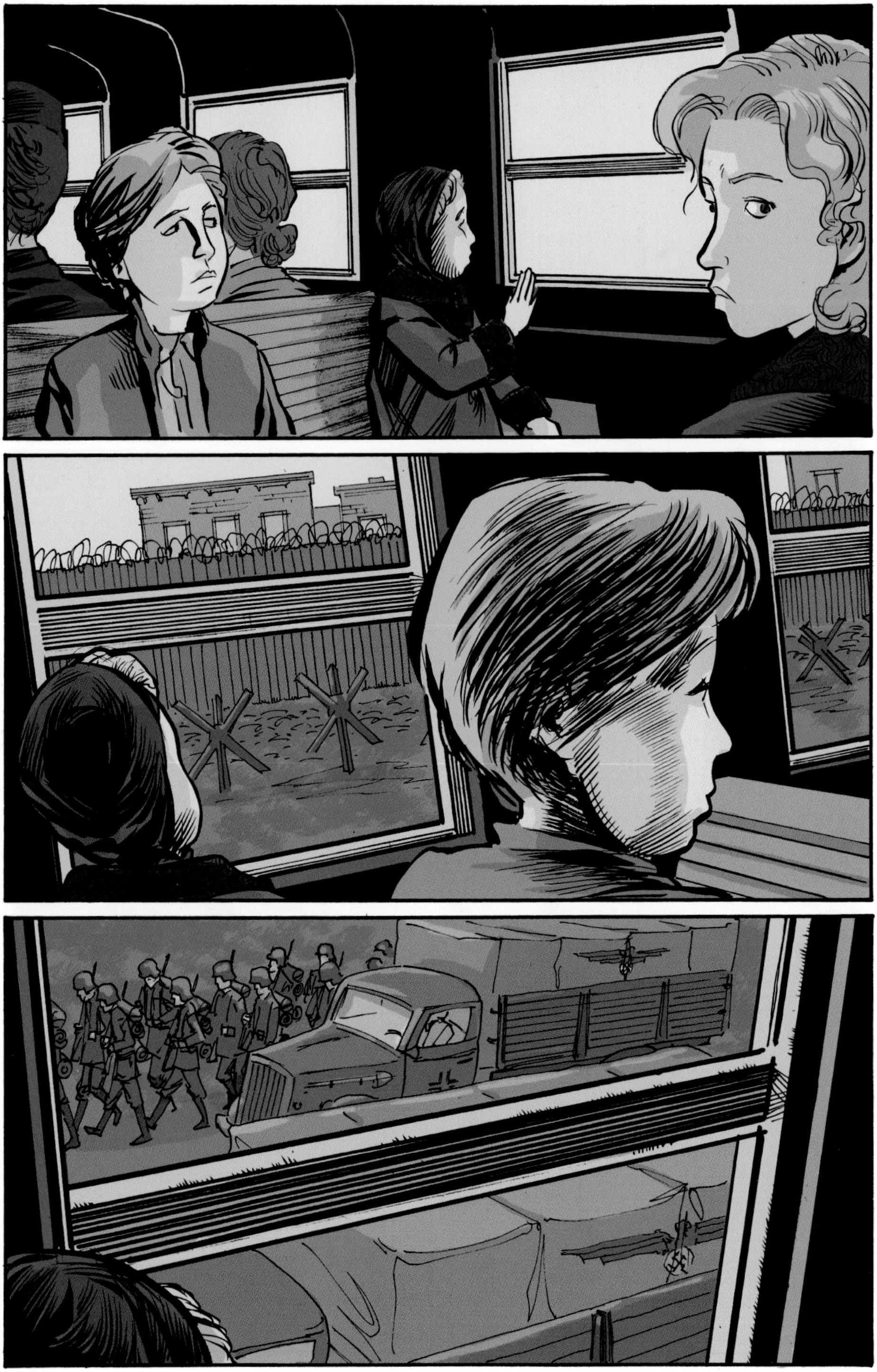

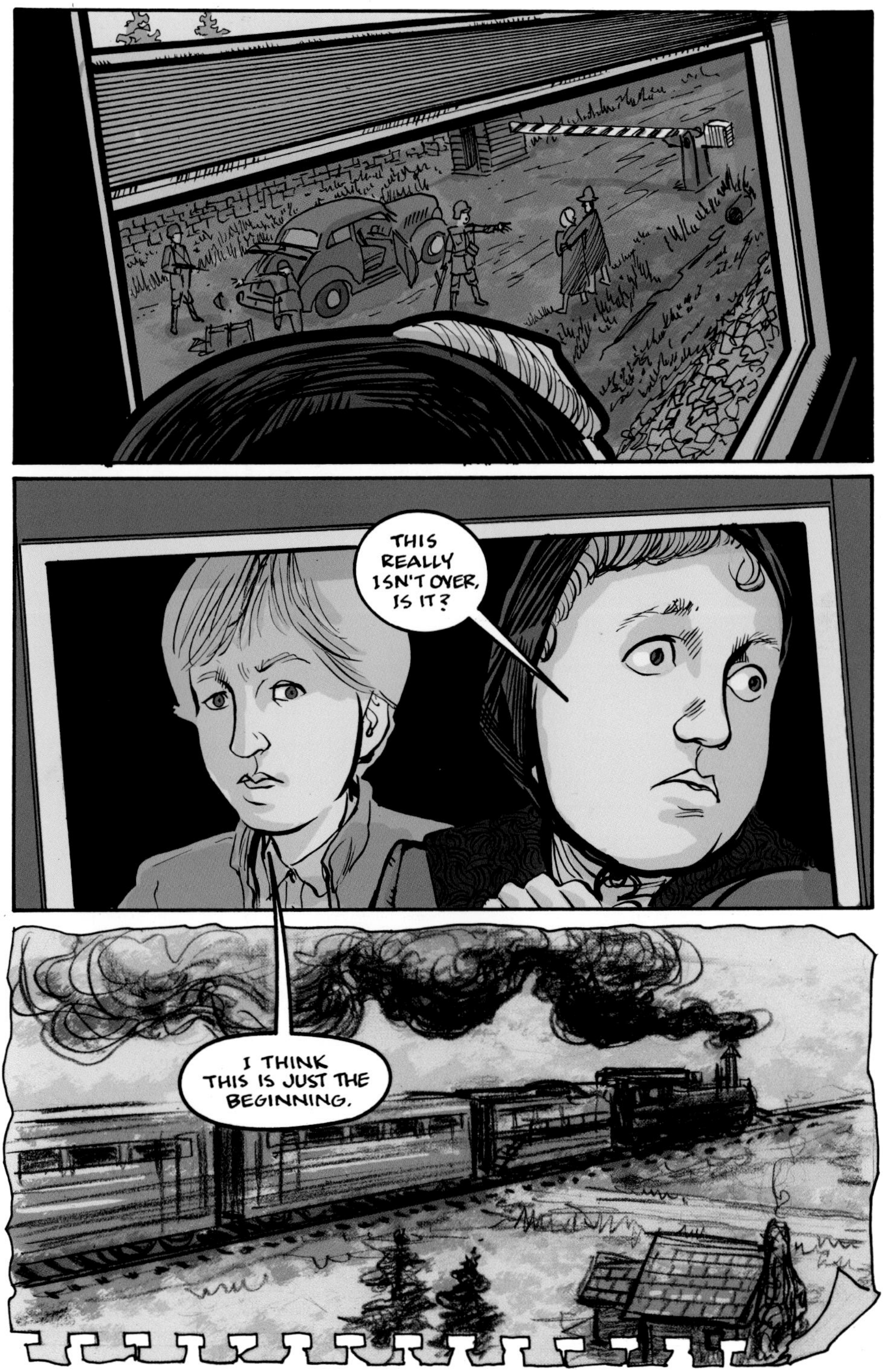
THIS REALLY ISN'T OVER, IS IT?
I THINK THIS IS JUST THE BEGINNING.